Martyn Burke is a film writer and director (*The Last Chase* and *Power Play*). He also co-authored the script for *Top Secret*, written with the team who wrote and directed *Airplane*. He lives in Malibu, California, and Toronto.

Panther Books
Granada Publishing Ltd
8 Grafton Street, London W1X 3LA

Special overseas edition 1985

First published in Great Britain by
Granada Publishing 1984

ISBN 0-586-06337-4

Printed and bound in Great Britain by
Collins, Glasgow

Set in Times

'How little you know of knighthood, Sancho!' answered
Don Quixote. 'Peace, and have patience, for a day will
come when you will see with your own eyes how fine a
thing it is to follow this profession. Now tell me: what
greater contentment can the world offer? What pleasure
can equal that of winning a battle and triumphing over
one's enemy? Undoubtedly none.'

To Marcella

THE
COMMISSAR'S
REPORT

Martyn Burke

PANTHER
Granada Publishing

Russia

1

Before the Great War, when I was a boy, we used to dream of what life was like in Enemy Number One.

It was a time when dreams were precious. Terror hung like a fog in our city, and even though we were very young, we still knew about the midnight arrests and the deportations going on all around us. And what we didn't know, we could sense from the fear-etched faces of our parents, who would talk even to us in heroic and heavy phrases of Socialist Realism like we heard from the loudspeakers at the May Day military parades. It was as if our parents were afraid that we would turn them in.

Enemy Number One seemed like a distant paradise to us then. We knew all about it from the pages of smuggled copies of *Life* magazine. Of course it was dangerous to be caught reading such a foreign magazine. (But how were we to know you could be shot for it?) All we cared about was hurrying home after school, running through the freezing streets where steaming horses wheezed under heavy loads and trams clanged and clattered among the grim, ragged throngs.

No one was home in our apartment for at least an hour after school, so my brother Yuri and I spent those precious moments staring into the pages of *Life*, with its photographs and advertisements of all those sleek people and those big Cadillacs and the skyscrapers in New York and Chicago. My imagination would stampede and before I knew it, I was walking around our high-ceilinged parlour with its overstuffed furniture and peeling plaster, pretending I was in a glittering ballroom in Philadelphia. I danced through the ancient odours of boiled cabbage as the after-school gloom fell away in the light of some distant candelabra.

I hated the smell of boiled cabbage. I was sure that Enemy Number One did not smell of boiled cabbage.

The copies of *Life* magazine belonged to my father. Yuri and I decided that he had probably smuggled them into Russia after his last trip overseas two years ago. Or maybe he had taken them from someone he had executed. Father was a very important member of the Party. I remember him in those days being a big man with fierce, prowling eyes that burst into their own form of laughter whenever he picked us up and kissed us. His moustache was like the bristles on a scrubbing brush, and it tickled so much we screamed and threatened to wet our pants. Father and his friends in the Party and the Army were always scheming to have one another shot. It was just the way life was during the purges, when millions of people were slaughtered by Comrade Stalin.

Father kept the *Life* magazines in a locked, hidden compartment in the parlour wall. He thought no one knew about this compartment, but Yuri and I knew about it because we had spied on him one night when he had come down to the parlour to get one of his balloons. His balloons and *Life* magazine were the only things he kept in the hidden wall compartment.

The first time we opened the compartment and took out one of the balloons, we didn't know what it was for. It was white and rubbery and rolled up so it formed a perfect little circle. It came in a small package with English writing on it. Yuri unrolled the balloon and blew it up, occasionally letting air out of it in small farting bursts that made us laugh. Then he let the balloon go and it shot across the room like a demented airship, crashing into the portrait of Stalin that hung near the wood stove. When Yuri tried to blow up the balloon again, he found it was impossible. There was a tiny hole in it. We didn't

4

know what the balloon was for, but we knew Father would thrash us if he knew we had been playing with it. He didn't keep things in the hidden compartment for nothing. So we rolled it up very carefully and put it back.

That night Father got drunk on vodka, as he often did. We heard him opening his hidden compartment, singing away to himself and then hurrying off to their bedroom. My mother always made strange yodelling noises after Father went in there with one of his balloons. Yuri and I thought he must have been tickling her. There was a lot to tickle. Mother was very heavy, with a flat, wide face and thick legs.

Later we realized that Father must have got the balloon with the hole in it. That was how my little sister Natasha was born. Father was furious. As Mother swelled up even more, he ranted about shoddy capitalist merchandise. The capitalists are still screwing us, he would say over and over again when he got drunk. And late one night, we sneaked a look at him spreading all his balloons out on the dining room table and then holding each one up to the light to see if there were any more holes in them. Stalin looked down serenely.

This mishap didn't stop us from reading *Life*. It became even more of an obsession with us as things got worse in our city. In the final days of a bitter winter, everything outside the heavily curtained windows of the parlour seemed to bring either coldness or fear. So we let our imaginations soar in the glorious childhood images that leapt from the pages of *Life*.

Enemy Number One was a magical place for us. We lost ourselves in visions of the big cars driven by sleek men in the advertisements. For myself, I had taken a Buick, while Yuri waved to me from a DeSoto as we drove down marvellous roads with white lines in the middle. And clothing! Not the baggy, shapeless suits that even someone as important as Father wore. But tailored elegance that made us dashing as we lit our Lucky Strike cigarettes with gold lighters and stared out from under our wide-brimmed fedoras.

From every photograph, Enemy Number One drew us into its secrets and mysteries and its power. We soared in its planes and raced its big cars. We could stretch out on the overstuffed furniture that stunk of boiled cabbage, and suddenly we were in Florida where the big nightclub echoed to Latin music and gangsters with blondes sat in velvet chairs watching the floor show. Or in Hollywood, where I was that big movie star Clark Gable who was probably able to have all the women he wanted without having to inform on any of them to the commissars.

It was the women of Enemy Number One that sent us into ecstasy. The brassiere ads totally wiped us out, as they say. We sat there gaping at these nearly naked creatures with their two shiny white cones beckoning us to illicit thrills. We laughed and clutched at our crotches, and rocked back and forth knock-kneed as these sleek visions of sexual enticement moistened their full red lips and pleaded with us to touch — *just touch it!* — their shiny white cones. There was nothing like it in our city. Almost all the women were like our mother. Shaped like the wood stoves. With pushed-in faces and a beaten-down quality. On the clotheslines their brassieres looked like two tents sewn together. Tents that smelled of boiled cabbage.

We lusted after so much in Enemy Number One. All the shiny and beautiful things that we in our drab and fearful lives did not have. But there was nothing that attracted us so much as its women. And it was because of them that we really got ourselves in trouble.

One day Yuri and I invited a school friend named Lavrenti over to our home after school. We knew that he would enjoy the forbidden delights of the white cones as much as we did. Lavrenti was my age but was smaller than either of us. Even then he had big round eyes, made larger by his thick glasses. Although he was small and wore such thick glasses, no one at school ever picked on Lavrenti, because his father was important in the Party. Almost as important as our father. On many official occasions his father and ours would be together on the reviewing stand with other commissars and sour-looking Army generals. Our father often got drunk with Lavrenti's father, and together they would toast the revolution and how much they loved each other and how they would defend each another against the insidious enemies of the motherland.

So we figured it was okay to share our secret with Lavrenti. When we opened the pages of *Life* to the treasures of Enemy Number One, his eyes almost fell through his glasses. He too was immediately swept off into our world of gangsters and big cars and movie stars. And of course the brassiere ads. When he saw those, he seized the magazine away from us and giggled uncontrollably. Yuri and I were both afraid he would tear the pages out. We had to stop Lavrenti from running into the bathroom and locking the door. The only way we could get his attention was to blow up one of Father's balloons and then let it go careering around the room. When Lavrenti saw the balloon, he was like someone who was having a vision. He picked it up in awe, holding it like a skinny limp fish.

"It's to put on your Raskolnikov," he said.

Both Yuri and I had no idea what our Raskolnikov was. But we acted as if we knew and said, Oh sure, we've whipped it onto the old Raskolnikov dozens of times.

"You have?" said Lavrenti, amazed and envious. "I've always wanted to. Can I?"

Sure, we said. Suddenly Lavrenti unbuttoned his pants and pulled them down. It was then that we realized what

7

a Raskolnikov was, as Lavrenti's was hastily fitted with Father's balloon. Lavrenti chortled and gasped as Yuri and I looked on, stunned.

"Why do you call it a Raskolnikov?" asked Yuri. "I thought it was your pecker."

"My father always calls it that," said Lavrenti, proudly hobbling over to a mirror, his pants still down at his ankles. "He keeps on telling me what will happen if I stick it into one of the worker's daughters who live in the shacks down near the river. He says it will turn black and fall off. That's what these balloons are for. To stop it from turning black and falling off."

"For capitalist tools," said Yuri, and we broke out in fits of giggling. But it was true. The balloons were made by the capitalists. Suddenly it all became clear to us. That was what the men wore in Enemy Number One! Under all their sleek tuxedos in Hollywood or their elegant pin-striped suits on Wall Street, all those gleaming, powerful men were walking around with balloons on their Raskolnikovs! That was why they had such style. That was why the blondes clung to them in their big cars.

Yuri and I immediately dived into the balloon supply and began unwrapping one each. Soon we were each taking turns standing in front of the mirror under Stalin's portrait, staring at ourselves wearing the balloons. Standing there trying to act debonair with our pants around our ankles.

But there was an obvious problem: too much balloon and too little Raskolnikov. It confirmed our belief that everything in Enemy Number One was bigger and better.

It was Lavrenti who came up with the answer. He was very smart for a twelve-year-old. "It's because the capitalists have all those women," he said. "It's like any muscle. The more you use it, the larger it grows. We need some women."

8

Of course. It was simple. So we pulled up our pants and put on our heavy greatcoats. We went outside into the cold greyness of our city to find women who would be enlisted to do their patriotic duty in our struggle to maintain national pride.

There was still snow on the ground. People hurried through the fading afternoon light, bundled up in their drab clothing against the cold. No one stopped to talk to anyone else. In those days everyone was too afraid to say anything. You never knew who would be arrested next, and anyone recently seen talking to the poor wretch might be taken in too. Only members of the Army or the secret police seemed to be in groups. There were few cars on the wide roads that had been built to resemble the boulevards of Paris. But nothing could have been less like Paris. The buildings were dingy and ill lit. Lantern oil was rationed like everything else, and a lot of places had neither gas nor electricity. And because the coal rations had got smaller after the failure of the Five Year Plan, many of the trees on the boulevards had been cut down for the stoves. The result was a kind of unending bleakness in the silent, fearful streets.

But on this afternoon we were true soldiers of the revolution. We saw none of the bleakness. We ran along the big road that led past the statue of some dead poet and then went down to the workers' shacks by the river. The shacks had been there since before the revolution. Most of them were made of wood, but some were made of hardened mud. Toothless old women hauled sacks of coal and stared suspiciously at us as we approached. Just by the way we dressed they knew we were outsiders — *Oktyabryata*, Children of the October Revolution. Privileged ones. Troublemakers. The old crones jabbered at the children to go inside.

We walked among the shacks imagining that we were movie stars in Enemy Number One waiting for the blondes. But I discovered that there must have been a certain skill to being a movie star, because my balloon started coming off. Yuri was having the same difficulty. Again it was Lavrenti who solved the problem.

"You walk with your knees together and your hands in your pockets," he said with an air of authority.

So we walked the way he told us to. We looked like three demented chickens. The children all started laughing at us. But that was their problem, the little peasant fools. How were they to know that this was the way movie stars walked in Hollywood?

When we were almost at the edge of the shacks, we saw Irina. She was a real woman. At least thirteen. At school we had watched her carefully and decided that she must be growing breasts under those layers of shapeless and ragged sweaters she wore. Irina had long braids of light brown hair framing her face. In ten years she would start to turn into a wood stove like her mother. But now she was cute. I tried to imagine her in one of the brassiere ads in *Life*.

Lavrenti informed Irina that we were on a mission of highest patriotic importance. He told her that she had been selected to help overcome a strategic advantage that the capitalists held over the sons of the revolution. Irina looked at us in a way that seemed almost intimidating. Lavrenti informed her that it was a matter of such significance that it could not be discussed in our present surroundings. Bourgeois spies were everywhere. A secure place had to be found.

Like the nearby woods.

The moment we got into the woods, we jumped her. That was only one of our mistakes. She was bigger than any of us and obviously had carried a lot of coal, while we had lifted nothing heavier than *Life* magazine. She immediately hammered the glasses off Lavrenti's head, sending him into a groping panic in the snow. His

10

greatest fear was to be without his glasses. Then she pitched me into a log. Yuri was our only hope. He was almost as tall as she was. But before he could make his move she landed a foot right smack in his balloon. Yuri keeled to the snow like a felled tree.

Then she sat on a tree stump looking at us. Several minutes passed. The daylight was almost gone. The only sounds were our wheezing and groaning.

I wondered if they did it this way on Wall Street.

Then she took off her coat and laid it on the snow. She sat back on the coat, hoisted her skirt above her waist, and peeled off the layers of long woollen stockings and underwear. She lay there half naked. Daring us. Lavrenti stared through his shattered glasses, an idiot's grin on his face. He began making unintelligible noises like a monkey. With his knees together, he staggered over to the white legs that were raised to form a canyon of flesh and teetered into its depths. Grappling with his pants and chortling to himself, Lavrenti pumped away like a jackhammer until Irina disdainfully pushed him off and motioned to me.

I tried to act as if I knew what I was doing. I imagined how Clark Gable the famous movie star would have done it. First of all he would just walk over to the women in the brassiere ads and stare them down. They would fall at his feet. Because if they didn't, Clark Gable could always denounce them to the commissars and they would be sent to labour camps.

So I walked coolly over to Irina and stared, like the movie stars would do. That was a mistake. She burst out laughing. I felt humiliated. I had no idea what to do next. My uncertainty ended abruptly when Irina reached up and grabbed my crotch. Raskolnikov instantly sprang to life.

It was perhaps the most political moment of my life. I realized why the men of Enemy Number One all looked

11

so sleek and powerful. And why they made the balloons so big.

I was dragged onto Irina, pulled down into the canyon. Swamped by the musty layers of ragged sweaters that stank of boiled cabbage. I unleashed Raskolnikov. I had no idea what to do, so I did what Lavrenti had done. I pumped like crazy, feeling a surge of excitement unlike anything I had known before. Suddenly Irina pitched me off into the snow, muttering insults. I lay there dazed and suddenly cold as she motioned to Yuri.

Yuri redeemed our honour. He did it differently from us. He began slowly, kissing her. I had never thought of kissing her. Then he began rubbing her all over. It was quite something to see. She began breathing harder. Then he climbed on top of her, and instead of doing it like a jackhammer he was a series of waves. She began to call out. First in low moans, then in loud, breathless cries.

Lavrenti and I sat there fascinated. I was proud of my older brother.

Suddenly, her cries were mixed with other, more distant voices. Angry male voices. The flames of torches could be seen in the darkness. The forest echoed to the voices that called out Irina's name. Lavrenti and I heard them long before the other two. They were too busy making their own noises. We did not want to interrupt them. But another group of voices and flames came bobbing up from a nearby hill. They were so close that even Irina heard them this time. She looked terrified.

"Help!" she screamed. "Rape!"

She grappled with her clothes and screamed. Almost immediately we were surrounded by a group of angry, sour-faced workers (in the old days they would have been called peasants). The flames of their torches made them look like demons from the woods. They reeked of the potato vodka they drank. Irina was still trying to put on her clothes when her father, a small man with a flat face,

12

hit her and called her a whore. She whimpered and cried and said that we had raped her. More men arrived. They were all very hostile. One of them kicked Yuri in the rear end while he was pulling up his pants. Others grabbed Lavrenti and me. There was talk of flogging. Or cutting a hole in the ice and throwing us into the river, where we would drown.

Again it was Lavrenti who came up with a solution. "Comrades," he said sharply, "you are fortunate that your stupidity has not got you shot already."

His boldness surprised them. Suddenly they looked unsure. I remembered what my father had said about the peasants either being at your throat or at your feet.

"Do you know who you are dealing with?" Lavrenti continued even more forcefully, peering up at the coarse, angry men through his shattered glasses. "You are dealing with sons of Heroes of the Revolution! Patriots. Our fathers are men of influence who are always vigilant in defending the motherland against agents of imperialist aggression."

He needed to say no more. His message got through immediately. You could see the fear settle across the men, some of whom took off their caps as they would have done in the presence of their masters in the old czarist days. They coughed and mumbled and shuffled away in frightened clusters. Irina was still snivelling about rape, but her father cuffed her across the head and told her to shut up. They had reason to be afraid. Those were the worst days of what was called collectivization. We had heard the word used often by our fathers, who were very important in the programme. What it meant was that the government was taking the land away from the *kulaks* — the richer peasants who had owned it and had farmed there all their lives. The *kulaks* were being herded onto state farms, where they suddenly decided they had been tricked into being slaves on their own land. They rebelled against collectivization.

And so they were slaughtered.

People like Father were sent out to solve the problem. The secret police, the Committee for State Security as it is now called, also sent out many men. The Army moved in reinforcements. The butchering was unlike anything our century had known until the Nazis got hold of those millions of Jews a few years later.

I remember one Saturday when there was no school Yuri and I were being driven with Mother in an official car. We were to meet Father at a place we thought was a farm outside the city. It was really a prison camp. It was a very cold day, and while we were inside one of the offices some kind of trouble broke out. A riot perhaps. Gunfire sounded from not far away. We were hurried away to a safer part of the camp. I could see guards with machine guns on tripods firing into the screaming crowds. Men, women, children. The snow ran red. A few were being dragged away from the others by men with clubs.

We had to stay there for several hours until the trouble stopped. When Father finally met us, he looked very shaken. He whispered something to Mother and then told us sternly to say nothing to anyone about what we had seen that day. Nothing! he said over and over. We were hurried out to the car, past the place where the shooting had been. There were hundreds, maybe thousands, of dead *kulaks* frozen in mute and bloody hordes. In the biting wind, arms and legs rose stiffly from the pile, protruding up to the slate-grey skies. Mouths were opened in silent screams on frozen faces that stared sightlessly at the gathering blizzard. I remember those faces even now.

But it was not just the *kulaks*. It was a time when everyone was afraid, even people like Father. The terrible purges were at their worst. There were whispered stories of Army generals returning from the war against the fascists and being decorated with medals in the morning. Then in the afternoon they were taken out and executed. It happened. No one was safe. High-ranking Party officials were suddenly dragged away by the secret police and shot. Within a day their friends would deny even having known them. Informers were everywhere. The catch phrases of the purge — *enemy of the revolution, anti-socialist elements*, rang out like death sentences. Guilt or innocence was of no importance. The main aim was to create fear so intense that it paralysed everyone. It worked.

Fear was the shadow cast by Stalin's light. It was part of our lives. Or more accurately, our parents' lives. We were just children then.

So the workers who were departing with the wailing Irina were no doubt thankful for the darkness. Hoping we could not recognize them in the daylight and report them to our fathers. But our immediate problems were of a different magnitude: the balloons.

Yuri had lost his balloon. It had disappeared in the snow. And mine was all warm and damp, so I washed it in a nearby stream that was not completely frozen over. Lavrenti tried to do the same but lost his balloon immediately in the cold water. And when we hung mine on a branch to dry, it froze solid. We struggled to get the frozen balloon down from the tree. It came away in two pieces.

That night Yuri and I went to bed with a different kind of terror. We listened to our father getting drunk in the parlour. We could always tell when he was really drinking heavily, because he called out sweet names to our mother, who was usually asleep and snoring by then. Yuri and I lay in our beds listening to those early stages of the mating process. Usually we snickered, but on that night we were holding our breath.

"Ludmilla, my flower," he called out drunkenly, "the

little commissar is stirring with desire." I realized for the first time that this was his own particular name for Raskolnikov. If Yuri and I hadn't been so scared, we would have laughed. We heard him open the hidden wall compartment. Then there was a terrible silence.

Finally there was a breathless mumbling coming from the parlour. He was counting his balloons. Several times he lost his place and had to start over, but when he finally finished he let out a roar that sent us both diving under the covers. First he lurched into their bedroom, bellowing at my mother about thieves, demanding to know who had been in the apartment who could have stolen his balloons. (It was the first time we had heard him refer to them. He called them "the commissar's raincoats".)

Then, as if answering his own question, he burst into our room, grabbing Yuri, who was closest, and thrashed him until he cried. Then he grabbed me and spanked me so hard I saw stars. He yelled at us, calling us dirty names we'd never heard before. Then he stopped and dropped me to the floor.

"Why three?" he said, looking suddenly stricken. We dared not answer. "Why did you steal three?" he bellowed at me. I just whimpered. "Have either of you idiots grown an extra pecker?" he yelled, and beat us both again until we told him. It was Yuri who mentioned Lavrenti. At this news, my father's knees almost buckled. My mother gasped fearfully and went very pale. Then she began to weep. My father grabbed me and desperately demanded to know if Lavrenti had seen *Life* magazine. Suddenly he had forgotten all about the balloons. All he cared about was *Life*. Tearfully I said that yes, Lavrenti had seen *Life*. My mother was almost hysterical at the news. She howled at my father, saying that we would all go to the firing squad for possessing counter-revolutionary magazines. My father yelled at her to shut up and pounded his fist into my clothes cabinet.

16

Clutching his bleeding fist, he lurched into the parlour.

"Do you know what Lavrenti's father will do to us?" he said. "That swine. That illiterate informer. He'll have your father shot. And your mother too. If you're lucky they might only send you to the *gulag*."

Yuri and I had always thought of Lavrenti's father and our father as being friends. Whenever they met they always shook hands and embraced and laughed at each other's jokes.

All night my parents stayed up. My mother cried and my father drank. At dawn when I awoke, my father was fearfully pacing the floor. In silence we got ready for school. Before we left, my father gave me a very large, plain brown envelope and told me to listen as I had never listened to him before. He told me to take the envelope to school and keep it hidden in my knapsack until after school that afternoon. Then I was to give the envelope to Lavrenti and tell him to take it home to his father.

It was a present, my father said. A present that would help smooth things over with Lavrenti's father. I was not to open it or write anything on the plain, unmarked surface of the envelope. And after I gave it to Lavrenti, we were both to come straight home.

I did just as he told me — almost. After I gave Lavrenti the envelope, I started to return home with Yuri, but something made me decide to go over to Lavrenti's home. I wanted to see if his father would be pleased by the present. Yuri refused to accompany me, so I went on my own. Their house was on a wide street next to the park. I took the short cut through the park, and when I got close I realized something strange was happening. I saw several black cars parked outside. They were the kind secret police drove. I knew because I had seen those cars in places like the prison camp. There were several men in long coats standing outside Lavrenti's house. I crept through the trees in the park and watched as another car

17

drove up. My father got out. He looked very nervous. From the house, one of the men in the long coats emerged and walked quickly towards Father. The man was holding the envelope I had given Lavrenti. From the envelope, he took out the two copies of *Life* magazine and gravely showed them to Father, who shook his head.

Just then, Lavrenti's father came storming out of the house cursing at Father. He was stopped by two secret policemen who were very rough with him. Father merely seemed to sigh and shake his head again. Lavrenti's mother came out wailing. It was just like my mother had wailed the night before. His mother called out to my father, begging for mercy. Father just looked very regretful and gave a few orders. Lavrenti's father was put into one car and his mother into another, which sped away. Then Lavrenti and his two sisters were dragged out of the house. I remember thinking how much Lavrenti looked like his father and being impressed by how fiercely he struggled until one of the secret policemen slapped the thick glasses off his face. Then he panicked and yelled terribly as he was heaved into another car.

I ran home. I sat trembling and staring at the big portrait of Stalin until there was no more light left. I couldn't figure out what I had just seen. I was sure Stalin was smiling.

Father came home very late. It was almost dawn. Both Yuri and I were catapulted from a hair-trigger sleep by his arrival. We crept down the hall as far as we dared and listened to our parents talk in the bedroom.

Lavrenti's father and mother had been tried and executed. In a midnight trial they had been found guilty of possessing counter-revolutionary propaganda. The only evidence used against them was the two copies of *Life* magazine. The ones I had given Lavrenti to take home. Both Father and Mother were very upset. And somehow relieved.

Much later they talked about Lavrenti and his two sisters. All three had been sent to labour camps.

I cried for the rest of the night. So did Yuri. Lavrenti had been our friend. I was sure I would never see him again.

How could I have been so wrong?

Enemy Number One
New York City

2

But that was a long time ago. A very long time. Yet ever since those magical afternoons, lost in the images of *Life* magazine, my fascination with Enemy Number One has remained the one constant element of my existence. The allure, the seductiveness, the power of that amazing country has been my own polestar during my darkest moments.

Of course, in my childhood days I thought that everything about Enemy Number One was superior to our own fearful and tattered country. We all did. But now, after having risen to various positions of power, and after having travelled across Enemy Number One on many occasions, I know the lesser reality behind the images. But even so, that country still slightly intimidates me. As it does most of my countrymen.

Perhaps I remember too much of those boyhood images. I constantly ask myself how we could even have the audacity to take on that awesome and overpowering nation. But now there are those with whom I have worked in Moscow who spend their spare time dreaming of what life will be like when Washington is ours. Years ago I would have laughed at them.

But of one thing I am sure. If we ever do smash Enemy Number One it will not be because we defeated them. They will have defeated themselves. Like the Romans, when their empire was crumbling and they had neither the will nor the wit to save themselves. It has been astounding for me to watch them do themselves in. It reminds me of a saying I heard there once: "He shot himself in the foot." (I love their expressions.)

Of course we have helped the process along·in any way we could. Over the decades we have gnawed away like an army of termites inside a glorious old mansion. With infinite patience and an unchanging goal we have persevered, labouring towards the day (which some say is already here) when only the magnificent façade remains and the wind alone will topple it.

I am responsible for part of our success. An important part, I suspect.

After World War II, in which we all suffered hardships that are almost unimaginable nowadays, my father decided I should rise above my surroundings and enjoy the material comforts of life. In other words, I should become part of the regime in Moscow. This was shortly after my brother Yuri was killed in the war. He was only nineteen at the time. His death shattered our family. For weeks, my mother sat in the greyness of our musty apartment, rocking back and forth and weeping, her face growing older every day. I tried hard not to cry. For a while I succeeded. But I felt alone for the first time in my life. I kept expecting Yuri to walk into the emptiness of the room we'd shared, smiling and making jokes. It took me a week to realize that he never would. Then, in the middle of a night when the snow was piling up outside and there was no heat in our apartment, I burst out of a nightmare-drenched sleep and ran over to Yuri's bed, sobbing and pounding against the empty pillow. My mother came running in and bundled me in blankets and pressed me against her, singing what I later learned were hymns. We remained huddled in the cold, sitting on Yuri's bed until I fell asleep, just as the steel light of the winter dawn came through the ice-caked windows.

Only my father did not cry. At least in public. But I know that in private he must have wept, even though he would not have admitted it to me. On the day after we learnt Yuri had been killed, his eyes were red like coals against the whiteness of his face, which seemed drained of all colour. It was from that day that his hair began to go white and his once impeccable moustache grew wild, like a bush gone to seed.

It was also when he began spending more time with me, as if he was afraid of losing me too. I knew the terrible things my father had done to Lavrenti and his family, but I couldn't help loving him. It was the time when he and I grew very close and now, so many years later, I treasure those moments. My father would sit with me for hours each night, helping me with my homework. It was very important, he said, to excel in school. Only the brightest would get the really good jobs in Moscow. I didn't let him down. After Yuri died I never stood lower than second in any class. School had always been easy for me anyway. The only thing that caused me problems in school was my own imagination, which was always running away into a wonderful world of fantasies whenever I got bored with what was being taught.

That fantasy world was my escape. I would actually see different places and people right in front of me, as if I had some kind of mental projector that was blotting out reality with overpowering images. Usually while I was sitting in class I would see people from Enemy Number One, like Hollywood movie stars, walking up to me and asking for a light and then wanting me to direct their next film. But sometimes I would see terrible scenes too, like our school being blown to bits in slow motion and the teacher melting like wax in an eternal millisecond.

It was always embarrassing when the teacher asked me a question while my mental projector was turned on.

By the time I was twenty I was taller than my father and thinner, with a shock of straight blond hair that I forever fought to keep from falling across my forehead. My face was what might be called angular, with the kind of almost sharp features that are softened by age. My

25

father had decided that I should try to get into the Ministry of Foreign Affairs. It was a good place to begin, he said. After being trained at their school, anything would be possible. Secret police. The Kremlin. The embassies. My father's position and influence in the local Party apparatus opened the necessary doors.

Within a few years I was one of the young assistants who sat quietly in the empty, echoing offices of the Kremlin bureaucrats while older men talked. It was at one of these meetings that my talent for devising schemes to be used against Enemy Number One was first discovered. One day I simply spoke up and said, why not regard the entire global struggle as just a kind of judo? Use Enemy Number One's strength against itself. Let them defeat themselves with their own superiority, I said, feeling suddenly very uncertain as the cynical eyes of the old men in the Kremlin slowly turned to see who was the possessor of this reedy voice that blurted out such heresy. For a moment there was silence, a cold marble emptiness, and I felt the wrath of Comrade Stalin's terrible stare as he looked down from his portrait high on the wall in front of us. Stalin's little Mona Lisa smile hid the corpses of millions of government and military men whose ideas had fallen from his favour. So original thinking was neither common nor wise.

And in those days it was accepted that we would some day be fighting a war with Enemy Number One. (It still is among the generals.) That was the conventional thinking.

But my thinking was different. I thought war would be unnecessary. We could win without firing a shot.

Unnecessary? The old bureaucrats rose up one by one from the murky depths of their protective cynicism. They had caught a faint whiff of the dangerous scent of innovation. The silence held. I was in agony. But then one of the old men from the Kremlin smiled, his lips coming tightly together like a slender scar on that parchment face. Go on, he said.

We are wasting our time worrying about Enemy Number One's great wealth and material superiority, I said. We should be doing just the opposite. We should be encouraging it. And then waiting. Let them grow so wealthy that they wallow in their own decadence, and kill off all their gods. And we should exalt all their much-trumpeted freedoms. The day will come when we can drown them in their own freedoms. We will set fires in the hearts of the masses (theirs, not ours) until the clamour for freedom will shake their temples. And when all are as free as they have demanded to be, none will be free. They will have torn themselves apart. They will lie spent and grovelling before us, their conquerors.

Their liberators.

Smiles crept into the corners of those cynical mouths.

I was on my way. Soon I was regarded within the Kremlin as one of the brightest of the young officials. My ideas were filtering ever upward. I was instructed to attend more important meetings. My opinions were asked on problems in the Balkans. And I was very good at my work. Where others could see only brush strokes I could see the whole canvas.

Even my father was impressed. He made sure that all of his associates knew that his son was at the forefront of the great battle to destroy Enemy Number One. (I later realized that he had told his cronies about my success in case any of them were planning to have him shot. I became insurance against his friends who, like him, were basically smiling old murderers. He made sure they all knew I was destined for the Politburo.)

But in those early successes there was one desperate problem: I really had no desire to destroy Enemy Number One. I *loved* that incredible country! Without having even been there. It was the source of my fantasies.

The flame of my dreams. All I had ever wanted to do was go there. Just to step into the pages of *Life* and walk the streets of Chicago and Hollywood and dance myself into exhaustion at Mardi Gras on the packed streets of New Orleans. I wanted to *see* the gangsters — just once. And to sit behind the wheel of a Buick. And go to their movies. And stare up at the Empire State Building. And eat their hot dog, or whatever they called it. And see Niagara Falls.

That was all.

But the only way I could ever get there was to help destroy what I loved.

There were scores of bright young men fiercely competing to be sent to Enemy Number One. It was the most prestigious posting in the diplomatic and espionage services, and only a very few would be sent. So I competed more fiercely than the rest. I made sure that my strategies about Enemy Number One were the most destructive of all.

Within a year after I had blurted out my theories at that Kremlin meeting, I stood on the deck of a Russian ocean liner, clutching the railing, afraid I would disgrace myself by jumping up and down like a five-year-old as the skyscrapers of New York rose slowly out of the horizon. *New York!* The very name leapt from those distant pages of *Life*. Suddenly I was in the middle of my own fantasies.

I can only recall those first euphoric days in New York as a blur, a memory refracted into beams of joy and nervousness. I was like a child in a massive candy store. I remember walking up Fifth Avenue staring at the stores and being overwhelmed by all the merchandise in the windows. I wondered if perhaps Fifth Avenue was not a special street where only members of their political parties were allowed. Like our special stores at home. But when I walked onto other streets the stores there were filled with the same amazing display of things to buy. And the people all looked so well dressed. As if they had stepped out of the pages of *Life*. And no one smelled of boiled cabbage.

I walked a few more blocks and began to feel a kind of panic. I was not prepared for this tidal wave of materialism, this surge of humanity and traffic and commerce. A kind of dizziness overcame me. The colours and the motion of the streets seemed to blur. Like a drunk, I needed a lamppost for support. There was a collective raw energy to those people, to those streets. It frightened me to the point of despair. How, I asked myself, can we ever compete with this?

I decided that perhaps it was all a massive trick. Like we have at home, where the big department stores for the ordinary people display windows filled with merchandise and none of it is available inside. Or anywhere. So I walked into a store whose windows were a static avalanche of cameras, watches, radios, and whatever else could be made of chrome or plastic.

To my amazement, I emerged ten minutes later with a shiny new watch. At the time I had no idea it would stop working four days later, so I was pleased. And to show the assistant that even though I was wearing my only baggy suit, I was really a sophisticated man of the world, I bought an art object. A pink flamingo. The kind you put in the lawn. (You laugh, do you? Originals like mine are now being sold in antique stores.)

Suddenly my fear and despair had vanished. I walked proudly down the street, clutching my pink flamingo and my watch. I was exhilarated. And in my exhilaration, I made a discovery as significant as the one revealed to me over Irina's half-naked form fifteen years earlier. I realized that the way to relieve fear or tension in Enemy Number One is to buy.

It is that simple. *Buy!*

Of course the converse applied too. When you didn't buy, the fear, the despair would build up. I realized that this was the way the country worked. Buying — whatever — was the key to happiness. And because I had just bought, I was ecstatic.

I was also pleased because I had discovered something about life in Enemy Number One that might be useful for my theory of strengths and weaknesses. (Indeed it has.) It was definitely a moment worth celebrating. So I went into a bar and ordered a vodka. The bar was filled with men staring drunkenly at a television set and looking at something called a baseball game. After my second vodka I became interested in the game. The Yankees were playing the Dodgers. I decided to cheer for their Dodgers. I could never cheer for anyone called the Yankees. Most of the people in the bar were fans of the Yankees, so we Dodger fans had to stick together. I sat with a taxi driver from Brooklyn and several of his friends. Whenever they cheered, I cheered. I became so emotional over my Dodgers that I almost broke my precious flamingo over the head of a Yankee fan.

Two hours later I lurched from the bar, a Dodger fan for life. (When we take over the country, I would like to keep the Dodgers. But the Yankees will definitely have to change their name. Perhaps to something like the Dynamos.) I weaved contentedly toward the large old East Side building where those of us in the Russian embassy lived. On the way I stopped in Central Park and sat on one of the benches, clutching my pink flamingo and staring at the traffic on Fifth Avenue. It was a warm autumn night, and people were still strolling along the lanes of the park. I watched to see if anyone was stopping them to check their papers. I could see no one. I realized that all day I had seen no one checking identity papers. I decided they must have other, better, means of controlling the masses. But I didn't really care. I was reasonably drunk, I had my flamingo, and my Dodgers had won. What more could I want?

But suddenly my contented little world shot out from under me. On the park bench directly opposite me sat a man who smiled. It was not a pleasant smile. I felt my insides turn to ice. Fear leapt through my mind, scouring off the drunkenness. The man rose and stepped into the light. I had not been mistaken.

It was Lavrenti.

I would have known that face no matter how many years had passed. The same quizzical eyes behind those thick glasses. Framed by an owlish face that seemed to be smiling even when it was not. Looking like a younger version of his dead father. Staring at me. Through me.

"I have been waiting for you. I will make your life absolute hell," he said quietly. In English.

I fled. Clutching my flamingo, stumbling through the park, I ran, yelling back at him in incoherent phrases. Insisting that I had not meant to get his father shot. Or his mother. In the darkness I fell over a rock and looked back in terror. He was gone. Without a trace.

I rushed back to our embassy apartment building. Arriving drunk, dishevelled, and out of breath was not a good career move. If one of the *stukachi* — the snitches — were to see me, I would be in trouble. They were the informers, whose job it was to report anything that seemed even slightly suspicious. They all loved their work. They could destroy careers, or lives, on a whim. They lived and worked among us in seemingly ordinary positions, from chauffeur to diplomat. But their real task was to spy on us. To find the slightest hint of disloyalty. The rest of us feared them.

I was in luck. Yakir, the youngest of the guards, was in the lobby when I arrived. He was our most stupid guard and lacked even the essential bullying stare that the others had perfected. He admired my flamingo as I hurried past,

31

praying that the elevator would be there.

Katya was waiting up for me. Katya was my wife. I had married her at least partly because there was little danger that she would ever turn into a wood stove. She had a figure that stepped right out of the brassiere ads in *Life*. Actually better. Her naturally golden hair would have sent the old-time peroxide starlets of Hollywood sulking back to their beauty parlours, and her flawless face with those pouting lips unleashed forbidden thoughts in men who stared too long at her. Although we had been married for only two years, every lust-ridden day confirmed the purely anatomical brilliance of my decision to marry her.

But other areas of our marriage were a disaster. (Although I don't think she would have thought so. Then.) The essential problem was that she was stupid.

A gloriously beautiful creature of almost bovine intelligence. And often given to flights of wild enthusiasm over things she had forgotten an hour later. But just as nature doles out defences, selectively giving many of her creatures speed but not strength, or protective coverings instead of either, so Katya was blessed with an awesome sense of cunning. Behind that dewy and voluptuous face lay a mind of traps and snares that a trial lawyer would have envied.

I had first met Katya on a trip to one of the republics, a dreary place to which we junior officials dreaded being sent in case the posting became permanent. Her father was a petty bureaucrat, harassed by his own family. In the hovel they lived in, resentment hung in the air like stale smoke. I have often wondered whether Katya saw me as simply a means to get out of that terrible life. The life that had crushed her parents. Her protestations of love were too quick and too easy. But who was I to argue, as we thrashed our way around her steaming bed on the second night we knew each other.

Her parents had suddenly developed a theatregoing urge, leaving us alone in that one-room apartment. Every night while I was in their town, they went to see the same play. They were no fools. They knew my father was important in the Party. And that I was a rising young official. Our wedding was held two months later. It was a properly drunken affair with endless toasts to us and the Party. Katya displayed an instant skill at mouthing whatever rhetoric had to be uttered in order to advance the career of her new husband and thus acquire a proportional share of any rewards the revolution dispensed to its favourites. It was at the wedding that I first observed the phenomenon of paunchy Party officials listening intently to whatever inanities flowed from her lips. Nodding sagely and giving greater weight to her opinions while staring into her breasts. Men will listen for hours to such splendid idiots when the identical opinion advanced by one of their subordinates would earn bureaucratic thumbscrews.

It was not that I was unhappy with Katya. At least not at first. But I realized that the marriage was a mistake. It was my fault. For a while I laboured hard to convince myself that I was in love. But I soon had to admit that what I had really done was acquire an ornament. A beautiful, lusty display piece.

I cannot recall a time when Katya ever really talked about anything other than objects or people. If it was tangible she could comprehend it. Ideas or theories were of no interest to her.

In this respect she was perfect for Enemy Number One. And it for her. From the moment she stared into the glittering display windows of all those incredible stores, she had found nirvana. The clothes, the jewels, the cars — she craved it all. And the happiness she could achieve from the act of buying was utterly pure. Erotic even.

But of course, as I had found from my own

observations, there was the converse of this happiness. Her frustrations, her tensions that seethed from *not* buying were at least marginally volcanic. And living within the financial resources of a junior-grade diplomat-spy from a workers' state was not helping her to lessen those tensions.

So that night, before I stumbled through the door to our apartment, I had decided to tell her that I had bought the pink flamingo especially for her. But when I got inside, it was I who was surprised. She sat there coyly smiling at me — dressed in a stunning red gown. An expensive, stunning red gown. I stood there gaping as she glided across the floor, turning around as the models do in fashion shows and smiling seductively at me.

"Do you like it?"

What could I say?

Then, with an unerring sense of the dramatic, she reached into the front of her low-cut gown the way I had seen dance-hall girls do in the western movies. From her cleavage she removed a large roll of money — there was space for more — and threw it joyously into the air. I looked at this paper-money shower.

And panicked.

I dashed for the radio, turning it on, frantically twisting the dial to find loud music. Anything to drown out our voices. I had no way of knowing if our apartment was one of the ones bugged by our own secret police. And I knew of people who had been sent home and executed for far less than what I had just witnessed.

"Where did you get this?" I whispered desperately. She just winked seductively and danced barefoot through the pile of money. I dropped to my knees and stared into that awful pile of money. There were twenty-dollar bills. And fifties. Hundreds even! Images of the secret police bursting through the door sent me scurrying after the dreaded dollars. In a flash, the remaining days of my life sped before my eyes: accusations of taking bribes; secretly working as an enemy agent; being drugged and stuffed into a steamer trunk; flown back in one of our military aircraft. Then the torture in some basement cell. And finally, mercifully, the bullet in the back of the brain in that infamous white-tiled room with no windows.

I scrambled across the floor until every last dollar was retrieved. I hissed my terrified question at her once more, but it was as if she was in a trance, drugged by the vapours from the money. It was only when I succumbed to my panic and grabbed the front of her dress, threatening to rip it from her body, that she reacted. It was as if I had thrown cold water over her.

"I won it. In a contest."

My Katya. Money was merely iron filings to the magnet of her soul. Within a week after arriving in Enemy Number One she had entered a contest at the Safeway supermarket on Third Avenue. And won second prize.

One thousand dollars.

It was a small fortune in those days. You could buy a new car with it.

After buying her gown she had eight hundred dollars left. It settled in my hands like hot coals. But she was drifting back into her own particular form of ecstasy. I tried to get through to her. To explain the danger we were in. I told her that she could never wear that gown outside our apartment. Even having it in the closet was a terrible risk. "Don't you realize what Stalin would think of all this?" I yelled, hurtling down the most obvious route of logic.

One that even she could understand.

"Comrade Stalin would approve, I'm sure," she murmured coyly. "After all, look at the colour. It's the brightest red I could find."

It was useless. I watched her standing there, swaying

gently back and forth in time to some inner music, and realized that either God or Marx was trying to tell me something. So I started to undress myself. And her. In a low voice she was telling me of the physical act of buying the gown. Her account became more and more breathless.

And at that moment, for the first time, I understood true quality in material things, because there was something utterly electrifying about the way that magnificent gown fell around her feet.

The radio station I had tuned into signed off for the night, leaving only its static to accompany our rapturous moans and cries for anyone who might have been listening in. If some lonely police goon had been eavesdropping, he would have suffered that night, because we went on for hours. Spectacularly.

The next morning I confiscated the money. I took it with me to a drop I had established. (A drop is a place where spies leave the information they have secretly gathered for their control officers. Or used in reverse, we could leave money or instructions for the spies. Eventually, I became very creative in finding drop points. Magnetic boxes on low bridge girders. Containers at the end of unused piers. That sort of thing.) Because I had been there just a short while, I had established only one drop. It was in a hollowed-out section of a tree in the park not far from the reservoir. I wrapped the money in foil, left it in the drop, and then went about my business of learning how to destroy Enemy Number One from within.

Part of my business that day consisted of attending a boring diplomatic cocktail party. As I was to discover, these were invaluable for spotting blackmail targets or willing dupes among the diplomatic corps at the United Nations. It was like picking mushrooms after a summer rain. They were all over the place. But my attention that evening necessarily had to be riveted upon Katya. She was furious because I had taken away the money. And even worse, I had forbidden her to wear her magnificent new gown. On the way to the reception she rode in glacial silence, wearing the shapeless general-issue dress she had brought from home. In that respect, she blended in superbly with the rest of the embassy wives. But most of them were built like wood stoves. And smelled of boiled cabbage.

The situation was not improved when we arrived at the reception and discovered most of the wives of the diplomats from the Western countries looking as if they had stepped out of the pages of a fashion magazine. It was all I could do to keep Katya from throwing a career-destroying tantrum. My career, that is. I was too nervous even to begin to operate effectively. So I tried simply to get through the evening as best I could and figure out a solution afterwards. But my composure was almost shattered for good by the man whom I suddenly noticed across the room, smiling and raising his glass in a toast to me.

It was Lavrenti.

I tried to pretend I didn't see him. I engaged in desperate small-talk with those around me. I took refuge behind the table of canapés. But he was relentless. Smiling, almost gliding after me. Finally he trapped me in a perspiring circle of South American diplomats.

"I will make you suffer in places you never knew pain could exist," he said in our native language. He said it so smoothly. Charmingly. The South Americans, who understood not a word of Russian, smiled and nodded smoothly. Also charmingly. Lavrenti put down his drink and headed slowly for the door. I rushed over to Ivchenkov, my immediate boss, and pointed out Lavrenti. He had already seen him.

"He is the worst," Ivchenkov said grimly. He was a

little man with a disproportionately flabby face and narrow eyes. Whenever he became nervous or angry, the broken veins in his cheeks glowed brighter. His face looked like a road map now. "He is our fiercest enemy here," he continued. "Do you know him?"

"No," I lied. It was perhaps the wisest of all my lies. Had I told them how I knew Lavrenti, they would probably have requested that I be sent back to Moscow. They wanted to avoid attracting Lavrenti's attention in any way possible. He was making their life difficult enough as it was. And to have someone in their midst acting as a lightning rod, drawing his wrath to them all, was too much to cope with.

Lavrenti was now working for what was known in Enemy Number One as the Central Intelligence Agency. His speciality was in exposing our agents, destroying our operations, and harassing our diplomats. He was our most implacable and ruthless foe.

And only I knew the true reason for his zeal.

For over five years after his parents were shot and he was dragged into the secret police car, Lavrenti had fought to survive in the worst camps of the *gulag*. He had endured worse horrors than anyone else I knew. As I had learned later, on the day his parents were shot he had been thrown onto a cattle truck filled with other prisoners. The truck broke down on its way to one of the labour camps. The guards and the driver left the truck with its imprisoned human cargo for two days in the middle of a blizzard. When they returned only Lavrenti and one other prisoner had not frozen to death. He had taken clothing from those already dead and used it to warm himself. In the first camp, he survived starvation and a terrible spotted-typhus epidemic. On several occasions he was horribly beaten by a guard who had tired of raping the female prisoners. And finally he was shipped off to some experimental camp that was rumoured to be the worst of them all.

According to our files, when the Germans overran the part of Russia where Lavrenti was being held prisoner, he was one of thousands who were used cruelly as cannon fodder. Stalin had ordered that the slave labour battalions were to be used as a delaying buffer against the advancing Nazis. Most of the wretched prisoners Lavrenti was with were literally shredded by artillery fire as they desperately built tank traps and fortifications. Lavrenti was one of those sent ahead of our troops to build a pontoon bridge. Bits of flesh from his fellow prisoners were plastered across his body as he threw down his shovel and with magnificent audacity ran straight toward the enemy lines, waving a white piece of cloth. He established his value to the retreating Germans immediately by being able to warn them of partisan attacks on their flanks. There was a story that I could never confirm of Lavrenti seizing a machine gun from a dead German and joyously killing dozens of our own soldiers.

There was another story of what he did to one of our officers who had been captured. When I heard about it, I had nightmares. But again I cannot confirm it. However, it is known that he made his way into western Europe during the chaos of the last days of the war. And from there he became one of the millions of post-war refugees who emigrated to Enemy Number One.

There were perhaps twelve million people who died in our labour camps. More than twice as many as the Jews in World War II. And for one scrawny boy to have survived was truly awesome. He endured those terrible years by the grace of a fanatic's will power fuelled by a lust for revenge against those people who had made him suffer.

People like me.

It was those qualities that made him so terrifying as an adversary. For most of the others in their Intelligence

Agency, it was just a job. A game with its own rules. With victories and sacrifices that were best not explained outside the profession. Of course, I'm not trying to imply that they didn't care deeply about what they were doing. They did. But most of them cared in the same way that company managers in Enemy Number One care about selling more products than their competitors.

What they lacked was a kind of passion. Lavrenti had passion. And as I have learnt, passion in its purest form burns off reason like a blowtorch. I was beginning to realize that we would some day confront one another in a way that I dreaded. There would be no chance for talk. No possibility of appealing to the good old days of *Life* magazine and the rolled-up white balloons.

Katya could not understand why I was so nervous that night. My thoughts of Lavrenti were replaced early the following morning by a more immediate concern: the money. I was informed that my drop was to be activated for use by one of our spies working in an aircraft company on Long Island. The thought of the spy reaching in and coming up with a tinfoil wad of money was somewhat unsettling. So I retrieved the money and spent the morning walking the streets and wondering what to do with it. The answer, when it finally came to me, was to change my life in ways that are still difficult to convey.

The answer was brilliant in its simplicity, ridiculous in its contradictions, and best of all it made me laugh. I love jokes.

The answer was the stock market.

I actually did laugh out loud when the idea came to me. In fact I roared with laughter. I was standing on a crowded street in front of a big window. On the other side of the window was a huge office with numerous desks piled high with pieces of paper. Behind the desks were harried-looking men talking on one and sometimes two phones at the same time. They seemed to be doing a lot of yelling. At the front of the big office was a large board that covered almost the entire wall. On the board were a lot of letters, and clerks were running back and forth on a platform changing the numbers beside the letters. It was as if they were performers for the audience that sat in front of them. The audience consisted of several dozen men who just sat and stared at the changing numbers on the wall. Most of the men were old and pasty-looking. Some smoked big cigars and muttered to themselves or slapped their foreheads. Occasionally they yelled at the harried men behind the desks.

I had never seen a stockbroker's office before. Not a single thing I observed made the slightest sense.

On the window in front of me, written in gold letters was: *Taylor, Wendell, Bulmer & Carr*. I decided to go inside and ask for Mr Taylor. The woman who received my inquiry at a big mahogany desk in the lobby had a stare that needed no translation. I was obviously put into the category of *nut*. And looking back, perhaps there was some justification. I was dressed in my baggy suit, which some of the local winos would have passed up. And with my thick accent and my awkward manners, I needed some help. So I engaged in my own ploy, which needed no translation. I pulled out the stinking wad of money and dumped it on her desk.

Then it was my turn for the icy stare. She became fawning immediately. Mr Taylor had been dead for years, but someone else would help me. She offered me a seat. I accepted, laughing to myself and thinking that when we chose to make the revolution in this country, she would have much practice in being obsequious. After several minutes, Mr Smith came out to meet me.

Smith. Perfect. If I had thought of it, I would have insisted on doing business with a Smith. The perfect archetype of Enemy Number One. Sam Smith, it was

41

immediately apparent, was the lowest man on the corporate totem pole. The receptionist's revenge.

Sam Smith was also probably the youngest. He looked like he should have still been in school. He was what they call in Enemy Number One "Ivy League". He was thin and somewhat nervous, as if he was not used to dealing with anyone outside his own kind. He had short blond hair that was greased over with something that smelled sweet. He wore those heavy wing-tip shoes that his kind think are stylish. I insisted on going into an office with him. I did not want to sit there in front of all those people. He became even more nervous and explained that he did not have an office. So we settled for standing in the stairwell of the fire escape.

I put the money in his hands and told him to put it into the stock market. I told him I wanted nothing on paper ever sent to me. I wanted no phone calls. He told me he at least had to know my name, but I said no. He insisted, so I told him to call me Mr Yagoda. That was the name of the man who had been boss of our secret police a few years earlier, until Stalin shot him too. Sam Smith had obviously never heard of Yagoda. He dutifully wrote the name down. Then I said the words I'd been waiting to say ever since I read about the movie stars years ago in *Life* magazine.

"Don't call for me. I'll call for you," I said with my best Clark Gable look, which I could tell made him nervous. I was sure he thought I was a big-time gangster from Miami with gum-chewing girlfriends all over the place. I walked out the door, not knowing it would lead me to the back alley, leaving him standing there with the money. I laughed once more. Me! A Marxist fomenting world revolution. Walking into the very command post of the enemy. The heart of Wall Street capitalism that we were pledged to smash.

I knew it was something Humphrey Bogart would

have done. *What style*, I told myself, standing there in the trash of that back alley.

Now I could get to the business of coming up with ways to destroy the country. I felt pleased that I wouldn't have to worry about that money anymore. But like so many other things in my life, I was wrong.

How was I to know that Sam Smith was an absolute genius in his field?

3

But after one month in New York, I was filled with despair. My career, my whole life, was about to slide into oblivion. All because of Lavrenti. He was relentless. I was unable to concentrate on anything but the fear he made me feel.

I began to think that was his main purpose. Gradually to wear me down, torture me with fears real and imagined. He was like a ghost. I would catch sight of him for an instant in places like Macy's department store or in the subways. Sometimes I would only think I saw him. But I would still flee from this vengeful spectre, rushing into elevators or pushing my way onto different subway cars past irritated passengers. I began to develop nervous habits. I was always looking over my shoulder. And I lost weight.

Once I zigzagged from Madison to Fifth Avenue for several blocks, and when I was sure that no one was following me I hurried into Central Park, exuberant in the cool autumn twilight. I loved the park. Its winding pathways and the craggy walls of granite that suddenly opened onto meadows allowed me my memories of home. I would sit on one of the benches, half closing my eyes, and drift back into the Russian summers of my youth, a world of gentle birch forests and villages of wooden homes painted bright blue and green.

Because I had never seen Lavrenti in the same place twice, I felt Central Park was my refuge now. I was wrong.

On that quiet evening while I was lost in my memories, a sudden tiny puff of smoke exploded from the boulder next to the park bench where I was sitting. In the same instant there was a screeching whine. Nobody had to tell me what that sound was. I had seen enough John Wayne cowboy movies at private screenings in Moscow to know a bullet ricocheting off a rock when I saw one. Yet strangely, there had been no sound of gunfire. I was too frightened to run. Besides, I didn't even know which way to run. The sniper could not be seen. Then Lavrenti stepped out from behind a tree only a few feet away. In his hand was a huge pistol with a silencer on it – the kind they used in the spy movies. He aimed the pistol straight at my head and walked slowly toward me. He was smiling.

"This is for the memory of my father. And my mother. And for all the years I rotted in the *gulag*."

He was very close. My eyes had seized upon the tiny lethal image of that finger wrapped around the trigger, and even in the fading light I could see it getting whiter and whiter as it pressed against the sliver of metal that would send my brains hurtling against the granite like an explosion of glutinous worms. The finger pressed *more*. I shrieked, but no sound came out. And *more!*

Click!

Lavrenti smiled pleasantly and lowered the pistol. My knees gave way and I sank back against the rock, terrified. "I will kill you not just once, but a thousand times." He smiled. "You will never know when it is really coming."

"I had no idea that there were copies of *Life* in that envelope," I gasped.

"I think I believe you," he said thoughtfully, putting a single bullet into the magazine of that terrible pistol. "But I don't really care. You see, your father is still alive. I'm sure he's very proud of you. Your death will shatter him. Which is what I want. Actually, I would prefer to kill him. But since I am now an agent of the other side, I am no longer exactly welcome in the Workers' Paradise. So if

I cannot get to him, you have to take his place."

I babbled something about an unwritten understanding between the two countries that we never killed one another's agents and diplomats on home ground. (Well, almost never.)

It made him laugh. "I could get into a lot of trouble with my superiors. They wouldn't like this sort of thing at all. If our people have to kill each other, it's always much more refined than this. More professional. You know that as well as I do. But then this isn't your average professional mission." He peered at me inquiringly. "Is it?"

And then he was gone.

The only good thing about the situation with Lavrenti was that he was not my worst problem. Katya was. Her red dress had become a banner leading the raging forces of materialism that had broken loose within her. Our fights over the dress were growing worse every week. I could not make her understand that the dress was a threat to our very lives. That Comrade Stalin did not always smile as he did in his photographs. That when the embassy secret police came around to ask how a junior official's wife was so well dressed, they would never believe the story about winning the prize at the supermarket. That they would accuse me of taking bribes. Tales of people being drugged and packed in steamer trunks to be shipped out of various embassies on special flights back to Moscow had no effect on her. She was like a gorgeous, wilful child. She just wanted her dress.

I thought of burning it. But I realized that she was capable of throwing a fit of hysteria in public. Young officials with what were termed "unreliable" wives came under heavy scrutiny. She knew this too, the crafty peasant. When she saw me eyeing her dress during one of our arguments she became very sweet and said what a shame it was about poor Novikov being posted back to some remote Soviet republic just because he could not control his wife's outbursts. Checkmate.

Even during our worst arguments I never thought she was acting out of simple maliciousness. It was much more complicated than that. It was just that some incredible need had overtaken her. (She alone proved my theory about wealth in Enemy Number One.) That dress was like the missing jigsaw piece to her existence. So I tried to be nice to her. To help her through her addiction. And save my career, of course. One of my ideas was an elegant dinner party for just the two of us. Candlelight. Wine. Loud music for the benefit of whatever secret policeman there was listening to us through the bug hidden somewhere within the walls. The first part of the dinner was a roaring success. Katya and I sat opposite each other, she in her beautiful red dress and I in my best baggy Moscow suit. As the traffic noise of New York filtered into our small embassy apartment, we toasted one another on our chic, stylish way of life. I made sure she understood that this was really no different than if she was out wearing her dress at the Copacabana. Or the Plaza.

Mistake. The more I talked about it, the more I could see images of the Copa and the Plaza dancing before her eyes. I was suddenly a man desperately treading verbal water as the storm gathered around him. I spun marvellous tales of the imaginary elegance surrounding us. She started to drink too much wine.

"Comrade Stalin is a turd," she cried tearfully.

All the blood must have instantly left the upper part of my body. *Siberia!* I scrambled over to the radio, turning it up as loud as I dared.

"A hot, steaming turd. Plop. Plop. Plop." She giggled and bounced around the room. My first impulse was to clap my hand across her mouth and drag her onto the bed. But that would probably have created an even more vocal outburst. So I did the only thing I could think of. I ran to the bathroom and turned on the shower. The noise of the water helped to muffle her babbling. Then I raced back to our living room and embraced her.

"I'll take you to all the best stores tomorrow," I whispered in her ear, pretending to be dancing with her. "Macy's. Gimbels. We can go to them all."

"We can?" She brightened instantly.

"We'll go and look in them all."

"I don't want to look. I want to buy. I want to be like the women who live here."

"Of course, my darling. Of course. But you must be nice to Comrade Stalin, otherwise we won't even live here. We'll live in Siberia. Or maybe worse."

"I need gloves. And a purse like the one on the cover of *Vogue*."

"Soon, dearest. Soon."

"You promise?"

"Of course I promise. Now let's just sit down," I whispered. "And let's drink a toast to our beloved Comrade Stalin," I said in a loud voice. Loud enough to be heard over the music and the noise of the shower. She sat down uncertainly and raised her glass. I could hardly see her because of the steam coming out of the shower. The entire room was filled with steam. But I was afraid to turn the shower off in case she said something else that would get us in trouble. We sat there and finished our elegant dinner, smiling at each other through the fog. Her make-up began to run. We were both drenched in sweat. The candles went out. But somehow it was better. More erotic. I took off my jacket and tie. And then my shirt. Sitting there in my baggy pants held up by my suspenders, I proposed many more toasts. I had switched over to vodka now and murmured messages of eternal love while pointing out that her mascara was running

48

down into that gentle white valley between those magnificent breasts of hers. She giggled and stood up to take off her dress. When she sat down she accidentally kicked one of the legs of the folding card table that we were using. It collapsed, sending the food crashing into her lap. We both giggled.

I'm not sure of the exact sequence of the events that followed. I remember being on the floor eating some kind of dessert off her thighs. And I remember the sound of sirens. And loud voices and hammering noises. Then suddenly a strange, helmeted face looming up through the fog outside our window. The window was a hundred feet off the ground.

Someone had seen the steam pouring out of our windows and thought it was smoke. The fire department had been called. Aerial ladders zoomed into the night. Searchlights crisscrossed the building. I dimly recall my one brilliant decision: I grabbed Katya, ripping the few remaining pieces of clothing from her body, wrapped her in a towel, and then thrust her in front of the firemen on the ladder, who were about to take an axe to our window. The sight of Katya in the slipping towel almost caused the top fireman to step off the ladder. And suddenly our apartment was filled with embassy security guards yelling at the firemen to go away and staring into Katya's breasts. There was much yelling and cursing in two languages and people bumping into each other. Our security guards were sure the firemen were really enemy agents looking for an excuse to get inside the embassy and install listening devices.

I remember most clearly the chilling sight of Ivchenkov, my boss, walking into the apartment, his eyes dark with anger and the veins on his face glowing like neon in the windows of a cheap bar. I immediately began yelling at a fireman about not even being able to take a shower in this fascist country without having people

49

trying to break in on you. I hoped my outburst would save me.

What saved me was Katya's towel. Ivchenkov cleared everyone else out of the room, waved the firemen away, and then he too stared into those two splendid puddings of hers. As the towel inched its way even lower, Katya sniffled convincingly, big tears rolling down her cheeks. The petty tyrant consoled her with soothing words and pawed and patted and manoeuvred for a better look.

The next day I took Katya to the big department stores. I thought that the excursion might at least help bank the fires within her. Once again: mistake. She stared at the mannequins dressed in all the stylish clothing. And the elegant New York women in the better stores. Then she stared at herself in the mirrors.

She saw a peasant from the steppes looking back at her.

"What happened to the rest of my money?" she said with a certain icy determination that I did not like the sound of.

"I put it in the stock market," I said before I realized that I should have told her nothing.

"What's the stock market?" she said suspiciously.

"You buy stocks."

"Is that like furs? Or jewels?"

"No, it's sort of . . . pieces of paper," I said.

"Paper?" Her eyes went wide. Nothing of her past life as a peasant had prepared her for the stock market. I tried to explain. She began yelling at me, right there in Saks Fifth Avenue, and customers and salesgirls turned to see who was causing this outburst in the strange language. I took her over to the street where Taylor, Wendell, Bulmer & Carr had their offices.

"So?" she said defiantly. "Go in there and get our money back."

"Are you crazy? I can't be seen going in there again. I was risking my life even setting foot in there the first time. Comrade Stalin says those are the people we are to crush."

"So why did you give them the money?"

"As a joke," I yelled, exasperated.

Irony was not among her strong points. She peered in through the window at the grey men sitting sombrely behind their desks. Her gorgeous blue eyes narrowed into slits. All she understood was that she could be looking at beautiful clothes in a store window, but here she was staring at a bunch of dull-looking men. Who had her money.

"Comrade Stalin is right," she yelled at me. "They should be crushed so I can go out to buy the new purse." She stormed off into the lunchtime crowds. I was about to follow her when I heard someone calling me.

It was Sam Smith. He hurried to me, his pale, thin face glowing with unaccustomed exertion. "Congratulations," he said proudly. "You've made a small fortune."

Standing there on the streets of Enemy Number One with a broker – *my* broker – shaking my hand was more than I could take. For a moment I was too terrified even to look to see if anyone was watching. Inside the office, Sam explained. He had taken a few chances, he said almost apologetically. But they had paid off. "First I bought options," he told me. "Better leverage." I nodded as if I knew what he was talking about. "Then I exercised the options and rolled them over."

"Of course."

"I bought into a couple of little companies that no one has ever heard of. One called IBM. Office machines and that kind of thing. And something called Polaroid. They're into fancy cameras. Risky stuff, but with any luck we might make another dollar or two."

For a long time I sat on a bench in my beloved Central Park. I was a capitalist! I chuckled out loud. Me, a peasant boy, son and grandson of commissars who had liquidated capitalists by the thousands. Here I was playing chess from both sides of the board. Tomorrow morning in the meeting with Ivchenkov and the others, I would be presenting plans to smash Enemy Number One from within. But for tonight I was content with my little private joke.

It was to change my life. I didn't realize at that time how much I liked owning something. It was amazing. Me, a member of the Party, owning a tiny chunk of those companies. It was all mine. Not the Party's. Not the State's. Not the People's.

Mine!

And after all, as long as I was careful, what harm could there be in that?

4

My life had changed for ever.

For a while I tried to tell myself it was just a phase I was going through. But it was no use. I realized that the thrill of owning something — anything, other than the suit I was wearing — was not going to go away. I began to dream of owning other things. And I began plotting strategies for the companies that I now owned little pieces of. One night I stayed up late and pretended I was the president of this IBM outfit. I destroyed Remington Rand and two other electronics companies in no time flat. All their executives were sent to the *gulag*. A few were given show trials where they confessed their sins.

Comrade Stalin's methods applied to the business world of Enemy Number One. A natural blending. It was brilliant. While the secret police of my beloved IBM were rounding up a few revisionist suspects, Katya came out of the bedroom looking very tired and irritable. She told me that it was three o'clock in the morning and that I was crazy.

She was right.

It was the beginning of my double life. I was forced to admit that I was thrilled to be living in Enemy Number One. Although it was different from the images that leapt out from the pages of *Life* when I was a boy, Enemy Number One was still more exciting and colourful than the greyness that seeped into almost every corner of our lives back home. A greyness shot thought by intermittent bolts of fear.

I wanted to stay in Enemy Number One. There were only two ways I could remain. One was to defect. But in those days our secret police hunted defectors to the ends of the earth. A bullet in the brain would be the most merciful retribution a defector could expect. And then there were my parents and my little sister. Comrade Stalin would make their lives hell on earth. The thought of Natasha alone, slowly freezing behind barbed wire, was enough to make me give up all thoughts of defecting.

The second way to remain in Enemy Number One was to continue what I was now doing — devising schemes to destroy it. My schemes would have to continue to be brilliant and devastatingly effective. Otherwise I would be sent home to some obscure posting in places like Moldavia or Kiev. There was fierce competition for jobs like mine. The various ministry schools and secret police academies were still crammed with young men with inventively diabolical minds. As long as my ideas were more destructive than theirs, I could look forward to a long career of either living in Enemy Number One or being sent there on a regular basis.

So I was caught.

I brooded about that for a day or so until I came up with what seemed to be a marvellous solution. I decided I would add another level of intrigue to my already convoluted life. I would find ways — quiet, secret ways — to rally the citizens of Enemy Number One to defend themselves against my schemes.

If my profession required that I destroy Enemy Number One, my soul demanded that I save it.

Or was it my soul and my precious IBM?

5

A few days later I set in motion the first of my plans.

I had spent the day up in the Bronx, first riding the subway as far as 175th Street and then taking several taxis, each time doubling back on my route to see if any cars were following me. It was all classic espionage stuff, the kind any junior-grade spy handler gets taught early in his training. I had several purposes in going to the Bronx. My official purpose was to service one of our drops. This was something we all took turns doing. And we always had to be careful that the counter-intelligence people in Enemy Number One had not discovered any of our drops. Servicing a drop was always a time of tension.

There was more tension than usual on that day, because I was late. Hours late. On the way up to the Bronx, I discovered from a taxi driver that my beloved Brooklyn Dodgers were playing the terrible Yankees at the stadium just a few blocks from the drop. The taxi driver was going to the game and had an extra ticket that he sold to me for an outrageous price. (I paid for it out of the money I was leaving for our spy, who was supplying us with information about the submarines being built in Connecticut.) For the whole game the taxi driver and I sat next to each other, screaming insults at one another's teams and drinking beer. A lot of beer. By the seventh inning, the taxi driver had lapsed into Armenian epithets, while I was threatening the entire Yankee team with Siberia. A couple of hours later in the middle of my victory celebration at a nearby bar, I realized that I had forgotten to make my drop.

Actually, drops. The first drop was my official one. It

was for the submarine man. The second one was more personal. It was for Sam, my broker. After my last visit to Taylor, Wendell, Bulmer & Carr, I decided that this tycoon business was just too risky to carry on in broad daylight. Unless I kept my visits to Sam's office to an absolute minimum, sooner or later someone would spot me going in there. So I began leaving instructions for Sam in some of our drops in the downtown area. When I had explained it to him, he thought it was a rather strange way of doing business. But then Sam had always thought my ways of operating were slightly bizarre. Fortunately, I was blessed with a broker who was not only a young genius, but also had almost no curiosity outside his own field.

When I was returning along Madison Avenue toward the embassy, I saw a rather rotund and familiar figure walking slowly up and down the block on the opposite side of the street. It was Anatoly, my closest friend in the embassy. And a complete misfit. Chubby, nervous, and capable of admirable fits of Slavic passion even without vodka, Anatoly was definitely not equal to the embassy scheming that swirled around him. But somehow he blundered through his job as a second secretary. A whale among sharks. Anatoly was the only one there I could talk to — not about everything, of course. More than once the two of us had closed the bars on Second Avenue while loudly lamenting the demise of Pushkin, Tolstoy, and literature in general since the revolution. What I loved about Anatoly was that he really meant it. I could not see how he could survive for long. I felt protective toward him.

When he saw me he hurried across the street. "Where have you been?" he exclaimed breathlessly. "They're very upset with you back there." He nodded towards the embassy.

"Dodgers 3, Imperialist Yankees 1." I grinned. I

showed a bravado strangely out of character with my normal reactions to such a situation.

"Not again," Anatoly groaned. "You idiot. You had a meeting with Ivchenkov two hours ago. He's furious. Boris is in there with him now. And Katya's upset too."

Katya did not worry me. Boris did. He was the *rezident* — the head of the secret police within the embassy. Anatoly drew closer to me and stuck his nose in front of my face. "Breathe," he ordered. I breathed all over him and he grimaced. "Capitalist beer spoiled by the vodka of the proletariat. A terrible mixture. No wonder you're late. Your breath is practically combustible, comrade. Here, drink this." He shoved a thermos of bitter hot coffee at me.

The coffee was a mistake. With sobriety came fear. As I walked the remaining block back to the embassy, my bravado suddenly crumbled. Ivchenkov was bad enough, but Boris terrified me. He too was listed as merely a second secretary, but his real position — as a colonel in what was then called the NKVD — inspired fear in us all. With his sharp, thin face and his oily, receding hairline, Boris always managed to look sinister until he smiled. Then he became charming. A killer but charming. His smile even gave him a kind of innocence. But we all knew that his survival through the terrible purges that had wiped out so many of his colleagues a few years earlier had not been the result of loyalty or gentleness. I had always suspected that the last living image in the eyes of more than one doomed man was that terrible smile of his. Whenever Boris smiled at me my spine turned to ice.

I walked straight into that smile. In Ivchenkov's office they were waiting for me. But I made one of those instant, almost unconscious decisions that sometimes change our destinies. I seized control of my own terror, swinging it around until it pointed at them like a cannon. Offence, of course, being the best defence.

"Where is my poet?" I demanded irritably. Just like that. No explanations. No greetings. No grovelling. Just an angry demand for a poet. What could be simpler?

"I beg your pardon?" Boris looked at me as if I were crazy. I was staring right into the line of fire of that chilling smile.

"My poet! How many times, comrade, do I have to ask for a lousy poet?"

The smile faded, replaced by a hint of uncertainty. I was winning.

"Poet?"

"Yes, Comrade Colonel. My poet. The one that I've asked you for a dozen times in my written reports." Boris was lazy. That was his weakness. I knew he had not read any of my reports about my big scheme. It was my plan to bring over a Russian poet and begin to infiltrate and then recruit intellectuals in Enemy Number One by holding poetry readings. Later would come other cultural exchanges on a more lavish scale. But for now all I wanted was one lousy poet. And I said so.

"What kind of poet do you need?" asked Boris.

"A standard secret-police type of poet," I said in a tired voice, as if I'd said it a thousand times before. "Craggy features, unruly hair, rumpled clothes, and a tragic air about him. The usual, comrade."

Boris tried to regain ground. He could feel Ivchenkov reassessing whatever they had discussed about me before I arrived. "Comrade, this matter of your poet is all well and good. But it obscures the fact that you have been outside the embassy totally unaccounted for during the past three hours." His smile reappeared. His voice was dry with menace.

But I was ready for him. "*Four* hours."

This admission of what seemed like further guilt took him by surprise. "Four hours, then," he said with somewhat less certainty.

"And next time it might be ten hours, comrade. Unless I get my poet. I mean, how many times am I expected to meet with the intellectuals of this country, promising them a poet, when none shows up? How do you expect us to bring about the revolution in this country when the intellectuals are not being won over by us? I have to sit there listening to them quote all their great poets — Whitman, Sandburg, Picasso! And I have no poet to show them. As I had promised them weeks ago. So I have to spend hours talking this rubbish, when I should be leaving that to my poet. Turning him loose on them. Drowning them in the fuzzy meanings that they love. So I can then move in and recruit those who can be of use to us, comrade. Instead of wasting my time away from my job. And my Katya. Besides, I was under the impression that Moscow had ordered us to carry out such plans."

My last remark echoed silently among us. I knew it would. It was only partly a bluff on my part. Normally I would never have dared quote Moscow's desires without a bushel of official cables to back me up. (It was probably the vodka making a comeback. Vodka always made me brave. Or stupid, which was usually the same thing.) But it was one of those times when several of the ministries in Moscow were being purged. Comrade Stalin's paranoia was again sweeping through them like a scythe, and the bloody, whispered tales reverberated out to all of us. The result was yet another bout of bureaucratic terror. No one was sure who was in or out of favour.

The following day it was announced that my poet had been ordered and would be shipped over within a week.

However, I was not at the embassy to receive the grand news. I was out in the Bronx frantically trying to correct a terrible error. That morning one of Boris's assistants came into my office and told me that the loose brick had been removed from an old factory wall not far from the Hudson River. We checked on that brick regularly. If it was ever removed it meant that our submarine spy was in some kind of trouble and needed an emergency meeting. I raced up to the Bronx, going through the usual diversionary taxi rides. In an empty old warehouse I met him at three o'clock, the appointed hour for such emergencies. He was a fat, nervous little man with access to the blueprint room where the submarines of Enemy Number One were refitted.

"You keep pushing me for more. Always more," he said in his whining little voice. "But this is too much. I ain't trying to be a hero, you know."

"I realize that."

"It's too much, I tellya."

"What's too much?"

"This!" He handed me the envelope I had left for him yesterday in the drop. "I tellya, I ain't got no other options."

"What are you talking about?"

"What you asked for. It's too much. You want the option of getting stuff out of IBM? Not from me, buster. I toldya once, I toldya a dozen times — subs I can get. But anything else, forget it. I toldya, I'm just in this until the house is paid off."

With suddenly heavy fingers, I opened the envelope and read the message: "Options — IBM?" It was the message I had intended to leave for Sam. I stared at my submarine spy. I could not think of a thing to say. My silence unnerved him even more. "*IBM* is a tough nut to crack," he said. He was sitting on the edge of a packing crate, his left leg jerking up and down like a jackhammer. "And where's my money? The three hundred you usually leave for me?"

I just stared.

"Okay, okay, so the information I got you last time wasn't that hot. But it's getting tough, I tellya."

On my way back downtown, I risked a phone call to

Sam, who asked me why the two hundred and eighty dollars I had left for him was not accompanied by any instructions. I could not tell him that the blank piece of paper the money was wrapped in was really crammed with invisible coded writing requesting blueprints on submarine sonar devices. But Sam had taken matters into his own hands, as usual. "I put the money into a neat little defence stock. Defence is going to be very bullish, you know. Because of the Russians and all that."

My poet arrived at the weekend. He was perfect. His name was Alexei, and he was dead drunk when he got off the plane. Alexei had the requisite craggy features, his deeply lined face framed by an unruly profusion of white hair. When he read his poetry, his voice sounded the way people thought God would probably sound. And best of all was the tragic air that hung around him as visibly as his long scarf, which always trailed dramatically in the wind. His tragedy was real. In his twenties Alexei had been a brilliant poet. But after the revolution he was slowly drawn into the demands of the Party, that he write more "socially useful" poetry. Glorifying the workers. The Red Army. Or denouncing counter-revolutionaries. At first he resisted. His works were no longer published. His books were removed from the stores. And former friends could no longer look him in the eye when they met on the street. The books of these former friends were filling the stores. They glorified the workers or the Red Army or denounced counter-revolutionaries.

One day Alexei got drunk and wrote a poem that was exactly the opposite of everything he truly felt. It was a poem claiming that Stalin was the wisest, most loving leader in the world. He laughed ferociously as he wrote it. The poem was published all over the country. He was given a car and an apartment, and he told himself that it was just for a year. Anything to keep from being forgotten by the public. But after a year he found that something terrible had happened to him. He was now unable to write about what really mattered to him. Somehow the images no longer soared with imagination. Instead they dropped onto the pages with the same leaden solemnity that marked his official writing. It was a time of panic. Alexei did everything he could think of to regain his genius. But the flame had died.

By the time I got to him, Alexei had thoroughly embalmed the remains of that genius in decades of vodka. New York was to be no exception. Anatoly and I bundled him into a taxi and had to physically restrain him from fleeing every time it stopped at a traffic light. Drunk as he was, he wanted to get drunker. Poetry reading was not for Alexei. He had long ago decided that anyone who would listen to the poetry he wrote was not someone he would want to associate with. Anatoly and I made the mistake of allowing him one drink at the bar a block away from the elegant East Seventy-first Street brownstone of Harold Leonard Dawes, the famous playwright. It was a mistake because we needed drinks more than Alexei did. By the time we stood in front of Harold Leonard Dawes's front door I was debating whether or not to take a raincheck, as they say in my beloved baseball. Alexei was drunk and belligerent, and Anatoly and I were not far removed from his condition. But on the other side of that door were forty people who were waiting to see their first real, live Russian poet.

"Comrade poet is shit-faced," said Anatoly in his heavily accented English. We were trying to figure out what to do and did not want Alexei to understand what we were saying.

"Is part of image of comrade poet," I said.

"Much more better to get heroic artist of the motherland away from imperialist counterparts."

Alexei roared with impatience. Each of us was holding him by one arm. It was now or never. My entire scheme was in jeopardy. "Is too late," I said, ringing the doorbell. Inside we could hear the sound of music and many voices that chorused expectantly at the sound of the chime. The waxy, parchment-pale face of Harold Leonard Dawes himself — known to his friends as H. L. D. — opened the door. As if we had been practising it all our lives, Anatoly and I pitched our drunken poet through the doorway with a precise and synchronized heave. H. L. D. was almost knocked off his feet. The effect on that roomful of elegantly casual and generally brilliant citizens of Enemy Number One was stunning. It was as if the canapés had suddenly been electrified. Or as if we had pitched a live bull into that china shop of reason and rational thought.

For an instant I thought it was all over. But then I looked around into excited faces and said to myself, comrade, it is not only the heroic Brooklyn Dodgers who can come from behind.

Just the sight of Alexei thrilled them. Here he was! At long last — Revolutionary Man! Roaring with passion and filled with art.

He was far better than any bloodless clerk of a poet I might have been given. This was just what they had expected. The printing presses within a dozen minds immediately rolled with reviews, journal articles, magazine pieces, and even musical scores. H. L. D. was delighted. He had been responsible for bringing one back alive. His introductory remarks were made over the irritable mumbling of Alexei, who just wanted another drink. It was well known, said H. L. D., that revolutionary man was at a higher stage of development than others. And that mankind had been born into a blissful state of innocence, only to have it poisoned by the institutions around him. Alexei was described as one of the brilliant artists of this newly rekindled state of innocence and hope that was practised in Russia.

Anatoly and I applauded heartily and exchanged glances. I had been counting the house with the beady eye of a showman. It was dripping with names. Alexei did not disappoint them. Or me. From the instant he stood up and lurched into his first poem, he set loose all the images that he had lost so many years ago. But it was not his words that did it. It was his performance. No one in the audience understood a single word of Russian. But that chiselled face, which so obviously had the pain and the glory of the workers' revolution etched upon it, set loose the phantom horde of heroic images. That rich, rising voice rolled like purifying thunder across the steppes in forty minds. Nature and mankind had been fused at last through Art. Happy peasants cheered, heroic Cossacks took up arms, and finally life had meaning.

Alexei was reciting his poem about the young Party member who fulfilled his monthly quota in the tractor factory. It was the poem that had earned him his new Zil with the whitewall tyres.

When the applause finally died, there was a difficult moment. "Comrade," said a woman who had removed her diamond necklace as a show of solidarity during the poem, "we *must* have a translation!" There was a rush of approving voices. Anatoly and I hastily conferred.

"The goose of the revolution, as they say here, is cooked," whispered Anatoly.

"I know. They think they've been to a literary banquet."

"Now they find out the oats they've been eating have already been through the horse." Anatoly was perspiring heavily, his chubby face glistening in the soft green glow of the elegant Victorian lights.

"No problem, comrade," I said. "All we do is scoop up the oats and push them back through the beast."

I stood up and motioned for quiet. A revolutionary

64

hush settled across the packed room. I told them I was sure that they would not want me to translate in any way that would not do justice to the greatness of Alexei. There was a general murmur of agreement. It was impossible, I said, to translate the whole poem they had just heard. Perhaps another time. But what I could do was recite one verse of it. It was the verse that every schoolchild in Russia had learnt by heart.

Anatoly looked over at me as if I were crazy. For a moment I thought he might be right. I stood staring into that silence and began saying whatever seemed remotely what I imagined they wanted Alexei's poetry to sound like.

> *"The eye turns inward*
> *Filling the soul with a universe*
> *of nothingness . . ."*

For a moment I went blank. I stalled for time by pretending to be translating as I went along.

> *"Until when God has died*
> *I have found the chains*
> *Of my soul cast off*
> *Into the glories*
> *Of those dark nights*
> *When I rode on swift fears . . ."*

As I said — not only my Dodgers! I knew I had them. It was truly thrilling. Even Alexei had stopped drinking and gaped with expectation, hanging onto every one of my/his words. But where did I go from "swift fears"? I stalled for a moment. The silence was deafening.

Alexei, who of course had not understood a word of it, came to my rescue. "You must be at the part where the commissar is warning them to look out for counter-

65

revolutionary tendencies in the factory."

"Ah, yes, thank you, comrade."

> *"Through the fires of that*
> *Terrible new dawn*
> *That burned away*
> *My guilt."*

Neither Anatoly nor I had seen an audience like this one since we saw the stripper drop her G-string at a Forty-second Street burlesque house. The applause swept through the room. H. L. D. rushed to Alexei and shook his hand. Alexei, for the first time in decades, was caught up with the power of his own work. Within minutes there were invitations for him to speak in front of dozens of other high-powered gatherings.

I had hit the jackpot. Finally, my plan was working. The plan was simple: I had convinced my superiors at the Kremlin that we had never made enough of an effort to win over the intellectuals of Enemy Number One. Because of their influence in what has come to be called the media, and in public life and opinion, everyone understood that they were an important group from which to try to win friends. So I proposed cultural exchanges. What could be more harmless than a poet or a bunch of dancers? Give me a handful of artists, I had argued in front of the old men in the Kremlin, and I will deliver a hundred intellectuals on your very doorstep.

But what I had not told the old men in the Kremlin was that I intended — secretly, of course — to make the plan backfire once the intellectuals were in Russia on their tour. It would backfire in such a way that those cynical old men in the Kremlin would suddenly find themselves responsible for the fiasco.

After all, how could I still be expected to destroy Enemy Number One when Consolidated Edison was about to split two for one?

6

The next day the phones at the embassy did not stop ringing with requests for Alexei's presence at various literary or society functions. Ivchenkov read through the list of names, chuckling and shaking his head. Even Boris was impressed. My status within the embassy rose immensely.

I had decided that I would turn Alexei loose on only one more gathering and then ship him back to Moscow. There was too great a risk that someone who spoke Russian might show up at one of the poetry readings and realize that my translations were not about the tractor factories of which Alexei had just spoken.

Besides, there was the problem of Alexei himself. For the first time in thirty years his poetic ego had risen up from the depths. Suddenly he was convinced that his writings about the factory workers' quotas and the kindly commissars had been works of genius after all. He became even more impossible to deal with. When he was drunk, which was often, he would berate us with lines from the poem he had just started writing. It was about workers completing a hydroelectric dam on schedule.

Anatoly finally had to shut him up by threatening to have his Zil taken away when he got back to Moscow. It was the only thing that worked.

I sifted through the sheaves of invitations and finally decided on the party hosted by Miriam Nelson at her elegant apartment overlooking Central Park. Miriam Nelson was an author. She was a good friend of H. L. D., so I knew he would be there too. I wanted to close the deal, as they say, with him. Miriam Nelson also had the advantage of having been to Russia once, during the war. I knew that my father was one of the commissars who had been ordered to escort her on a tour behind the lines. He had talked about her for weeks afterwards, until my mother had bitterly yelled at him. And once, I had peeked out into the living room late at night and seen my father taking one of his rolled-up white balloons out of the hiding place, where he stored them under the copies of *Life* magazine he was once again collecting. I knew that the next evening he was again supposed to be escorting Miriam Nelson, the woman from Enemy Number One, on a tour up near the front lines. One week later I actually saw them together, walking near the barracks that were not far from our school. I remember her as being much younger than Mother. And very attracted to Father.

Miriam Nelson no longer seemed so young. Her features had become sharper, and her eyes had a defensiveness that her smile could not erase. Like Mother's. When she found out who I was she threw her arms around me and gave me a hug. And searched my face for traces of Father's features.

Her party was my triumph. The names of her guests would have been like my shopping list. Novelists, journalists, scientists, historians, sociologists. Names that even the old men in the Kremlin would recognize. But best of all was Miriam. She did most of my work for me. My presence had triggered memories, and even before Alexei had a chance to read his first poem she was talking about the old days on the Russian front. The stories came rolling out in waves of nostalgia that swept her audience into worlds of train rides across the frozen steppes. Heroic peasants. Happy women workers who were side by side with their men. Revolutionary songs. Clear-eyed soldiers preparing to fight the fascists in the name of the revolution. And Father — even Father strode forth heroically exhorting the troops to defend the motherland.

My memories were not like hers at all. I remembered only the cold and the terrible hardships that we all endured. And the fear in the eyes of the young soldiers whenever Father was in their presence. On orders from Moscow, Father was in charge of a rearguard company of secret police, whose job it was to follow the troops into battle and shoot down those who showed any signs of retreating.

But who was I to argue over details when Miriam was filling the room with magic?

Her stories taught me a crucial lesson. That roomful of supercharged intellects was locked in a desperate quest. Not for reason. Not for the rational, desiccated thought that most of them claimed to pride themselves on.

What they wanted was romance. Passion. Heroism.

It was the very thing that their reason and enlightenment had cut to pieces. Scorned even. But all their lives they had really been engaging in their own form of Social Realism, purging from their existence whatever could not withstand the cold glare of rational inquiry. Yet that was what most attracted them. From that moment on, romance — passion, heroism, call it what you will — became the door opener in my sales pitches to intellectuals. (Later I refined it, after watching their tendency to be existential flame throwers burning off whatever meaning in life they happened to encounter. I began pitching revolution in such a way that it seemed the ideal thing to fill the void, giving their existence some purpose after all. It was like selling water to camels. A stampede. And as the clincher, as the salesmen in Enemy Number One say, I threw in a big one — dignity. Dignity was very big. Because, oddly enough, many wore a sense of irritable humiliation around them like a cloak. They felt slighted, even mocked, by the more practical citizens in their own country who held positions of power and acclaim in politics or business. A dangerous mistake. Starve them and they would come grovelling for food; but humiliate them and they would fuel their high-powered minds with venom and plot your demise in a million ways.)

By the time Alexei lurched to his feet he could have recited the minutes of the last Politburo meeting and still have been crowned poet laureate of the revolution. I stood up and made my usual halting translation, thinking up lines as I went along, stopping for the continual bursts of applause. (I suddenly discovered artistic jealousy. I found myself seething whenever Alexei staggered up and took another sweeping bow. For *my* poetry.)

Then Anatoly and I really got down to work. After the poetry reading, we let the requests to tour Russia start flooding in. We were very careful to let them come to us, almost appearing disinterested. And by ten o'clock we had eleven definites and seven maybes. We discovered that the more vague we were about arranging such a tour, the more insistent our new friends — led by Harold Leonard Dawes — were about going. Soon the room was filled with excited planning and talk of solidarity with the masses.

I remember listening and thinking, Aha, my budding revolutionaries! Wait till you find out what is in store for you. For I had decided that they were going to see more than anyone bargained for — not just what the old men in the Kremlin wanted them to see. What no one in that room knew was that I had anonymously entered their names on the mailing list of one of the small magazines published in New York by Russian exiles who had fled for their lives from Comrade Stalin. These magazines always contained amazingly accurate articles about the labour camps, the purge trials, the executions, and other facets of life back home that Comrade Stalin tried to hide from the world.

I knew that at least some of these intellectuals would read those articles. Then, no matter what they wanted to believe, they would demand to see the truth. At least to refute what was in those articles. The old men in the Kremlin would be besieged by these reluctant truth-seekers. And my budding revolutionaries would *have* to realize they were being lied to by those old men. There would then be angry voices. Furious departures. Back in New York, articles, broadcasts, and learned essays spewed in all directions, telling the citizens of Enemy Number One what they had discovered.

I did not envy the poor wretch who was to escort them on their tour.

How was I to know that the poor wretch would be me?

7

Less than a month later I stood next to Harold Leonard Dawes in Red Square. H. L. D. was having what could only be described as a religious experience. His pale green eyes almost clouded over as he stared at the Kremlin. It was, he murmured, a spiritual homecoming.

My eyes also clouded over when I stared at the Kremlin. From fear. I knew Comrade Stalin was inside. I also knew that my life now literally depended on this cranky playwright's state of ecstasy continuing with undiminished fervour.

I had known there would be trouble from the moment I returned to the embassy after the party at Miriam Nelson's. I was carrying Alexei's feet, and Anatoly was holding him under the arms. We walked right into that chilling smile. Boris had been waiting for us. For me. He would have waited till dawn just to break the news. He and Ivchenkov had been sending cables back and forth to Moscow. It was decided that the first tour should be made up of just one intellectual: Harold Leonard Dawes. If it went well with him, the others would follow in small groups. And there would be great rewards. But if it went badly with H. L. D.? I did not have to ask the question. The answer was in that terrible smile.

He saved the worst news until we had almost got Alexei into the elevator. When Boris told me that I was the one who was to escort H. L. D. to Russia, I dropped Alexei's feet. As the elevator door closed he informed me that they had decided it would be nice if Katya accompanied me too. A holiday, he said. I almost fainted. When the elevator door closed, Anatoly dropped Alexei onto the floor, where he lay mumbling fragments of poetry about a steel mill. For at least five minutes Anatoly and I rode up and down in the elevator, the same thoughts rushing through our heads. Whenever they sent both the husband and the wife back to Moscow it was always a sign that they might be liquidated. (I ask you, is there any more hideous word than *liquidated?*) During the purges of the previous fifteen years, our embassies around the world had been filled with stories of diplomats and their wives ordered back to Moscow for celebrations, meetings, or awards. And then being tortured or imprisoned or shot. Or all three. Sometimes it did not happen. Sometimes the relieved, joyous couple returned. But you could never be sure. In my case, the old men in the Kremlin, or even Comrade Stalin himself, would be waiting to see what happened with H. L. D.

I had always planned that it would be those soft and corrupt old men in the Kremlin who would be the ones in trouble. With their grasping for credit of other people's ideas. But now I understood why they were in the Kremlin while I was standing with a drunken poet at my feet. Those old men, so cunning, so cynical, had not survived all these years without refining their lethal sense of timing. While flunkies like me walked a tightrope in the dark, high above the mounds of corpses, they waited on the other side with patient smiles for the moment when the spotlight would shine.

In the ten days that remained until we departed, I made my preparations, almost paralysed with fear. My first desperate priority was Katya's red dress. There was just no way we could ever leave that dress sitting in the closet of our apartment while we were gone. Boris and his men would surely find it. But what could I do with it? If I tried to take the dress out of the building in a package, I would probably be stopped and searched by one of the secret police guards at the door. They were always on the lookout for anyone taking things out of the embassy. And because there were no fireplaces, burning it was out of the question. I finally decided that there was just one way to get the dress out of the embassy. Katya would have to wear it out, underneath her long winter coat.

But perhaps I made a mistake. Maybe I should have told her what I had in mind before we went out that night. Instead of merely saying that it would be a nice night for a walk. And why didn't she wear her dress?

When we left the embassy compound, walking arm in arm past the guards, I should definitely have known there would be trouble. She had hitched up the bottom of her red dress above her knees so it would not show under her coat. She was thrilled just to be wearing the dress. Too thrilled. I was beginning to panic because I did not know how I was going to break the news to her that she would be returning to the embassy without her precious dress. And while I was beginning to panic, she hugged me and gave me a big kiss, telling me how much she loved me. And then asking where we were going. I knew she wanted to go somewhere like the Copacabana. Or the Plaza. Or "21". Any of those glittering places where sleek men escorted their beautiful women out of the limousines.

Instead we went to a bar on Madison Avenue. Actually what happened was all my fault. But I was just too nervous and crazy in that terrible period to be thinking properly. After many drinks — too many — I suggested that we take a walk. I manoeuvred us over near Central Park. It was still early in the evening, and it was a cool, pleasant night. So it did not seem unusual when we walked through the edges of the park.

"I think you should take off your dress," I said when we came to a quieter area. She misunderstood what I meant. She looked at me seductively. "So, the commissar is stirring, is he?" She smiled, rubbing her hand slowly

75

across the front of my pants. (I mean, after all, doesn't every couple have their own names for such things?) She pressed herself closer to me, as only she could do. "You don't understand, Katya. I want you to take it off."

"I understand, Dimitri Nikolaevich." We were pressed together. She was breathing into my ear and her other hand was loosening the straps of her dress. We had backed up against a tree behind some bushes.

"No, my beloved. I want you to take your dress off . . . and leave it here."

I felt the motion of her hands slowing down and then stopping, as if they were powered by a battery that was wearing out. She pulled back and looked at me to see if I was joking.

"What do you mean — leave it here?"

"We cannot go back to Moscow and leave that dress in the closet."

She pulled away from me, her eyes filling with indignation. They almost glowed. "This is *my* dress!"

"Do you want to get us killed? Boris will search the apartment. If he hasn't already. He hates me. Any excuse to get rid of me is like a gift for him."

She had backed farther away. Her dress was down to her waist.

"Then the answer is simple," she said. "I will just have to take it with me."

What was the use? Here I was fighting Bloomingdale's for my life. I lunged after her, yelling things that I was later embarrassed about. Telling her that she would be packing fish in Murmansk if it were not for me. She was too quick. She raced onto the path, teetering along in her high heels. I soon caught up with her. She swung her purse at me as I grabbed her dress and began pulling it off her.

At that moment a cop came along. A cop on horseback.

It was, as the French would say, an existential moment. For Katya it was simply a choice between being married and being the owner of that exquisite red dress. No contest. "Rape!" she shrieked in Russian. The cop did not need an interpreter.

The sight of a ton or so of horsemeat thundering toward you is quite fascinating. It requires absolutely no intellectual activity for a decision to be reached regarding what to do next. I released Katya and took off like a shot through the bushes. Images of Cossacks thundering down on peasants leapt from some genetic memories and gave me the pure fear to really get up speed. For a few precious seconds I thought I would be safe. The horse was having trouble in the darkness just like me. I could hear the cop yelling and cursing behind me.

And then I ran into a tree.

The next four hours were terrible. Handcuffs. The ride in the back of the squad car. Then the fingerprints, the photographs. My angry demands for diplomatic immunity. Followed by grins from fat men in uniforms bulging at stomachs congealed with decades of doughnuts and bad coffee. The Commie. Pinko. Red sex fiend. Comrade Hard-onski. Hah, hah. Then the stinking jail cell filled with winos moaning on the floor and junkies trembling in the dark. And angry men threatening me with their eyes. But I was already too frightened to feel fear from them. What would happen when news of this got back to the embassy? No fear known to humanity could ever compare to that.

Then I was moved from the big cell and put in a smaller one by myself. My suit, which was splattered with mud, was taken from me, leaving me shivering in the darkness. I could not understand what was happening. Less than an hour later a man walked down the corridor toward my cell. He was carrying my suit, holding it out in front of him on a hanger. My suit had been cleaned and pressed. It was only when the man stopped in the light in front of me that I could make out who it was.

It was Lavrenti.

"You have nothing to worry about," he said. "It has all been hushed up. Your suit is clean. And it's only eleven o'clock. You'll be able to get back to the embassy before anyone asks any questions."

"Why are you doing this?"

He smiled. His eyes did not smile. Through his thick glasses they just peered at me accusingly. I felt the same chill I did when Boris smiled at me. "Because I wouldn't want anything to stop you from going on that trip."

"What trip?" Never give anything away. Rule number one.

"Please. Spare me. That old fraud has been running around telling everyone who would listen that he's going off to join the revolution. *Comrade* H. L. Dawes, I think it is now."

He was beginning to make me angry. "I'll get you a ticket for his lectures when he returns."

"I'm not sure you'll be able to." He grinned. "Because I'm not sure you're coming back. Pity. I'd prefer to finish you off myself. But in this case I'll defer to the masters. I hear they have a new man handling tortures in the Lubyanka. The word we get is that he's almost blind. Operates by touch. And by the kind of screams he produces. They call him the blind violinist. He can produce sounds from the human body never before heard." I felt my knees go weak. I tried not to show fear, but I knew I was.

Lavrenti opened the cell door. "Wouldn't it be awful if the old fraud just happened to feel he *had* to find out if all these nasty rumours about mass executions and labour camps in the Workers' Paradise are true?"

In the embassy everything was normal. I opened the

door to our apartment. Katya was sleeping. A picture of innocence. On the dining room table was a note saying she was sorry for yelling rape but it was my fault for trying to force her into giving up her precious red dress. And if I touched it again she would get *very* upset.

What could I do? Her mind was a battlefield of Stalin versus Fifth Avenue. And Fifth Avenue had won. At least for the moment.

But a few days later, on the morning we set sail, Katya had to sit through a bon-voyage party for Harold Leonard Dawes wearing one of the drab Moscow-made dresses she loathed. The party was exuberant and the champagne flowed freely. I noticed that Katya had drunk a little too much of it, so I stayed close to her. Never knowing what would happen next. (She was, as they say in Enemy Number One, a loose cannon on the deck.) I watched her eyes narrow with fury as she sat among a group of women who were dressed like the mannequins in the windows at Saks or Bloomingdale's. They were all telling her how fortunate she was to be going back to Russia.

There were speeches and toasts to the revolution and much talk of solidarity with the masses and of trading in the Buick for a Chevrolet, which was more acceptable along class-struggle lines. At one point H. L. D. introduced me to someone as "my comrade," and Miriam Nelson asked me, almost ordered me, to tell Father that she still had fond memories.

And that they would meet again.

It was a small, triumphant procession of cars that drove up to the docks. A few of them flew red banners from their aerials, and the sound of their horns blended into the blasts from the mighty foghorns of the ocean liner. Everyone was laughing and yelling slogans and passing champagne bottles between the cars.

Everyone but me. I sat clutching at the armrests and

staring rigidly at the waterfront. I felt like a condemned prisoner being driven to the scene of his doom. Confetti swirled around the thousands of passengers and those who were seeing them off, but to me it might as well have been snow. We struggled through the chaos of farewells and flashbulbs to the gangplank, where H. L. D. stopped to make sure the press photographers would properly record the moment.

And then it happened.

I can remember that instant so clearly that I can still replay it in my mind like running a piece of film over and over. Somehow in that tumultuous mob of waving people my eye caught a solitary figure moving quickly through the background, heading inexorably toward us.

Lavrenti.

He was dressed as a messenger. He picked his way through that crowd with grace and speed. He was carrying a large brown envelope. I turned and tugged at H. L. D.'s sleeve, hoping to flee from whatever it was that Lavrenti intended. But as usual he was relentless. We had made it to the top of the gangplank when Lavrenti caught up with us. He looked only at H. L. D. "From your publisher, sir," he said, thrusting the important-looking envelope into the playwright's hands. And then shooting a fiendish grin at me before fading back into the crowd.

A large brown envelope. I knew what was inside. My thoughts shot back to the day Lavrenti's father was dragged off to be shot, and my heart hammered me mercilessly as my knees seemed to lose their vertical capacity. Puzzled, H. L. D. opened the envelope. Inside was an advance copy of *Life* magazine. (What else?) H. L. D. turned to a page in the magazine that had been marked by a paper clip. There before my widening eyes was a big article about Russian prison camps in the *gulag*. Complete with photographs that had somehow been smuggled out. Attached to the page was a handwritten note on the stationery of his publisher. I caught only phrases of it: *"For God's sake, Harold . . . your reputation . . . don't let them accuse you of being duped again. . . ."* H. L. D. irritably jammed *Life* back into the envelope and went back to waving at the crowds.

I grasped the railing and sank against it, looking blankly down at the docks as the huge liner was pulling away. Lavrenti stood out in that mob as clearly as if a spotlight had shone on him.

He was waving to me and laughing. Uproariously.

I stared at the ocean for a long time after the other passengers had gone below and New York City had become just faint grey spires in the distance. I tried to think through my dilemma as clearly as I could. I vowed that if I survived, which at that moment looked somewhat doubtful, I would have to confront the problem of Lavrenti in a very direct manner. Strangely enough, I still liked Lavrenti, just as I had liked him when we were little boys back in Russia. And I even wished we could be friends again. But his devious wrath was now more than I could cope with. It was implacable. And perhaps truly mad.

If I lived through the next few weeks, what other choice was there but to kill Lavrenti?

8

Three days later, a cold grey sky stretched to the horizon. Harold Leonard Dawes and I sat in deck chairs, faces to the wind, bundled up like Eskimos. It was his idea, not mine. We were the only ones on the deck. He was reading the article in *Life*, shaking his head and muttering.

"What do you make of all this?" he said finally, thrusting the magazine at me.

"Typical bourgeois propaganda," I said too quickly.

"Just as I thought!" he exclaimed, as if I'd provided him with some scientifically verifiable truth. He flung the magazine overboard and sat staring irritably into the cold wind. I could almost feel his thoughts. *Duped . . . your reputation.* I was sitting next to a time bomb.

My other problem was that in just those few days I had come to loathe him. He was vain and arrogant, falling instantly into foul moods when the other passengers did not recognize him, and was contemptuous of them when they did. He loved all humanity as long as he did not have to come close to any of them. He treated the waiters and stewards like dogs and yet could rhapsodize on the essential dignity of the working man. I decided that he believed the revolution he was beginning to crave would not affect him in any way. Except perhaps to make him more famous. Fame was something he cared desperately about. He pretended he didn't. And there was something about this revolution business that definitely gave a little lustre. A little controversy. He had run the course of three marriages. Two divorces and a suicide. To make matters worse, he was fawning all over Katya. The old fool. She loved it.

It was the only time I saw his long, stern face soften. He exuded charm the moment she came into his presence and patted and pawed away at her, obviously in the hope of greater delights. At dinner it was as if I didn't exist, and when the band began playing he danced with her for an hour. I was just glad to get him out of my sight.

After the boat landed we took a train first to Finland and then to the Russian border. As we got closer, both H. L. D. and I experienced rising emotions, for totally opposite reasons. He peered out of the window, his eyes gleaming.

"I can see it!" he said exuberantly, motioning for us to look at the guard towers, barbed wire, and secret police patrols that were coming into view. We had to walk across the border into Russia. He looked like a man who was going through the gates of heaven. In his arms he was carrying a large, elegant parcel of food that friends had given him before leaving. Standing on the exact border, he stared at the parcel and suddenly threw it contemptuously back into Finland.

"You see," Harold Leonard Dawes said triumphantly, "there is no food shortage in the motherland. It's all bourgeois propaganda." He walked imperiously ahead. Behind him the secret police guards fought off the workers and each other in the scramble for the food.

For the next week I witnessed adulation in its purest form. Everything we showed him he perceived as a tribute to the dignity and justice of mankind. Of course a lot of preparation had been made by our people. The factory workers knew just how much they had to smile and be happy. At the collective farm, the peasants were booted out for the day and the secret police moved in their own people, who were experts at being cheerful. But even if all the arrangements had not been made, I was convinced he would still have loved everything he saw.

83

He was always comparing it to *back home*. And somehow *back home* was a place he wanted to get even with. This vindictiveness against his own country fascinated me. It made it possible for him to see everything as a mirror image of what I saw. The numbing drabness of the city. The secret police. The fierce propaganda. Somehow he managed to see it all as being dignified and just. Not like *back home*.

The fact that Gorky Street had almost no cars showed proper concern for the environment. And because the government ministers — even Stalin — earned only 250 roubles a month, they were not cut from the same greedy cloth as those crooks in power *back home*. (Who was I to point out that they had absolutely no need of money when they were given all their big cars, their luxury food from the special stores, and their huge apartments and their *dachas?* Crazy I was not.)

After a week in Moscow, I knew we had a live one. The secret police guides and I could smell success. H. L. D. was already writing glowing speeches and articles in his head. Word spread throughout the bureaucratic crevasses. Suddenly the old men in the Kremlin could sense the spotlight. They appeared out of nowhere. Dinners by candlelight after the Bolshoi. Speeches of interminable eloquence and flattery. And replies bursting with fervour.

Then the call came. Stalin would see him.

My nerves burned holes in my mind as we drove to the Kremlin. At the gates we were transferred into a different car and accompanied by an officer who pointed out the various cathedrals inside the Kremlin walls. We drove through the immaculate courtyards, past the gold-domed bell tower of Ivan the Great and the smaller, crenellated splendours of the Cathedral of the Assumption. The security was awesome. Terrifying even. Which was exactly what it was intended to be. We were searched several times by steel-faced men from the Guards' Directorate, who would lose their own lives in an instant if any weapon ever got past them. The car stopped in front of a long, low building where another officer took charge of us. Uniformed NKVD troops were discreetly stationed everywhere we looked. From behind us someone called out, ordering us aside, and we waited pressed up against a wall as somewhere in my mind muffled drums sounded. Suddenly dozens of huge black cars — Lincolns and Chryslers, just like they had in Enemy Number One — appeared out of nowhere and roared past us. The NKVD troops held their arms out in front of us, pressing us harder against that wall. In the midst of all those cars was one with murky green windows through which you could see nothing. It was a Packard, and as it sped by I could see that those windows were as thick as my finger.

This was Stalin's car.

Everywhere there were cars and rifles and secret police. Then suddenly they were gone, and a kind of silence hung about us as the NKVD troops seemed to catch their breath and lower their arms. Like everyone else I saw around Stalin, their ferocity simply seemed to be fear pulled inside out.

Inside the building we were taken to an elevator, which opened at the second floor into a long, red-carpeted corridor. I was amazed at how immaculate everything was, the floors all gleaming fiercely and the brass doorknobs looking as if they were never touched. At every corner of that corridor, another stern young guard saluted with an intimidating click of the heels.

We were escorted into a large, dark room with heavy curtains and overstuffed chairs. For at least an hour we sat there, just H. L. D., myself, and a guard who wore a suit that looked as though it had been measured for several different people. Through one of the windows I could see the tip of the coloured domes of St. Basil's Cathedral, perched on top of that bizarre building like the swirling turbans of a pasha gone mad. I remembered being told that when it was built centuries ago, the czar had expressed his gratitude to the architect by having the man's eyes gouged out, so he could never build anything as beautiful for anyone else.

Gratitude made me nervous, sitting there in Stalin's antechambers.

H. L. D. was also nervous. I had never seen him like that before. It was probably because it was the only time he was encountering anyone he considered to be his equal. Or at least close to him. He got up and paced nervously around that large room. The eyes of the guard never left him. H. L. D. went over to a desk on which there was a typewriter and neat piles of paper. He picked up a piece of carbon paper and studied it. "At least this is honest," he said. "Do you understand me?"

I didn't have the slightest idea what he was talking about. And what do you say to a man standing in Stalin's offices bestowing integrity upon a piece of carbon paper? I nodded numbly.

"This only creates a copy of what the writer himself does. Instead of stealing from others like the voracious capitalist mentality," he exclaimed passionately. "Do you know that one of my neighbours, a scientist, is prostituting his genius to create such theft? He has invented part of a machine that can photographically copy anything! Books, plays even! In an instant."

I said I hadn't heard about it.

"Not surprised," he muttered. "No one knows about it yet. It was only perfected last week. A company called Xerox. Who else but the capitalists could think of stealing the fruits of others' labours like that?" He threw down the carbon paper and resumed pacing across the room.

I sat there. Thinking. *Xerox?*

He paced and talked until suddenly there was a flurry of motion at the far end of the room. Several fierce-looking men entered. One of them told H. L. D. it was time for his appointment with Stalin.

I was left behind in that big room with the stern, silent plainclothesman. *Xerox?* I couldn't believe what was going through my mind. *Stop!* I told myself. Have you gone totally mad? *Only perfected last week?* On the desk was a telephone. My request to use it was met with a grunt and a nod. I dialled the ministry number that I normally phoned to relay messages to New York. (Ivchenkov had instructed me to stay in touch every couple of days. I figured it was his way of knowing whether or not I'd been arrested or shot.) I had to go through a Kremlin telephone operator to reach the ministry offices. The effect of phoning from Stalin's offices was amazing. The normally arrogant ministry officials were suddenly falling over themselves to carry out my every wish.

I was immediately put through to the woman in the ministry code room who had been assigned to take my messages. Mine and a hundred others. I was counting on that dry, disinterested female voice mirroring a mind of similar bureaucratic tendencies. A mind dulled by the endless incomprehensible and trivial messages she was forced to send. A mind without even enough curiosity to decide that something was very strange about my message. And that it should be handed over to one of the secret policemen who prowled the halls of the ministry. I loaded the message with the usual jumble of questions and instructions for Anatoly, who had been assigned to handle the drops for my spies while I was away.

But in the middle of it all, I included "*Xerox. Act on it immediately.*" And then gave the coded number of the drop that I had been using to get instructions through to Sam. I was still on the phone when there was a barrage of noise and motion from the far end of the room.

Stalin entered. As I stood there sending messages to my stockbroker.

The phone turned to lead in my hand. My limbs went as numb as wood. No words came from my mouth and it seemed that my stomach was on fire. I finally croaked, "That's all." And put the phone down.

Stalin stood talking to H. L. D., who towered over him. I was stunned by Stalin's appearance. Like everyone else I knew, I had never seen him in person. Only in newsreels of the May Day parades, or in the heroic paintings, where he looked like a giant. (If he didn't, we discovered later, the painters were dragged away and shot. Stalin was the ultimate critic.) Stalin was a midget compared to my image of him. His face was pockmarked and sallow, like the underbelly of a fish beginning to rot. His left hand hung strangely at his side, and I remembered the whispered rumours that Stalin had a withered arm.

H. L. D. stood there prattling away like an excited child, as the translator struggled to wade through all the flattery. It was obvious to everyone but H. L. D. that Stalin had lost all interest in the conversation. His eyes darted around the room, knifing whatever they saw. He noticed me standing there and inquired who I was. He was informed that I was from the embassy in New York and had brought this playwright over to Moscow. Stalin stared at me, through me, a tiny smile creeping across his heavy lips.

I thought I would faint.

That smile! What does it mean when Stalin smiles at you? Stalin — who, I once calculated, was personally responsible for creating enough corpses to fill the Yankee Stadium from ground level to the top deck; Madison Square Garden from ice surface to the height of the timing clock; Carnegie Hall as high as the second balcony; and with enough left over to fill the first fourteen floors of the Empire State Building.*

I tried to smile back, but my mouth would not work. When it finally did, Stalin had left.

All the way back to the hotel, H. L. D.'s face was lit up as if he had seen a vision. "Such a gentle man," he murmured over and over. "Such a nice, gentle man."

Saint Stalin.

I sat back in the limousine, now blessed by escort cars and motorcycle outriders, and watched the pedestrians leap out of the way as we turned onto Marx Avenue for the short drive to the hotel. You almost had to feel happy for H. L. D. It was as if his whole life was suddenly validated. He had something to believe in.

My vaguely charitable feelings toward that old fool ended abruptly when he turned to me, still glassy-eyed, and said, "By the way, there is just one other matter. The camps."

Camps?

I've just taken him to see Stalin and he's asking about camps? Hello?

"Yes, yes. Now how are they referred to in all that capitalist trash? Slave labour camps, is it? You know. That nonsense they're trying to foist on us. I'll just have to see one, I suppose. Just to be able to say that I've not been duped. Slave labour, indeed!"

Indeed.

I rushed into the hotel and threw up.

Word spread. Like cries of "Fire!" in a circus tent. And those soft and corrupt old men in the Kremlin were the first outside. The others, the secret police guides, the

---

* Calculations based on six cubic feet per corpse; allowing for settling and rigor mortis; packed head to toe sardine fashion. Calculations not subject to Baltic state corpses, which would bring it up to the forty-eighth floor of the Empire State Building.

bureaucrats, all fled too. Leaving me standing in the dark on that same tightrope. Harold Leonard Dawes was adamant. I was totally on my own. And wondering if this was why Stalin had smiled.

I phoned my father. He came up the next day on a military plane. As a survivor of many bloody power struggles, he was now sufficiently important that he could fly to Moscow when he decided there was a need to. I had not seen him in almost a year. As I had become more cosmopolitan, he had become more crude. He looked like the scheming old peasant he had become, his fierce eyes peering out over his vodka nose and wild moustache. Living by his wits, picking through the deadly thicket of Stalin's whims, had given him the mentality of a murderous gypsy. Flattering and servile in the face of authority, but with a deadly eye for the weaknesses of opponents. But he was my father. I loved him.

"Look at you!" he roared when we met. "They've ruined you!" We laughed and embraced. For an hour, my troubles were forgotten and we talked of home and New York and Mother and Natasha. My little sister was now nineteen and engaged to the son of a Party official. And Katya. "Why no grandchildren yet?" He grinned. "With a woman like that. You must be stealing the white balloons from someone," he said with a laugh.

"Miriam Nelson says to say hello," I shot back. His eyes leapt at me conspiratorially.

"She does?" He chuckled. And then slyly stopped himself. He waited for me to say something. I said nothing. We just stared for a moment. His wife; my mother. "Come on," he said, "I know a good restaurant." We walked up Gorky Street as a light snow was falling. It was so different from New York. Almost eerie, as if the life and the noise and the energy that I had unknowingly become used to on city streets had suddenly vanished. The absence of any advertising struck me. There was no colour anywhere. All the way up Gorky Street, we had walked through greyness. Somehow I missed the neon that I first laughed at. It was late afternoon and already it was dark. The streets were beginning to fill up with people going home. Their numbers only seemed to add to the silence.

We walked past the old English mansion that after 1917 had become the Revolutionary Museum and turned right onto a narrow cobblestone street with crumbling houses that were soon to be torn down, an Orthodox church that looked permanently closed, and a restaurant where the waiters owed Father a favour. The vodka flowed. I told him my problem. His eyes narrowed.

"Some of my best times have been with intellectuals. I've shot hundreds of them."

"I'm serious."

"So am I. This Dawes. What's he like?"

I told him. My father raised his eyes to the ceiling. "No wonder Stalin smiled! I'm surprised he didn't break out laughing at you." He had lowered his voice and looked behind him to see if anyone was listening. It was a habit with him wherever he was. Already we had drunk a lot of vodka. "Lenin was right. Useful idiots, he called those people. Always good for stirring up things before a revolution. Yelling for morality and justice and all that other nonsense. Then afterwards you take them out and shoot them."

I realized that this was the first time my father and I had ever talked as two men. Always before it was as man and boy. Even when we last saw each other and I was already working in the ministry. It was as if I was old enough now to know the way the world really worked. Instead of how it was supposed to work. For the first time we were sharing secrets that he felt I could keep. His murderous old eyes glowed with memories.

"It's different when you shoot intellectuals. When you were a boy we had carloads of them come through the camps. Poets. Journalists. Professors. All the bright ones. Lots of well-known names. They were quite amazing when you took them out to be shot. Not like the peasants, where there was always a lot of yelling and flailing about. The intellectuals reminded me of when I used to go to the farm and watch the pigs being slaughtered. You see, the pigs were always the smart ones too. Not like the cows or the sheep, who were too stupid to know what was happening to them. The pigs always knew they were about to be butchered, and I'll never forget the look in their eyes. As if you had betrayed them. Just like those professors and journalists and that bunch. They looked at us with the same shattered eyes as the pigs. 'How could you do this to us?' they used to ask. They couldn't believe what was happening to them."

"I'm not interested in shooting anyone. I just want to avoid being shot."

"It's all the same thing!" He burst out laughing and slapped me on the back.

We walked back towards Gorky Street. There were fewer people on the streets now. Once in a while an ancient trolleybus would clatter into view, its bell clanging as small knots of bundled humanity ran through the fresh snow to catch it. Soldiers wrapped in greatcoats and felt boots passed by, on their way to the steam baths with fresh socks and underwear in their arms. Theirs were the only voices to break the muffled silence once the trolleybuses had disappeared. And even in that cold air, the pungent scent of cheap tobacco rolled in newspaper trailed after them. It was quiet on Gorky Street, where the snow was almost undisturbed, and we sank up to our ankles as we walked. I loved the snow. When it was fresh like this it made everything in Moscow seem so clean and soft. And it reminded me of the fun

Yuri and I used to have throwing snowballs when we were young.

Thinking of those days made me think of Lavrenti. I told my father about my problems with him.

"Very dangerous," was all my father said, until he had drunk some more from the bottle he pulled from his pocket. He was now quite red-faced from all the vodka. "Lavrenti is like his father," he said. "No one ever worried me as much as that man. He would have had me shot for certain if I had not done the same thing to him first. Best move I ever made. Act, Dimitri, act! No more of your good-guy stuff."

We had come to a part of the street where there was construction equipment and scaffolding everywhere. The government was creating a square in honour of Pushkin, and his statue had just been moved over from Tverskoi Boulevard, where it had been for decades. It was a very large statue, and on that night it rested on a massive trailer next to the granite base that awaited it. Pushkin stood cloaked and sombre, a giant peering down at us. My father threw a snowball at Pushkin. He missed. He stared at the statue and drank.

"Pity," he said. "Writers are always fine to have around when they're dead."

"That's ridiculous," I said.

He laughed, his eyes bulging in his red face. He looked like a mad gypsy. "Perhaps. There's a few good ones around. Like that famous poet. Alexei something or other. He can write you a poem whenever you need him to. Now *that's* an intellectual for you!"

I had been waiting for him to offer some help, some solution to my problem. He just kept throwing snowballs at Pushkin. "I need your help," I said finally.

"Of course you do." That cunning grin. "And you'll get me shot in return."

"No, I won't. You've lasted this long. You'll figure

something out. But I don't have the experience to get myself out of this mess. I want to put Harold Leonard Dawes into a plane and bring him down to your area. I want to show him one of the camps."

"Why there? They're all over. Why pick on your poor father?" The same grin. But his eyes were like two glowing coals.

"I want you to do whatever you do with all your cronies. Make deals, bribes, whatever. Put on a show that will keep that old fool believing what he wants to believe."

"Let me tell you something, boy. When I was your age I had dozens of friends who I used to drink with. *We* made the revolution. Us! Now they're all dead. So I drink alone because they were taken away and executed. Except for the lucky ones who had heart attacks or drank themselves to death. Why am I the only one alive? Because I stay away from Moscow. I don't want to be a big shot in this place. Another rooster crowing on the shit pile. I like it where I am. But the others didn't. They were like you. And they got shot for their troubles. They were pleased when Stalin got to know their names. He probably smiled at them too."

He was talking too loudly. He was furious with me. And I was utterly without hope. "You're right. I'm sorry. I have to get back to the hotel. Please give my love to Mother." I turned and walked away. For many reasons I just wanted to cry.

A snowball hit me in the back of the head. I spun around in a fury. He was grinning. With his eyes, too.

"I have a plan," he said.

The next night, Harold Leonard Dawes boarded a plane as excited as a schoolchild. We had left Katya behind, as my father had instructed, and took the hourlong flight to my old home city. In his own little area, my father knew

94

how to do things. There were limousines, photographers, and girls with flowers. H. L. D. was impressed. He had never had such a reception. My mother gave me a sobbing, joyous hug while H. L. D. said all kinds of delightfully flattering things to my father, which I translated only in part. I decided my father would have made a good Mafia boss back in Enemy Number One. Even the mighty Al Capone would have trembled.

At the hotel, H. L. D. was like a wizened active child. In his huge suite, filled with the best Georgian wine, flowers flown in from Tashkent, and a small mountain of caviar, he paced back and forth. "At last we can put this nonsense about labour camps to rest," he said almost apologetically. My father sat sprawled in one of the big chairs, looking uncomfortably respectable. His fierce old eyes followed H. L. D. around the room.

I knew what was going through his mind. He was thinking of pigs.

The next morning we drove for almost an hour, leaving the city and heading out in the slightly rolling countryside. It had not snowed there yet and it was warmer than in Moscow. And when the driver pointed out that we were passing through areas that had been conquered by the Nazis and then retaken only a few years earlier, H. L. D. set his nose to the wind and sniffed at the heroism in the air. Twice he made the driver stop at remnants of burned-out German tanks that had not yet been carted off for scrap.

"Holy ground," he said solemnly.

As we approached Vamagad, I began to get nervous. I suddenly realized I had been there before. As a boy, with Father. It was a place I had blotted out of my memory until that moment. It had been a huge, intimidating place, ringed with gun towers, dogs, and barbed wire. I thought there had to be some mistake. We couldn't be going there! But we were. The car turned down the rutted road that merged identically with the one that leapt from my memory. My father must have got things all wrong.

But it was no mistake. Suddenly happy, smiling inmates waved to us as they walked along the road. They were singing. I looked back in disbelief. Then the camp came into view. More massive than ever. But somehow the gun towers had disappeared. And the barbed wire and the dogs. Even the guards had gone, except for a few jovial old codgers in sparkling uniforms. It was just as my father had said it would be. For the previous twenty-four hours, the camp had been the scene of frenzied activity. The gun towers were torn down and the barbed wire was dragged into the woods. The buildings closest to the main gate were freshly painted. Whatever might be inspected was cleaned. Busloads of Party office workers were brought in, dressed in prison clothing, and put into particularly sensitive areas. Most of the real prisoners were marched out into the forests or the distant fields until H. L. D. had departed. Then they would be marched in to put the camp back together again.

My father greeted us at the main gate. He looked tired but exuberant. He winked at me and then made the introductions. It was Comrade Volkov who was in charge of the prison, and he would be happy to take us anywhere the distinguished visitor would like to go.

"Of course," said H. L. D. "No restrictions. I must be free to see everything."

My father left us with Volkov, saying he had to inspect some important work being done in one of the fields.

"Where to, comrade?" said Volkov. When I translated for H. L. D., he beamed. Volkov had been taking lessons from my father. Short and barrel-chested, with an unruly mass of curly hair, he was the perfect host. Jovial, waving to inmates, and encouraging H. L. D. to see everything. Volkov immediately set a relaxed and candid tone to the visit. I wondered what immense favours he had owed my father.

All morning it was a celebration of friendship. Harold Leonard Dawes kept muttering that he would definitely set things straight *back home*. He inspected the barracks, which were immaculate, with warm blankets everywhere and a new coal-burning stove. A very new stove. In the library there were dozens of inmates reading and others being taught to read. To give them skills when they leave, Volkov said. In another large room inmates were standing around a piano, rehearsing a folk song that they would sing for the others the following Tuesday night. I recognized two of the singers. I had gone to school with them. I knew they were members of the local Army choir. One of them looked me right in the eyes, then looked at Volkov, and went back to the safety of his music sheets.

We came to an area where large boulders were being moved away to make room for new barracks to be built. It was hard physical work. The men there were leaner and tougher than the others we had seen. I saw Volkov tense. These were real inmates.

"Physical labour," said H. L. D. "Is there anything else that so truly dignifies the human soul?"

We said we couldn't think of anything. He moved closer to the inmates, who were struggling with a boulder. Volkov seemed on the verge of grabbing H. L. D. by the arm and leading him away. "They are building their own residence," he said quickly. "We let them design it in the style they want."

"Marvellous," exclaimed H. L. D., who walked over to two of the men who were swinging a sledgehammer against the boulder. "What did you do before you came here?" he asked them. They seemed confused and frightened, looking to us for instructions. I translated.

The man nearest me answered. "He was a school-teacher. I was a writer."

"They were both petty criminals all their lives," I translated immediately.

"Ah, marvellous, marvellous," said Harold Leonard Dawes, beaming. "Giving these poor men a chance to learn a proper trade."

Lunch was served in a building with round tables, and women brought heaped plates of food. Volkov apologized to H. L. D. for having to serve him a prisoners' meal, and then said goodbye. There were pressing duties out in the fields, he explained. H. L. D. was almost tearful in his farewell, thanking Volkov again and again. We left the camp belching under the weight of the huge lunch. I had never seen so much food. My father or Volkov must have threatened all the food black marketeers in the area. "Famine, indeed!" snorted H. L. D.

We drove happily back along a slightly different route. The car bounced across rutted roads, past burned-out old farmhouses and small hills that appeared through the forests. We came to a fork in the road and the driver headed toward the left. "Stop!" yelled H. L. D. suddenly. "That way," he said, pointing toward the right fork. The driver slowed down and yelled at him in Russian that the right fork was forbidden.

Panic showed in the man's eyes. But H. L. D. had seen more rusted remains of German tanks. And as usual, once he had made up his mind, he simply expected others to obey his wishes. The driver tried to speed up, but H. L. D. flung open the car door and was on the verge of tumbling out when the car screeched to a halt. "I damn well intend to see those tanks," he snapped. "And no driver is going to tell me where to go just because he wants to get home early." He was already out the door and striding up the right fork of the road.

The driver was almost hysterical. "Don't you know what's going on there?" he yelled.

"Know what?" I yelled back.

"The minefields. They're clearing the minefields!"

I still didn't understand. What did I know about minefields? But whatever it was, it wasn't part of the tour. I scrambled out to try and get H. L. D. back into the car. I was thankful that I would soon be rid of him. He was already standing by the rusted German tank that lay on the side of a grassy hill. I began to climb it when suddenly there was a tremendous explosion from the other side of the hill.

"What on earth was that?" he called out. Behind me the driver was running, and babbling something about us being finished. H. L. D. was already sprinting up the hillside as quickly as his long, spindly legs would carry him.

When I reached him, gasping for breath, I found myself looking down on a horrifying panorama. Below us was a small valley. Stretched across it, walking in several rows, were prisoners. There were hundreds of them, maybe a thousand, ragged lines of humanity moving across the quiet green fields. And behind them were prison guards, perhaps five, armed with submachine guns. Suddenly from the middle of the rows there was an explosion and a geyser of flames and smoke. From that distance it was hard to tell, but it looked as if several prisoners simply disappeared in the explosion. A second later the sound reached us, like a sharp little burst of thunder.

The lines of prisoners momentarily convulsed and stopped. Then they shuddered back into motion across the length of the whole valley. Almost immediately another explosion ripped through the lines. I could see men flung through the air. Harold Leonard Dawes squinted into the delayed shock waves of the blast. "What in the name of God is going on down there?" he demanded.

Then almost at once there were three, maybe four,

explosions, erupting like beads bursting on a tattered necklace. The lines shook and cries rose up from the valley and were knocked aside by the sound of the blasts.

Then there was another cry. Much closer. I looked down and saw my father, Volkov, and several other men standing around a man with mobile radio equipment. One of the men was pointing to us. My father spun round with the others. His eyes burned holes in me even from that distance. All of them seemed to panic. They began yelling conflicting orders. One of the men had a gun, which he raised to his hip. Volkov grabbed the radio and shouted into it, ordering that the lines should stop. From the valley below, his orders were yelled out by the men with guns. But before the lines stopped, another explosion ripped through them near the centre.

My father was storming up the hill, trying to smile because he was staring into the bony, confused visage of H. L. D., who kept demanding to know what was going on. I ran down the hill, yelling in Russian that I wanted to know what was going on too. "You fool," my father bellowed at me, still smiling that dead smile of his, as he clambered up the hill. "Fool!" He would have broken me in two if H. L. D. had not been there.

"I should put you down there with them," he seethed, pointing to the prisoners. "What are you doing here?"

"Maybe I should be down there!" I cried. But it was not really me that spoke. It was a voice that came from somewhere inside of me, pushed out by horror and desperation. I wanted to hit my father as much as he wanted to knock me senseless. But from behind me came the impatient shouts of H. L. D.

"Go on up and tell him something," hissed my father, looking ferociously at H. L. D.

"Tell him something!" I was almost hysterical. "Tell him *what?* The truth?"

Another prisoner blew up in the valley below us.

"How could I have a son so stupid? You fool! The truth is shit. It doesn't matter. He made up his mind what the truth is before he even got here, you idiot. Now go up there and tell him something to help him out."

H. L. D. was already bouncing down the hillside toward us. My father immediately went into his obsequious gypsy act, flinging his arms apart and roaring a lusty welcome. He embraced H. L. D., who was confused and not sure what to say.

"Tell him!" smiled my father, his teeth never parting. "Tell him that they are collective farmers who have asked permission to clear this land which they want to farm. They are so eager to rid themselves of the fascist legacy of war that they are willing to risk their lives in the name of the revolution."

I translated. H. L. D. looked down at the ragged lines in the valley. And then back at my father. His face was blank.

"Heroes!" my father roared, pointing to the valley. "They will be thrilled to know that you have come to visit them." Still flashing that revolutionary smile of his, he turned and bellowed to Volkov, ordering him to tell the prisoners that if they ran back and cheered loud enough they would not have to walk the rest of the valley. Others would be brought in. Volkov radioed the message.

"You see?" My father grinned, embracing H. L. D. "I have instructed that they will be told you are here. They know that you, like they, have been a fighter against the fascists. I feel they might be pleased to see you."

His timing was perfect. I had just finished translating when the valley swelled with cheers. The prisoners began to run towards us. First only a few. Then dozens. Then hundreds. Running and waving, filthy, ragged hordes. They staggered around the craters, lunging over the fallen, scrambling desperately towards us. There was a madness to it all. The cries that rose up from the valley were incoherent and fearful. But the sheer force of the noise was awesome and on that hillside it all sounded like cheering.

Cheering for H. L. D.

He looked down on the prisoners. His mouth had fallen open. "Marvellous," he said. "Simply marvellous."

But one prisoner had chosen not to run. I think I was the only one to notice him. He stood like a solitary black speck in the stillness at the far end of the valley. Then he turned and slowly began to walk in the same direction that the lines had been moving. I couldn't keep my eyes off him. I wanted to make him stop. To call out to him. But he was so far away. And from below the mad, ragged chorus of waving and cheering rose like a curtain in front of him.

The solitary prisoner kept walking. Then he blew up. Or was he just in my imagination?

9

Katya's red dress had been designed on the third floor of a famous salon on Avenue Montaigne in Paris. The designer was a young man who was later to become famous in his own right. He was then working for an older man whose name was on the front of the salon. The older man was in his fifties and felt he had lost some of his most productive years to the war. So he hired men half his age and took credit for their work.

The dress, when it was shown at the collections that spring, inspired such words as *dramatic. Sweeping. Stunning*. Every year the new fashions inspired the same descriptions arranged with a different variety of nouns. Buyers from the big New York stores bought the dress, expecting that it would show up a few times at society parties and then be discarded for next year's styles.

The dress was made of a fine red silk. It swept off the shoulders and gathered smoothly at the waist before plunging to an elegant fullness just below the knees. As much as anything, it was the colour of the dress that drew such attention to it. Realizing his gamble against garishness, the young designer used simple and flowing lines. One element daring; the other, conservative. It was to become his style. From dresses like this one he was to become famous.

The young designer was not in the slightest political. And wealth was a natural part of life. Without it, he would not be working at what he loved. And in those days, it also seemed natural that his dresses should hang in the closets of only a few areas of the world. The Sixteenth Arrondissement in Paris. Belgravia in London.

Zamalek in Cairo. The Upper East Side of New York. There were, of course, other areas where he thought his creations might be found in smaller numbers.

Moscow was not one of them. In Moscow the dress represented a political statement. It represented wealth and property and class. But to both Katya and the young designer this would have been utterly confusing. Infuriating, even. In their own form of simplicity they were kindred spirits. What was so wrong about beauty? Katya yearned to be covered in beauty, just as the young designer wanted his creations to be worn by the most beautiful women. He would have been pleased had he seen Katya in the dress. There was a perfect symbiosis. The dress and the woman — each made the other more spectacular. More beautiful even than when the dress was worn on the runways by the house models during the showings. Of course, now there was a fascinating structural stress around the top of the dress that had been missing when it was worn by the house models. Katya's far fuller breasts strained against the silk, even threatened to overflow in places. (Breasts were not much in favour in the fashionable salons of Paris. They were considered to be rather unfortunate and pendulous appendages best left for artists and sculptors to handle in whatever way they could. In fact, breasts were even to be banished; they were traitorous objects that kept poking through those sleek, vertical lines the designers made when they first sketched their creations on paper.)

Katya sat in the near-darkness of the Moscow twilight. From the eighth floor of the Moskva Hotel she could have looked along Marx Avenue and seen a new coating of snow that was dusting across the city. And she could have looked off slightly to one side to the Central Lenin Museum, with its profusion of Romanesque arches over the doors and windows. But she merely stared into the greyness until there was barely enough light left to make a silhouette. Then she stood up and took off all of her clothes. She went to the closet and removed the red dress from the bottom of her crude suitcase. It was the first time she had dared to take it out in Moscow. She had told no one she had even brought it. The more she could not have it, the more she wanted it. Needed it. It had become a part of her personality. It was as if the dress were the solution to the most basic problem of her existence. A problem that filtered up unannounced and unnamed from the mists of her memories, as a young girl unhappily enduring life in that single room shared with her parents and a grandmother whose face she could not remember. The grandmother had told her, even as a little girl, to make sure she married someone important. Someone of position and power. So she would not live like *this*. The grandmother would always say these things when her son-in-law, Katya's father, was home. Later there would be shouting. While the old woman's face would harden into a tiny smile, as she would go on warning Katya to make sure she was beautiful enough to marry someone important. So she would be important too.

The dress was confirmation that she was indeed important. Desirable. And would never again live in one room where there was all that yelling. To Katya, it was utterly natural that she should have the dress. But the awesome wilful streak she possessed — which had intimidated even her parents — had unfortunately not been matched by the development of other, more refined mental resources. So on the surface, there was the appearance of pure and simple greed in the making. Yet she was not that kind of person. She wished no one any ill will. She was often kind to others. And she was genuinely perplexed that anyone could be upset because of her beautiful red dress.

For it was really a matter of pure simplicity: what she wanted, she *wanted*.

And there in that dying light of a Moscow afternoon she let the silk fall in an opulent cascade down her body. And decided she probably wanted another dress.

I came back pissed to the gills — as they say in Enemy Number One. I lurched off the elevator, past the ferocious old woman who sat at her desk in the hallway controlling the keys to the rooms. And taking notes for the secret police. I bowed deeply and unsteadily and said in fractured English, "Frankly, my dear, I do not give for a damn." Ah, Clark Gable, you should have been born a Cossack.

I barged through the door to our room and there was Katya. In her gorgeous red dress. I could tell she expected me to be furious. I stood there swaying slightly, a stupid grin on my face. "You look like a million roubles," I said.

I swaggered up to her the way I had seen Gable do it. I could tell she was stunned by my reaction. But on that night I really, truly didn't care. And can you believe it, I told jokes. Jokes! I don't know why, but something inside of me wanted to make her laugh. And me — I desperately needed to laugh. We rolled around on the bed, laughing like children. I pawed and nuzzled and stuck my hand up under her dress until we both realized that I had left the door open, and the old woman at the hall desk was staring at us with a look that would have terrified the Politburo. I grinned crookedly, took my hand out from whatever crevasse it had sought warmth and waved at her while gurgling "Peekaboo". I crawled across the floor and closed the door.

We laughed even harder. It felt so good to laugh. If I hadn't laughed I would have cried. Or worse. Because I kept seeing those explosions in that quiet green valley. I *had* to laugh.

I don't know whose idea it was, but we went for a walk. With Katya wearing her red dress. It was the most insane thing I could have done. Even the thought of it before — or after — that night struck terror in me. But the cauldron of anger and fear and drunkenness had short-circuited all my normal defences. I just didn't care. Let them get me. I was daring them. And I kept seeing those damned explosions.

We walked through Red Square. It was still lit, and with the fresh snow it looked even more beautiful than usual. We had a snowball fight, laughing and running around like children. And while I was throwing one of the snowballs I started crying because I thought of my father. I loved him. I loved my whole family. But now, as I threw the snowballs, I kept seeing my father's face in front of the explosions. I was laughing and crying at the same time. Let the secret police come for me. I was prepared. I had my snowballs.

Now, so long after that night, I look back on it and wish that I had been like that more often. For Katya and me it was our best night ever. For that one night, a burden was lifted. The exhilaration of not caring about it all was breathtaking. That night we truly made love. And we were in love.

Because, after all, was it not reasonable to feel that tomorrow I might die?

10

The next day I was a hero.

Harold Leonard Dawes had talked to the correspondent for the *New York Times*. The story was published that same day. The old men in the Kremlin shook my hand and smiled. No one mentioned Katya's dress.

And Xerox went through the roof.

In New York, the news of H. L. D.'s trip was played up in all the newspapers. And a day later, in London. Paris. Rome. And in the rest of the world when AP and UP picked up the story in further detail, quoting him on the wonderful life people led over there. The generosity of Comrade Stalin. And labour camps? It wasn't even fair to call them prisons. Perhaps rest and rehabilitation centres was more appropriate.

Even before I left to return to New York, other tours were being planned. I sat in the ministry reading the coded cables from New York that told of the rush of names that had been put down on the list. Almost every one of the people at Miriam Nelson's party had been demanding to go. With friends.

So my plan had backfired. Of course, I was glad it did, under the revised circumstances. Otherwise I would have been in big trouble. I sat staring at the list of names and wondered how I could ever have gone so wrong? How was I ever going to save Enemy Number One, when its own people fouled up my plans? I had to admit the obvious — that I had chosen the wrong group. Intellectuals definitely did not have what it takes to save their country. I had to aim higher.

On the way back, I made my decision. I would aim for the politicians.

In New York, Ivchenkov and Boris welcomed me as if there was never any doubt that I would return. Yet our apartment had been turned over to another couple three days after we had departed, and now there were embarrassed explanations and a hurried attempt to find us other living quarters in the building. I decided on a small test. I demanded more than we were offered. When we got the corner apartment of the fifth floor, I knew I was really moving up in life.

The same with Sam. In that big stockbroker's office, his name was painted in gold lettering on the glass-enclosed cubicle he now occupied. I saw him sitting there as I made a hurried pass in front of his office building on my second day back. Through the huge front window, Sam still looked like a college student who was late for classes. I waited until after dark, when he was the only one still working. The curtains were drawn in front of the big street windows, but I could still see the light on his desk. The light went out and a few minutes later he appeared at the door to the building. I followed him for a few blocks until I thought it was safe to make contact. When I tugged at his arm, he turned round absent-mindedly and for a moment stared blankly. Then his face lit up.

"Wow!" was all he said. "Wow!"

That was Sam's way of saying that he was glad to see me. He shook my hand as if it were a water pump and grinned from ear to ear. I had never seen him so excited. "What a move," he said. "Pure genius. That Xerox stock has been incredible. We got in just two days before it went sky-high. Where on earth did you hear about it?"

So what could I tell him? In Stalin's office?

He saw my hesitation and held up his hand like a traffic cop. "Shouldn't have asked," he smiled. He began fumbling with his briefcase. "Got something to show you."

Standing there on the corner of Forty-fourth and Broadway with the traffic and the crowds swirling around us, Sam took out a file folder with the words *Yagoda Enterprises* typed on it. That was me! I felt an almost electric thrill surge through me. I leaned over him, eagerly peering at the pages. Balancing the papers on his briefcase as the neon lights from Times Square rolled over us in waves of different colours, Sam turned to the page that said "Holdings." I couldn't believe it. There they were, the names of at least a dozen companies, and I owned little chunks of all of them. And these were not just your dinky little *kulak*-owned bucket shops either. This was the big time. US Steel. IBM. General Motors. The very places that my communist soul had been trained to smash.

And believe it or not, I swear there was thunder in the skies at that moment. "Lenin!" I said, pointing upwards. There was more thunder and I yelled, "Marx and Engels!" I laughed, staring up at the neon-lit clouds that hung low over Times Square. Sam did not understand. And I did not pursue my little joke.

"How did I get so many?" I asked him.

"We've been lucky," he said modestly. "We've been buying at the right time and selling just before the peak. Also leverage. Great leverage on the options. And that Xerox thing was a killer. Keep this up and someday you'll be a millionaire."

A millionaire! I stared blankly at him. He was serious.

"But may I make one suggestion? I understand that you don't like to do business in an orthodox way. But I really think you should get an office."

The idea stunned me. It was the last thing I had ever imagined. Me, with an office for Yagonda Enterprises.

It started to rain. Sam hurriedly put his papers away. "Think it over," he said. "My God, you can afford it now, with all the dividends you're getting. Mind you, I don't dislike chasing around to these funny places where you leave messages for me. If that's what you really want."

I walked back through the rain, ecstatic. *Not bad for a boy from the steppes*, I told myself. The thought of becoming a millionaire fascinated me, but only in a remote way. People are surprised when I say this now, but somehow the money didn't mean to me what it means to most other people. I was not caught up with the idea of big houses or cars. I've read stories of very wealthy men who buy almost nothing for themselves. I understand that. Money is different for them. It's just a means of keeping score. Like when the Dodgers beat the Yankees. Money tells you how well you're doing in the game. And it is a game. At least that was how I regarded it.

Before I had gone even a block, I was sure that I was being followed. I turned and saw no one other than the normal pedestrians hurrying through the rain. But I knew I was not imagining things. I cut across towards Fifth Avenue, and when I came to the darkened doorway of a small store, I took a quick sideways step and spun round. I was just in time to see a figure lunge into an alleyway not far behind me.

So it had begun again. I cursed him under my breath. This was serious. I didn't mind losing a dozen agents. But not my stockbroker. Lavrenti had just taken things too far. There was no time to lose.

Through the tedious business of changing directions in various taxis, I think I finally lost him somewhere on the West Side. On Columbus Avenue I went into a corner store that sold hardware and various kinds of junk that had piled up over what must have been decades. The store was filthy. Behind a pile of mouldy magazines and newspapers sat a little old man who told me something

111

about needing a special permit when I said I wanted to buy a pistol. I slapped down two ten-dollar bills, and he just grunted and said, "Okay, bud. Which one do you want?" I walked out of there with the smallest .32 calibre pistol he had. It could be concealed perfectly in my overcoat.

Now, Lavrenti. Now we shall settle accounts once and for all.

Over that weekend, I was busy with my next scheme to save Enemy Number One. This one was foolproof. This time I would aim for the politicians. Or at least one of them. That was all I would need — one good, solid politician. I decided I would offer some really tempting bait.

My bait was our entire network of espionage.

I have to admit that the network was brilliant. I mean, Stalin may have had his ups and downs in other areas, but the man did know how to run a network of spies. In every country we went into, our orders were to burrow right into the woodwork of government. It became an automatic response. (I was always amazed when people were surprised or shocked about this. What did they think we were there for?) Most countries with pretensions to power do the same thing with varying degrees of fervour. But we do it the best. Every target country had its weaknesses which we exploited. In England, for instance, their class structure has led to no end of laws and customs designed to protect elegant fools and traitors in positions of power. We joyously ducked behind these social curtains and for decades almost ran the agencies that were supposed to be spying on *us*.

With Enemy Number One, the big weakness was its openness and its lust for publicity and constant change. We moved in decades ago and quietly set up a network taking these national traits into account. I must admit it was a superb network. We had our people in all the best places in their government. Treasury. State. Commerce. Defence. These were of course not your average trench-coat spies. These were most often very respectable-looking citizens of Enemy Number One. Well-educated, serious-minded. Sometimes pious. But for one reason or another each of them had decided that their own government was wrong. And that we were the wave of the future. Over the months and years, our people had patiently and secretly tried to work them into positions we wanted. Some were the inevitable fools who had to be humoured. Others were spectacular. For instance, we had one man to whom we almost owed eastern Europe. He was in Treasury, I think. At a time when our armies, fighting the Nazis, were bogged down far to the east of where we wanted to be, this man came up with a government plan that kept the war going for a few extra precious months. Just enough time to allow our armies to drive through all those forlorn and battered little countries.

I could see that such a superb network was definitely going to be a problem.

Because, after all, how could I possibly keep Yagoda Enterprises flourishing when that network was working to bring the roof down on it?

11

I liked the idea that my plan would also help Anatoly.

It was obvious that Anatoly was being set up as a scapegoat by Boris, for whatever happened to go wrong with the network. Around the embassy there was more than just the usual numbing fear of official punishment for any mistakes, real or imagined. There was a particularly carnivorous atmosphere, where weaknesses were probed and, when one was found, the wolves quickly circled for the kill. It was an atmosphere created by Boris and given at least indirect encouragement by Ivchenkov, who did nothing to stop it. We always thought that Ivchenkov was really afraid of Boris too.

At first I was the marked man. But then when I returned from Moscow trailing official blessings, the attention was quickly turned to Anatoly. He was called into Boris's office and informed of "excellent news." He was being put in charge of the Party in Enemy Number One. The news was conveyed with Boris's familiar chilling smile.

It was a form of death sentence. A slow death. Twenty years earlier the Communist Party in Enemy Number One had been the jewel of the superb network that was then just beginning. It had been a dynamic, hell-raising organization. Now the Party was in a shambles. And no one could make it what it had been. But officially it was still considered to be one element of the network, and the local Party chairman still went to Moscow every year to be photographed with the big shots there. Everyone knew the Party was an embarrassment but, so far, no one had been officially blamed for it. And we all knew that someone had to be. Several people at the embassy had been put in charge of the Party over the previous few years. And each one was reduced to a nervous wreck, wondering if he would be the unlucky one. It was like being in a roulette game, wondering if that little ball would land at your number when the wheel stopped. And the wheel was definitely turning slower. We could all sense it.

I hated Boris for what he was doing to Anatoly. I hated him for that lousy smile of his. And I hated him for playing his bully's game with our lives. I hoped that if my plan was successful, it would not only save Enemy Number One, it would finish off Boris. But as I sat there thinking about it all, I said to myself, Dimitri, my boy, keep thinking like this and one day you'll be blowing up prisoners.

Anatoly and I were in yet another bar just off Broadway. He was plunged into despair. He had just come back from a Party meeting held in a warehouse not far from the East River. "I'm finished. In three months I'll be freezing my *yaitsy* off in Siberia. If I make it that far." His chubby fingers twirled his glass nervously. I had talked him into coming to the bars because I thought it would take his mind off his problems. A few weeks earlier he had seen a dancer from one of the Broadway shows come into a bar he was in. He had fallen instantly and hopelessly in love. But he could not remember which bar it had been. Tonight we were trying to find it again.

"Is that her?" I said, pointing to a group of young women who had just come in.

"No," he said without even looking. I pretended impatience. "Well, why should I even bother looking for the poor girl? She'd just fall in love, we'd get married, and then she'd be a widow." He laughed. But not really. "You know, I'm not meant for this job. All I ever wanted to do was be like Tolstoy and raise hell and screw till I was ninety. Or Dostoevski, and gamble myself into ruination."

Anatoly was right. He was definitely not meant for that job. He sat there, staring into his drink, alternating between laughter and despair. His moods were written in the expressions across his pudgy face. He could hide nothing — which made him so honest as a friend. But terrible as a spy.

In so many ways, he reminded me of Yuri. Before Yuri was killed in the war, he was not only my brother, he was my best friend. After his death I went into a period of being closed off from those around me. You had to be very careful who you trusted. Even friends could give you away to the police or the commissars in a dozen little ways. That was just the way things worked. I grew very lonely. I missed being able to talk to Yuri about everything that came into my mind. And laughing at the crazy things we did.

I laughed the same way with Anatoly. From the moment we met in Ivchenkov's office, we each recognized a kindred spirit. Somehow I knew I could trust him. It was an absurdly foolish thing to do. But I literally bet my life on my instincts. A gut reaction, they call it in Enemy Number One. And I was not wrong.

"There she is!" he said suddenly, staring towards the door, where a group of women had come in dressed in slacks and carrying clothing bags.

Her name was Sara. She danced in the chorus line of *Oklahoma!* She laughed when Anatoly told his jokes, and she gave him her phone number when he asked for it. We walked back, bundled up against the cold, singing songs from *Oklahoma!* — which out of proletarian patriotism we renamed *Vladivostok!* — and dutifully pissing against a dark corner of Rockefeller Center. Suddenly Anatoly stopped and seemed to sag into his heavy coat. "I don't want to be purged," he said in despair.

116

"You're not. I'm going to help you."

"How? Shoot Boris?"

"Close."

He just stared, his eyes widening. "I was making a joke. I hope you were too."

I shook my head.

"What are you going to do?"

"I'm going to borrow one of your Party members." He waited for me to explain more. But I just grinned.

I borrowed Harry. Harold T. Simpson. Comrade Harry. I think it is possible he was one of the most decent men I ever met. And one of the saddest. Twenty-five years earlier Harry had been a young revolutionary. He had come from somewhere around Pittsburgh, believing that he would shake the world. He had seen men's heads broken in marches at the steel plants and listened to marvellous tales of other workers who now controlled their own destiny in a place called Russia. He went to New York, where he met other young revolutionaries. They jammed themselves into tiny apartments in Greenwich Village, joined the Party, and talked endlessly of what life would be like after the revolution. Moscow was the centre of their life. From there came incredible tales of the Workers' Paradise that was being created. Harry just wanted the people like those he grew up with in Pittsburgh to share in this paradise.

When I met him, he was an empty shell of a man. Every trace of vitality and originality within him had been eaten away. Like the others who had remained in the Party, he had simply become a mouthpiece, uttering slogans he was told to speak. Thinking thoughts he was told to think. The Party meetings were not like the old days, when those fine, rebellious minds and clashing personalities created flashes of oratory that moved men to action in those crowded, musty meeting halls in the unfashionable areas of Manhattan. Now the halls were

117

much less crowded. The rebellious minds had been driven out or beaten down. The oratory was just stale words that people far away wrote for them to say. And the younger members were mostly misfits. Or undercover agents from the FBI.

Harry's problem was loyalty. It replaced judgment. Loyalty was what got him and the others through those bewildering times when they were united in their loathing of the Nazis one day, and the next day told that Comrade Stalin had embraced the Nazis as allies. Judgment became suspect. Bourgeois. Do what Moscow tells you to do. And think what you're told to think. Many left. But Harry could not. As in a bad marriage where the love had gone, Harry remained true, clinging to memories of the old days. Telling himself those days would return.

The flashing smile of his youth had forever faded, and his face had become heavy with sagging cheeks and a wounded expression. He reminded me of an old and toothless basset hound. He had never married. His only life was the Party. He embarrassed Anatoly and me by his wooden fervour, his belief that everything he read from Moscow was absolutely true. He was totally without the ability or the inclination to read between the lines as we did. (*Bullshit* had become Anatoly's favourite new word. Spoken, of course, only in private.)

Because we were from Moscow, Harry regarded Anatoly and me as being sort of holy men. He would have done anything we ordered him to do. His loyalty had moved from being merely a duty to being the girders of his mind. Without it, he would have had to face the wasted decades of his life. If we had told him the Party required him to walk off the Brooklyn Bridge, he would have done it.

I was counting on that.

The first time I met him was at Alexei's poetry reading

118

at Miriam Nelson's. When he had learned that the famous Russian poet was arriving, he had pleaded with us to be allowed to attend. I was against it, but Anatoly was moved by Harry's apparent love of poetry. He had inadvertently found Anatoly's weak spot. Harry had stood apologetically at the back of the room looking awkward and out of place. He lacked the sleekness of the others. When Alexei had stood up to read his poetry I watched Harry's mouth fall open. It was the first time he had seen a poet from the motherland. I later thought that of all those in the room, he was the one whose ecstasy was the purest.

He also fell madly in love with Katya.

I became aware of it after Alexei's poetry was finished and everyone was milling around making plans to go to Russia. He stood in a corner, unable to take his eyes off her, as she sat straining to understand what the women around her were saying. I watched him out of the corner of my eye. I could always tell when some guy was zeroing in on Katya. It had happened so often, I had developed an almost sixth sense about it. But this was not just another case of watching old worthies stare into her breasts while nodding sagely at whatever words she happened to utter.

Harry was different. There was something almost touching about his obvious affection for her. He was like a hulking, bashful schoolboy in the presence of the girl of his dreams. And in a way she was indeed the girl of his dreams. Sitting there in her baggy Russian dress, Katya was as unfashionably attired as he was. But to him, she was the new breed of revolutionary woman. The motherland personified. Somehow he worked up the courage to talk to her. And she seemed to find his fumbling awkwardness a relief from the presence of the sleek women who made her feel so insecure. Soon they were happily labouring through a conversation in broken fragments of two languages.

119

With almost nothing in common, they became friends. And Harry, locked in the haze of a permanent puppy love, seemed not even to mind all her rattling on about clothes and jewels. Somehow his affection for Katya was the least physical of any man who took an interest in her. To him, she was practically the Party's Virgin Mary. In my presence, he was always apologetic, as if I had read his mind and caught him in the act of wanting to hold her hand. He began phoning me, and after the mandatory remarks on the state of the world as seen through politically correct eyes, he would hesitantly ask if I would mind him accompanying Katya on a walk down Fifth Avenue. I never minded.

When we sailed for Moscow, Harry was there in the crowd waving forlornly, and on our arrival back in New York we looked down from the deck and saw him on the docks, excitedly straining to catch sight of us. Or more correctly, catch sight of Katya. In the days after our return I was glad to have Harry around. His walks with Katya helped to take the pressure off me. She was driving me crazy again. It seemed that things changed the moment the terrible dangers of Moscow receded. Maybe we were just that kind of couple. Maybe extreme danger and hardship were the only things that could make us forget the fundamental problems that existed between us.

My first inkling of trouble came on the Sunday after we returned. Katya was looking at the fashion pages in the *New York Times*. Suddenly she put the paper down. "I think it's time to throw out my red dress."

I couldn't believe it. Throw it out? After I almost got lined up against a wall and shot because of it? Throw out the closest thing she had to a flag in her newly acquired religion? With its temples over on Fifth Avenue.

I was quickly initiated into the realities of fashion. *This* year everything was different. Hemlines. Necklines.

Padded this. And unpadded that. Sleeve lengths. And gathered at the waist. What did I know about all that? I who walked around with the bottom of my pants not even touching my shoes and my ankles sticking out like two cloth-covered twigs. And did they change the necklines on the collective farms? Were the steppes twittering with news about the latest fashion ads in the *Times*? A dress was a dress.

Wasn't it?

Katya's campaign was relentless. The more she stared at the clothes in Bloomingdale's, Saks Fifth Avenue, and Bergdorf's, the more she *wanted*. Our domestic life became so bad that I was ready to buy her another dress just to keep a semblance of tranquillity. The money was not what bothered me. I could have easily gone to Sam and asked him to cash in whatever was needed to get me some money. (One day after a walk with Harry, Katya asked me whatever happened to all that money she won. I just grunted and said, "I gave it away to the people in that office I showed you," and waited for her to ask more questions. But much to my relief she never did. Another crisis averted, I told myself.)

But I realized that buying a new dress would have stopped one argument and started an even worse one. Next, she would demand to wear the thing. And I would have to go through all the endless explanations about why the wife of a junior embassy official should not displease Comrade Stalin by being seen in a dress so outrageously expensive that even the wives of most capitalist oppressors could not afford it. And thereby bring suspicion down upon the already worried head of her generous husband.

Of course, the endless explanations would then create equally endless tantrums wherein Comrade Stalin got called a turd or some other name shouted into the loud music on the radio that I had just scrambled to turn on.

Praying to all the socialist gods I knew that Boris was not listening in, rubbing his long, bony hands with glee.

I was not the only one who had to cope with Katya. Harry was having his own problems. She awakened something in him. It was not physical. (I'm sure of it. But then every husband is.) For Harry it was something even more troubling. It was his long-dead dream. I first heard about it from Katya in between one of our arguments. At first I wasn't too interested, but then when I heard something about him leading an armed revolt, I decided it was definitely time to have a talk with Comrade Harry. After all, he was to be the unknowing centrepiece of my newest plan to save Enemy Number One, and I couldn't have him running around shooting up the town.

When I sat down with Harry and casually mentioned what Katya had told me, he was embarrassed. His jagged face went red and he mumbled something without being able to look me in the eye. But like most people from his country, Harry knew nothing about the art of drinking vodka. With a few quick toasts to the revolution, which of course he could not refuse, I had him stumbling through his story.

It was very simple. He wanted to lead a revolt. Ever since Harry was twenty-four, he had studied in minute detail the 1917 uprising of the sailors on the battleship *Aurora* in St. Petersburg. He knew the details far better than I did — and every Russian schoolchild has the legendary details of that epic revolt forever imprinted upon his or her mind. It was one of the sparks that ignited the entire revolution.

So Harry had decided he too could lead a rebellion. In the Brooklyn Navy Yard. The sailors would rebel. Rise up in one glorious proletarian fury. Just like they did on the *Aurora*. He knew they would. All they needed was a leader. For thirty years Harry had been waiting to be that leader. He had made his plans. He knew all the entrances to the naval yards. Every dock. Every security check-point. He had spent the last twenty years living alone in what he thought was the perfect apartment. It was on the third floor of a grim little brick building overlooking the docks. Just to be close. When the time comes.

It was a fire that had burned. And then burned out. But somehow Katya made him feel young. She made him remember. And now, for the first time, I had a glimpse of what the young Harry must have been like. As the story tumbled out and the Brooklyn Navy Yard resounded to the calls of revolution and the red hammer and sickle banners flew over the U.S.S. *Ticonderoga* I stared into those dead eyes and saw a tiny flame suddenly flicker back into life.

Its heat was searing.

For a few moments he was young. Passionate. And then whatever fuelled that awesome fire was suddenly spent, and he seemed to shrivel back into himself, leaving only a husk.

I remember staring at him, not knowing what to say, but thinking comrade, we do have a live one here. I began to worry even more about my plan. I couldn't have him running around fomenting revolution when I needed him to save the country.

And I also recall wondering about something else. Would a rebellion in the Brooklyn Navy Yard close off traffic to the Dodgers' home games?

12

The next morning I quickly began to put my plan into action. Harry found himself quietly assigned to the role of Party courier for the next few weeks. I knew it meant that he would be followed night and day by the counter-intelligence people of Enemy Number One. Anatoly and I were sure that the couriers were always tailed.

Next I found out where Boris was meeting with his own spies. They were the most important ones in our entire network. Like the man in the Treasury Department. Or the ones at State or Commerce. Officially, I was not supposed to know anything about these meetings. They were to be kept secret even from us. But Boris was as sloppy as he was mean. Almost every time we were in his office, there were notes lying around. *Friday 2:30/Morristown, New Jersey. Boardwalk café/Atlantic City/10:00 Wed*. With his peculiar sense of power, it never occurred to him that he could be making himself vulnerable to those he was trying to torment.

That same afternoon we met in his office. He had turned that smile of his on Anatoly and was saying how he was expecting such great improvements in the Party. As usual, Anatoly turned white and tried to act calm, which only made things worse because he was incapable of hiding anything. I sat silently through the meeting, reading the notes that littered Boris's desk. Finally I spotted what I was looking for. Read upside down, the meticulous writing told of the next meeting. *Tues/6:00/ Chesapeake Inn/Balt*. Baltimore? Because it was so close to Washington, he had to be meeting one of the big ones. Tomorrow.

As a test, at the end of the meeting, I asked Boris if we could get together again the following day. Impossible, he said. He would be out of town.

For the next step I needed Anatoly. This was delicate, because as usual after one of Boris's inquisitions he was reduced to emotional jelly. But I gave him a sealed envelope that I wanted to be delivered to Harry immediately. I told him it was personal. In the envelope were instructions ordering Harry to leave immediately on the next train to Baltimore. He was to go to the Chesapeake Inn in Baltimore just before six o'clock the following evening. He was to find an inconspicuous place to sit for an hour or so and wait. That was all.

In order to let him feel there was some purpose to his mission, I added that he might be contacted by a stranger who would use the code words *Dodgers 2, Yankees 1*. If no one contacted him, he was to return home. Twice during my instructions I referred to the absolute loyalty I required of him. In other words, don't ask questions. And tell no one of this mission. It was almost unnecessary because Harry would trundle off into the night on whatever mission he was sent, the silent and faithful Party servant.

So Harry went off to Baltimore, like some medieval disease carrier, unknowingly trailing a plague of eager FBI agents behind him. And five days later the notation *Statler/Phil/Sun/noon* sent him off to Philadelphia and what had to be another of Boris's meetings with one of the very top spies in our network. In either of those places the counter-intelligence people from the FBI had to spot Boris. He would be well known to them, his grainy surveillance photo imprinted on their memories. And when they spotted him, they would call out all the help they could get. Someone would have to spot the man he was meeting with. Then, within the FBI, all hell would break loose, as they say in Enemy Number One.

While Harry was away, I was busy going through our files on politicians in Enemy Number One. We kept files on a lot of local people in most of the countries where we had major embassies. They were important for a number of reasons. If we were negotiating, it was useful to know the personalities of those opposite us. Or when we were looking for weaknesses that could help us to blackmail someone into spying for us, it helped make the job easier if we knew who was badly in debt or was a secret homosexual. Messy personal stuff like that. And in extreme cases, when we took over a whole country, the files were needed to decide who got shot first.

Almost every one of the congressmen and senators had a file. I was looking for one who was not too bright, was relatively obscure, and needed help getting re-elected. That took in almost all of them, so I had to start over again.

I began looking for almost anything of interest, and after several hours I found the Senator. He was certainly obscure. I found a newspaper report — a small newspaper report — of a speech he had made a year ago, blaming almost all the troubles of the world on *the commies*. I had found my man.

I sent the Senator a letter. I signed it as a secret supporter at the FBI and I told him how much I admired his work, but wasn't it a shame that people like him weren't being kept briefed about the meeting at the Statler in Philadelphia on Sunday? Or the one five days earlier in Baltimore? *In the name of God, don't decent citizens have a right to know what's going on in this country? The real story of commies high up there!*

To write the letter, I needed a typewriter that could not easily be traced. And since every one of them has a distinctive and traceable type, almost like fingerprints, I had to choose carefully. The ones at the embassy were probably all on record with the FBI. Besides, it was too dangerous. I took a chance and went to Sam's office. It was a rainy Sunday afternoon. Because there were fewer cars on the streets, it was easier to see if I was being tailed. I was not. Sam, of course, was there, alone. He was used to me making unusual requests, and a quiet, hidden office with a typewriter did not seem all that much out of the ordinary. He was in a good mood. Pan Am was turning into a big winner.

And soon I was going to have a big tax problem because of the money I was making. My tax accountant should start looking into it.

Tax accountant?

What did I know about a tax accountant? Feverishly I pecked my way through the letter. When I got outside, it was already dark. I hurried over toward the anonymous confusion of Broadway.

But before I had gone a block, I felt that familiar ice-cold fear that shot through my insides. I was being followed. Even before I turned around, I knew it.

Lavrenti.

I fought to control myself. The letter almost crumpled in my hands. Thoughts of him wrestling it away from me almost caused me to break into a mad dash through the traffic. I spun around. Nothing. I walked some more and turned around quickly again. I saw just a shadow. That was all. Nothing more. It was more terrifying than if he had loomed out of the shadows, peering at me with his hauntingly boyish look magnified through those thick glasses of his.

He succeeded in totally unnerving me. I ran. Crashing through the crowds on Broadway, I trailed curses in my wake. But I had to get away. An hour later, after subway and taxi rides across Manhattan, I stood sweating in the shadows of a noisy street near the Apollo Theater in Harlem. Ten feet in front of me was a mailbox. I watched that street long enough to convince myself that there was no one around who would have any interest in forcing open the mailbox to see what it was I had mailed. Then I dropped the letter inside.

I walked back through several blocks of Harlem. I stopped in front of a club. A lot of Negroes — that was what they were called then — were making the most incredible music inside. It was jazz. Good, decadent jazz. I stood on the sidewalk and peered in through the frosted-glass window. All I could see was a whirlpool of colours. From the shadows of a large awning came a sly, curling voice.

"Hey, man. What's doing?" A young Negro in a suit stepped into the light and smiled. He held open the door. It was like opening the door to a blast furnace. The music and the lights roared out onto the street. Behind me there was the sound of a large car arriving quickly. A Cadillac convertible drove up and double-parked. Behind it came a Packard, and suddenly the sidewalk seemed filled with laughing young women dressed in expensive clothes and elegant-looking men. All of them were white. The men smiled at the Negro as if they had been there many times and tossed him their car keys in lazy silver arcs that caught the light and somehow added to the casual elegance of it all.

I had stepped into a movie. It was just like I had always imagined Enemy Number One to be when I was a boy back in Russia. The pages of *Life* had suddenly become real. I stood there on that sidewalk and in that instant, staring into all that laughter and happiness, I realized that I was a traitor. Mailing that letter was an act of utter betrayal. I hated the thought of being a traitor. I didn't feel like one. I didn't want my own country to be destroyed. But neither did I want all this laughter, this mad outpouring of energy that reached out and pulled me in, to be destroyed. I loved Enemy Number One. That was my problem.

I hurried inside. The club was filled with whites and Negroes. The band was going through Duke Ellington and Fats Waller music with even some Gershwin thrown in. It was late enough in the evening that everyone was loose and laughing. The coloured lights cut dimly through the haze of smoke and perfume, and when the saxophonist really broke loose, the dance floor filled with spectacular silhouettes. That night, I danced too. Usually I was too inhibited to dance. Or I would wait until I had drunk enough that my awkwardness had been oiled out of existence. But on that night everything was different. Of course, I didn't know how to dance what they called jiving, but there were girls there who stepped out of the shadows and showed me how. I didn't feel foolish. I was just enjoying myself, and I could laugh when I made a mistake. Have you any idea what a sense of relief that is? To be able to laugh at mistakes?

And when the piano player slid into a Count Basie number, I found myself dancing with a young Negro girl who looked up at me as we passed through the cool glow of one of the blue lights. "Why are you crying?" she asked.

I didn't know I was.

When I got back to the embassy, perfume and cigar smoke were trailing me like a faint mist. I sat for a long time in a chair staring blankly at the street below. Katya was asleep. The city was as quiet as it ever gets. Finally I rose, went over to the hall closet, and took my new pistol out of the shoe box I kept it in.

Lavrenti, my friend, the time has come.

The next morning, someone else was given Harry's tasks as courier. I got word to him that he was to meet me at the bus terminal near the Lincoln Tunnel. I was in a phone booth when he arrived, and he went to another booth opposite the one I was in. Before he arrived I had taken down all the numbers in the opposite phone booths. I simply dialled the one he was in and we talked for a few minutes. It was long enough for me to make sure no one was following him. In the crowded coffee shop a few minutes later, I let him talk first. The two trips of the previous week had been almost spiritually uplifting for him. "Finally," he said, rolling his huge hand up into a fleshy fist and pounding it into his palm. "Finally, we're getting some action. Man, the Party must be about to roll again. Isn't it?" His words came out both as a declaration and a plea.

"Yes, Harry," I said, pushing a parcel across the table at him.

"What's in here?"

"A pistol."

Those dead eyes widened in that sagging, houndlike face. "What do I need it for?"

"You're going to kill a counter-revolutionary."

I had already decided that I was not going to explain too much to him. Everything was going to be presented in the form of orders. Party orders. And Party loyalty. He was to do what he was told, just as he had for decades. There was no room for discussion. In the package there was a map of the area around Sam's office. I had drawn the map myself, and it included the exact place where Harry was to wait to kill Lavrenti. It was at the end of a small alley that delivery trucks used. At night it was badly lit. The next time I sensed Lavrenti was behind me, I would walk up that alley and out onto Forty-Sixth Street. As he followed me through the alley, Harry was to open fire.

Harry wanted to know who it was who would be following me. I refused to tell him. "Comrade Harry," I said, playing my man-from-Moscow role to the hilt, "surely you must know that such details are not important for you to know. You are simply to carry out *the Party's orders*."

130

The catchwords that sent a thirty-year weight slamming down on any mental trapdoors that still happened to be open. "Of course, Comrade Dimitri," he said quickly. And nervously.

The following day, Harry went to an abandoned factory near Coney Island, drew a chalk circle on the wall, and practised filling it full of bullets. He was ready.

Two days later, I waited until the evening rush hour had subsided and then I set off toward Sam's office. I walked down Lexington because it was a narrow street, and I might have a chance of knowing earlier if I was being followed. Nothing. Then over to Park Avenue. And Madison. Still nothing. I kept walking in zigzags through the cross streets, stopping at the Algonquin Hotel to buy a newspaper, which I immediately threw away.

That was when it happened.

It was like electricity shooting through me. I *felt* that shadow before I saw it. I was tossing the newspaper into a pile of cardboard boxes when my hair stood up. I turned just enough as I was throwing away the paper to see that same blur of blackness. My heart started pounding like a hammer in my chest. I didn't want to panic like I had a few nights earlier. It was all I could do to keep walking at a normal pace, while everything inside me screamed with that intolerable fear.

As I walked I began breathing heavily, like a person going into shock. So terrified was I of that shadow that my entire system was spinning out of control. I got to Forty-fifth Street. And then the alley.

I told myself there was no reason to fear Lavrenti any longer. It would soon be over. I knew that it was not far ahead now. Maybe fifty yards. And closing. My steps in the alley were heavy and too noisy.

I walked past Harry, silently frozen in the shadows, just where he was supposed to be.

131

I concentrated on the traffic that rushed past the end of the alley. Trying to make it pull me towards that street with its sounds and lights.

Then I heard the shot. One single shot. It sounded surprisingly small, like a twig cracking. It came when I was almost at the street, where people were passing by. The instant I heard it, a weight that had been pressing me down fell away. I was free.

I had planned to keep on walking. Even to run. But I was suddenly spent and exhilarated. Almost carefree. I remained at the end of the alley looking back. Out of the darkness, I could see Harry lumber into the middle of the alley. He stopped.

And then something strange happened.

He seemed to lurch. I wasn't sure if he stumbled or not. But he sank down and then I heard a moan. An unearthly moan that echoed off the hard brick walls. It was a sound that was easily swallowed up by the countless other noises of the city at night. But it went right through me.

I walked a few steps back in Harry's direction. He lurched toward me, passing through the faint rays of light from the painted and barred windows that faced the alley. His face was contorted. He made a hideous noise, like a strangled scream trying to escape. He raised his arms stiffly, pointing the gun right at me.

Harry stopped, his face twisting in a kind of pain. The gun shook. He tried to fire, but his body began to convulse. The scream escaped as a sobbing bellow. The gun slipped out of his hand.

He sank to his knees, tears streaming down his face. "I have always been loyal." His entire body shook. "Loyal! All my life." That was all he could say, over and over again. I took a step closer to him and he looked at me with pure hatred showing through the tears that flowed as if he was a child. He toppled over and sat sprawled in the

132

alley, his face in his hands, sobbing uncontrollably.

"Damn you," he said. "Why me? *Me!*"

I didn't understand.

"You knew I was loyal," he sobbed. "So did you have to make me shoot your wife just to prove it?"

13

It was put down as a mugging. An attack on a Russian diplomat and his wife as they were taking a short cut to go to the movies.

There were ambulances and flashing police lights with radios crackling. Then the desperate ride through the streets with the sirens screaming. The doors of the emergency ward blasting open. Hurtled into a white world of tense voices snapping quiet orders. Nurses shooting quick, worried looks over the tops of their surgical masks. Then the endless waiting in the marble hallways that smelled of chemicals.

And finally the words from the surgeon: "She'll probably live."

I discovered that Katya had been following me to Sam's office ever since she found out what a stockbroker was. Much to her amazement, a stockbroker was — in theory, at least — a person who took a little bit of money and made it into a lot of money.

Her little bit of money.

This astonishing revelation had come to her months earlier, at Miriam Nelson's party, where she had been sitting uncomfortably with all those well-dressed women. Two of the women next to her had been filled with guilt after hearing Alexei's impassioned poetry (mine, as you will recall). They immediately resolved to sell their stocks. Katya had no idea what they were talking about. And when those women told her that stockbrokers were social parasites who made vast fortunes for the wealthy while exploiting the workers of the world, she just nodded her head and wondered where she had heard of stockbrokers before.

Certainly it was not in the Caucasus where her hometown was. There, people talked mainly of getting enough to eat. Or who the secret police had taken away from the neighbouring towns. But no one ever mentioned stockbrokers there. So it had to be someone in New York. Katya just sat in that opulent apartment staring out over Central Park at the skyscrapers until she remembered the offices I had shown her — the offices of those people who had taken away the money she won in the supermarket lottery.

She grew excited just thinking about it. The money was not lost forever! In her peasant's way of thinking, she had presumed that the money had somehow been confiscated, the way they took away the *kulaks'* property in Russia. But after listening to these rich women, she realized that those stockbrokers were performing some kind of financial wizardry to make her small fortune into a vast fortune.

And maybe Comrade Husband was secretly hoarding those sums of money and not telling her. Vast sums that could be spent on beautiful dresses in Bloomingdale's.

She had decided to wait until we returned from Moscow. Then she would find out.

On the fifth floor of the hospital I was given a surgical gown and a mask before I was allowed in to see her. She was in a special room that was somehow more antiseptic than the others. The pale white light reflected faintly off the tiled surfaces of the room, and a small electrical machine made intermittent wheezing noises. She was still unconscious. Looking as white as porcelain, she lay with her life hooked into all those tubes and wires that were fastened across her body.

I stood in the corridor staring at her through the observation window. A nurse came up to me with a parcel of Katya's clothing, which they wanted me to take home. I had to sign a receipt for it.

"It's a pity about the dress," the nurse said while I was signing. For a moment I wasn't sure what she was talking about. Then I quickly opened the parcel. Inside was Katya's red dress. She had been wearing it pinned up under her coat.

Of course, there was a bullet hole in it.

Inside that tiled room, I sat beside her and held her hand. I looked first at her face, which seemed so fragile it might shatter. Her eyes flickered but remained closed. Then I stared at all the wires and tubes. I followed one of the tubes to a small machine with dials on it. The machine was plugged into a wall socket.

I wondered what would happen if something went wrong with that machine. Or if the tube came loose.

I couldn't believe I was thinking such things. I patted her hand and whispered loving words to her. But my mind was playing tricks on me. All I could think of was more dresses. More arguments. And one day being stood up against a wall in the Lubyanka Prison and shot because my wife had been caught with a closetful of Dior gowns. I told myself I was being irrational. I looked around that tiled room with its white light. Weren't the execution chambers in the basements of the Lubyanka also supposed to be tiled? So they could be hosed down easily afterwards? White-tiled, as a matter of fact. That's what we had heard. White-tiled, with a floor that sloped slightly toward a drain. For the fluids to run off.

I was hallucinating. I had to be. But why was she put in this white room? With this little life-giving machine? Was this her execution chamber? I tried to sit on my hands and rock back and forth, smiling and whispering to her. What was happening to me? Hours earlier, I thought I had murdered Lavrenti. But now Katya? I stared at the white walls and saw that lone prisoner at the far end of the green valley at the very moment he blew up.

136

I suddenly realized that I had grasped the tube in my hands. I looked at it in a kind of horror and then let it drop.

I discovered I was being watched by one of the doctors. I turned and smiled weakly, forgetting I was wearing a surgical mask. He too was wearing a mask and gown and cap. The doctor was standing on the other side of the observation window. The white lights reflected on the glass, making his face look almost surreal.

Katya stirred. Her eyes opened and she mumbled a few words. Then she drifted back into unconsciousness. I stared at that tube. The doctor was still there. Just watching. I glanced irritably at him. He beckoned me towards him. I got up and walked over to the observation window. The doctor said nothing. He just stared at me through his thick glasses. I stood directly in front of him, staring back through that window.

"What is it?" I asked, becoming even more irritable. My next words froze in my throat.

It was Lavrenti.

"My sympathies," he said, his voice barely coming through the glass. "It's terrible when someone close to you gets shot. I know the feeling." Those peering eyes, magnified by his glasses, went right through me. Then he switched over to Russian and said, "So, Dimi, you had success in the Workers' Paradise, did you?" Dimi was the name my father always called me as a boy. "Enjoy it while you can. I still have faith in your ability to destroy yourself. With my help, of course. By the way, did your father remember me?"

I could say nothing. I knew he was smiling behind that surgical mask. We were standing only inches away from each other. One of his hands was inside the long gown, and I knew he had a small pistol trained on me. And was thrilling to the knowledge that he could kill me but chose not to. Yet. Just letting me dangle longer, twisting slowly in the winds of my own fear.

My fist plunged right through that window. Straight towards his face. In the explosion of glass, he twisted imperceptibly and my fist flew past his cheek. But I grazed him just beside the ear.

He stepped back, leaving me caught with one arm sticking out into the corridor. He felt the side of his head. A tiny bead of blood smeared his searching fingers. He nodded, even smiled at me as the sounds of loud, questioning voices and hurrying footsteps filled the corridor. Quietly, professionally, Lavrenti blended into the chaos and vanished.

One of the nurses ran out of a nearby room and stood gaping at me caught with my arm dangling through the hole in the window. For a moment she didn't know what to say.

Then she asked, "Is something wrong?"

14

It began the way most forest fires probably begin. With a tiny flame unnoticed because of its apparent insignificance.

That tiny flame was a nine-line article buried deep within the second section of the *New York Times*. The Senator had made a speech somewhere in the Midwest telling some Rotary Club members that communists were swarming all over their government in Washington. The article was not in any of the other newspapers I saw. Nor was it reported on the radio. And it made no impact at all on the daily life of Enemy Number One.

Even inside the embassy it was regarded as just another disgruntled outburst from a politician in need of votes. People were far more concerned with their expressions of sympathy for Katya than with the obscure rantings of this unknown Senator. The embassy wives were busily organizing shipments of proper Russian food to be smuggled past the nurses. And the shooting was the only thing the staff could talk about for days. Anatoly wanted to know how the attacker jumped out of the shadows at us. And Ivchenkov seemed relieved that her chest area had not been touched by the bullet.

I answered all their questions and then retreated into my office and read that nine-line article for the third time. *Swarming over the government?* That was not exactly what my letter to him had said. I should have guessed what was coming.

But I was obviously too preoccupied with Katya to think much about the Senator. That afternoon she was taken off the critical list. I made sure I was in there before the police so our stories would be identical. And I took her flowers and chocolates. I lavished her with affection. I ran errands for her. I wanted to be the perfect husband. I told myself that things would change.

Her room was filled with flowers. The largest bouquet was signed *Thank you for so much — Harry*. He was not among the visitors.

The next morning, Boris cancelled the meeting we had scheduled. He hurried through the office looking pale and tense. From behind his closed door we could hear yelling. Ivchenkov entered his office and emerged looking worried. Anatoly and I were ordered to remain in close touch all day. Late that night we were summoned to a meeting in Boris's office. Something had gone wrong, we were told. One of our most valuable agents, the man in the Treasury Department, had got word back to us that he had been visited by men from the FBI.

Boris stared at us grimly. "It looks like they know about his meeting with me last week in Baltimore," he said, in a way that was almost inviting either of us to say that somehow we too knew about the meeting in Baltimore. I could tell that already Boris was setting traps. Looking for scapegoats. There was that tiny hint of fear that shone through the anger etched across that sharp, thin face. He unconsciously ran the palm of his hand across what was left of his hairline. And his stomach made noises that sounded like an old door opening.

Two days later, I returned from the hospital and was met by Anatoly, who was waiting near the front door of the embassy. His usually jovial greeting was missing. His chubby face looked very red and moist. "Trouble," was all he could say. "Trouble." In his office all the morning newspapers were spread out. In varying sizes of headlines the Senator was proclaiming that he had proof of our infiltration into the government of Enemy Number One.

And he would hold hearings to prove it. With the help

of this new gadget called television, the entire country would see the Red Menace — as he called it — firsthand.

This was not what I expected.

Hearings? Television? I stared at the photographs of my Senator, taken while he was making his announcement. He looked forceful, almost angry. This was his first time ever on page one. I realized I had made him famous.

"Boris is going berserk," Anatoly said fearfully. "He's pissing all over everyone. Me especially." The look in Anatoly's eyes told too much. A more polished intelligence officer would have been able to hide his worries. But Anatoly, as usual, could hide nothing. I slapped him on the shoulder and told him everything would be all right.

But I knew it wouldn't.

There was a sense of controlled panic around the embassy. And if there had been a switchboard for spies, it would have lit up. All day we kept getting secret signals from our agents. The entire network was twitching because of the news. It meant that we had to spend hours finding ways of reaching our people and reassuring them that everything was under control. I had to meet my submarine spy, who was more nervous than ever. His fat little body shook, and he rocked back and forth on a packing case in the old warehouse.

"Christalmighty," he said as if he were in pain. "This is a goddam disaster. I almost got the house paid off, and now this."

I sympathized with him as I had been trained to do back in Moscow, and then in a dozen subtle ways reminded him that he was in too deep to stop now. Then I moved on to the next one, a steely-eyed older man who owned a photographic studio in Brooklyn. He was really a colonel in our secret police. He had been sent over years ago posing as an immigrant, and quietly, over a decade, he had put together a brilliant network of his own. We seldom saw him. He insisted on keeping communications to a minimum. I met him at a wharf on the East River. He had one of those long, narrow faces, with his white hair combed severely back, and his cold, blue eyes peering out accusingly from behind wire-rimmed glasses.

His fury was in keeping with the way he led his life. Cold and controlled.

"Amateurs," he said contemptuously.

"You mean the Senator?" I asked. We all dreaded having to deal with this man. He was the most intimidating of all our agents.

"Him. And you people in the embassy. This should never have been allowed to happen."

This annoyed me. "And how would Comrade Colonel suggest we have prevented it?"

"If you lack the imagination to provide the answer for yourselves, I assure you that Moscow will send over those who can." He peered down at me like a hawk examining a cornered rabbit. "You obviously do not understand the people in this country. They are very bizarre. They crave big news events like an alcoholic needs his vodka. If they do not have one, they will make one. I am worried because there is not enough other big news now. This Senator may satisfy their cravings. Do you understand me?"

I said nothing about the colonel's remarks when we all met late that night in Boris's office. Only his desk lamp was turned on, and we sat on the fringes of its glow as he attempted to control his own fears by turning them into anger. He constantly rubbed the palm of his hand against the perspiring edges of his thinning hairline. "A disgrace!" he hissed. "This fiasco is clearly a result of allowing such a weak link as your Party apparatus." He glared at Anatoly, who sat speechless, clearing his throat too often. In the corner, Ivchenkov sat solemnly staring at Anatoly, the little red veins in his face almost glowing in the dark.

Survival was the word that shot through the thoughts of every man in that room.

The next morning, I could stand outside Boris's office and listen to the noise his stomach was making. He had just confirmed his worst fears. The man from Treasury had been taken in for questioning by the FBI. And whoever he met in Philadelphia had also been taken in for two hours and then released. His entire network was coming to pieces. Moscow had to be notified.

I watched his growing panic, knowing that if it got out of control, it could envelop us all. I was prepared for that. I knew before I began my scheme that Boris would be one of the risks. I was sure he was a risk that could be controlled. In one way or another.

But what I was not prepared for was the Senator. I had expected that he would use the information in my letter for a careful and quiet investigation of the situation. And then make public what he had found. But suddenly he was on every newscast, on every front page. Making accusations he had no way of proving. And then other politicians got involved. Dozens, then hundreds of them. Then more. All sniffing the wind and changing course. They all wanted to be like the Senator. They ran around announcing hearings. Evidence. Charges of spies being everywhere. They were like blind men operating searchlights in an air raid.

I smelled disaster.

I was right. The Senator himself seemed to go out of control, making even wilder accusations. Some were vaguely accurate. But many I knew were not. Already he had gone too far. And there was no way I could stop him. I had created a monster.

Just as the colonel had said, Moscow did send over men to provide the answers. We received word only hours before they arrived. There were four of them. Their names meant nothing to me, but Boris sunk into his chair as he read the list, muttering fearfully to himself. At least some of them had to be secret police. When they arrived, I recognized the man in charge as one of the most powerful and deadly bureaucrats in the Kremlin. He was old, with a wide face and eyes that bulged slightly, making him look like a frog. The other three men I had never seen before. They were cold, hard-faced men who acted as if they were behind enemy lines and had no time to waste. Their very presence sent fear shooting through the whole embassy.

The old man from the Kremlin called all of us into a meeting. He sat in Boris's chair as if he had been there for years. "I understand we have a problem here," he said softly, almost like an old friend who had dropped in to help. The other three men waited outside the door. I knew they were there to take someone back to Moscow. By force, if necessary.

I glanced at Anatoly, who sat stiffly in his chair. Before the meeting I had whispered to him to stay calm no matter what was said. "Keep control," I had told him. "Remember, they are like wolves when they smell blood."

"Unfortunately, comrade, we do have a problem with this senator and the others like him," said Boris. He then pointed to Anatoly. "This unfortunate situation has been created by incompetence within our own ranks. By having a man in charge of the local Party who allowed it to deteriorate so shamefully."

All eyes turned to Anatoly. He remained perfectly still, listening to the words that could get him thrown against a wall and shot. *Hang on!* I mentally whispered to him. A tiny bead of perspiration rolled down the side of his cheek. But he did not crack, even as Boris continued, and Ivchenkov joined in.

Their presentation was smooth and damning. And totally untrue.

I sat and said nothing. Instead I watched that old man's face. It might have been thought that he was faintly smiling as he listened. Encouraging them to continue. But I thought I detected something else. Something that my father would have also looked for in such a situation.

I thought I saw the false hope that Stalin was famous for giving his victims, just before he had them executed. And I knew that this old man would have had endless opportunities to study the master at work. In fact, he would probably have come here straight from Stalin's office — where he would have cringed as we were now doing. I tried to imagine what would go through Stalin's mind if he were sitting in that chair behind the desk. The answer was simple.

Blood.

Suddenly the old man from the Kremlin tired of hearing Boris explain his plans to save our network of agents and cut him off with a wave of his hand. He turned to me. "And what of our young friend over here?" he said coldly. "What would you do to save our network?"

I took a deep breath. "I wouldn't save it. I would let this senator destroy most of it."

The silence was terrifying. Anatoly's eyes closed. I thought he was going to faint. The others just stared, open-mouthed.

After what seemed like a very long time, the old man put the palms of his hands together, brought his forefingers up to his pursed lips, raised his eyebrows, and said in the softest of voices, "Really? Why?"

For an instant I was on the verge of panic. But voices shrieked at me *Go on! Go on! There is no turning back!* and my mental projector stripped all the sprockets as my father careened out of blackness, scolding me, and the lone prisoner blew up once again.

Very calmly I said, "This Senator is trying to light a fire here. So we should help him. Not try to stop him. We should take all the dead-wood in our Party that has built up over the years and feed it into the Senator's fire."

"And sacrifice our own people?" the old man said, his bulging eyes fixed on me like a frog facing a fly.

"You see!" Boris yelled. "What fools I'm dealing with here."

The old man from the Kremlin waved his hand again and Boris fell silent immediately.

"Precisely," I said.

"Why?"

"The Senator seems to be enough of a madman that innocent people will also get burned if we can keep the fire going long enough. Once he's run out of our dead-wood he'll look for anything he can get his hands on. Just to keep those fires going. And once the innocent are tossed in with the guilty, we will have this country's most powerful force in the palms of our hands."

"Really? What?"

"Guilt."

"Guilt?"

"What Marx cannot yet accomplish here, Freud can," I said. "Just get them feeling guilty and you've got these people for an entire generation. They'll flail themselves for decades over the Senator's sins. And they'll never investigate us again. No matter how many agents we pour in here."

"What drivel," exclaimed Boris.

"Silence!" bellowed the old man, his eyes flashing a fury that pinned Boris into his chair. The old man pointed to me and said softly, "Stalin would agree with our young friend here. There are times when a forest must be pruned. And when the trees fall, chips must fly."

And that was the way the meeting ended.

Later that night they stuffed Boris into a big steamer

trunk. I was not there when it happened. According to Anatoly, it was not at all pleasant. The old man from the Kremlin had told Boris that he would be returning to Moscow with them. They were to leave later that same night. Boris knew instantly what this meant. It was like being handed a death warrant. He attempted to escape by running out the back entrance of the embassy, but the three cold, hard-faced men caught him in a basement corridor, clubbed him into submission, and injected a powerful drug into his veins. Then they dumped him into the specially built steamer trunk that would not be opened until it was safely in the hold of the Russian ship that was docked in the harbour, waiting to sail for Gdansk.

As I said, I was not there when they stuffed Boris into the trunk. I was wandering around Bloomingdale's, Saks Fifth Avenue, and Tiffany's. Immediately after our meeting, the old man from the Kremlin had taken me aside, smiling, for the first time, those bulging eyes of his beaming. "Well done, comrade," he said. "We must be ceaselessly vigilant in finding and destroying counter-revolutionaries in our midst. Now then, I promised my wife that I would do some shopping while I was here.

"Perhaps you could show me the way to Fifth Avenue?"

15

At first I thought the old man from the Kremlin would expect me to take him to one of the more proletarian stores, like Macy's. When we arrived there, I could see immediately that I had made a miscalculation. He just peered at me out of the side of those bulging eyes with an expression of distaste.

"Better. Much better," he smiled as we went into the first of the elegant stores of Fifth Avenue. He had a list. A long one. I was stunned. The dresses he chose for his wife were almost as expensive as Katya's. But he ordered two of them in the first store alone. My astonishment at the number of expensive goods he was buying quickly became obvious. I realized too late that my naiveté irritated him. That I should have known that this was just a normal foreign shopping trip for someone in his position. So after Bloomingdale's he smiled, asked me to write down the names and addresses of the other stores, and said he could manage on his own.

I also had some shopping to do. All week Anatoly and I had planned to go shopping for a television set. It was to be the official embassy TV set. Over a week ago I had successfully argued that a TV was essential, now that the Senator had announced he was going to hold his hearings in front of the cameras. We had to see what was happening. Ivchenkov had agreed, and we had been given the money, part of which we had spent in bars, so we were now looking at portables instead of console models.

We took our time looking. We were both relieved to have an excuse just to get away from the embassy while those three secret police types were doing whatever they had to do with Boris and the steamer trunk. I felt ill just hearing about it. And after the events of the day, Anatoly was gloriously useless even at choosing a television set. I insisted that we go to several stores, where I could scornfully reject anything the salesman showed us except for the General Electric models. (Sam had told me something about a price-earnings ratio with GE. I didn't know what he was talking about. I just knew I owned some of it.) But I could see Anatoly's heart was not in the venture. Nor was mine. We were both haunted by what had happened that day. So we stopped at a bar in Times Square.

"That could have been me in that trunk," said Anatoly. His chubby hands were again wrapped so tightly around the glass that I thought it would shatter.

"Or me," I said, trying to make him feel better.

"Or you," he agreed. I felt worse. "But you know something else?" he went on. "I don't like this game. I mean, I didn't want them to stuff Boris into that lousy trunk. So they can take him back and shoot him."

"He wanted to stuff you in there."

"That's the trouble." He was almost weeping. "There's no need for people to get so intense about it all. I should have been a poet. They don't get put in trunks."

"Stalin has shot thousands of poets. Stay where you are. It's safer."

"Poor Boris. What does he do when he has to go to the bathroom?"

By the time we left the bar, the vision of Boris in that trunk had sent us both into a fit of depression. Anatoly was resolutely praising Boris as a charming, saintly friend. I stood on the sidewalk and counted our remaining money. There was not enough to buy even a portable television. We agonized over this for a while, until I remembered a place that sold used television sets. In the glare of blinding neon lights in a junk-filled appliance store, we chose a battered old Emerson. It was definitely a portable, the man assured us, but Anatoly and I both suffered various forms of personal distress as we sweated and heaved our prize back to the embassy.

The embassy was strangely quiet as we struggled to get the television up to my apartment. We were about to open the door when we heard voices. From inside. Katya was still in the hospital, and when I'd seen her early that morning there was no chance of her leaving for at least three more days. We stood wheezing and sweating, holding the Emerson and trying to listen. They were male voices. I struggled with the key and pushed the door with my foot. It opened, revealing the three cold, hard-faced men. One was cleaning a pistol. The other two were playing chess. They looked up at us blankly and then went back to what they were doing.

"No one was in here," said one of the chess players in a bored voice.

"We're departing for Russia just before dawn," said the gun cleaner. I stared around at the food they had helped themselves to. Suddenly Anatoly let out a little whimper and shot a frantic look across the Emerson we were still holding. I looked in the direction he was signalling. And when I saw what he meant, I almost dropped the television.

The trunk! It was right in the middle of my apartment! And they were sitting there playing chess on it.

"Boris is in there!" whispered Anatoly, suddenly breaking into a sweat.

"Checkmate!" yelled one of the players. The other gave the trunk a kick and got up. He noticed the television. "Hey, put it here," he said, pointing to the trunk.

You could tell he was used to giving orders. And that no one ever disobeyed him. Anatoly and I struggled over to the trunk. The chessboard was cleared away and we put the television on it. Very gently. But the secret policeman giving the orders thought that it was too low, so they turned the trunk on its end. Anatoly and I placed the television on the trunk a second time. We plugged it in and it flickered to life. The other lights were switched off.

"It's sitting on top of Boris," Anatoly said in a desperate whisper.

"Shut up," I hissed under my breath as the Gillette Cavalcade of Sports came on. It was a boxing match with Sugar Ray Robinson fighting someone from Cleveland. All three of the men were fascinated by the television. They had never seen one in a home before. The vodka was broken out. My vodka. But they only consumed the smallest of amounts. They let us do the drinking. They were professionals and they knew the price of letting their guard down.

So we sat around and watched the boxing match. And when that was over, the news came on. Much of the news was about the Senator. He was making a speech.

On top of Boris.

The Senator was wildly denouncing communists of all kinds. I was asked to translate for the three men. "He must have a very big *dacha*," one of the men said.

Suddenly the picture on the television made both Anatoly and me sit up. It was Miriam Nelson. She was testifying in front of a group of congressmen who were asking her if she was a communist.

The trunk stood like a shiny slab rising up out of the centre of the darkened room. It glistened in the cold light of its own eye. Anatoly and I both sat there, fixed in our own quiet horror, watching those congressional hearings while peering at — into — that trunk, wondering if we would hear a whimper or see a trickle of urine ease across the floor.

Harold Leonard Dawes came on the screen. He was being questioned and was angrily asserting his constitutional rights.

"Who are these people?" asked the man who gave the orders.

I explained.

"So why do they show them to the masses when they're going to take them out and shoot them?"

I explained that they wouldn't shoot them. The three men debated this among themselves with various degrees of scepticism. "Do they send them to the *gulag* in Alaska?" one asked. Anatoly said they didn't.

"Well, that's just plain stupid, then," said the man who gave the orders. His long face was outlined in the pale light of the television. Thin with no cheekbones, his face descended straight down, almost inward, from his eyes. A jagged nose told of long-ago beatings. He stared thoughtfully at the television. A professional considering the problems of other professionals. "How do they ever expect to control their peasants?" He seemed genuinely puzzled by it all.

When the news was over, the national anthem came on and then the screen went blank. Anatoly quickly said good-night, and I was left with the three men lying on the couches and rugs in my apartment. Within minutes all three were asleep. Almost in unison. As if they had been trained to sleep on command. For several minutes I just sat there slumped on the couch. I got up to turn off the television. As I rose from the couch, I accidentally brushed against the sleeping form of the man who gave the orders.

In one terrifying instant, the room was filled with the deadly reflex motion of flashing metal, like the springing of some animal trap. I found myself frozen with fear, staring down the barrel of a Mauser pistol that had come from nowhere. In that single, almost humanly indivisible moment, the sleeping form on the couch had been catapulted into a lethal state, with every mental and physical capability racing at hair-trigger ready.

Around the living room, other pistols were also trained on me. One by one, they put the guns down, slumping back. "Don't you know better than to approach a man when he's asleep?" said the man who gave the orders.

Within minutes they were all sleeping again. I did not even bother to turn off the television. Or get up and go to bed. I just sat there staring at the empty screen, which glared back at me from on top of the trunk with Boris in it. My plans for saving Enemy Number One were definitely not turning out as I had expected. For the second time in a row I had chosen the wrong group to help me save the country. The politicians were as bad as the intellectuals. If they had done it all differently, I would not have three killers and a steamer trunk in my living room.

I drifted off. At 2:30 A.M., the three men awoke almost in unison. By three o'clock, they had moved the big steamer trunk quietly out of my apartment. I just lay there watching it go through the door. As they tipped it over I heard a clunking noise coming from inside. I wondered how long it would be before the drugs wore off and Boris began regaining consciousness. The three men left the door open, and I made no move to close it. I just stared.

A couple of minutes later, I found myself confronted by the old man from the Kremlin. I had no idea he was even still in the embassy. He had obviously found another apartment to sleep in. Perhaps even Boris's. Unlike the other three, the old man from the Kremlin seemed tired, almost disoriented by lack of sleep. His froglike face seemed wider, his chin spilling out across his collar in all directions, as he stood blinking in the doorway.

"Get ready," he said sternly. "You're coming with us."

Me?

16

In the basement of the embassy there was a garage where our cars were kept. I was led down there by one of the secret policemen. The others were waiting beside one of our black 1951 Fords. The steamer trunk was sticking out of the boot of the car. It had to be tied down with heavy rope that had been wound around the bumper several times so it wouldn't fall out.

The old man from the Kremlin reappeared. "You're driving," he said.

For a minute I thought it had all been a trick. That I was also being taken back to Moscow with Boris. But the old man from the Kremlin gave me a detailed map of New York with a route outlined precisely on it in red ink. It must have been done in Moscow. "You will follow this route to our freighter, the *Berezovska*. They are waiting for you. When you arrive, they will immediately unload the trunk and take it onto the ship. Then you are to return here. Now, I presume you are familiar with the area on the map?"

I looked at the map. The line went from the embassy, across the Brooklyn Bridge, and through Brooklyn itself to the harbour. The map showed Ebbets Field, where my beloved Dodgers played. Ever since the last baseball season it was the area of New York I knew the best.

"And I also presume that I do not have to tell you that you are transporting a commodity of considerable importance. You will, of course, be held personally responsible." Those bulbous eyes of his stared at me threateningly. I nodded, but the words I intended to speak wouldn't come out of my mouth.

154

A vision shot through my mind. In it I was drugged, inside a trunk.

"Now then, for obvious reasons I will not be accompanying any of you. I will be departing on a commercial air flight later today."

I stared at the Ford. The weight of the trunk had pushed the car down so it was almost resting on its back axle. "There's already too much weight. It won't hold three more people," I said, hoping to find a way out of this entire affair.

"They will not be accompanying you," he said, impatiently nodding toward the three secret police thugs. "They were not seen entering this country, and they will not be seen leaving it. Moscow is absolutely determined that no trace of their stay here should exist. So you will drive by yourself." He waved his gloved hand in the air, and from the other end of the parking garage an engine roared into life and headlights suddenly flashed through the damp gloom. One of our vans drove away from the far wall and stopped in front of us. Yakir, the embassy guard, was driving. He was trying to act very professional to impress the men from Moscow. You could tell that he was thrilled to be playing in such big leagues. He gave me a jaunty thumbs-up sign over the steering wheel.

The old man from the Kremlin turned to the three cold, hard-faced men. "You are to remain in the back of this truck until the driver assures you that you are at the *Berezovska*. Under no circumstances allow yourselves to be seen. Good day, comrades."

They went to the van and climbed in the back. I went to the Ford, sat behind the wheel, and wanted to throw up. The van drove up the ramp and out onto the street. I was to wait for exactly two minutes before leaving.

I was carting a man off to his execution. And he had to be conscious now. No drug could keep him under this

155

long. Or could it? Two minutes. I drove out onto the deserted streets of New York. A light rain had been falling. The reflections of the neon and the traffic lights shimmered on the streets. I went to Second Avenue, just as the map said, and then drove slowly, trying to avoid the potholes. A couple of times I ran right into one. I felt every vibration on that street as if it was an explosion. I could hear the steamer trunk clattering against the back bumper. Once, around Thirtieth Street, I thought it was on the verge of falling out, so I pulled over and got out to check it. One of the ropes was working itself loose. I tightened it and was about to get back into the car when I noticed something.

Across the street at the far end of the block a taxi was parked. I noticed it because there had been almost no other cars on that wide, one-way street except a few way back around Fortieth. The taxi had its engine idling. Then it flashed its lights at me.

It was a distinct pattern. The lights were flashed in short and long bursts. After two short flashes and one long followed by another short one, I realized from my Army days that I was looking at Morse code.

The taxi spelled out the letter *R*. Then the next letter, *U*. Finally the word came together in my mind. *RUN*.

And a split second later I realized it had been spelled in Russian!

And I leapt into the car and sent it hurtling through that intersection, the tyres making a sizzling squeal on the wet pavement. I got as far as Twenty-eighth Street before the light changed to red. Gripping the steering wheel and yelling at myself to calm down, I ran the light. Horns blaring. Other cars careening toward me. Spinning like toys on the wet roads. From every corner of my vision something was shooting towards me. And the trunk was making jackhammer noises against the bumper.

The taxi stayed serenely behind me.

To hell with the map, I told myself, suddenly making a left turn from the farthest right lane, cutting across those six lanes at high speed with my eyes closed, hoping that nothing would hit me. Nothing did. But the taxi made the same turn in a graceful arc.

Somewhere in the midst of that kaleidoscope of lights and noise flashing past me, I decided that I might as well run every light, dodge every pursuing policeman's bullet, and drive through oncoming traffic whenever necessary. If I got killed, at least it would be over. But if I didn't deliver Boris I would die a thousand Siberian deaths. Or worse, if this episode of smuggling a drugged diplomat out in a trunk ever hit the newspapers, Stalin's killers would hunt me down to the ends of the remotest jungle hide-out.

I ran three lights in a row. I could see the entrance to the Brooklyn Bridge. And in the rearview mirror I could see the taxi. Suddenly a huge tractor trailer made a partial U-turn almost directly in front of me. Then it began backing up, blocking the entire street. I yelled and honked the horn, but it was no use. I braked so hard the Ford skidded almost sideways with a loud squeal.

The taxi came up almost leisurely behind me. Like a cat that has backed a mouse into a corner. It drew up beside me. Lavrenti was smoking a big cigar, wearing a porkpie hat and a loud shirt with flamingoes all over it. "Hiya, pal," he called out through the open window. I could see a bandage just beside his ear from our last encounter. But now he was grinning, one hand casually draped across the back of the seat, the other waving at me.

"Out for a little night air, are we, pal?" He chomped on his cigar and wiggled his eyebrows, giving me a devious grin. "The air is better in Brooklyn, is it?"

I clenched the steering wheel.

"Relax, pal. We're stuck in traffic. Tell you what — I'll even switch the meter off." He reached over, and with that same big grin, he flipped a switch on the meter. Then he blew smoke rings. Perfect smoke rings.

"Remember those, pal?" he said, looking at the smoke rings. But now he was speaking in Russian. And his voice had suddenly turned very distant. "Remember us going out behind those burned up *kulaks*' houses and smoking that terrible *makhorka*. Yecch. What lousy cigarettes they were. We were too dumb to steal the good Moscow cigarettes from our fathers' supplies. You know, my father was the one who taught me to blow smoke rings." He blew two more smoke rings and stared at them, his face suddenly as still as a mask.

"Ah, well, you know what they say." He had switched back into English, using his Brooklyn accent. "L.S.M.F.T. — isn't that what the commercials here say? Lucky Strike Means Fine Tobacco. Isn't that the way it goes, pal? Or maybe it means something different. How about Lotsa Stalin's Men Fill Trunks? Huh?"

I panicked. I blasted the horn and raced the engine. The tractor trailer was still in the way. Lavrenti grinned. "Okay, okay, so you didn't like it. No need to get insulted about it."

He eased the taxi back a couple of feet. "Hey, pal, what *have* you got in that trunk? Goin' on a trip, are you? Extra charge for trunks, you know."

I did the only thing I could think of when I saw him start to reach for the door handle. I rammed the taxi. There was just barely enough of an angle to catch it on the front bumper. I backed up and desperately positioned for a second hit before he could recover from the first one. This time I hit him broadside, hurling the taxi sideways. And in the midst of that explosion of glass and metal and rubber, I could hear him laughing! "Okay, okay, pal. So I won't charge for the trunk." I could see him grappling to keep his glasses on.

And laughing.

There was just enough space behind the tractor trailer. I swung the Ford around, praying that Boris wouldn't fall out. The car spun and swerved its way onto the street leading to the Brooklyn Bridge. I almost stripped the gears getting up to top speed. The bridge resounded to car horns. I felt as if I was driving through a brass band. I didn't care about anything but getting to the *Berezovska*.

But Lavrenti stayed in the rearview mirror. Waving.

And halfway across the bridge he drove right up behind me. The taxi was only a few feet away. I had my foot to the floor. The engine in the Ford was screaming as the RPMs climbed past all its endurance. But Lavrenti stayed with me.

And then at one hundred miles an hour on the Brooklyn Bridge, he actually rammed me! I couldn't believe it. Not hard, mind you. But hard enough to hear metal striking metal behind me. Suddenly I remembered Boris. "Have you no decency?" I screamed at Lavrenti. "There's a man in there, for God's sake. You lousy savage."

I swerved all over the bridge. But he hit me again, the same sharp little jolt. All I could think of was poor Boris. "Hold on, comrade!" I screamed, hoping he might be able to hear me. "I'll get you there, Boris. Don't you worry about a thing."

At the time it seemed like the right thing to say.

The end of the bridge was in sight. I had no choice but to slow down. I got off the bridge, made a quick right turn, and suddenly there was nothing but blackness in the rearview mirror. I had lost him. Struggling to hold myself together, I hurried toward the part of the harbour where I was to rendezvous with the others. Because of the high speeds, I was still on schedule with only a couple of miles to go. I grabbed the map and drove through the darkened streets, taking a slightly different route from the one that had been marked by Moscow. I went almost parallel to the harbour, past the big Navy Yard with the destroyers and old battleships outlined faintly behind the high wire-mesh fences. From a few shabby cafés and bars music could be heard faintly blending into the perpetual humming noise of generators on the ships.

I checked the map. Only eight more blocks to go. I sped past a few groups of sailors heading back to their ships. Six blocks. Four. Then the car suddenly lurched for no reason. I had to fight to keep a grip on the steering wheel. I couldn't understand what was happening.

Then I saw Lavrenti. Standing on a deserted street corner with a high-powered rifle. I could see he was firing a second time. The car shuddered and careened in the opposite direction, with a loud, slapping sound suddenly coming from somewhere below me. I fought the car to a halt and stumbled out to find the front tyre on the driver's side had been shot to pieces.

Lavrenti walked toward me, looking ridiculous in his porkpie hat, his flamingo shirt, and the cigar jammed into the side of his mouth. And the high-powered rifle dangling casually at his side. The overall effect was chilling.

"You know, pal," he said, "one of these days my bosses are gonna wise up and fire me. I mean, we know all about those three goons you guys import to do a little dirty work. And instead of going after them, I decide to have some more fun with you." He grinned, his eyes twinkling with delight behind those Coke-bottle glasses of his.

"I don't even want to do anything else to you. Like opening the steamer trunk, if that's what you're thinking. Nope. Much more fun to watch you try to squirm your way out of this one, pal. Better hurry. The *Berezovska*'s supposed to sail in a couple of hours. And you know what Stalin does to those who miss the boat!" He guffawed.

160

He backed away, still smiling. "Of course, you did remember to bring the spare tyre?"

Spare?

I raced around to the back of the car. Boris and his trunk took up all the space. They must have taken the spare tyre out at the embassy. But would Stalin care who took it out?

Lavrenti got into his taxi. His laughter filled that deserted street. "Say hi to Stalin for me," he called out. Then he waved and drove away. I was alone.

Telling myself to stay calm, I tried to assess my situation as rationally as possible. At 3:45 A.M. on a deserted Brooklyn waterfront street, with a flat tyre and a drugged Russian in a steamer trunk, I rationally concluded that my situation was close to hopeless.

I ran to a phone booth across the street. But the receiver had been cut off. Lavrenti. The map flashed back into my mind. Four blocks. I raced down that street, running as I had never run before. After the second block my sides ached. And after the third block I stopped, gasping for breath. I turned in circles gulping air. And saw something move back at the car. Someone was opening the door. And someone else was wrestling with the steamer trunk. I yelled at them. It made no difference. I saw the steamer trunk tumble out onto the ground.

I ran back, shouting and gasping for breath. I yelled at them to stop immediately. I could see them more clearly. It was two sailors. Drunken sailors, from the look of them. They heaved the trunk against the fence. And then, to my horror, they began pushing it up against the fence. High over their heads, sliding it up to the barbed wire.

From a block away I shouted at them. They were balanced on tiptoes, trying to get the trunk over the fence. One of them gave a little jump, and the trunk rested horizontally like a seesaw on the straining barbed wire for a split second.

And then the trunk — Boris! — toppled down on the other side of the fence and the barbed wire. I staggered breathlessly up to the fence. A sign in front of me said RESTRICTED ENTRY — U.S. NAVY.

The sailors had already run off, laughing and talking loudly. They were heading towards a security gate surrounded by a lot of bright lights and guards and signs telling people to keep out. They went through the gate. I stood outside the fence, clutching the wires and yelling at them to give me my trunk back. The two sailors were hurrying back towards the trunk. They did not seem at all disturbed by my presence. "That's private property," I yelled to them.

"It's our property now," said one of the sailors, grinning. He was the older of the two, with a weathered face and huge forearms.

"You cannot take a person's property," I yelled at them again through the fence, as they began to lift the trunk.

"Yeah?" sneered the other sailor with a thick southern drawl. "Well, we're the government, Mac." He laughed as he pointed to the insignia on his dirty uniform.

"This is an outrage!" I yelled.

They picked up the trunk and carried it back towards one of the sheds near the big moth-balled destroyer that was anchored in the harbour. I could see them struggling with the lock. One of them kicked it several times. I yelled, but they paid no attention. I was in an absolute panic at the thought of Boris tumbling out onto the docks of the Brooklyn Navy Yard.

Brooklyn Navy Yard?

I raced over to the nearest light and checked the names of the streets. I thought they sounded familiar. Then I fumbled through all the scraps of paper in my wallet with coded phone numbers scrawled across them. Even before I found what I was looking for, I started running. And when I finally stumbled up to a pay phone that worked, I strained to make out my own writing as I dialled. I was still gasping for breath when the sleepy voice finally answered.

"Harry? Is that you, comrade?"

17

After the first two critical days, Katya had made a quick recovery. Every day I could see a change in her. And by the end of the first week she was sitting up in bed looking utterly stunning, with her long, golden hair falling naturally around her shoulders. Like many Russian women of that time, she normally kept her hair braided and knotted sternly behind her head in a bun. It was considered almost indecent to be seen with hair falling naturally around the shoulders.

During her first week in the hospital, nothing was said about her dress, or why she was following me to Sam's. We both just pretended it had never happened. I did everything I could to help her recover, getting up before dawn to collect bortsch, blinis, and other delicacies cooked by the women of the embassy, and smuggling them past the nurses so that she could eat the food she was used to. The nurses thought I was crazy anyway. After I punched that hole in the observation window, I could hear them whispering whenever I walked by.

I arranged to rent a television set for her room, and soon she couldn't live without the next episode of "I Love Lucy". I made a great flourish out of saying I would buy a television set for her when she got out of the hospital. (Of course, I already had the money in my pocket for the embassy TV set I had not yet purchased.) On the Monday night, after "Lucy", she began planning how she was going to become an actress and star in her own television series back in Moscow. Of course, there was no television in Russia at that time, so she knew she had a few years to plan for it. Her series would be called "I

164

Love Katya". I knew it would be like every other idea she had dreamed up since I had known her. For a week or two it would be fervently discussed, and then suddenly there would be something new that had attracted her attention. She was a butterfly of schemes, always flitting off to brighter colours. But in that week she had a great time planning "I Love Katya". During my nightly visits I joined in. And by the time her stitches came out we had made Katya a lovable, crazy, red-headed (dyed from blond) Party member who is married to Rocky Ricardrovnzia, the famous Cuban balalaika player who is the leader of the liveliest band in Moscow.

Creative matters can be very touchy. The artistic temperament and all that. The first real fight we had after she entered the hospital was about "I Love Katya". Our story had Katya being asked to look after a few of a kindly neighbour's pets while he was away. The pets turn out to be furry little creatures called sables that get into everything and even eat Ricky's balalaika strings on the evening his band is playing at the big dance for the delegates to the Party Congress. Soon there are sables all over the apartment and Ricky gets fed up. But Katya suddenly discovers that these are the animals that make the beautiful fur coats.

It was at this point that our story broke down in a heated argument. To Katya it seemed perfectly logical that the kindly neighbour was just a nice old man with a few pets who would give her enough pelts to make a luxurious fur coat.

Patiently, I pointed out to her that the nice little old neighbour was obviously a black marketeer running an illegal sable operation. It was Ricky's duty to inform on him and have him shot for economic crimes against the state.

Katya was horrified at the thought of losing those luxurious pelts that would make such a gorgeous fur coat.

If Ricky dared inform on that poor little man she was going to tell about the Cuban cigars he had been smuggling into the country in his bongo drums. We started to argue fiercely. Of course, I took Ricky's side.

"How do you expect to get it on television if you don't shoot the little counter-revolutionary bastard?" I yelled, getting carried away and thinking like a bureaucrat at Moscow Television.

"Well, shoot him *after* I get the coat," she yelled back. "This is a comedy, for your information, Mr. Know-it-all."

We were yelling so loudly that the nurses came running in. Of course, they had no idea what we were saying, but they took one look at both our expressions and immediately began taking Katya's pulse, temperature, and whatever else could be poked, probed, or measured.

But except for that one episode, Katya's stay in the hospital was as enjoyable as it could be. Besides the Russian food that I took in to her, there were plants and chocolates that friends at the embassy brought. Her room was overflowing with gifts and food. But the most spectacular presents of all were Harry's flowers. Every day, he sent a larger bouquet. And on the most recent cards were guilt-ridden messages like *Only Party loyalty could have made me do it — your best friend, Harry*. Of course I translated the messages differently when I read them to Katya, and then quietly destroyed the cards.

Harry did not come into the hospital or even phone. And after the fourth huge bouquet arrived, I decided that it was time to do something. I met him after a Party meeting down near Greenwich Village. At first he would not even look me in the eye. Only when I told him that I wanted to take him to see Katya did he show any emotion. He said he couldn't face her, and he almost bolted and ran away when I persisted.

I took him to a nearby bar and for an hour I tried to

convince him that shooting Katya had been an accident. That he was supposed to shoot somebody else. I realized he believed me, but it just didn't matter; he had still shot Katya and nothing could change that. To him, Katya was the flower of the revolution. Harry was in a kind of pain for which there was no cure.

But pain or not, somehow he was going to help me get Boris back. Just after 4:00 A.M. I stood, sweating and gasping, in front of the door of a crumbling apartment building. I checked the address Harry had given me over the phone. Inside, the hallway reeked of stale food and the paint was peeling layer by layer. Harry opened the door only a few inches. "Comrade Dimitri, good evening."

"Harry, there's an emergency. I've got to talk to you."

"It couldn't wait till morning?"

"I told you, it's an emergency. I can't explain it standing here in the hallway."

"I'm sorry, I can't let you in."

"The Party orders you to let me in." But strangely there was no response. His sad eyes remained expressionless in the houndlike face that peered through the crack in the doorway. "We're attacking the Brooklyn Navy Yard," I whispered fiercely. "Tonight!" His eyes widened. He seemed to search my face for an instant, waiting for me to say I was joking. He saw I was serious.

He hurriedly unfastened a big chain lock and, with a small flourish, let me enter. I did not have to be told that this was a momentous tribute. That no one else had entered his apartment in years. In an instant I could see why. The entire apartment was filled with plans for Harry's assault on the Navy Yard — for that one moment when his entire life would take on meaning. When the echoes of the uprising on the battleship *Aurora* would overwhelm the sailors of Brooklyn with the revolutionary fervour that would sweep Enemy Number One.

167

As it had swept Russia all those years ago.

I stared in awe at his living room. The walls were covered with stolen maps marked 'top secret' and blueprints of the harbour and the ships. There were lists of naval commanders and civilian employees and official cars. And aerial photographs with coloured markings for oil depots, munitions dumps, security gates, administrative offices, water mains, electrical generators, and the bars where the sailors drank. There were phone numbers of the prostitutes who got information for him, charts of the mean average temperatures, harbour depths, and the number of personnel present by hour of day. There were paintings of Lenin, Stalin, and the sailors storming the *Aurora* in St. Petersburg. There was a very large painting of Harry leading a group of comrades against a destroyer anchored in Brooklyn harbour. It was a crude imitation of the Socialist Realism kind of painting we turned out at home. There were arms upraised heroically and valiant men charging through gunfire. Harry had painted it himself. He was portrayed in the painting as being young and handsome.

And there were stacks of rifles piled in the corner.

As Harry feverishly dressed, I told him that there was a trunk that we had to get out of there. It was crucial to the Party. To Moscow. His eyes lit up as he threw a gun belt around his waist. "A sign," he muttered. "It's a sign. I knew it would happen like this. When I didn't expect it." He stopped, suddenly sceptical. "What's so special about a trunk?"

"The continued success of the revolution depends on that trunk," I said. "Moscow has ordered us to get it to the *Berezovska*."

"Hah! I wondered why it was anchored just up the harbour!" He was ecstatic. "I *knew* the Party would want me to go in there. And, comrade, when we get in there, watch those sailors revolt. Just like the *Aurora*. You just watch!"

168

I said I would. I walked to the window and looked out onto the harbour. What I saw made me yell for Harry to come over and look. In the distance, under the lights of one of the destroyers, were the two sailors with the trunk. They were still trying to open it.

With a sledgehammer. Or maybe it was an axe. I felt weak.

Harry grabbed a rifle. I stopped him and for a moment we argued fiercely. I wasn't going to be caught on the streets with any rifle-toting communist. But Harry was no longer the same docile creature. He was a man possessed by the dream of his lifetime. That awesome fire was back in his eyes. Finally he grudgingly agreed that three hidden pistols and two hand grenades would do just as well. Just before we left, he quickly consulted several of his charts, smiling and muttering to himself. Then he grabbed a bright red banner with a single gold Soviet star on it. "To fly from the bridge," he said, his eyes gleaming.

Harry's thirty-year obsession got us inside the fences of the Brooklyn Navy Yard. He knew every short cut, every weakness in the security, and every hidden entry point. We raced through a dry storm sewer and climbed up metal rungs, pushing a manhole cover aside. We came out in the motor pool. Racing low behind the staff cars and jeeps, we stopped at an electrical box, which Harry opened with special keys. He pulled a lever, cutting power to the nearby fence. We ran through the gate and had to sprint past fuel tanks. I could hear the terrible smashing sounds of the sledgehammer hitting the trunk.

"Hurry up," I whispered loudly.

But Harry was even more out of shape than I was. In fact, he was in terrible shape. It was the one element in all that planning that he had not taken into account. He wheezed and gasped like a man being choked. He stopped and leaned against a huge fuel tank.

"Wait," he gasped.

I stopped. The sound of the sledgehammer was very near. I motioned him ahead and he began running again. Before he reached me, he was lurching from lack of breath. "Be with you in just a second," he wheezed. I waited and watched him try to recover, but the hammering noise seemed to come faster now. *Boris!* An image of him waking up inside the trunk flashed through my mind.

I ran towards that noise. Past sheds and equipment and jeeps, with the darkened form of a destroyer looming above me. Suddenly I was almost on top of the two sailors, as they stood cursing and pounding at the locks on the trunk. The older sailor, with the powerful arms, held a chisel and a large hammer. Other tools lay scattered on the ground. The trunk was battered out of shape. But it had not been opened. The trunk makers of Moscow had done their work well.

I yelled at them the instant they came into view. Instead of showing any fear, they reacted with fury. Or maybe frustration. The older sailor turned and threw the chisel at me. It whistled past my head, splitting a board in a wooden create. The younger sailor started yelling at me and swinging a small hammer. He was about to throw it when Harry staggered around the corner.

"You wanna get cut open too, fat man? Huh?" drawled the younger sailor. "Open that trunk," he said to me, circling around with the hammer clutched in his hand. Harry reached into his coat, took out a pistol, and fired. He was gasping too hard to hold the gun steady. But the desired effect was instantly achieved. The sailor stopped wide-eyed, dropped the hammer, and fled.

"To arms!" bellowed Harry. "Workers of the world."

"The trunk! Harry, don't hit the trunk," I screamed. He was firing wildly at the two fleeing sailors. Harry paid no attention to me. After thirty years he was actually inside the Navy Yard firing a gun! The dream became more real with every shot he fired. He ran after them and then turned and stood staring at the gangplank of the destroyer anchored nearby.

"Sailors! Proletariat!" he yelled, labouring up the gangplank. He stopped halfway up and looked around.

"What's the name of this ship?" he called out to me.

I looked at the bow as I scrambled over to the trunk. "*Ticonderoga*," I called back.

"Moth-balled," he said grimly. "No one on it."

"Get down here and help me with the trunk," I yelled. Harry looked uncertain. He wanted to get on with the rebellion. "I order you, comrade," I shouted in my sternest voice. "The Party orders you!"

He wobbled back down the gangplank while I was already tugging at the battered trunk, pulling it across the ground by the handles. Harry lifted the other end. "Gotta get it out of here fast," he said. He was puffing with every step. Sweat poured off his forehead. "I'm going back in to liberate the sailors on the other ships."

"No, you're not!" I yelled as we heaved and shoved. "This trunk is more important. It's the *Aurora* and the battle for the Winter Palace all rolled into one."

"Will it make the history books?"

"I've told you that the future of the revolution depends on it. Don't ask any more questions, comrade."

Suddenly, from the corner of a storage shed, the silhouette of the younger sailor appeared out of the blackness. I saw him just in time to yell, the instant before the tiny bursts of flame shot from that same blackness. Bullets clanged into the piles of empty oil drums just behind us. We both dived for the earth, but Harry seemed to roll over in a motion he had obviously practised many times. He threw something. A second later there was an explosion and a burst of flame where

171

the grenade had gone off. When it exploded, I'm sure I heard Harry laugh with a kind of joyous release. I could see him crawling back toward the trunk. "*They'll* know their hour of liberation has come."

He threw a pistol. I seized it. And realized that I was now an armed Russian involved in a grenade attack on the Brooklyn Navy Yard. My panic knew no bounds. There was not a tree tall enough in all of Russia for Stalin to hang me from now. My fear-driven strength was awesome. Alone, I almost picked that trunk off the ground and waddled toward the perimeter fence.

But more gunfire erupted. From the other sailor. "Take cover!" yelled Harry. I dropped the trunk.

It was at that moment that bullets raked the trunk.

"Boris!" I screamed.

Harry was excitedly blazing gunfire back at our attacker. "It's simple now," he yelled through the noise. "This place is like a grid. We just neutralize one place, and all the rest of the yard will go. A chain reaction." He pitched his second grenade in a different direction.

"Boris?" I yelled through the noise. "Answer me!" There was another explosion. A gigantic one. It hurled me off my feet. The heat was a searing wave that sucked the breath out of my mouth. I struggled back to the trunk as the fireball billowed up into the blackness. Across the entire Navy Yard, lights flickered and died. Sirens began to wail.

"Just as I planned it," Harry shouted into his fireball. "For thirty years."

"Boris, I'm going to get you out," I shouted into the roar of the hot winds. I fired the pistol at the locks. One opened. Then the second one yielded to a volley of bullets.

I flung open the lid.

And something silky flew up from the trunk and plastered itself against my face. I peeled it off and

172

squinted through the inferno.

What were bags from Tiffany's and Bloomingdale's doing where Boris was supposed to be?

18

So Harry's revolution was for Bloomingdale's. Among others.

In all that inferno of confusion I was unable to persuade — or even order — him to leave the Navy Yard. He insisted on taking that trunk out with us. Of course, I had already slammed the lid shut so he couldn't see what was inside. And when he wasn't looking I fired my last bullet into that damn thing and wished the old man from the Kremlin had been stuffed inside it.

I did not even stop to wonder if that last precious bullet would pass through the Bloomingdale's bag with the chinchilla fur coat or the Saks Fifth Avenue bag with the pure silk dresses and the card attached saying, *To Olga with Love.* Or perhaps it went through the elegant dressing gown, *For me!* Or the smaller dresses and the necklace from Tiffany's, *For Natasha if she's good.* And the entire set of Lionel toy trains, *For little Ivan.* And cashmere overcoats. And more dresses. By Dior. And perfumes by Chanel.

I just left that trunk there in the middle of the gathering flames. I yelled at Harry to get out.

"The trunk! We can't leave it here," he screamed. The light of the flames danced off his sweating and blackened face.

"Leave it!"

"No! The sailors of the *Aurora* didn't turn and run when things got dangerous. This is history, for God's sake!"

What could I do? I couldn't tell him what was in that trunk. Sirens wailed all around us, and something else

174

erupted with a roar that blew the remaining windows out of the sheds.

Harry had run over to the trunk and hoisted one end of it. "The revolution depends on this. Remember?" he screamed at me ferociously. The red banner was tied around his neck like a scarf. In the heat-driven winds, it flew behind him, beating against the gale.

In that instant, Harry looked heroic. Just like the painting he had made of himself.

He heaved the trunk forward. And then seemed to stiffen. The trunk fell from his grasp and clattered onto the ground. Harry clutched at his chest. His mouth formed a bellowing circle, but no sound came out. Or if it did, it was lost in the roar of the explosions. He staggered a few steps and sank to his knees. I raced over to him, crawling crablike to get underneath all the debris that had begun pinwheeling through the blackness in deadly arcs of flame. He was moaning and clutching at his chest as I dragged him away.

Harry was having a heart attack.

I crawled and scratched my way across that steaming ground, tugging at Harry until we were behind a wall. Then I picked him up, staggering under the weight, and headed toward the fence. In the distance a group of military police appeared as silhouettes, soon joined by firemen, sailors, and civilian police. The whole area behind me filled with flashing red lights and the static of walkie-talkies, which sometimes cut through the noise of the fires. And the terrible moaning that came from Harry.

I made it to a gate that was normally locked electronically but now flapped in the winds. Yelling at Harry to hold on, I lurched through it, out onto a kind of gravel parking area that felt instantly cooler. I could see the Ford near the other end of the street. I was determined I would drive it, no matter how many flat tyres it had. All I wanted to do was get Harry to safety.

And of course there were other, less humanitarian motives. I wanted to get the Ford away from the area so that the headlines of FOREIGN SABOTEURS!! that kept flickering through my mind would go away.

"We're almost there," I called out as I put him down. I tried to get him to drape one arm around my shoulder so we could reach the car before I crumpled under his weight. I could see tears were running down his cheeks. He kept shaking his head.

We got to the car just as Harry collapsed with a fierce cry. He sank to the ground, illuminated by the glow of the flames that gave no warmth to the cold gravel near that Brooklyn street. "We left the trunk behind," he rasped.

"We had to."

"But what about the history books?" His voice faltered and was lost for a moment. I had cradled his head in my arms and had to kneel closer just to make out his words.

"Listen, Harry. Can't you hear? The revolution has started." I pointed to the harbour, where loudspeakers and sirens and voices fought against the roar of the fires.

He strained to listen, but I could tell that the sounds were congealing within his mind. His eyes stared vacantly at the fires. "How can you tell?"

"Just listen! Can't you hear the revolutionary cries? The calls to arms?"

"Thirty years," he said, the words being pushed out in weak little gasps. "it hurts." His hands groped for his chest. He was crying and smiling at the same time.

Suddenly a shadow fell across us. I looked up but could see only the outline of a man in naval uniform. "What's the problem here?" the man asked.

"My friend hurt himself," I said.

"You're foreigners, aren't you?" I froze. I still could not see the man's face, just his outline framed against the flames.

His voice was soft. "Diplomats. I can tell by the licence plates on your car."

All I could do was nod. I tried to make out the form of a gun. In my confused and exhausted state, the first thing that crossed my mind was to overpower him. Do anything just to get away.

"You sound like a Russian," he said, and my thoughts shot out of control.

He knelt down, his face turning slightly into the light. He was young. Even younger than I was. With searching eyes behind thin glasses, and an open yet earnest face. A shock of sandy brown hair stuck out boyishly from under his Navy hat. A strong, almost sharp chin gave him a determined look.

And underneath that chin was a gleaming white clerical collar.

He looked at Harry. Then he looked at me and silently shook his head once. He sensed instantly that Harry was dying. He reached for Harry's wrist to take a pulse. "Who is it?" asked Harry in a distant voice.

"A priest," I said.

"Chaplain," the young man corrected me gently. He reached into his pockets and took out a small black book, which he held up to the light. "The Lord is my shepherd. I shall not want. He maketh me —"

"Father," rasped Harry. "I want to be honest with you."

"Now is the time to be honest, my son."

"I've been going to blow this place to kingdom come since before you were around to call me son." Harry smiled. Or maybe grimaced — it was hard to tell. "You're out of work. We blew it all up."

"He's delirious," I said frantically, but the young minister seemed not to hear me.

"Thank you, my son," he said to Harry.

"Thank you?"

"These are instruments of war. I'm ashamed to be a part of this. Smashing these instruments of war will help me in God's will."

I stared from Harry to the flames to the young chaplain. In awe. To see if he was serious. And all I could think of for that moment was a saying I once heard that these Christians use. Something about their Lord giving at the same time as he took away from them. Just like what Stalin was always doing to us.

"I want to tell you something else," Harry whispered.

"Tell all."

"When we take over, all you righteous punks are going to get shot."

"Of course, my son."

Of course? I stared at him, fascinated.

"Nothing personal." Harry's voice trailed off. And then he died.

We remained in that parking lot for several minutes. The flames still soared into the night, and all around us there was confusion and noise. But somehow it was peaceful. The young minister muttered things from his black book about walking through the valley of death, and Harry's head rested against my knees. Then for a while neither of us said anything.

Then he asked me why we were there. Ordinarily I would follow the usual practice and lie. And then lie some more, until the gullible believed you. That was part of my training. Just lie your way through brick walls. But in this case, the truth sounded more like a lie than anything else I could think of. So I told him about the sailors stealing my trunk. I even told him the truth about Harry's thirty-year quest to blow up the Navy Yard.

"I'm sorry for blowing up your harbour," I said finally.

"Don't worry," he said. "I may wear this uniform for now. But God is my true commander in chief."

"I understand."

178

"And I must tell you. I'm ashamed at the way my country has treated you people. And now with these hearings in Washington. Where that Senator is smearing people. Decent, honest people who just happen to want to share and share alike."

"There has been a lot of suffering," I said earnestly.

"There has. Just because these people believe in peace and justice and sharing. Why, Jesus shared that one loaf of bread and those few fishes with all those people. He didn't do it for profit."

I looked into those shining, innocent eyes and thought: *Go for broke, comrade.* "I've often thought that Jesus might have been a communist."

"You know," he said fervently, those shining, innocent eyes almost glistening with emotion, "so have I!"

He reached out his hand. "Reverend Kent Filmore," he said, smiling. And so, over Harry's dead body, we shook hands.

He was my first Christian. And through him I came to believe in miracles. Small ones, but still miracles. Like flagging down a racing military police jeep and getting a spare tyre for the Ford. Not only that, an MP changed the tyre for us. And then after we had put Harry's body into the car, the chaplain walked in front of the car while I drove. He led me right into the midst of the firemen, the military police, and the sailors. It was a whirlpool of running men and lights that flashed through the black smoke.

But such was the power of that little white collar that they parted to let us through.

I was getting a new respect for Christians as I sat behind the wheel of the Ford, inching through the chaos. No one questioned anything. Not the diplomatic licence plates. Not the tyres marked "Property of U.S. Navy" that rolled slowly round on my Russian-embassy Ford. And not the body of Harry, bobbing in the front seat.

179

The Reverend Kent Filmore made all of those questions vanish.

I decided that I definitely had to get one of those Christians. It would be great to have one around. Especially for when I had to face that old man from the Kremlin. The thought chilled me. I knew he was as close to Stalin as anyone could be. For that reason alone, he had the power to hurl me into the depths of the *gulag*, just for having got all his fur coats and silks burned to a crisp. I wondered if I could dig up a surviving Russian Orthodox priest from one of the Siberian labour camps. Maybe they could come up with a miracle for me back in Moscow. I definitely needed one.

And it happened.

When we passed through the crowds and the firefighting equipment, the Reverend Kent Filmore got back into the car and said, "By the way, I presume you've heard the news about your Mr. Stalin?"

19

Stalin's death was my miracle.

I was saved. No one would know what to expect now. Purges. Power struggles in the Kremlin. Mass deportations to labour camps. But no matter what happened, that old man from the Kremlin would be far too busy scrambling to save his own neck to worry about his missing trunkload of expensive clothes.

I later learned that the *Berezovska* had sailed right on schedule, not even waiting an extra five minutes for me to show up with the trunk. Boris had been in an identical trunk, taken to the ship in the back of the van with the three secret policemen. (The fact that there had been two trunks made me wonder if Moscow kept any others around. So Anatoly and I began a quiet search and found three more in a basement room off the parking garage. The room could only be opened with a key we found in Boris's now unused desk. We sat in the damp little room one Saturday afternoon, drinking strawberry milkshakes mixed with vodka, and loosened all the screws holding all the lids on those trunks. Just in case.)

But on that night my most immediate problem was what to do with Harry. Neither the Reverend Kent Filmore nor I had known what to do with him after we drove away from the Brooklyn Navy Yard. I didn't want to take him to the police. Or the city morgue. That would have raised too many questions. So for a while we just drove through the deserted streets with poor dead Harry bobbing around on the front seat between us.

Somehow it didn't seem all that strange at the time. You had to be there.

We finally went to an all-night diner, where we left Harry locked in the car, sitting in the front seat. It was a cold night, so we figured he would be okay for a while. From a window booth we could look out and make sure he was all right, while we figured out where to take him. As he was eating a pastrami sandwich, the Reverent Kent Filmore's eyes suddenly lit up the way they did when a miracle was coming. "I don't know why I didn't think of this before," he exclaimed. "Part of my job at the Navy Yard is to look after arrangements for the deceased." He stopped for a moment, suddenly lost in thought.

"What's the matter?"

"He'd have to be transported in a Navy hearse. Complete with Navy flags and all that kind of thing."

I looked out at Harry, sitting dead in the front seat of the car. "He won't mind," I said.

"Are you sure?"

"Not if the Party orders him."

So Harry was checked into the Navy morgue and the Reverend Kent Filmore handled all the paperwork. It became very tricky. We had to invent a rank for Harry. And a naval history. I made Harry a ship's captain. A destroyer in the Pacific. Thirty years engaged in naval strategy. Retired to Florida. Next of kin requested burial in his hometown: Brooklyn, New York. After we filled out the form, I felt proud.

I'd just infiltrated Harry into the Navy.

The next few days at the embassy were filled with nervous speculation. No one knew what would happen after Stalin's death. And to complicate matters even more, the Senator was on a rampage. Our espionage network was reeling from the hunt for communists that the Senator was conducting on nationwide television. But even though we suffered some important losses, I was still regarded as a hero in Moscow. Why? Because the guilt button was about to be pressed all over Enemy Number One. Just as I said it would be.

Now that the innocent were being hunted and humiliated, as well as our own agents, you could hear cries of "Witch-hunt!" rising across the land. (What a great description. We tried to find out who came up with it but we never could.) And as the Senator veered wildly out of control, accusing more and more people of being communists, everyone began describing him as the great witch-hunter.

And when the country realized the damage he had done, people would rather be called a thief than a witch-hunter. The entire country felt guilty over what had happened. And nothing in Enemy Number One is more powerful than guilt. I knew that we would have a picnic, as they say, for at least a generation, maybe more. Flailing them with endless reminders of their witch-hunting! (I never understood it, really. We murdered millions under Stalin; they throw a dozen or so in jail for a year and let a few scoundrels loose on the country. Yet *they* feel guilty. We don't. Explain that to me.) It became our golden era. We rebuilt our network and flooded Enemy Number One with spies. Illegals. Agents of influence. Useful idiots. We had them all.

And whenever someone started investigating any of our best people, we would sit back and let the others yell "Witch-hunt." Our work was done for us by the decent citizens.

I cursed that stupid Senator. And, of course, I cursed myself for getting him started. Sitting in front of our battered Emerson television set, I began to despair. Once again I had been forced to destroy my own scheme to save Enemy Number One by coming up with a counterplan that made me a hero in Moscow.

There just *had* to be a way to save that country.

*

For a few days after the big fires at the Brooklyn Navy Yard there were stories about it in all the newspapers. The damage was massive. At first it was blamed on vandals. Then on an electrical malfunction. And finally it just faded from the public's attention, the way all those things do. By the day of Harry's funeral it was already what they call old news. I was thankful the Reverend Kent Filmore was around to make all the arrangements for the burial, because things were chaotic at the embassy. Not only was there the uncertainty caused by Stalin's death, but we suddenly got news that a number of Washington politicians would be making a quick trip to New York. One of them was the Senator. The witch-hunter as everyone now called him. We had to rush around the whole New York area calming nervous agents who'd left signals requesting emergency meetings. They all wanted to know why the senator was arriving.

By the time Anatoly and I showed up for the funeral, we were both exhausted. Anatoly had the difficult task of explaining to Harry's old cronies why he was being buried by a minister. And in a Navy hearse? And why were we all assembling at the Brooklyn Navy Yard? Harry's friends were all grumbling old communists whom he had known since his Greenwich Village days. There were only a few dozen of them left now, cringing old dogs who would occasionally snap toothlessly. Like Harry, they had been beaten down over the years, but occasionally you could see the flicker of faraway fires in those wrinkled faces.

Harry was being buried on the same day as Stalin. With almost as much ceremony. From the moment we arrived at the Navy Yard in our rented car, Anatoly and I knew that the Reverend Kent Filmore had got carried away. He met us at the main gate, wearing his full naval chaplain's robes. "For two days I have prayed, asking for divine guidance," he said. "And more than ever I know that we are all equal in God's eyes."

I agreed wholeheartedly. After all, Marx had said the same thing.

"There is no place in this life for political beliefs to separate brother from brother," he continued, his robes blowing in the stiff breeze. "Nor shall we be separated in death. The more I prayed, the more I knew that God would be angered if Harry were to be consigned to his eternal resting place with an inferior funeral. Just because his earthly beliefs were different. And just because he sought righteousness as he truly saw fit."

I looked into those wonderful blue eyes of his. They were beacons of innocence in that boyish face. "Absolutely," I said, wondering what was next.

He stepped aside and pointed towards one of the destroyers. I almost fell over at what I saw. Anatoly, in a reflex action, grasped my arm. There was a full naval honour guard. And behind them was a Navy band. And behind the band was a ceremonial gun carriage.

And on top of the gun carriage was Harry.

Harry lay in the open coffin looking somehow very angry. Or perhaps it was just my imagination. Anatoly and I just gaped. He suddenly remembered all the old communists who were about to show up. This would have to be explained to them. We both ran back through the main gate just in time to flag down half a dozen old cars and trucks bearing Harry's former comrades. Earlier we had been forced to order them not to wear hammer-and-sickle badges. Reluctantly they had agreed. But we allowed them their wish to wear two black armbands. One for Harry and one for Stalin. However, no one had expected to have to march behind a full Navy honour guard.

"Maybe you'd also like us to kiss Rockefeller's ass?" snapped one of them when we broke the news.

"Or join the board of Standard Oil," grumbled another.

Anatoly and I just did our tough-Russian number. We snapped out ultimatums of absolute obedience to the Party's wishes. And of course they came to heel immediately, although there was a lot of grumbling and muttered curses about how the Navy was part of the military might that was keeping the workers' uprising from happening. A tool of the capitalist élite.

After we had confiscated a couple of lapel buttons with Stalin's picture on them, we all went through the main gate. Anatoly was worried about the old men. I was worried about Anatoly. "Why are we doing this?" he hissed, talking out of the side of his mouth.

"We've got no choice. I can't upset that minister."

"Upset the minister? *I'm* upset! I'm terrified. Do you realize where we are?" Sweat was dripping off Anatoly's upper lip. Always a sign of impending inner crisis.

"Don't talk in Russian," I whispered.

"I'm going to end up in a trunk, I know it."

"You won't. Just be calm."

The Navy band started playing, and the Reverend Kent Filmore led us over behind Harry. I suddenly realized what was on top of the coffin. Wrapped around the usual Stars and Stripes was a thin piece of red cloth. It was Harry's banner with the Soviet star on it.

"I found it tied around him," the young minister said. "It must have been important to him."

"It was. Very. Now tell me — why are we marching in this direction? Through all this burned-out part?" I asked.

"I thought it fitting that Harry's last earthly journey should be through the scene of his attack on the war machine."

"I see. You don't think that this short cut to the main gate would do just as well?"

"I'm sure Harry will enjoy this route. By the way, I'm leaving the military in a few weeks. My conscience will no longer permit me to stay. Too much emphasis on war."

"That's always the problem with armies."

And so we marched through the wreckage of the Brooklyn Navy Yard. With a Navy band playing mournful hymns in front of us. And a dishevelled collection of old New York communists muttering behind us. The majestic lockstep of the honour guard moved slowly past the blackened wasteland. There were burned-out oil tanks, jeeps, and charred remnants of wooden buildings. A rotted old battleship listed badly at the dock, steam still rising from her hull like a veil across the Manhattan skyline.

And Harry gliding serenely through it all.

I was almost beginning to enjoy it. I loved parades. And this one was not bad. The gleaming brass, the starched uniforms, and solemn faces. And the music. But then I looked across the debris and thought I was hallucinating. Going utterly mad, with nonsensical fears dancing through my mind.

There, in the midst of the wreckage, was the Senator!

But it was not my imagination. A chorus of muttering snarls broke loose behind me. Anatoly tugged desperately at my sleeve, and motioned in the direction of what I had seen. The Senator was standing with some congressmen and Navy officers who wore an awful lot of gold braid. Flashbulbs went off all around them.

The Senator was pointing to the fire damage. I could see film cameras recording the event. "The Navy wants a new yard," said the Reverend Kent Filmore in a low voice. "So they flew all those politicians up here to see the damage."

"I see," I said numbly, as I realized that the road we were on curved around and went right past the Senator. Behind me the grumbling turned to gnashing sounds. Somehow I had to keep a riot from breaking out. I turned around and glared at them. Half of those old communists were cringing, while the other half acted like they smelled raw meat. I furiously hissed out something about Party orders. As always, it worked. But barely. We marched around the road, drawing closer to the Senator and the congressmen. Anatoly was on the verge of boiling. I could sense it. I grabbed his sleeve.

"The trunk," he whimpered. "This means the trunk."

Behind me the gnashings had been beaten down to an acceptable murmur. But then a grizzled old voice began croaking away at some kind of song. It was unrecognizable. I glared fiercely. But other ancient voices began joining in. That song spread through the ranks. Louder, lusty old voices joined the frail ones.

I realized what it was they were singing. Stalin's ghost could not have scared me more. Those old dogs were belting out the "Internationale". The communist anthem.

From the front of the procession I could see the band leader looking back, confused. His mournful hymn was being stridently drowned out by the unruly chorus behind me. He looked back several times, each time appearing more worried. Finally I could see him motioning his band into silence, and for a moment there was only the singing of the "Internationale". The band leader was feverishly telling them something. Then one of the trumpets began trying to play the "Internationale" by ear. It was obvious that the trumpet player had never heard it before. But he was giving it a good try. Soon the drummer got the right beat. Then the tuba player. Next came the cornets and flutes.

By the time we approached the Senator, the entire Navy band was blasting out a reasonable interpretation of the communist anthem. And the honour guard had adjusted the tempo of their march to fit the music.

It reminded me of a May Day parade.

The Senator, the congressmen, and the officers with all

that gold braid immediately cleared a path for our procession. Proper respect was shown to the dead. A couple of admirals saluted Harry as his gun carriage glided into view. The politicians all removed their hats and paid their respects.

"Who is it?" one of them asked.

"Looks like Horner. You shoulda seen him in the Pacific," someone said.

"Helluva man, that Horner," said the Senator.

"Did you know him well?" a reporter asked.

"We fought together," said the Senator grimly. "Saved each other in flak-filled skies at least a dozen times. Never thought either of us would die with our boots on."

The Senator put his hand over his heart as the band passed by blasting out the "Internationale".

"What's the banner with the star on it?" someone asked.

"Elite fighting unit," said an admiral, standingly stiffly at attention and saluting. "Only a few dozen men in it."

The funeral procession seemed to have gained momentum. I don't know if it was because of the music. Or the singing. Or a combination of fear and exhilaration. But we had all picked up our step and were definitely marching with what even appeared to be exuberance. Of course, I kept flashing dirty looks back into those grizzled old faces that were belting out the "Internationale" with eyes that cringed and hated at the same time.

Just in front of us was the Senator on one side, and across from him were the admirals. The singing behind me veered into momentary snarls that I beat back again with another sharp look. In a solemn, imposing voice, the Senator picked that moment to say, "I want you all to know that Horner here did not die in vain. We're going to give the Navy the funds to build the best new Navy Yard on this coast. To make us all more secure against the communist threat."

From somewhere deep in the dishevelled ranks of the old communists there was a strangled little cry. Someone else sounded like he was gagging. Others cleared their throats as they tried to keep singing.

"Who are all those men?" I heard a reporter ask.

"Deckhands," said an admiral. "He always was popular with even the lowest sailors."

The procession kept going until it reached the edge of the Navy Yard, where we all got into Navy cars for the trip to the cemetery. The Reverend Kent Filmore had thought of everything.

Except for the congressmen. Two of the politicians from the Brooklyn area decided that the funeral might be a good way to make the local newspapers. So they just blended in with the rest of us, and almost got put in a car with a bunch of the old New York communists, who knew who they were. Muttered insults rippled through the group until I had the Reverend Kent Filmore quickly transfer them to another car. Ours.

Anatoly and I were introduced as grief-stricken nephews from the old country who did not understand English. I did not want these congressmen to hear our accents, so we kept quiet as we all got into the big Navy staff car. One of the congressmen was short, with a big stomach that bulged out over a belt he wore under the lower end of that protrusion. He sat in the back seat, his clasped hands resting on his stomach, his feet barely touching the floor, and his eyes sweeping the surroundings like a vacuum cleaner. Everything was sucked in and stored away. He had a smile that looked as if it was turned on by a switch. Beside him sat the other congressman, a taller, skinny Republican. (I never could really figure out the political parties in Enemy Number One. They obviously had to be faking the fact that it was really all one big party, but that they got together and secretly agreed that some should be called Democrats and

190

some Republicans. The more I thought about it, the more I knew I was right. Why? Well, imagine in Moscow if Stalin had been head of the Democrats. Do you really think that Stalin and his Democrats would not have shot every Republican they could find? The dungeons of the Lubyanka would be jammed with Republicans unless they had made an agreement that they were all Democrats but some just called themselves Republicans to make it look good.)

The short, fat congressman kept sucking at something in his teeth as he looked out the car window. We were at the head of the procession, just behind the hearse. The photographers were in the car behind us. Anatoly just looked straight ahead. I wanted to laugh. Maybe it was all the pressure. But I held back, afraid it would send him into hysterics. Perspiration was still beading on his upper lip.

The congressmen felt free to talk politics. They began making deals to support bills each of them wanted to introduce in Congress. The short, fat one was the real wheeler-dealer, as they say in Enemy Number One. He told the Republican about the bill his party was going to introduce the following day. He was sure it would be passed into law. It was to build a vast system of superhighways all over the country.

It would take years, he said. And cost billions.

I totally forgot I wasn't supposed to speak English. "*Billions?*" I blurted out.

They both stared at me. I yelled at the driver and made him stop at the next street corner, three blocks from the cemetery. That was where the nearest phone booth was. And while I dialled, Harry, the honour guard, the band, and the mourners all waited.

"Sam?" I said when he answered. "I'm in a real hurry, so just answer my question, please. What kind of things are used to make big highways?"

191

"You mean bulldozers?" he said. I strained to hear him over the passing traffic.

"I guess so. Who makes bulldozers?"

"Well, there's Caterpillar and —"

"Buy Caterpillar," I said, and hung up. The whole honour guard was glaring at me as I walked back to the waiting cars. So were the congressmen.

"His eighty-seven-year-old mother," I said solemnly. "An invalid. She wanted to know the exact moment he was about to enter the cemetery. So she could be with him in prayer." All those hard faces softened instantly.

As I got back into the Navy staff car, I looked over at Harry lying there in the hearse and thought, comrade, if our kind ever gets into Heaven you deserve it. You see, I felt guilty about all the indignities Harry was being asked to perform even after his death.

(And it got worse even when he was in the ground. Because who would have thought that the Caterpillar stock would nearly double over the next few weeks?)

20

It got worse in other ways too.

The moment we arrived at the cemetery an intense, dark-haired young man — he was even younger than I was — hurried up to me. "Hi, I'm Lou Swackhammer from the *New York Post*," he said, grabbing my hand and shaking it. He talked so fast I could hardly make out what he said. "Understand you're the relatives of the deceased. I want you to tell 'em to leave the coffin open long enough so that my photographer can get a shot of the congressmen here in front of it."

Before I could even answer him, Swackhammer had turned away and was giving orders to the funeral director, his photographer, and almost everyone else around. The photographer immediately started shooting pictures of Harry surrounded by the congressmen, us, and the snarling pack of old communists.

Anatoly gripped my arm, muttering something I could not hear, and the Reverend Kent Filmore looked over at me uncertainly. My mental projector suddenly clicked on, and before my eyes was the fearful scene of Tuesday's *New York Post* pinwheeling out on the screen — just the way they did it in all the old movies, with a big front-page photo of Harry under the headline WAR HERO BURIED. That was immediately followed by Wednesday's *Post*, which spun across the screen with the huge headline COMMUNIST BURIED IN NAVAL CEREMONY. HOAX REVEALED WHEN . . . Etc.

I rushed over to Swackhammer and said in my most fractured English that for the sake of the rest of the family we did not want our poor Harry to be seen dead in some newspaper.

He seemed irritated, as if I were telling him how to run his business. "Well, we're not going to press on this story without a good shot of the captain there," he said, motioning toward Harry. He was still talking quickly and paced back and forth in front of me as if he were wired to some kind of internal energy that had surged out of control. Swackhammer was shorter than I was, but much thinner, with ears that stuck out a little too much from the almost-shaved sides of his head. His suit looked as if it had been worn too much, and his skinny tie had stains of something oily on it.

"Tell you what," he said, suddenly, becoming even more excited. "Your Uncle Harry was a war hero, wasn't he?"

"Glorious hero," I said.

"So your family must have photos of him from the war."

"Thrilling ones," I said. Anatoly looked at me, his eyes getting wider, a sign that panic was about to overcome him.

"Terrific," said Swackhammer. "Here's the deal. You get me a great shot of him, and we won't use this stuff here. But we need something really patriotic. Know what I mean? Juicy patriotic stuff is what the country wants now. But I need it by six o'clock this evening."

After the funeral, Anatoly and I raced back to Manhattan cursing that obnoxious little punk of a reporter. We had seven hours to come up with a miracle.

We did it in four.

Our initial solution was to go to a bar and wait for the real solution to appear. Neither of us had any idea how we were going to get out of this mess, and we consoled ourselves by telling one another not to worry, that only a million or so people read the *New York Post* and that at worst, we would only appear on the front page beside the

Navy band and poor dead Harry. "Siberia for sure," muttered Anatoly. But no sooner had we gotten out of the Queens-Midtown Tunnel than I yelled at Anatoly to pull over. There was a movie theatre on Thirty-fourth Street not far from Second Avenue, and emblazoned across the marquee were these words:

OPERATION PACIFIC
WITH JOHN WAYNE

"What are you doing?" he said.

"I'm not sure." And I wasn't. I just sensed good fortune in the presence of that famous movie star, John Wayne. Even in the old days of *Life* magazine I was a fan of his. (He made me wish that Russia had cowboys.) I got out of the car and went over to the theatre. In glass display cases were black and white photographs of scenes from the movie, showing John Wayne playing some kind of military hero in World War II. I had found my answer.

A few minutes later I hurried back to the car, clutching my precious photograph of John Wayne in action. For ten dollars some sly usher had given me what I would have paid him a hundred for. Anatoly immediately sensed what I intended. "Are you crazy?" he said. "If John Wayne finds out he'll come and break us in two." It was something to think about. John Wayne was always playing the great patriot, accusing us Russians of the foulest deeds. He hated communists. And with his money, it was no wonder.

"So? Who would you prefer to have to face?" I asked. "John Wayne or our secret police?"

He thought for a moment. "John Wayne."

The rest was easy. We stole an old photo of Harry from his apartment and then had our forger in the embassy reprint both photographs and blend Harry's face into John Wayne's body. Harry had never looked so good. "Terrific!" said Swackhammer when we got the photograph to him. "Now that's a really patriotic shot. That's what we're looking for. Helps keep the country great. I don't know if you immigrants can really appreciate that yet."

Later that evening Anatoly and I sat in a bar just off Broadway, waiting for the first edition of the *New York Post* to be delivered to the nearby news-stand. Just before midnight, I grabbed a copy right off the delivery truck. On page twenty-eight was the picture of Harry-John in action in the Pacific. (I later found out it had been filmed in Malibu.) Beside it was another photo of the Senator saluting the coffin. Of course, I was ecstatic. But Anatoly could barely manage a smile. Over the course of the day he had become a nervous wreck.

Anatoly's problem was death.

The real impact of Harry's funeral was catching up with him. Like other funerals he had attended, this one had plunged him into an existential crisis. "We're only here on this earth for a few lousy decades," he said. "We're just puny fish, swimming against the tides of time, desperately trying to reach the shores of our own personal destiny."

"I think I'm going to be sick."

"I'm serious."

"That's why I'm going to be sick."

"I can't help it," he said, staring forlornly into his vodka. "I feel that my life is slipping away from me. And I haven't even started to fulfil my life's goal. I should be writing Broadway musicals."

"What happened to being a poet?"

"Things change."

"Thought you wanted to be like Pushkin. Or Tolstoy."

"That was until I saw *Oklahoma!* and *Porgy and Bess.* You know that there's never been a Russian Broadway musical?"

"And I take it you want to do the first one?"

"I've already written the first act," he said, proudly patting a thick briefcase. His chubby fingers had been clutching it the whole time we were in the bar. I had presumed it was something from one of his spies. Anatoly beamed as he showed me the pages.

"You know, I think you're right about one thing," I said. He looked at me hopefully. "You're not made for working with spies."

His features seemed to sag immediately. "I know, I know," he said, looking like an overgrown schoolboy. "I'm not tough enough for all this. Moscow's going to have me stuffed into a trunk any day now."

"That's ridiculous."

"No, it's not. Have you any idea how much trouble I'm really in?"

21

Anatoly did have troubles.

One of his early assignments under the late Boris had been to blackmail a well-known Broadway producer — the man called himself an impresario — who thought he could make a fortune bringing Russian dancers, circuses, and musicians to New York. The impresario was a flamboyant, opinionated man of about sixty. He was bald, with one glass eye over which he wore a monocle. He loved vast quantities of good wine and very young girls. When he went on a negotiating trip to Moscow, the secret police were only too happy to supply him with both. And to photograph him in great detail with the cameras hidden in the walls. It had fallen to Anatoly to confront him with the photographs and then make sure that he did not complain when we slowly filled his operation with our agents, who would be used for various espionage duties.

But the impresario was as tough and shrewd as Anatoly was uncertain. Just looking at the photographs made Anatoly blush. And at first he was too embarrassed even to confront the impresario. But he had finally worked up his courage, marched into the man's office, dumped the photographs on the desk, and sat back to wait for the pleading, the hand-wringing, and the abject promises to cooperate in any way.

"Thank you," said the impresario.

Thank you? At the training school in Moscow that was not the way it was supposed to go.

"Of course, my boy!" boomed the impresario, finally opening his good eye and standing up to tower over the desk and over Anatoly. "Quite an accomplishment for a man my age. Wouldn't you say? Of course no one would ever believe it, if you people hadn't been so thoughtful as to take a few snapshots." He leaned even farther over the desk. He held one of the photographs out to Anatoly and, with his finger, made a little circle around the central area.

"Could you get me an enlargement of this part?" he said, smiling ferociously. "I'd like to frame it."

It got even worse. The impresario ended up blackmailing Anatoly, who had been reduced to his usual emotional jelly after such an encounter. Desperate to change the subject, he began to pour out his love of Broadway musicals. And the story he wanted to write some day.

"Brilliant!" boomed the impresario. "A Russian musical! Why, of course. What genius!"

An hour later, Anatoly bolted onto West Fifty-Seventh Street, his life suddenly blossoming before him. Dreams of Rodgers and Hammerstein and Cole Porter and George Gershwin danced in his head. Soon the world would be humming *his* tunes. Laughing at *his* story. It was all arranged. In that feverish hour, theatre owners had been phoned, production managers located, directors' availability checked, contracts signed —

Contracts?

Anatoly had stopped right in the middle of the intersection in front of the Plaza Hotel and groped through his pockets, pulling out the official-looking piece of paper. In the euphoria of that mad hour he had signed it. After all, it was his preliminary contract. Until the proper one could be drawn up. And who cared about fine print when they were talking about leading ladies? *If only Garbo* . . .

Standing there in the cold wind that blew down from the park, with car horns blaring unheard all around him,

Anatoly looked at that piece of paper. It read merely *For services rendered*, with a mass of other fine print that referred to nothing in particular.

Anatoly had made the classic blunder that he had been trained to get others to make. He had accepted money. Even worse, he had signed for it. No matter how innocent the circumstances, it was the one thing we tried to get any prospective spy to do. We would call it expenses. Taxi money. A tiny fee. Gratitude. Anything — as long as they took it. And then we had them. Because then the next step was to inform them that unless they worked for us, we would report the fact that they had already been taking money. To their employers. To the police. To the government. There were many variations, some of them gentle, some cruel. But they all worked.

As the impresario well knew. A few days ago, he had informed Anatoly that the musical *Siberia!* had been put on the back burner, as they say. Then he demanded that Anatoly arrange the contracts with the Moscow circuses and dancers immediately. And with very little money as payment. Otherwise he would be forced to report to the embassy officials that Anatoly had been taking money from him.

Sitting there in the bar near Broadway, Anatoly had only one bright spot in his current existence. It was Sara, the girl from the chorus line of *Oklahoma!* He was madly in love with her. He had been to see the show a dozen times and had spent all of his three-hundred-dollar *Siberia!* advance on dinners and presents. She was also very much in love with him, even though you could tell she was a little frightened by the fact he was a Russian. She was not very tall for a chorus girl. She had short brown hair and a round face with remnants of freckles. She laughed easily. And she made Anatoly laugh. They were perfect for each other.

"Tomorrow it's the trunk," said Anatoly glumly. When Sara arrived I excused myself, phoned Sam, and told him I needed some money. That night I went to one of the dead letter-drops that we used for the submarine spy and picked up the money Sam had left me after selling off an odd lot of Westinghouse. Accompanying the money was a note saying he had to see me urgently.

I went back to the embassy and began going through the files in Boris's old office. Because of the chaos in our offices after Boris had been shipped out, there were a few weeks when no one was really sure what was happening. Until a new man arrived, we had each taken over some of Boris's spies just to keep things going. So there was nothing unusual about looking through the files. When I came to the records of the impresario, I read the file carefully, noting any peculiarities like the glass eye. Then I destroyed it, leaving no trace that the man had ever been approached.

The next day, I went to several stores, and then just before lunch I went to the impresario's office. I was dressed in a long, black leather coat, the way I often saw secret policemen dressed in the movies. I had walked slowly past several mirrors, trying to look very menacing. Some people are naturally menacing. Even when they smile, there is a quality of evil that comes from somewhere deep inside. Others have to work at it. By the time I walked in that door, I think I was menacing.

I told his secretary that I had been sent over instead of Anatoly. A few minutes later I was shown into the impresario's office. He reached out to shake my hand. I just stared at his hand, and then stared at him. I was careful to keep the slightest hint of a smile. Very deliberately, I put three hundred dollars on his neat mahogany desk. The exact amount he had paid Anatoly.

"Very generous," he said sarcastically. "But I'm not

interested in getting the money back. I'm after, shall we say, certain contracts."

He pulled the same intimidating trick on me, closing his good eye and staring at me through his monocle with the fake one. But I was ready for him. I reached into my pocket and pulled out a glass eye I had bought a few hours earlier.

He reopened his good eye to find a glass eye sitting in the middle of his desk staring back at him.

He suddenly became very nervous. He looked from the eye to me and back again. "What is the meaning of this?" This time there was no sarcasm.

Still staring at him, I reached into my leather coat and pulled out a small hammer. I held it up and smiled. This made him more nervous. Then, with a perfectly aimed swing, I brought the hammer crashing down on the glass eye.

It literally took his breath away. His monocle seemed to shoot out from his cheek. On his desk the eye lay pulverized, bits of it still staring at him.

I walked out of his office, leaving him shovelling little blue pills into his mouth. I knew Anatoly would never hear from him again.

Just being able to help Anatoly made me feel good. It brought back all those memories of Yuri, my brother. And of what it was like before he went off to the war. The memories of those times kept coming back to me. Especially now, when someone had trusted me enough to confide something personal, as Anatoly had done. To allow yourself to be vulnerable was the ultimate trust. And because we had grown up learning to trust almost no one, such moments were precious to me.

Before I realized where I was, I had walked all the way to Madison Square Garden, cursing the fates that had taken Yuri. I wanted to be vulnerable in the way that I didn't care about what I said. All my grown-up life I had been watching what I said. The only time in my whole life that I had been truly free was when Yuri and I were boys and we said whatever we wanted to.

I sat on the bumper of a parked car watching the congestion of midtown New York traffic. Trucks were double-parked, unloading barrels of fish for the huge old seafood restaurant nearby. Horns blared. Angry voices crossed. The colours of the cars and the people's clothing merged into blurs in my mind. I thought of the Russian proverb my father always used to tell me: "Feed the wolf as you will, but he will always look to the forest." For the first time I understood it. I was the wolf. And at that moment I would have given it all up just to be back in Russia as a boy playing games with Yuri.

I went off to Saks Fifth Avenue, and with the remaining money from my Westinghouse odd lot, I bought Katya a new dress. This one was blue. It was spectacular. Or rather, she was spectacular in it. When she tried it on in the hospital, she looked like a movie star. She jumped up and down and threw her arms around me, kissing me and saying that I was the best husband she could ever have. I had to calm her down in case she did something to her stitches.

Buying that dress was very difficult for me. I thought about it a lot. I was still terrified that one day Katya and her clothes would be my downfall. It was okay for the old men in the Kremlin to be seen with wives dressed like that. Everyone knew that they were the new upper class. With all their cars and houses and opulent clothes. But even if I lasted, it would take me twenty-five years to reach that stage. And by that time, the genetic odds were that Katya would look like a bag of potatoes. So in a way there was a kind of logic to her thinking. It was a crime against nature for her not to look even more spectacular than she already did.

But already I could see the real problem emerging, like dirt being brushed away from a buried bomb. She knew enough about what I was doing with Sam to sense that money was involved somehow. And over the time she had been in the hospital, I could almost see schemes forming in her mind. Instinctively she knew that whatever I was doing, it was her supermarket lottery money that had made it possible. It was the seed money. Or venture capital, or whatever they called it. And she was equally instinctive in knowing that such risk money brought high rates of return.

While she was recuperating, she had accumulated a pile of magazines with pages carefully marked at ads for furs and diamonds. And holidays in the Caribbean. And Acapulco. Many times, I had sat by her bedside idly flipping through the magazines, pretending not to notice the pages that were marked, as my insides went numb with fear.

I had hoped that a new dress might put a stop to it all. And after all, her old dress had been shot up. So fair is fair, I told myself. But even as she was hugging me with ecstatic little squeals of gratitude, I knew the stakes had been raised over these past few weeks. A dress was no longer enough. Not even this stunning blue creation that had come direct from the *défilés* in Paris. As she swept around like a joyous model, there was a look in her eyes that told me this was merely the opening round of negotiations.

It was my first true lesson about money and what it can buy: a lot is never enough once you have it.

And for Katya, the yachts, the furs, the jewels had all become part of her obsession. In her own way, she was my impresario. She was blackmailing me. Gently. Lovingly.

Skilfully.

But I could sense it was all leading to an explosion. A

terrible and unfair fight. And what really began to worry me was that she was capable of putting my little Yagoda Enterprises out of business. Single-handedly. If you added up all the discreetly printed prices on all those glossy advertisements, the total came to more than the value of the company — if you included the home in Palm Beach that Katya now wanted.

I left the hospital smothered in kisses and feeling very worried. But I knew it was all my own fault. I kept on asking myself: Why didn't I marry the girl my mother wanted me to?

22

I left the hospital and went to meet Sam.

For some reason, Sam was even more insistent than usual that we had to meet. Over the past four days, he had sent me increasingly urgent signals on the one-time pad. (One-time pads are pairs of identical notebooks with random numbers printed across each page. Each of those pages represents the key to a code that can only be deciphered by the person with the matching notebook. After the secret message is sent and decoded, each party tears off the top page. Usually we only gave one-time pads to our important spies. But I figured, what the hell, if I used them for my spies, I should use them for my broker too. It was the least I could do.)

When I deciphered Sam's latest message there was a strange address on it. It turned out to be an old building on East Thirty-eighth Street. When I arrived there, it was almost ten o'clock, and no one else was around. I took the elevator to the third floor and went along the darkened hallway, wondering why I had been told to go there. At the end of the corridor, light was shining through the opaque glass in one of the office doors. It was the kind of old-fashioned door you used to see in all the Humphrey Bogart movies. I walked towards that light, feeling uneasy. When I was close enough to make out the lettering on the glass, I stopped.

For an instant I almost lost my breath.

YAGODA ENTERPRISES, INC. said the lettering. I laughed out loud. Sam opened the door. "I thought you'd like it," he said.

I stepped into *my* company offices. Me! A boy from the

206

steppes! A communist, no less. I was thrilled.

"And I must tell you," he said. "You're incredible. I don't know where you get your information from. Caterpillar's just going through the roof."

"Does that mean it's good?"

"Good?" said Sam, beaming and looking pale under the neon lights. "Have you any idea of the way Yagoda Enterprises is growing? Why, that Caterpillar alone meant we had to open up these offices. It's got way too big to operate out of my desk drawer any longer."

I walked through the offices. There were two small rooms filled with old wooden furniture and grey metal filing cabinets. A radiator that had been painted too often made clanking noises in the corner, and one slat of the venetian blinds was missing. "I love it," I said. Sam seemed pleased that I approved. He stood among the cardboard boxes, his starched white shirt ballooning out at his skinny waist. His slicked-back hair gleamed in the light, and his neck moved around in his stiff, white collar without always touching the sides.

I reached out and shook Sam's hand. "I think you should run Yagoda," I said. It was one of the best decisions I have ever made.

After the Xerox and Caterpillar moves, Sam thought it was really me who was the genius. In the interests of corporate success I did nothing to correct that false impression. And I told Sam he could have half the profits and whatever else he felt he deserved. The arrangement between us was that simple. No big contracts or lawyers. Just a handshake. It was an arrangement that suited both of us perfectly. Sam was like a scientist who cared only about tinkering around in the lab. He had no interest in owning the lab itself.

So, naturally, I kept control of Yagoda merely by owning its stock. (Of course, that too had been a problem, because the government in Enemy Number

One requires all kinds of identification for anyone owning stock in anything. But I had been able to have our forgers back in Moscow create everything from phony birth certificates to Social Security cards for one Dimitri Yagoda, born in Newark, New Jersey. Our forgers, naturally, thought they were doing this for one of the illegals we were sneaking into the country. Our forgers were the best.)

The next day Sam took several hours off work at Taylor, Wendell, Bulmer & Carr, while I postponed an important meeting with an H-bomb spy from the morning to the afternoon. The spy was one of Boris's people, whom I was handling until his successor showed up. This was not any ordinary spy. The man was a clerk at the nuclear testing lab in Alamogordo, New Mexico, and he was bringing in secret data on the design of the H-bomb.

But I had no choice. My meeting with him simply had to be postponed. We were hiring staff for Yagoda that morning.

Our method was somewhat unusual. Sam would meet and interview the job applicants, while I pretended to be a janitor cleaning up the offices. When I first changed into the janitor's uniform, Sam thought I was crazy. But I explained to him that I still did not want to be identified with Yagoda in any way. Of course I couldn't tell him the real reason for that. But I didn't have to. He had long ago decided that I was simply an eccentric, amiable immigrant investor who did things in a bizarre way. The kind who kept his money in a sock under the bed because he didn't trust banks.

So that morning, while Sam interviewed bookkeepers and office managers, I swept up and emptied wastepaper baskets at least a dozen times. Believe it or not, it was an effective way of hiring. No one paid any attention to me, so I had the chance to observe the applicants as they really were. The woman who stuck her chewing gum under the chair didn't stand a chance.

By noon we had hired the staff. *My* staff! I still couldn't believe it. I almost skipped along Thirty-eighth Street. I hurried because I was late for my meeting with the H-bomb spy. I jumped into a taxi.

"Ebbets Field," I said to the driver.

Could I help it if this was opening day of the baseball season? All the way out to Brooklyn in the back of that taxi, I came up with reasons to make myself feel less guilty for going to the game. Where else was there a better place to pass information than in a crowd of fifty thousand people? What was more innocent than going to a baseball game? It was obviously the safest place for any spy to be. By the time the taxi was on the Manhattan Bridge I was already starting to feel less guilty.

I had decided baseball should have been a Russian game. I could not understand why we had not stolen it from Enemy Number One and then claimed that we invented it. I was sure that from Murmansk to the Caucasus there would be baseball diamonds all over. In a way the sport was like chess, which was our national passion. Only it was chess with real players living out the strategies of when to sacrifice pawns and when to go for the queen. And that diamond on which the game was played was every bit as symmetrical as a chessboard. I used to glory in sitting there, trying to guess what my beloved Dodgers should do next. Jumping to my feet, screaming at the umpire in Russian. Threatening him with the *gulag* when we took over. It was chess with passion.

I was almost late. Ebbets Field was packed when I got there. It was a thrill just hurrying through that old stadium with the loudspeakers calling out the names of my Dodgers, and all those people cheering. There was so much excitement in the air. I began to run toward my seat, weaving in and out among the ushers and the peanut vendors. My seat was behind what they called the first base. It was the only empty one in a bobbing sea of people. And sitting beside it was a nervous-looking man holding a long cardboard tube, the kind you put posters in. This was obviously my spy. As I approached, he looked at me out of the corner of his eye. Before the first pitch was thrown he said, "I hear it's raining in New Jersey."

Those were his code words. I answered back as I was supposed to: "Yes, but the rain is moving east."

He seemed to relax a little. He was tall and middle-aged, with a deeply lined face, thinning hair, and a worried expression that I suspected was normal for him. "I was afraid you weren't going to show up," he said. He lowered his voice and leaned closer. "These are the plans you people wanted." He passed the cardboard tube to me.

"You keep it until the end of the game," I said. I didn't want to hold a bunch of H-bomb plans for nine whole innings.

"I don't want to stay. I hate baseball."

I didn't have a chance to answer him because at that moment the immortal Pee Wee Reese got a hit and I, like every maniacal Dodger fan, was jumping up and down, whistling and yelling. As far as I was concerned, the matter was settled. The spy stayed.

By the end of the seventh inning I was a nervous wreck. The game had gone back and forth, with the disgusting New York Giants now leading by one run. Even worse, a man behind me was a supporter of those disgusting Giants. He had become louder and drunker, and several times I had turned around and yelled at him in Russian. This made him laugh drunkenly in my face and call me a D.P. turd. He was fat and very hairy, with big fleshy cheeks that seemed to bury his eyes. I was getting more and more angry. The spy kept telling me to calm down.

And then it happened. The brilliant Carl Erskine struck out the Giants, three in a row, and the incomparable Jackie Robinson came up to bat and hit a home run. In the midst of all the cheering I turned around and laughed, right in the fat man's face. He threw a beer in mine.

I went berserk. I tried to punch him but missed. In the fray, arms and fists were all over the place in a blur. People were yelling and laughing and pointing. I snatched the cardboard tube out of the spy's hands and began beating the fat man over the head with it. Part of the tube broke, and the H-bomb plans began to come out. But I didn't care. I was like a windmill, flailing away with those plans until people pulled us apart.

I must have hit a hot dog with those plans because somehow there was mustard over the part that said "U-235." The spy was trembling as we wiped the mustard off. "Jeez, I dunno. This is the critical part," he whispered as we tried to make out the writing on the plan. "This is the part that blows everything up. And you got hot dog mustard on it, for Christ's sake." He was very upset.

"Can you read it?"

"No, too much mustard after the word *detonator*."

I had to admit it was a problem. But almost immediately there was another one. It was in between innings and various announcements were being made over the loudspeaker. One of them made me stop what I was doing: "Will the owner of a blue Buick with Florida licence number 786543 please return to your car. You left your engine running."

Such messages were made once in a while when people left on car engines or lights in the parking lot. But the blue Buick with the Florida licence was the emergency signal from Anatoly at the embassy to me, via one of the head ushers who was a Party member. I hurried to find a telephone, but the only one in our section had a line of

211

two people. Even worse, I could not see what was happening on the field. I ran back to get the H-bomb spy and made him stand at the archway, calling out the action on the field while I waited for the phone. When I finally phoned the embassy, I could hardly hear Anatoly's voice over the cheering. And the spy was yelling that the Dodgers were about to score.

I couldn't believe what Anatoly was saying to me. "Moscow is ordering you to return there immediately."

"For how long?" I yelled.

"For good. You're being recalled."

"Why?" The cheers were deafening. All the old fears flashed in front of me. Boris. The trunk. The one-way trip to doom. The old men in the Kremlin. Labour camps. The white-tiled basement at the Lubyanka.

"They want you to be a poet!" Anatoly's voice came through that phone like a distant echo.

"A poet?" I yelled, confused and frightened.

How could they do this to me? In the bottom of the ninth inning, with the score tied, the bases loaded, and the immortal Pee Wee Reese coming up to bat?

Russia

23

Stepping by rote through sunlight
I have hung fears on the rack
Of my own darkest night
And flailed memories
With a vision
Of blackness
Beckoning

So I was ordered back to Moscow to write poetry for Alexei. He was too drunk to write his own name anymore. But after I had brought him over to New York, his fame had spread throughout the world, and the proper literary salons were clamouring for more poems.

That became my job. A ghost poet.

Years passed. Difficult ones.

At first there were the joys of just being back in Russia with my parents and my sister Natasha and her new baby. I still couldn't get used to the idea of my little sister being a mother. After the welcoming parties came the drab reality of living in that single-room apartment in the large grey building located in the suburbs of Moscow. Everything was relentlessly grey. The view from our window of other identical apartments stretched off into a bleak infinity. It was a difficult time for both Katya and me.

Especially because of our memories of New York. And every morning those memories danced in my head, as I boarded the subway at one of those ornately immaculate subway stations and rode into the centre of Moscow.

I had been told that my job as ghost poet was a promotion. But I knew that wasn't true. My new job had much less influence than my old one. It was obvious that the new regime had just wanted to shake up the centres of power and put people they trusted in those places. And so began yet another struggle that would convulse the Kremlin. That old Russian saying, "when you cut down the big trees, chips have to fly," was true once again. I had no interest in being one of the chips. A lot of people were either shot or jailed — including the head of the secret police. Even in our office, I saw cases of people suddenly not showing for work one day. It was as if they had vanished. And no one was naïve enough to ask where they were.

So I was content to work in obscurity. I had a desk next to a small window on the third floor of the old czarist building in which we had our headquarters. I would often look out across the square with the sparse traffic moving around the statue. Occasionally a motorcade would roar through it, with motorcycle outriders and secret police cars enclosing a black Zil with curtains pulled down over the rear windows as it sped on to, or from, the Kremlin. But mostly there was just the hypnotic circling of the few cars.

Sometimes I would stare down at those cars and my mind would play tricks on me again. I would see Fifth Avenue with all its kaleidoscope of colours and noise. And if anyone asked why I was just staring out of the window for hours, I would tell them I was thinking up another poem. After all, that was my job, wasn't it?

I actually began to love writing poetry. It became an escape from the numbing boredom of everyday life. But it also became a kind of agony for me, because I hated seeing my poems in books with Alexei's name on them. I grew to hate that fraud. It was as if he were stealing my children. But because the cultural exchange programme had become vital to us for infiltrating agents into the West, I had to be very careful. Alexei had become a superstar. His exalted status made it even more painful for me to have to take each new batch of poems over to his *dacha* up by Arkhangelsky Park near the banks of the Moscow River. Usually he was sitting surrounded by pieces of torn-up paper, vodka bottles, and the occasional fawning admirer. Believe it or not, he sometimes yelled at me for destroying his genius! But he never minded his genius being destroyed when he read *my* poems to the adulation of thousands in Enemy Number One.

After the purges ended, the Kremlin settled down to its usual level of intrigue. One day I was ordered to meet with some old men there. It was as if I had been lifted out of my obscurity by the memories of those old survivors who recalled my earlier schemes to destroy Enemy Number One. Everyone had acknowledged that my schemes were brilliant. And now those old survivors needed that brilliance. They showered me with flattery, gave me warm, fraternal embraces, and asked me where I had been for the past couple of years. They promised me promotions. Apartments. A *dacha* in the Crimea if things went well.

All I had to do was get back to the work I was so brilliant at. Destroying Enemy Number One.

We were rounding the final turn, they said. Coming into the home stretch. And didn't I want to be in on the action?

I nodded and acted pleased that they had thought of me. I promised I would get back to them with my ideas. But I never did.

Soon, I was allowed to labour on undisturbed in my obscurity. I acquired the aura of a burned-out genius.

It was not that I didn't want the cars, the apartments, the *dachas*, and all the rest of it. I did. My life was generally boring and often uncomfortable. I would have given almost anything to change it. But I had made myself a vow that I swore to keep, no matter what.

I vowed I would not use my skills to destroy Enemy Number One. I had come to feel fiercely protective of my little Yagoda Enterprises. And if I could not be there, at least I would not do anything to destroy it.

My problem was made worse because I missed my life in New York more than I ever imagined I would. After a year in Moscow I was desperate to return. But the only way I could would be to give the old men in the Kremlin more of my devastatingly effective schemes to hasten the final destruction of Enemy Number One. Only then would they consent to my return.

So I was caught. If I didn't agree to destroy what I had come to love, I would be doomed never to see it again.

After a couple of years Alexei died. He had been drinking for hours before he went outside and went to sleep in a snowdrift. They thawed him out, put him in a coffin, and gave him a huge state funeral at which I was forced to be one of the pallbearers. We moved through hordes of weeping literati to deposit Alexei in the ground in front of a huge tombstone on which were to be chiselled lines of his poetry that I had written.

Even though I wanted more than ever to go back to Enemy Number One, I still kept my vow. I drifted through a series of obscure middle-level positions. For a while I was put to work training illegals. Most of the illegals I dealt with were Russians, Czechs, or Germans who had been born in Enemy Number One and grew up there until their parents returned to the homeland for one reason or another. Even though they often spoke perfect English, they had only hazy memories of what life there was like. So before they were smuggled back to begin their espionage, I had to make them familiar with all the details of everyday life there.

Mostly I used movies, which were far more effective than just reading the New York newspapers or the *Saturday Evening Post*. The illegals could watch how people talked to each other and see actual street scenes in those movies. And of course — most important of all — I loved them. Soon I had acquired a library of Hollywood movies. I would sit for hours with my trainee-illegals watching those films. I became an expert on the early Marlon Brando films. But we had to be careful. After a screening of *A Streetcar Named Desire*, one of the trainees showed up for days afterwards wearing sweaty T-shirts just like Brando's. Another one came in with his hair cut and dyed just like James Dean's in *Rebel Without a Cause*.

Every time I saw a new movie with street scenes, I looked at how the cars and the clothes had changed since I was there. It all seemed to change so fast. Between Humphrey Bogart and Robert Redford was like two different worlds. I began to worry about losing touch in more ways than one. I realized I was living out my fantasies in those movies. Seeing a film like *Hud*, I rode through Texas for a couple of hours. Me and Paul Newman in that battered convertible. While I walked right down Park Avenue with Dustin Hoffman in *Midnight Cowboy*.

And then I would put on my coat and walk out into the greyness of Gorky Street. Sometimes, on cold, clear Moscow nights, after spending hours locked in my fantasy world of Enemy Number One, I would walk across Dzerzhinsky Square all the way to the Sadovoye Ring and then cut over towards the big skyscraper on Vosstania Square. It had been finished only a few years earlier, a part of Stalin's attempt to imitate the buildings in New York. On a clear night the skyscraper loomed above its surroundings, its central spire rising like a missile with a huge star mounted upon it. At each side of the building two smaller towers rose up, like enlarged naves in some redesigned cathedral.

I went there several times before I realized it reminded me of the San Remo apartment building on Central Park West. The one I had sat and stared at for hours from my favourite bench in the park.

My most anguished time in Moscow was not caused by the Kremlin. It was caused by the Brooklyn Dodger crisis. When I read the news in a two-day-old copy of the *New York Herald Tribune*, I was so upset I immediately left the office, claiming I was sick.

How could anyone ever imagine moving my Dodgers to Los Angeles? It was treason, pure and simple.

I cursed, I schemed. I looked through all the KGB files to see what we had on this evil O'Malley character who owned the Dodgers. There had to be some way to stop him from sending the immortal Pee Wee Reese to Los Angeles. And Duke Snider and all the others. It was February when the news first came out, and the final decision on the move was constantly postponed. All spring and summer I grabbed the sports pages of the New York newspapers, which were closely guarded within our department. Research on infiltrating athletic teams, I told my colleagues.

For a while it looked as if my Dodgers would stay in Brooklyn. That this perfidious O'Malley was just bluffing. But then toward the end of August you could see signs of doom. I tried to stop it. I got word through to Anatoly, who was still in New York, asking him to run an operation against this O'Malley. Rent a suite at the Waldorf. Fill it with hookers and put cameras in the walls. Anything. Just stop my Dodgers from being moved out of Brooklyn.

But in September it was all over. They were now the *Los Angeles Dodgers*. It was just like seeing your wife out with someone else.

Or in my case, the way things were between Katya and me, was it not perhaps a little worse?

24

Katya let me know that I was still in a trap.

Subtly, lovingly, she reminded me in a hundred ways that what was mine was hers. And just because we were stuck in Moscow for the time being was no reason to think that the future would not be filled with treasures. Her treasures.

Of course, it was a trap of my own making, and many of the Moscow worthies would have envied me, if only because Katya had become even more beautiful over the past ten years. Her face had softened just enough to lose the slightly angular quality it had when we were first married, and now with those large blue eyes framed by the carefully arranged windswept look of her naturally blond hair, she resembled one of the voluptuous Swedish movie stars who had recently become so popular.

Leaving New York had been even more difficult for Katya than it was for me. It was almost like having to cure an addiction. Suddenly there were no more store windows filled with spectacular clothes. And no more trips to Henri Bendel or Bloomingdale's or Bergdorf Goodman, where she could spin out her dreams to dress herself in all that finery. After the first week in Moscow, when she stared into the barren displays of Bulgarian dresses at the GUM department store, she wanted to go right back to Enemy Number One. Her withdrawal symptoms were awesome. For a while she wore her blue dress from Saks Fifth Avenue every night around our tiny Moscow apartment, and stared hopelessly into her old issues of *Vogue* for hours on end. During the days, she even tried keeping the curtains drawn so she would not have to look out at that unrelenting greyness of the other concrete-slab apartments facing ours. A greyness broken only by the tiny park below us, where aged pensioners sat during their endless days and sturdy old babushkas watched over their infant grandchildren. For Katya those days were filled with fantasies of sleek fashion models on Caribbean beaches and at New York salons.

For a few weeks I thought she might go truly mad. But Katya's thoughts were too uncomplicated to sustain the weight of prolonged fits of imagination, and soon the entire fantasy began to collapse under its own weight. In the end, she was saved by her ability to act in a simple direct manner. She went out and found a job in the nearest thing Moscow had to offer to the luxury goods business. She became an employee of Food Shop Number Five, one of the special stores reserved only for the Moscow elite. While the ordinary stores sold inferior merchandise to the average citizens who had queued up for hours, Food Shop Number Five lavished its restricted client list with whatever luxury foods and delicacies they wanted. Foreign cigarettes, cognacs, champagnes, and wines were all there to be purchased for only a fraction of their normal price.

The place was as close to Fifth Avenue as she could get. And much to her delight, she discovered that her new job brought her endless opportunities to get involved in the black market, which had spread throughout the entire society. Everyone, even the most righteous ideologue, was scheming to buy or sell luxury goods in his spare time. Of course Katya took to this new venture like a Cossack to horses. She was a natural at it. Within weeks she was fiddling the foreign cigarette accounts. Then she jumped to liqueurs, and then got herself promoted into meats. With each step she manoeuvred favours and began bartering for luxuries for us. Soon our apartment was graced with meats and wines that even my bosses could not get. And, of course, perfumes, silk scarves, and once an Italian purse.

Her progress in Food Shop Number Five was quite incredible. Too incredible. She began returning later and later at night, always claiming to have been working and always smelling just a little too much of strong perfume that never quite masked the smell of even stronger cigars. I knew that Adamov, the lecherous old manager of Food Shop Number Five, smoked Cuban cigars. Once when I unexpectedly called for her just after work, she seemed flustered, almost frightened, and in a loud voice announced to one of her coworkers that her husband had come to call for her. Adamov instantly appeared at the office doorway, staring fiercely before ducking back inside.

I said nothing about my suspicions. Not even when she became third deputy manager within a year. And not even when she began hounding me for not being more important and having the power and the privileges that her Food Shop clients had. And Adamov had. I had almost stopped caring, even in the strange way that I once did. For one thing, her affair coincided with mine. I had met an Intourist guide, a young, dark-haired woman from a town near the Urals. She had a sharp wit and a sense of fun. Soon I began arriving home only minutes before Katya. Our marriage was disintegrating day by day.

And strangely, infuriatingly, *I* began to feel guilty. This is ridiculous, I told myself. She cheats, so I cheat, and yet I'm the only one who feels guilty. My guilt showed in many ways. I began to get angry at her for small things, and only later did I realize I was just looking for an excuse to justify my affair. Then I moved on to being angry with her for not feeling guilty, like I did, but after a while I had to admit that guilt was not her strong point. So I began to blame her for not having children, but that only worked for a while. After all, I had been the one responsible for Harry firing that bullet into whatever it was inside her that could not be sewn up properly by the doctors.

Finally I ran out of things to get angry about. The truth, I thought (and still think, worldly cynicism to the contrary), is that she still loved me and that in her simplified way of thinking, she was sacrificing herself into the cigar-reeking clutches of an old man from whom she would extract certain favours to make our life more tolerable. That was Katya's great strength; she could justify anything she did and truly believe the reasons.

But it no longer mattered to me. One day, I made my decision to leave her and phoned her at work, telling her to be home early that night, because we had to have a talk. Without saying it, I left no doubt what the subject of the talk would be, and looking back on it I suppose that was a mistake. From a military point of view, you might say that I lost the key element of tactical surprise. I hurried home, endlessly rehearsing and refining my impending speech to her, demanding a divorce. By the time I reached our apartment, my oratory was nothing short of brilliant.

And it all disappeared the moment I opened the door. I thought I was in the wrong apartment. The soft light from candles in the silver candelabra sparkled in the elegant French crystal, while classical music played softly on the German stereo. Nineteenth-century silverware and starched napkins were arranged around the Limoges china, on which sat mounds of caviar, whipped Devon cream, and other delicacies only dreamed of by the grey masses on the other side of that door. It was all elegantly arranged on a huge, antique dining room table. Katya must have called in every IOU in the State Warehouse and in her Food Shop. Money alone could not have bought or borrowed that display of opulence. Katya appeared from the kitchen, wearing her blue dress and looking even more beautiful than usual.

"Ah, darling, you're just in time. You sit over here," she said, as if this was just a normal dinner. She poured the French wine. We sat across from each other, smiled, toasted one another's health, and politely talked about things like the weather. I could not remember one single line of my brilliant, incisive oratory. I just sat there stunned. She had completely upstaged me. After dessert, she looked at me seductively over the top of her wineglass, pinning me down with those big blue eyes, and said, "Now then, darling, you wanted to tell me something."

I was helpless. All I could do was blurt out, "Divorce. I want a divorce."

Those blue eyes never left me for an instant. "Of course you do, darling," she said in a strangely soothing voice. "These little difficulties come up from time to time. But I'm afraid a divorce is out of the question."

"You don't have to agree to it. I can still get one just by —"

"No, you can't," she said in that same soothing, soft voice.

"Why can't I?"

"Because we have our own little partnership, darling. After all, your Yagoda Enterprises . . ." She paused for dramatic effect. I was aware that my eyes must have been suddenly as wide as kopeks. ". . . is *mine* too. Comrade."

I blew up, throwing my napkin into the caviar and marching around the room. I should have known right then — I had lost. "I have no idea what you're talking about! This is a ridiculous conversation, and I'm not going to put up with it any longer."

"Of course not, darling. But tell me, have you any idea how many times I followed you over to your Mr. Smith's office? What is it called? Taylor, Wendell,

226

Bulmer, and somebody. Harry told me all about what stockbrokers do, and of course I couldn't let him know, but I was so proud of you, Dimitri, when I found out. I always knew you'd be fabulously rich."

"I have nothing to do with any of that anymore," I yelled.

"Of course not, darling. But tell me, would they still take you down to the Lubyanka and shoot you if they found out you were a stock market tycoon?" The words came out so lovingly, so gently, that I couldn't believe what she had just said.

"Shhh!" I yelled, scrambling to turn up the stereo, because I knew without a doubt the walls had to be infested with hidden microphones.

"I simply couldn't bear to lose you," she said with that same devastatingly warm smile.

"Would you mind telling me what the hell that means?" Already I could see those white-tiled basements.

"To somebody else, darling." But it sounded like an afterthought.

"This is blackmail!"

"Oh, Dimitri, don't be so silly. It's just a little business discussion between two partners who love each other." She raised her glass in a toast, not so much staring at me as impaling me for an instant. "To yachts and furs and tropical islands."

"This is absurd! We're never going back to New York, anyway."

"Are you sure of that, darling?" That old seductive warmth flowed from her eyes again. "You'll thank me for this eventually."

I sat there just staring into all that food. She reached out and ran her elegantly manicured finger through the cream, then slowly licked it.

"Don't you think food is sensual?"

"I beg your pardon?"

"Food. Don't you find it erotic?" She ran her finger elegantly down her neck onto her bare shoulders. It left a white creamy streak, which was then duplicated just above the neckline. Some of the cream dribbled into the cleavage at the top of her breasts.

"What has this got to do with what we were talking about?"

"Everything." I thought the cream might melt under the heat of that smile. With a practised and deft motion she reached around behind her, and suddenly the top of her dress fell away. She sat across from me, nude from the waist up, smiling as the cream continued silently on its journey. I found myself gripping the edges of the table as something very warm surged through me.

She reached out into the caviar and drew a slow circle around one of her breasts. With the other hand she reached into the cream and drew more circles that blended in with the caviar. "Everything," she whispered again. Suddenly I dimly perceived a kind of logic to what was happening. Others ate expensive foods.

But Katya wore them.

It was as if whatever was expensive and opulent had to be engulfed by her entire being, sucked in until the physical boundaries between her and it ceased to exist. A memory of something like this happening once in New York flashed through my mind, and suddenly I realized how unobservant I'd been. For Katya, working at Food Shop Number Five was almost a spiritual fulfilment. Maybe that was Adamov's secret, tempting her in ways that tortured her very soul, draping her with imported salamis, green peppers, and smoked salmon until she achieved a higher state of consciousness.

Like the source of the Nile, the cream and the caviar travelled down in rivulets that ran together in the centre and continued on toward some yet unseen mouth of the river. I found myself leaning forward to see if it would run into the top of her blue dress, which was now around her waist.

At the last moment she stood up and the dress fell away completely. The effect took my breath away, it was done with such supreme confidence. She stepped onto the chair and then kneeled on the table, slowly smearing herself with those creams and sauces. "Still hungry?" she smiled, reaching out to me as whatever music was on the stereo thundered and crashed.

"This is embarrassing," I said, feeling very uncertain.

"Of course it is, darling," she whispered, reaching out for my tie and tugging me onto the edge of the table.

"Katya, please, I'm a respected member of the People's—"

"So let them respect you even more," she murmured, reeling in my tie and me with it. Suddenly I felt the gravy from the silver platter of filet seeping through my pants. I lurched to my feet on top of the table, balancing between the sherbet and the mints, and tore off my suit. "My best suit!" I said in horror when I saw the stain. But Katya was not paying attention to me. She was embellishing that river of cream and swaying blissfully to some inner rhythm. I watched that river of cream like an eagle floating high above some luscious terrain looking for a place to land. I realized that I was swaying too. I wanted to be free and throw myself down upon her, because there was a part of me that thrilled to what she was doing, arousing me beyond anything I had known.

But there was another part, built with the puritanism of decades, ringing in my ears and in my eyes, with images of stern old Party officials yelling ferociously, "Decadence! Disgrace!"

And were the curtains pulled?

I ripped off the rest of my clothes and looked down to see her holding up a bowl of whipped cream like an offering. "Put the commissar in the cream," she said with a blissful smile.

229

"I will not," I said, suddenly taking refuge behind those stern Party officials. But it was too late. She did it anyway, and in an instant I forgot all about the cries of "Decadence!" and reached out, clasping her to me, sinking down onto that huge table, and rolling through those delicacies that had become part of us. For joyous hours we thrashed through the paté and writhed opulently through the sherbet, making love as we had never done before. And I nuzzled that cream at the source of the Nile and then kissed and licked my way right to the Mediterranean.

My next memory is of two burly workmen gaping down at us. One looked at the other and said indignantly, "I told you the bosses have all the fun."

It was dawn. I rose from the table, dazed, naked, and caked with food. "We knocked, but no one answered," said one of the workmen, smirking. "We've come for the table and all the rest of it," said the other one. They were talking to me, but they were both staring at Katya, who was stretching blissfully and nakedly across the table.

"Wait outside, will you please," she said to them, yawning contentedly. They backed away, staring at us wide-eyed until reluctantly they closed the door. "It all has to be back at the State Warehouse by eight o'clock," Katya said, still stretching as if nothing had happened. She winked at me. "The sherbet was fantastic," she said.

We hosed each other off beside the laundry sink, and then she put on a housecoat and called in the waiting workmen, as if all this were just another ordinary morning. I was too embarrassed to go out into the other room as they were tossing the silverware and the china into boxes. Through a crack in the doorway I could see them cleaning up the mess. They never took their eyes off Katya for a moment.

They took the table and the boxes down to their truck,

which was parked on the street below. I looked out our window and watched them throwing buckets of water across the table. I could see them laughing and making obscene gestures as they pointed to our apartment.

Katya emerged from the bathroom, dressed and looking immaculate. She kissed me on the cheek, said she wouldn't be late, and left the apartment. I watched as she passed those two workmen below. She smiled serenely at them. They just stood there, staring at her with a kind of awe.

And so my attempt to free myself from Katya had failed. What emerged between us was a truce that spanned an emotional spectrum from love to a business arrangement. And my little Yagoda Enterprises became the unspoken tie that bound us. From that day, Katya did not come home from work late, and my affair with the Intourist guide dwindled out of existence. Oddly enough, it was probably the happiest time of our married life, mainly because so many things were in limbo. All those luxuries that Katya was waiting to harvest, the yachts and furs and tropical homes, were obviously not even a possibility as long as we were still in Moscow. But she was content to wait for what she thought would be a year or so, serene in her certainty that we would be back in Enemy Number One, whereupon she would claim her share of the wealth. I, on the other hand, was equally certain we would never go back, even though I longed to. Since it was a topic that was not discussed again, we both achieved a state of marital tranquillity that had been missing for all those years.

A month after Katya's dinner party, I decided to take a daring gamble that I thought would please her. I had received an invitation for both of us to attend an evening reception at one of the institutes not far from the Kremlin. I suggested something that only a few years earlier would have been impossible — that she wear her blue dress in public. She was thrilled, throwing her arms around me, smothering me with kisses, and telling me I was the best husband in all Moscow. (My real reason was simply an attempt to get her to forget New York. Every little bit helped.)

Until then, it would have been suicidal to have been seen with her wearing such a piece of capitalist finery. But since our return I had become aware of a large number of officials and their wives who were dressed in clothes that came from the West. The old ways were changing, and in their place had come a subtle corruption that affected us all. Various forms of smuggling, black marketeering, and bribery were practised on a mass scale. And seen by almost no one. With them had come the first trickle of decadent bourgeois clothing, as the dresses from the Fifth Avenue racks occasionally began turning up on the wives of the bureaucrats. No longer were junior officials automatically in mortal peril because of their wives' inexplicably expensive tastes in fashion. Now it was just presumed that they had been somehow successful in buying well on the black market, like so many others.

Of course, you had to be careful, because calling attention to yourself in material ways could still lead to an investigation driven by the envy or ambition of others. And it was still possible to get shot for what they called economic crimes, but everybody played the odds, figuring they'd run out of bullets before they got the job done properly.

So I decided the risk was worth taking, and at first it seemed I was right. All the way to the reception Katya was more excited than I'd ever seen her. We took a taxi, which in itself was a luxury. I was beginning to think my plan would work — that Moscow would suddenly blossom as a cosmopolitan fashion centre in her eyes. But it all fell to pieces once we arrived at the Great Palace, because there, under the glittering chandeliers, stood the wives of some visiting French officials. They were wearing absolutely the latest styles, only days out of the salons on the Avenues Montaigne and George V.

Katya forgot all about the excitement of the occasion and circled those women like a dog sniffing at its rivals. Hemlines, shoulder height and cut, fabric, gatherings, bias, and necklines were all checked, itemized, and evaluated.

Whereupon she pronounced her new blue dress hopelessly out of style.

In an effort to minimize the damage of the evening, I tried everything I could think of to draw her away from those French women. I plied her with the caviar and the wine, I introduced her to colleagues, and I told her how lovely she looked. It was no use.

She wanted a new dress and that was that.

The ornate ballroom swelled with polite talk and diplomatic niceties from the hundreds of guests. We were standing next to a group of colleagues at one side of the room when something made me look away. I had the feeling I was being watched. I scanned the crowd and saw nothing. But then the human ebb and flow created a parting that momentarily extended all the way to the other side of the room. In that moment I saw a man staring at me. Instantly I turned my back to him, the way you flick your hand away from an open flame a split second before actually feeling the pain.

I knew the instant I saw him that he was trouble, but the reason why came in a slight delay. I clutched Katya's arm and whispered that we had to go. Quickly saying good night, pleading illness, I rushed the two of us toward the door. But I could see the man weaving hurriedly through the crowd, trying to cut me off. The voice of my own panic almost sent me running through that ballroom, and for a moment I thought I would make it. But a waiter with a tray of food stepped in front of me.

When I reached the doorway he was waiting. His wide, flabby face was flushed with exertion and anger. He glared at me with his bulging froglike eyes.

"Thief!" he hissed. "What did you do with my trunk?"

25

Years passed.

But the fury of the old man with the bulging eyes burned on, his own personal eternal flame. Or maybe it was his wife. His anger had been tranquil compared with hers. She had come ploughing through the crowd, her eyes fixed malevolently on Katya's blue dress. His wife was wearing a shapeless, drab cotton dress obviously designed by some local factory manager for ease of manufacturing, so he could make his monthly quota. All the way out of the reception hall they hounded us, accusing me of stealing that steamer trunk crammed with silk gowns and Fifth Avenue treasures. They threatened me with the most awesome fates.

What had saved me were the old man's bureaucratic misfortunes. In the years after he had escorted Boris back to his doom, the old man had found himself on the wrong side of the Kremlin power struggle. He had been lucky enough only to be pushed aside into some obscure position. But recently there were signs that he might be making a spectacular comeback. Perhaps even be appointed to the Central Commitee.

For a while I worried about him. But then I forgot about that sinister old man. I had other things to worry about.

My real problems in Moscow began, strangely enough, with one of my happiest times. It was when Anatoly returned for a few days. He occasionally came through Moscow on his way to or from Havana, where he was now stationed. Only then would it be like the old days, where we drank and laughed and told the truth to each other. The unnoted irony of his success and my career stagnation did not bother me. I was truly happy for him. He was thriving in Havana where he was working with cultural exchange groups.

I had never seen him so relaxed. All the way down Gorky Street one night, he showed me the six different Latin dance steps he had learned from the Cuban dancers with whom he was now working. By the time we got to the rhumba, with his huge torso jiggling across the sidewalk in quick little back-and-forth steps, we were both laughing too hard to stand up, and a militia car stopped and warned us of public drunkenness. But we weren't drunk. It just felt so good to laugh.

Later we did get drunk. Just a little. Not enough so that Anatoly couldn't suddenly look very serious and say, "What's happened?"

"Happened to what?"

"You."

For a moment I acted as if I didn't understand him. But we both knew I did. "I just lost it." I shrugged.

"No, you didn't."

"You've changed," I said. "You were never so assertive before."

"Maybe it's just because we don't have much time to talk. I don't know what your problem is, but you didn't lose all that talent you had. They still talk about your operations back in New York, as if they were the good old days."

"I can't explain it."

"Is it Katya?"

"Don't be ridiculous."

"I'm not. Is it Lavrenti? Are you afraid of having to face him again?"

"Yes, I am. But no, he's not the reason," I said.

"Glad to hear it," said Anatoly, pulling out an envelope and handing it to me. "I opened it," he said.

There was only a postcard inside, with a glossy photograph of a brand new baseball stadium. *Beautiful Dodger Stadium! Los Angeles!* said the writing across the photo. "It came in the mail to me a few weeks ago. Postmarked out of Canada," Anatoly said. "I presume he knew it was the best way of reaching you."

On the other side was a typewritten message: *Forgotten the old team? Come on back. The game is still the same! Regards Larry (Lavrenti to you, pal).* I just stared at it as all the old memories of Lavrenti, the boy and the man, rushed back. After a while I said, "No, that's not the reason."

"Then let's try this one." Anatoly shoved another piece of paper in front of me. It was a crumpled message from Sam. *Where are you? I must talk to you! Incredible news! Sam. P.S. I presume you saw what Xerox did yesterday!*

"When did you get this?" I was stunned.

"Nine years ago," he said. "Just after you left New York. But it wasn't me that found it."

"Who did?"

"Ivchenkov. Remember him?"

Sudden images of a sinister and flabby face with its broken veins glowing in silent fury. And those fearful encounters with him and Boris. "I thought he died of a heart attack?"

In the threadbare splendour of that ancient Moscow restaurant, with its musty velour curtains and patched tablecloths, Anatoly sat by the edges of a lamp's glow, oblivious to the irritable stares of sturdy waitresses anxious to be rid of their remaining customers. I watched him change back to his former self as the veneer of his self-assurance crumbled, leaving only the beads of perspiration forming above his lips and the moist glaze of uncertainty settling in his eyes. "Ivchenkov wasn't sure what the message meant. But he said he was sure there was no agent code-named Sam. He was going to launch

237

an investigation. He smelled blood. Yours."

I remembered the stories from the time. About how Ivchenkov had suddenly keeled over dead of a heart attack. In a New York coffee shop. No one had paid much attention at the time. He was in his fifties, smoked too many cigarettes, and had high blood pressure.

But now, years later, those details fitted together differently, as fragments of Anatoly's emotions seeped out from that sad stare.

"So you killed him?"

"Yes." Something in his throat was pulsing up and down. He infuriated the waitress by calling for more vodka. "I kept in my pocket at all times a tiny pill that you could either bite or dissolve in liquid and it would kill within seconds. I'd stolen a couple of them from one of our people in Department V in case I was ever going to be put in the trunk. I'd told myself I would rather die than be put in the trunk.

"So when Ivchenkov and I were sitting in that coffee shop and he got up to buy some cigarettes, I just dumped that little pill into his coffee. He came back and sat down, excited as a ten-year-old about finally finding a way to have you shot for treason. He gulped down that coffee and shoved a Danish pastry into his mouth as he talked. And then it suddenly happened. He went red all over and clutched at his chest. I could see him trying to form words in his mouth as he began to keel over sideways, and his eyes never left me. He knew! I could tell from that hideous stare he knew I had poisoned him, but he couldn't get his lips to move to scream out that one word — *murderer!*"

Anatoly's hands were wrapped around his glass in a death grip. The glass suddenly shattered, sending a burst of vodka and cheap crystal across the table. He swept it away as if nothing had happened. "Ivchenkov just keeled over into his Danish and lay there. The whole restaurant erupted in yelling and pandemonium and people were giving him artificial respiration and thumping him on the chest. I just stood around and tried to keep myself from thinking that I'd just killed someone. I was afraid I was going to burst out crying. But I had no choice. I mean, it was either him or you. Wasn't it?"

I nodded. But Anatoly could only stare off into the distance. He had reached for another glass and was drinking in great gulps. "Anyway. The next day I went back to that same drop and left a typed message with no signature. It said *Sam — Will be gone for a long time. Proceed as normal. Absolutely no further contact until I initiate it.* A couple of days later, I went back and checked the drop. The message was gone."

I realized I had been holding my breath. "Thank you."

"You don't have to. After all, you saved me from Boris. So now we're even — with one slight difference."

"What difference?"

He had finally looked up at me with his glazed and nervous stare. "I've spent nine years wondering if I did the right thing. I checked through all of our code names, and Ivchenkov was right — there never was any Sam. Or any operation called Xerox. What is that all about, Dimitri?"

"I can't tell you."

"You've got to." It was both a plea and a command. "I've spent all these years wondering if you were really working for the other side. Betraying us."

"Supposing I was betraying the motherland. Would you have still saved me? Would you still have dropped that pill in his coffee?"

He stared into the tablecloth for a long time before nodding. "Yes. I would. I've told you I'm not meant for all that spying business. I'm okay working with Cuban dancers. There I can be clear and precise, and I just follow my instincts and have fun. But for what we did in New

York, I'm afraid that my instincts sometimes get in the way of my head. So I'm not good at all that. And I don't want to be, either."

I told him the truth.

I told him as I would have told Yuri. I made up my mind in an instant without fully knowing why, and only later did I realize how much I had wanted — needed — to trust. Even though I would be vulnerable beyond all my past fears. Anatoly would have the power of life and death over me with that knowledge of Sam and Yagoda Enterprises. But then he had possessed that power nine years ago in some New York coffee shop.

When the waitresses began flashing the lights on and off, we left and walked back through the old part of Moscow University. The leaves were beginning to appear on the trees in front of the huge stone columns of the front portico. I loved the spring, and suddenly I too felt truly alive for the first time in years. Somehow just talking about it all had been exhilarating, as if the burden of keeping that secret had been lifted.

Anatoly began muttering about how he should have blackmailed me into financing his Broadway play. The one he was still working on.

"Better me than the impresario." I grinned and we were instantly lost in the old days in New York. Until I remembered what it was I wanted to ask him.

"You said you stole two of those poison pills. What happened to the second one?"

He reached into a pocket of his coat and took out a tiny plastic bag. Inside was the pill. "Just in case," he said.

He was still smiling, but it was not a joke. "Why? Are you still expecting to get put into the trunk?"

"No."

"Then what?" He just stood there holding up that pill. I had seen one of them a few years earlier in a secret police office. Those pills were legendary. A century after they were made, they were capable of stopping the heart of an elephant. In ten seconds.

"Actually, I don't need it now. I just keep it as a habit. But for a couple of years afterwards I kept having nightmares, seeing Ivchenkov's face staring at me. I was almost driven crazy with guilt over what I'd done. At one point I couldn't take it any more and . . ." His voice trailed off as he stared at the pill.

"So give it to me." I wasn't going to let him take any chances. I could see he didn't want to give it to me. "I said give it to me!" He hesitated.

And finally he shrugged and tossed the poison pill to me.

We walked across to the new Rossiya Hotel, where he was staying. A few lights still dotted the windows of its massive sterile façade, and as usual only one of the long bank of glass doors was open. Before Anatoly got to the small queue of late-night guests waiting to enter through that single open door, he turned suddenly and said, "I wasn't sure if I should tell you this, because I didn't want to worry you any more than it worried me. But when I was in that coffee shop with Ivchenkov, I think there was someone there who you know."

"Who?"

"Lavrenti. Young, owlish-looking guy? Big, thick glasses?"

I nodded. And began to feel very numb.

"He was in the next booth."

The next day, while Katya was still at work, I sat in the front room of our apartment holding Lavrenti's Los Angeles Dodgers postcard under special equipment for reading microdots. Something about that postcard had been nagging at me all the previous night, and now, under the special enlarging equipment, the full stop beneath the question mark in *Forgotten the old team?* came

241

into focus. That tiny dot separated into entire words and then sentences.

There were four stops in his typewritten greetings on the back of the postcard, and each one was a microdot containing a sentence or two of his new secret message. Several times while I was working, I was interrupted by the barking of the dog down the hall. The barking grew worse, until I could not concentrate on what I was doing. During the year Katya and I had lived in that apartment, the barking of the German shepherd down the hall had almost driven us crazy. The dog was the prized possession of a red-faced sergeant in the militia who lived at the very end of the hallway. Officially, the dog was the property of the militia, which used it for guard duties. But because the dog was as mean as its master, no one else could handle it. So the sergeant brought it home, and when he went on drinking binges, he left the dog tied to the outside handle of his apartment door. Whenever any of the other tenants complained, they had been subjected to the most foul verbal abuse hurled at them in various stages of drunkenness, questioning their loyalty for hindering a militiaman in his efforts to protect the Party against counter-revolutionaries.

And a couple of times the dog had got loose when its lunging charges had ripped the handle off the door. Terrified, tenants had barely managed to make it inside their own apartments ahead of those slashing fangs.

But now, as I sat there in the middle of transcribing those microdots, I reached into my coat pocket and removed the poison pill Anatoly had reluctantly yielded. The partner to the one that had killed Ivchenkov. I stared at that pill, and eventually I began to smile. I went over to the door, opened it, and peered down the hallway at that snarling man-eater.

"Nice doggie," I said.

I went to the kitchen and removed the solitary piece of

meat from the refrigerator. Using the hand grinder, I made three little meatballs, and in the centre of one of them I inserted that pill. Then I ventured out into the hallway, leaving our door open just in case the dog broke loose and came after me.

The closer I got, the more the dog snarled and lunged. When I threw the first of the meatballs, the dog caught it in midair and swallowed it in one gulp. The second meatball also created only the smallest interruption in all that barking. And then the big moment. I held the third meatball, the one with the pill in the middle. I was determined to aim it perfectly.

"Three strikes and you're out, Fido," I whispered at those lunging fangs. Suddenly I knew how the mighty Carl Erskine must have felt pitching against those New York Yankees.

I threw it. With one snarling gulp it disappeared. I almost cheered. I stood there and waited for the inevitable. I had heard stories about the victim's leg shooting out from under him as if he was poleaxed. I wondered if all four legs of this beast would suddenly fly out in mid bark.

I decided to time it. Twenty minutes later I was still waiting.

Why wasn't that stupid dog dead?

26

The dog barked all night.

I lay there with the pillow over my head, trying to block out the noise, and wondering what had gone wrong with those famous pills. The elephant killers. My mind was running away with its own thoughts, each one more crazy than the last. Could Anatoly have made a mistake and given me the wrong pill? But that was impossible. Their strange rectangular shape and mottled white colouring made them impossible to confuse with anything else. But how could one pill kill Ivchenkov and the other have no effect on that stupid dog? Could someone have switched the pill on Anatoly?

Or could Anatoly have . . . ?

Don't be ridiculous, I told myself. Anatoly is my friend. He had no reason to invent the story. Or to give me a harmless pill, hoping I would think it was the same as the one with which he had poisoned Ivchenkov. Supposedly in order to save me. Anatoly was incapable of such scheming.

Wasn't he?

And why would he want to do such a thing? I suddenly remembered my burst of truthfulness, telling him all about my little Yagoda Enterprises, and about Sam. Just twenty-four hours earlier I had been so proud and so relieved to have finally trusted someone. With my life! I sat bolt upright in bed, reliving all those admissions compressed into that one instant of fear.

That barking dog kept reminding me that I was getting careless. Years ago in New York, before I had really become serious about Yagoda Enterprises, I had sat myself down as calmly as I could and told myself that since I was now doing something not strictly legal in the eyes of Comrades Marx, Lenin, Stalin, et al., I had better do it well. It took very little research or thought to figure out what every policeman knows: the most unsolvable crimes are those where only one person is involved in the offence. One very careful, very close-mouthed person. Once others knew about the crime, no matter how friendly they were, the chances of getting caught increased by a logarithmic progression of blunders. Anything could happen. A casual, careless remark overheard by the wrong people. Bragging about a friend. Momentary anger and hasty words.

I had started out so carefully with only Sam knowing, which of course was unavoidable. But now I had included Anatoly. Not to mention Katya — who of course had included herself.

I looked over at her, sleeping as if the only sounds to be heard were the gentle ocean winds caressing the open shutters in whatever Montego Bay mansion her dreams were allowing her to buy tonight. (Montego Bay had replaced Miami Beach, which in turn had replaced Acapulco several years earlier.) While I lay there listening to that damn dog howl.

Finally I got up and crept into the other room. I took out the Los Angeles Dodgers postcard and went to work on the last microdot, the stop at the end of *Lavrenti to you, pal*. Before the first wedge of light appeared behind the neighbouring apartments, I had finished the task. Transcribed in my own writing, Lavrenti's message lay on the desk in front of me. And I wondered if it was cold outside, or if it was just me. His message read:

> *Way to go, Dimitri! You figured it out. I knew you would. Must be wondering about your friend now, huh? With just one of his little pills Ivchenkov bites the dust.*

245

What a guy! But a little word of advice, Dimi — don't ever, ever trust friends. They just get you into the worst trouble. I should know, shouldn't I? Just a little friendly advice, pal.

So when are you coming back? Don't think you'll escape me by staying over in the Workers' Paradise. If I have to chase you across Siberia, I swear to God (we capitalize it) that I'll find a way to do it. And if necessary my sons will hunt your sons. And their sons — well, you get the idea. You're very important to me. You know that? You're the last surviving heir of those who put me in the Village. The reunion is almost complete, pal. See you soon . . . L

What was the image and what was the mirror? That Anatoly should be trusted after all? But who was Lavrenti to tell me who to trust? Anatoly was my friend and that was that. But the *Village*? I had no idea what he was talking about. "Reunion?"

I phoned my father.

I arranged the tickets for my parents to stay with us that weekend. As always, it was a joyous reunion filled with crushing hugs, laughing stories of former neighbours, endless toasts, and, of course, photographs of Natasha and her family. My little sister, already thickening rapidly behind that heavy dress, her face widening below those tired eyes that stared out from the photo with her three children and her pompous-looking husband. He looked as if he was practising his pose for the official photographs taken by the Party District Council. His eyes were two dead spots of blackness. I felt sorry for my sister.

My father had lost none of his fire and exuberance. He roared toasts across the table as quickly as my mother could yell at him for making a scene. Those fierce, scheming eyes still sparkled, and once I caught him staring voraciously at Katya's rear end as she leaned over the table beside him clearing away dishes. He saw me watching him, and his face broke into a broad, evil grin as he wagged his finger at me. By the end of the evening that red nose of his glowed with the fuel of fine vodka, and that wiry white haystack that now passed for a moustache flew in several directions at once.

If the rest of us had not been exhausted, he would have stayed up and talked all night. We went to bed, leaving him muttering about the abysmal lack of stamina of all those present, while my mother tried to hush him up and whispered to him twice to go to the bathroom before he came to bed.

It was the first night in a week that that damn dog was silent. He was smarter than I thought. There was no way he could compete with my father's snoring.

The next morning the two of us walked over to Kalinsky Prospekt, the wide new street lined with high-rise apartments and offices. My father looked at it distastefully, declaring that so far none of the towns in his district had been foolish enough to make people live in places like that. Where would you grow the turnips? And what if a plane hit the top floor? The modern ways were definitely not for my father.

"I need some information," I said as we turned onto a quieter street.

"Of course you do, you young whelp. When else do you invite your aged father up to see you?" The glint of the crafty gypsy danced from the corner of his eye. It had become almost a ritual way of starting any discussions between us.

"It's serious. Someone is trying to kill me."

"So? What's the problem? Kill him first."

"It's not that simple."

"Bah! Of course it it. That's the trouble with your milk-fed generation. You make everything complicated.

For us everything was clear. We drank, screwed, followed Stalin's orders, and schemed to shoot one another."

"And lived in terror."

"Fear is good for you. Keeps you alert. You don't even know what it is."

"I remember watching you the night before you shot Lavrenti's parents. You didn't look like you enjoyed all that fear."

"Well, of course not!" he roared. "You idiots had given him all he needed to have me shot. My own sons!"

"I need to know more about what happened that day."

"Your father saved his own skin and those of his two informer sons. That's what happened." He grinned at me and walked over to a small cluster of wildflowers sprouting defiantly amid the concrete that had encroached on their domain. "What lovely little flowers," he said. "You know, I always wanted to have a flower garden. I'm serious. When you were little, I planted seeds for three years in a row. But then I'd forget where I planted them and walk over them with my boots. Oh, how your mother used to yell at me for that."

It was his way of trying to change the subject. "So tell me what happened to Lavrenti."

"It's none of your business."

"It is. He's the one who's trying to kill me."

"*Still?* This is the longest unconsummated murder since Rasputin. Just shoot him before he does it to you."

"It's not that easy anymore. Things have changed."

"Dreamer!" he roared. "All the wolves are just too well fed now. Just you wait."

"What does Lavrenti mean when he talks about the Village?"

"Village? What Village? Don't talk nonsense." His irritation this time was real and not just for effect. We came to a small park, an oasis of grass in the midst of the high-rise apartments. Because it was a weekend, the park was filled with parents playing with their children. We sat down on a bench and my father stared blankly into the commotion of young children swirling around us. For several minutes he said nothing.

Then he looked off into the distance and said, "Funny, I'd forgotten all about the Village."

"What was it?"

"It was a labour camp. The one where Lavrenti was sent. The strange thing about it was that it was run by an academician. In those days the country was suffering from a lot of things, and one of them was the idiots who wrote learned papers proving scientifically that Stalin was superior in everything from the smell of his shit to the shine of his shoes. The universities were filled with these fawning frauds. And the problem was that a few of those academicians were turned loose on the citizenry. One of them insisted he knew how to grow a new kind of wheat, so Stalin gave him the whole country to play with. Millions starved in the famines that resulted when the wheat wouldn't grow. And another was this one who somehow convinced Stalin that mass suffering could be measured scientifically. And that it was possible to predict exactly when the masses would finally revolt. Since Stalin was obsessed with the people someday rising up against him, he gave this old fraud a labour camp to play with. Nobody paid much attention to it. When you needed fishermen's boots to walk through the blood in the Ukraine and the country was filled with labour camps, who had time to notice such a thing? But that's what became known as the Village."

"Where's the academician now? Is he still alive?"

"I think so. I heard he lives here in Moscow, but he must be at least ninety."

"What's his name?"

"Ivchenkov . . . What's the matter? Do you know him?"

27

Academician Ivchenkov was now Pensioner Ivchenkov. He was eighty-two years old, went for a long walk every day, and laboured each afternoon on completing the findings of his experiments in the Village. He was a thin little man with wiry grey hair and sharp features. His grey eyes looked out from behind rimless glasses at a world he felt had not recognized his genius. Only the broken veins in his face bore any physical resemblance to what I remembered his son looking like.

He lived in one tiny room of a large old apartment building, sharing a kitchen and bathroom with five families. His room was piled with old books, yellowing academic journals, and bulging files of newspaper clippings. The walls were almost entirely covered with huge charts and graphs that he had meticulously drawn himself. He was pleased to have company for the first time in years and wanted to make sure that I understood the significance of his work. I sat on a pile of books drinking weak tea as he thrust old pamphlets and papers at me.

"Stalin was thrilled with my work," he said, smiling. "No one else had ever thought of scientifically measuring the human-suffering potential of different groups. And if you can tell how warm it is by looking at a thermometer, you should be able to tell when the population *perceives* itself to be suffering. Because that's when the revolts start."

"Of course."

"So we gradually increased the suffering in the Village. Measuring it very scientifically. So many points for a beating, so many for lack of food, and so forth. There were emotional factors too, like having someone in the family shot. If I recall, we gave that seven points on the scale. You understand that this was all in the interests of the state."

"Of course." He sat under the single light bulb that hung above his desk, becoming more impassioned as the memories came back.

"I ran it just like a normal town. It was the perfect laboratory experiment. There was nothing that we could not scientifically control and measure. Nothing and no one got in or out without being part of the experimental plan. And see! We proved it!" he said, leaping to his feet and hurrying over to the largest chart, which covered one entire wall.

At the top of the chart, with a score of 221.4, were *Aztec Slaves under Montezuma*. Below them, with 214.6, were *Roman Galley Slaves*, followed by *Russian Peasants* with 209.6.

"You see!" he exclaimed triumphantly. "No other living group can withstand hardship like our own people. And it's all perfectly scientific. Of course, for the Aztec, Roman, and other slaves I had to rely on published accounts of their lives."

I looked at the chart more carefully. It kept going, through *Plantation Slaves* and *Chinese Coolies* all the way down to the bottom groups, which were *Sopranos* with 70.9; *Second Sons of English Upper Class* with 65.8; something marked simply *Rich Suburbs* with 61.7; *French Intellectuals* with 46.5; and tied for last place were *Freudians* and *Former Royalty* with 42.3.

"The Aztec slaves won easily because of Montezuma's live sacrifices, when thousands of them at a time had their hearts cut out of their bodies while they were still alive," he said.

"Tough competition," I said, and he nodded sombrely.

251

I listened to other theories and looked at more of his charts until it was almost time for me to go. Then I asked him if he remembered a boy at the Village named Lavrenti. His face changed in an instant.

"Him!" He snarled and began rummaging through a pile of old photographs before shoving one of them in front of me. It was a picture of Lavrenti looking fifteen years old, standing in front of a row of mud houses, defiantly sticking his tongue out at a much younger Academician Ivchenkov, while a guard ran up towards him with a club. "Utterly disrespectful young savage," he said. "No manners at all."

He kept delving through other piles of photographs and removed two of them. The first one he showed me looked like a police photograph of his son, my former boss in New York, lying face down in that Danish pastry. In the background, various police officers and ambulance attendants could be seen moving around the coffee shop. "And now look at this!" said the old man bitterly, thrusting the second photograph in front of me.

It was a photograph obviously taken only seconds after the previous one, from the identical angle. But in this photograph, Lavrenti was clearly seen smiling into the camera as the lifeless, jam-covered face of Ivchenkov Jr. was being raised up from its resting place. "There was a letter that arrived separately but on the same day. It's from him. Who else?" He turned his attention to another musty pile of papers, from which he removed an envelope bearing the imprint of the Waldorf-Astoria Hotel. The letter inside was also on the hotel's stationery, and on it was the typed message: *Seven points! Just a little souvenir from the graduating class (total: one) of your Village.*

"He knew my son was the pride of my life," said the old man, shaking his head stiffly. I wondered if my father had indicated similar sentiments about me. "I gave this information to the authorities, but they did nothing about it. I think my experiments are something they have no wish to publicize in the slightest way, now that the late Comrade Stalin is no longer in such favour with the new leaders."

I stood up to go. I didn't know whether it was the stale air in his room or just the feeling of being closed in by all those papers, but I suddenly needed to get out of there. Before I left, I remembered what I had intended to ask him — about how Lavrenti escaped from the Village with thousands of others when the Nazis overran that part of Russia.

He interrupted me. "The Germans never overran my Village," he said almost indignantly. "They were stopped forty kilometres south of us."

"Then how did he escape?" I asked, trying to remember what I had read in that file on Lavrenti in New York.

"A mystery. To this day I don't know," said Pensioner Ivchenkov, looking very troubled. "I blamed myself for his escape. I was too lenient, I suppose. After all, I found the way to terrify him into complete submission. And I didn't use it."

"What way?"

"Why, his glasses, of course," he said, almost surprised that I didn't know. "If you take those big, thick glasses of his away from him, he's almost blind. He panics. It's the only time he's not in control of his surroundings, and it terrifies him. I should definitely have taken his glasses away from him." He shook his head sadly. "You know that out of four thousand three hundred and sixty-four people, there were only four that were ever foolish enough to try. Three died before they got a thousand metres away. And only *he* escaped. But you can see that with such a large statistical sample to work with, the coefficient of error is still well within acceptable limits — even losing those four."

He looked down at the photograph of his dead, jam-faced son, and shook his head bitterly.

"What kind of person would do a thing like that?"

28

There were many things I was no longer sure of. Like who had really killed Ivchenkov. And why the dog didn't die. And why I remembered so clearly reading in some file that Lavrenti had escaped only because the Germans overran the prison camp.

And Anatoly, my friend. *My friend?*

But, as usual in my life, these uncertainties were balanced out by elements of impeccable clarity. I knew, for instance, that staying in Moscow was no protection against Lavrenti. If he wanted to, he would find a way to get at me, just as if I were still in New York. And I also knew that any day now I would find myself confronting the bulging eyes of that old man with the froglike face. Rumours of his promotion to a position of power within the bureaucracy had increased greatly since a recent favourable mention of his name in *Pravda*.

In both cases, Moscow was no longer the refuge it once seemed to be. For a while I wondered about getting transferred to remote places like Murmansk or Vladivostok, but I quickly realized that Katya would rebel at even the mention of such a scheme. Besides, the words *If I have to chase you across Siberia* kept echoing in my head.

One day the answer was suddenly thrust in front of me almost by accident. It left no room for uncertainties, and my life was changed forever.

My job at that time was to read the newspapers of Enemy Number One, looking for reporters whose articles seemed to favour us in any way at all. We would then study their reporting carefully and classify them as either *Potentials* or *Useful Idiots* in our vast computer bank of names of Enemy Number One's citizens. An important part of this job was to go to official functions where the Moscow-based reporters from Enemy Number One would be working. The more of them I could get to know the better. So one evening I was sitting in the third balcony of the Bolshoi Theatre, peering out over all that red plushness at yet another performance of *Swan Lake*, while the usual contingent of reporters fidgeted below me and the visiting Washington politicians stared glassy-eyed at the ballet dancers. I did my usual mental checklist, and most of the heavyweights were accounted for. The *New York Times*. CBS. The *Washington Post*. *Reuters*. *UPI*. Among others. But suddenly I sat bolt upright and peered into the gloom, not quite believing my own eyes. At the interval I raced down the stairs into the lobby so I could be at the doors when the reporters emerged.

I found myself staring at Lou Swackhammer, the reporter at Harry's funeral.

I hardly recognized him. He was still short, of course, but his ears no longer stuck out, his hair was longer, and he had lost his Brooklyn accent. I walked up to him. "Mr. Swackhammer?" I said.

One of the other reporters he was with began laughing, and a flicker of embarrassment shot across his face. "It's Hammer," he said irritably, grasping me by the elbow and steering me away from the other reporters. "Louis Hammer. What can I do for you?"

"We know each other." His dark eyes scanned my face and showed nothing. "From your days at the *New York Post*."

"Ah, yes, of course. I remember now," he said, but we both knew he didn't. "Sure, and you're . . ."

"Dimitri."

"Dimitri! Of course. Look, Dimitri, things have changed since our last encounter. Just make sure you remember it's Hammer, huh? Now then, what brings you here?"

More than his name had changed. Swackhammer was now one of the top network television correspondents in Washington. His natural state of seething tension was overlaid with a carefully manufactured sense of tranquillity and an uneasy smile that was supposed to soften up potential interview subjects or information sources. Of which I was one. After the ballet, he met me in the lobby again and this time greeted me like a long-lost friend. "Dimitri!" he said. "What say we go out on the town?" Which is what we did. And by the time we reached a restaurant over near Kalinsky Prospekt, we were both smiling and pumping each for information in the name of our old nonexistent friendship.

Even after several drinks, I found it strange that he never asked where we had met before. He seemed to have wiped his Swackhammer days out of his professional memory. It was difficult talking to him because he seemed to get bored with any topics of conversation that lasted more than a few minutes. And he kept staring over my shoulder as we talked. Actually, we yelled, because the eight-piece band was playing at full volume in that crowded restaurant. It was almost impossible to talk normally, so we spent the evening bellowing at each other and trying to harangue the usual surly Moscow waiters into serving us.

This was Swackhammer's first time in Russia, and after spending a week touring with the Washington political delegations he had formed a lot of theories about how the country worked. He was amazingly certain of his theories.

"What's going on in the Kremlin?" he asked me after ordering more drinks.

"What are you talking about?"

"Ah, come on, Dimitri. For old times' sake. Look, I've got two minutes to fill tomorrow. There's gotta be

257

something you can tell me about what's going on in the Kremlin. Scandals. Bribery. Anything. I won't even use your name. I'll just call you a source close to the Kremlin."

At first I thought he was joking. "I don't know what's going on in the Kremlin," I said.

"Dimitri, it's between friends!" he yelled with great passion, his dark eyes darting across me, searching for a place to rest. "Hell, if you come to Washington I'll turn you on to a thousand clerks who can tell you what time the President takes a dump."

I just shook my head. What could I tell him? He began to realize that I really was of no use to him. He sat back and stared at me as if he had been betrayed. Instantly he lost all interest in dinner. He looked at his watch, and ten minutes later we were in the taxi riding back to his hotel. Conversation was difficult because his mind was already somewhere else, but this time it was me who did the probing.

"What other stories are you working on?"

"Oh, the usual Washington stuff," he said as the taxi roared past the entrance to Red Square.

"Like what?"

"Just the usual," he said, with a smile that told me I was asking for something for nothing. But just to be polite he said, "You know, all the normal political stuff. And also a couple of oddball stories, like the one on the rise of Yagoda."

Yagoda? *Yagoda!*

"What Yagoda?" I almost pinned him to the seat, grasping his arm as the taxi pulled up to the Metropole Hotel. But he was in a hurry to get out.

"You know. Yagoda. The company," he said. "Look, if you get to the States, we'll have lunch." He slammed the car door and hurried into the hotel. I jumped out of the taxi and ran after him, but the driver pounded on his

258

horn and yelled that I was a thief for not paying him. One of the militiamen standing near the hotel reached out and grabbed me. The driver and I yelled insults at each other until I hurled four roubles at him and rushed inside the hotel. Swackhammer had disappeared into the elevators.

I stayed awake most of that night. *Yagoda?* A few minutes before 6:00 A.M., I was standing in the cold darkness, waiting for the Kutuzovskaya metro station to open and watching the eastern sky for any faint trace of light that might make me feel warm. Before anyone else arrived at work, I was already reading the business sections of the old newspapers from Enemy Number One. Because I was one of the few people in Moscow allowed to read those newspapers, it was not unusual that I should be working alone in the restricted area. *Los Angeles Times. Chicago Tribune. Buffalo Courier Express. Miami Herald.* The piles were endless. By midmorning, when two researchers from our department came into the area, I had already read through four of those huge piles of papers. And I was still there when the researchers went home for the evening. My eyes stung, and I had to massage my neck with whichever hand was not turning the pages.

My mind began to drift. I wondered if Swackhammer was playing some kind of game. Could he know? But that one word *Yagoda* shimmered in my mind like a mirage. I had no choice. I had to go on.

By eight o'clock I had passed from hunger into a kind of numb exhaustion. I was labouring through the pages of the *Memphis Commercial Appeal* when my eye darted to an obscure single-column headline on a tiny article buried in the back pages. YAGODA OFFICIALS SEEK SITE IN STATE. I seized that page, my heart pounding. *My* Yagoda? . . . *searching for a site in Tennessee for one of their new aluminium division plants. In keeping with the company's low-profile policy, board chairman Sam Smith said . . .*

It was!

My thoughts suddenly bunched into one baying, howling pack, chasing themselves senseless around that little piece of black print. I let out a yell of joy and laughter and threw the newspaper into the air.

The meaning of it all was joyously obvious: I would return to New York.

I had to. It was a compulsion. For years I had tried to shut my little Yagoda Enterprises out of my mind, and failed. But now, after this, I was like a mother suddenly glimpsing a photo of the child she had been forced to put up for adoption years ago when she was very young. I simply had to go back and see it with my own eyes. That night I began making plans. All the original problems of returning were still there. Especially Lavrenti.

But the biggest obstacle was to convince the old men in the Kremlin that I had suddenly regained my genius for devising ways to speed the demise of Enemy Number One. This was personally very difficult, because of the vow I had made never to use my skills for this purpose again. But I began convincing myself that it was my duty to go back to New York. After all, other Russians were being sent over there and were doing a reasonably devastating job. So staying in Moscow was fine for my conscience but useless for helping Enemy Number One. Unless I was there, how could I get the citizenry to defend themselves?

For days I hardly slept, working far into the night, studying whatever secret police or ministry documents I could get my hands on. Within a week I had refined the approach I would take. I made the first of my phone calls to the offices of the old men in the Kremlin. I was hoping they would still remember me, the one they had urged to work for them years ago. Three of them remembered; two did not. That was enough. I was invited over to see those three, and every meeting was the same bemused, almost cynical encounter. Those old men looked at me as if I was some bureaucratic Rip Van Winkle who had just emerged from the forests. I could tell they were sifting my words carefully, searching for signs of the irrational. I had to be both careful and daring. I knew I only had one chance to get back to New York.

So I stood in front of them and said:

"It is a mistake for us to try to destroy Enemy Number One ourselves. In this case destruction is best carried out by the victim itself. The conditions now exist in Enemy Number One for us to encourage them to bring about their own demise faster than anything we could ever do. Our most crucial task is simply to assist them in smashing their own centre, breaking down that core that holds them together, attacking all those who give hope until they are certain of nothing about themselves. And when the centre no longer holds, and they are wallowing in confusion and self-doubt, our opportunity will have arrived.

"To seize it, we have only to confront that truly strange phenomenon of theirs known as public opinion. It has become the way they govern. It is the oracle to whose lights their leaders nervously hold up the maps, as they chart their course. But if we seize the mechanisms of this massive force and turn it around in the night without their knowing what has happened, it can be made to rule them instead of the other way around. If we succeed, their public opinion will come to reflect *our* wishes and not their own. The doubts and confusion will be awesome, as the messenger becomes the master. It will be too late when the problem is finally understood. By then they will have been softened and paralysed forever."

And that was all I said.

One by one, the old men raised their eyebrows. Their faces were like masks. Yet each of them reached for a pen and wrote quickly. Then came the questions. Were there ways of putting all these ideas into practice? I reached into my briefcase, removing thick proposals. There were polite nods of approval. A few days later there were phone calls and then more meetings. Sometimes with a dozen people present and sometimes with only one of the old men. And finally, the call came.

I was told that I would now be working for the Institute.

It was like being accepted into some holy order. The Institute was filled with some of the finest minds in all the Russias, who laboured brilliantly towards the primary aim of destroying Enemy Number One and the secondary aim of denying any such attempt was being made. I must say that from a theoretical standpoint, the Institute was an exhilarating place to work. Unlike years ago, I really felt the competition from the ideas of my co-workers. In fact, at first I panicked, wondering if I could come up to their standards. Some of the work was truly fascinating. One small department was studying how Rome fell when it ceased to be populated by Romans and then devising scenarios that would swamp Enemy Number One with millions of illegal aliens. Others were analysing the collapse of their religious beliefs and how it weakened their ability to fight. Someone else was working on the strategy that all negotiations should really be just an extension of warfare, while other departments were looking at what lessons could be learned from how Chinese society was destroyed by drugs in the nineteenth century, or ways we might encourage Mexico to demand the return of California and Texas, which had been stolen from them in past centuries. Some of the work at the Institute was more offbeat, even bizarre, like the one that measured the correlation of Enemy Number One's national self-confidence and the design of its cars. (Tail fins, convertibles, and lots of chrome mean war. Imitations of foreign designs mean they're vulnerable.)

Of course, it was never pointed out that most of their

problems, like racial differences, loss of faith, and historical border disputes, were also our own problems. It was a case of one shaky empire trying to get its enemy to crumble faster than it was itself.

It took me less than a year at the Institute to really make my mark. My work on public opinion soon reached up into the higher levels of the Kremlin. Soon others were using my analogy of Enemy Number One as a huge choir where a few well-placed voices singing slightly off-key could completely change the concert.

And finally, one afternoon, one of the old men from the Kremlin came to the Institute. He sank into an armchair in the Director's office, stared into the pale early-afternoon light, and said to me, "I presume you would not mind going back to New York?"

Enemy Number One
New York City (Again)

29

I stood there staring numbly at the huge stainless-steel letter *Y* that hung above the entrance to the building. The Yagoda Building. On Park Avenue.

I had never, ever, imagined anything like this.

Just to make sure that I really did have the right address, I ran back inside the telephone booth on the street corner and thumbed through the ragged phone book. Perhaps my exhaustion was playing tricks on me. It was not even twenty-four hours since we landed on the Aeroflot flight from Moscow, and in the blending of day and night my mind was still eight time zones behind, scrambling to catch up with the confusion and the noise of that New York street corner. I wanted to pull the glass of the phone booth around me and shut out that barrage of colours. It was as if the street itself was moving, with the yellow of the taxis fusing into one long stream that was constantly clipped by those rushing bodies that threw themselves past my little refuge in that phone booth.

Twice I had phoned the number listed in the book, and each time I had hung up in fear when the operator answered "Yagoda." What would I say after all these years? Suppose Sam never wanted to hear from me again? After all, I had left without a word. I dialled a third time and this time forced myself to stay on the line. I had no more dimes, only kopeks. Each time, a different voice came on the phone and asked me very politely what it was I wished to talk to Mr. Smith about. Suddenly one of them was interrupted by another, exuberant voice. "Dimitri? Don't tell me!"

"Sam?"

Less than a minute later I ran like a schoolchild across a playing field. I had to restrain myself, to make myself calm down as I went through brass revolving doors into a glass and marble lobby the size of a small cathedral. Another huge letter *Y*, this one chrome-plated, was mounted on one of the marble walls. For a moment I just stared in awe. All around me people were hurrying, most of them following invisible paths to or from the elevators. At first I got on the wrong elevator, the one that only went to the thirty-third floor. When I finally reached the top floor, Sam was waiting for me. He was as excited as I was. I almost leapt off the elevator into the carpeted, softly lit opulence of the seventy-fourth floor. We shook hands, and then I embraced him in true Russian style. Sam still had the same boyish-looking intensity that I remembered him for. Only now it was an older boyishness. His hair was fashionably longer and still as blond, maybe more so because there was no longer any greasy hair oil on it. But the oversized white shirts and the wing-tip shoes could have been bought decades ago. "I always knew you'd show up again." He smiled. "But tell me, where have you been for God's sake?"

When I started to answer in my usual evasive way, he laughed and said, "Forget it. I'm sorry I asked. Nice to see nothing's changed."

He wanted to introduce me to other people — "Your staff," as he called them — but I politely declined, saying that the same ground rules applied now as in the old days. I just didn't want anyone knowing I was involved. Sam grinned and rolled his eyes. "You're the boss," he said. He escorted me into an office with a large desk, big couches, and a coffee table. I'd never seen furnishings as luxurious as this before. "This is your office," said Sam. I realized he wasn't kidding, and I burst out laughing. "Didn't I tell you I knew you'd be back?" he said. From the windows I could see for miles, across both the

Hudson and the East rivers. I walked around the office like a cat in unfamiliar territory, and only when Sam urged me to did I sit carefully behind the desk in the black leather chair. On the desk in front of me were phones with buttons marked *London*, *Tokyo*, *Frankfurt*, *Toronto*, *Rio*. I swivelled slowly around in the chair and stopped when I was staring down at that huge blossoming patch of green in the midst of all the Manhattan concrete.

An hour later I was sitting in the twilight haze of Central Park, eating peanuts from a paper bag and pondering my new secret status as a tycoon, or whatever they called it. I was still too dazed and excited to know what to make of it all.

Me, a boy from the steppes. I could even see the top of *my* building through the trees. I laughed out loud. I did. I actually sat there alone, slapping my thighs and laughing.

A passing mounted policeman stopped and asked me if I was crazy. I was embarrassed and started to make up a reason for laughing to myself when he interrupted. "I ain't interested in your sense of humour, Mac. Don't you know no one comes in this park after dark? Unless you're looking to get knifed, robbed, or screwed." I couldn't believe it. My beloved Central Park? I hurried over to Fifth Avenue, wondering what other changes had come over New York in my absence. Just walking on the streets, I could sense a whiff of anarchy, a tinge of madness, that was not there when I left years ago. You could almost reach out and touch it. Its energy frightened and excited me at the same time. With every block I walked, my mind was tuning to a higher pitch, and by Fifty-seventh Street my exhaustion had fallen away and I was striding briskly with those early-evening crowds. I was thrilled to be back.

I walked into several bars and began cheering for whoever was playing against those terrible New York Yankees. In the third place I went, I found kindred spirits, old-timers who still remembered the days of the Brooklyn Dodgers. We all got drunk together cheering the memories of the mighty Pee Wee Reese and booing the Yankees on the television screen. I felt at home.

By the time I got back to the embassy, with all its guards and surveillance cameras, I was in a good mood. I had stopped off in some store that sold everything from cameras to rugs. It was so bright I thought I was in a neon blizzard as I groped to buy Katya a silk scarf — a sort of peace offering. A tiny banner of marital truce thrust into the winds of the gathering storm. Katya had been even more excited than I was about returning. Her reasons were as obvious as they were unspoken. Within half an hour after our arrival, she was off to the stores on Fifth Avenue, just to stand in front of their huge display windows, breathing in the vapours of that opulence.

I went back to our apartment at the embassy feeling that my life was indeed a bed of roses, as they say. Even the apartment we had been given was superb — number 31, the corner one that so many others within the embassy had wanted. It was one of those signs of status that counted for so much in that world. I opened the door and tiptoed inside the apartment, not wanting to wake Katya. All the lights were out except for a faint glow from the bathroom. I crept towards the bedroom holding the scarf, wondering if perhaps I should have spent a few more dollars on the pure silk version. Suddenly I tripped over something. In the faint light I could make out the shape of a large shopping bag. On the side it said Bloomingdale's. Beside it was another large bag that said Henri Bendel.

I lit a match. The room was filled with shopping bags. From expensive stores. And dresses! They were draped elegantly all over the place. With labels like Christian Dior. Halston. Balenciaga. The match singed my fingers.

Katya was sound asleep when I burst into the bedroom,

tripping over yet another pile of shiny shopping bags. She looked up sleepily and murmured, "Isn't it wonderful?"

"What," I demanded, "is so wonderful?"

"All that." She yawned. "It's all free."

"Don't be crazy!"

"It is. They gave it all to me just for signing my name with those marvellous little cards." She pointed to the dresser and sank back into the pillow. On the dresser was a pile of credit cards. American Express. Visa. Diners Club. All in Katya's name.

"Where did these come from?"

"Your friend," she said, her voice slurring with sleep. "Whatever his name is. He had them delivered. Said he'd get in touch with you later. He left a note for you. By the way, I saw the Yagoda Building. Nice, isn't it?"

And with that she was asleep, curled up beside the pile of travel magazines with the pages marked. Inside the envelope under the credit cards was a handwritten note.

It said *Welcome back pal. How about lunch sometime?*

30

I tried very hard to get Enemy Number One to save itself.

This time my plan was superbly simple. I would go to the press. After my work in Moscow it was a natural. I would provide them with information that would create a firestorm of controversy across the whole country, rousing the citizens of Enemy Number One to their very ramparts.

So one morning a couple of weeks after I had returned to New York, I sat in a phone booth in Grand Central Station juggling a bag of small change and dialling Swackhammer in Washington. The phone number on his business card turned out to be the network news bureau. My call was transferred to a studio of some kind where Swackhammer came on the line, his voice edgy, even irritable. "Hammer here," he said as other voices boomed out in the background. I told him who was calling. "Who?" he said twice before a quick "Oh, yeah. What's up?"

"I've got some information for you," I said.

"Shoot," he said.

"Not on the phone."

"Is it important?" He still sounded irritable.

"Very."

"Is it worth two minutes on the six o'clock news?"

"It has to do with the fate of the nation."

"You're not answering my question."

"I think so."

"Gimme a hint," he said, becoming a little more friendly.

"It's information I found out in Moscow."

"You mean like the scandal we were talking about that night?"

"Sort of."

"Hold on, fella." He must have clamped his hand across the phone because I could hear only muffled voices. Then he came on the line again. "I'll be in New York on Thursday."

We met in a remote corner of Central Park in the late afternoon. Somehow Swackhammer looked out of place in the park with his Burberry raincoat and his heavy-soled brogues as joggers in brightly coloured sweatsuits circled around us in the paths through the woods. He tried to do a professional job of smiling a lot and putting me at ease while he pumped for information, but he was still the same old Swackhammer, firing off invisible volleys of his own tensions. "So," he said, as we walked towards a clearing. "What's doing?" To the west, the big apartment buildings were becoming silhouettes as the sun descended behind them.

"As you know, I am Russian."

"Right, right."

"So I must insist that nothing I tell you be traced back to me."

"I never betray a source," he said firmly. "Professional ethics, you know. We'd go to jail first before we'd reveal our sources."

"And I will do nothing that will hurt any Russians."

"Goes without saying."

"But I want to help your country. So I am going to tell you what no one else except for a handful of men in Moscow knows. We have moles operating here — your own countrymen secretly working as agents for us. Our people recruited them decades ago as students and now they have risen up to important positions in this country. A year ago, when I was in Moscow, I discovered the identities of two of these moles by going through some files I think I was not supposed to see."

Swackhammer stopped and stared at me, his eyes widening with amazement. "One of these men," I said, "had been recruited by us at Yale, the other at Cambridge University almost thirty years ago while he was doing graduate work there. The Cambridge man comes from a wealthy family, but in his student days he saw us as the way to atone for his family's robber-baron sins. He is now a Wall Street financier with great influence on the money supply of this country. He has been adviser to two of your presidents. His name is —"

"Wait! Wait," Swackhammer said, his face turning suddenly pale. I thought it was because he could already see the headlines forming. I was wrong. What was forming was panic. "Do you realize what you're saying?" he yelled at me.

"Yes. I'm giving you the names of two moles."

"To do what?" He was still yelling.

His question confused me for a moment. "So you can expose them to the whole country," I said.

"For Christ's sake!" he yelled. "We don't persecute people for their political beliefs here."

"But they're working for us as spies. Trying to destroy the nation."

"Well, goddammit, it's a free country!" Now he was beginning to turn very red in the face. Something was terribly wrong with his reaction to my news, and I couldn't quite put it all in focus.

"Why bring me all the way up here to listen to this crap?" he said angrily.

Then I remembered my original reasons for wanting to approach him. "Because of all your talk about patriotism."

"Me? Patriotism?" He seemed aghast.

"Back when you used to be Swackhammer."

"Well, goddammit, it's Hammer now!" he snapped instantly. "Look, fella, you don't realize that was *then*. Things change. You don't go running around acting patriotic now."

"No?" I was getting very confused.

"No. It's just not done now. Unless you're some extremist flag-waver. Maybe in a few years things will change and it'll be okay again. Shit!" he muttered. "You foreigners just can't understand the way things operate in this country, can you? I mean, my God, man, I've got to work here, you know. How the hell do you expect me to walk into any newsroom and hold my head up high if I get involved in this — this *witch-hunting* of yours?"

He just shook his head and glared at me for a moment. "All this way here, and for what? Is this *all* you've got?"

I nodded.

"No scandals?"

I shook my head.

"No dirty stuff that *our* government is doing here? I mean, that's what we're here for, you know. To protect the basic freedoms of this country."

I shook my head again. I didn't know what to say to him.

"Shit," he muttered. Then he turned and walked away. I watched him recede into the gloom of the park, thinking that perhaps I should move on to some other group who could help me save Enemy Number One. Maybe the press was just too difficult for me to figure out.

I hurried across the hills towards the east side of the park. The green of the trees and the grass was darkening, and was broken only by the bright colours of the joggers' outfits as they crisscrossed the park at varying distances from the horizon. They all appeared out of the trees or the small hills and ran huffing and wheezing across the park until they disappeared from sight.

All but one.

I had gone halfway across the park before I realized he was there. A man in a blue sweat suit. Somehow he always managed to stay even with me in spite of the fact he was running and I was only walking. He would disappear behind the hills and then reappear when I had walked a few hundred feet further. He was too far away for me to make out his face, and the trees acted as a kind of shield that blurred what little of him I could see. But it didn't matter. Every alarm bell in my body was madly beating itself to pieces.

Lavrenti.

I had prepared myself as best I could for that moment. Before I arrived in New York, I knew that sooner or later I would have to come face to face with him again. I had decided that I could drive myself crazy worrying about it. Which was probably what he wanted. So, for the sake of my sanity, I had taken the only rational approach possible to such a horrible problem. Which is to say, no approach. I had decided to treat him like a car accident, or cancer, or any of life's other calamities. When they happened, then I would worry about them, but definitely not before.

Now, as I walked faster and then slower, turning to the left and then to the right and never losing that blue sweat-suited shadow for a moment, I cursed myself for being such an idiot. At least I could have stayed out of the park. Or carried a gun. I began to run as that familiar panic swept over me, that fear I had forgotten about for all those years. I looked over my shoulder as I changed course, running straight towards the edge of the park, which was still several hills away. I saw him clearly for an instant, that same owlish face with those heavy glasses and that strange smile that never seemed to leave him, even when he was not smiling.

But in that instant he was definitely smiling. Maybe even laughing, as he dropped to one knee and in the fading light two small bursts of flame flashed from somewhere in front of his face, and the big rock next to me whined as the bullets smashed into it. Even now, I can remember thinking that I was not going to be killed. At least not immediately. If he had wanted to, he could have killed me with those first two bullets, but that was not Lavrenti's style. What he wanted even more than my death was the ultimate revenge of finite terror stretching out mercilessly for as long as he could make it.

Just as his parents must have known in those last few hours.

Scrambling across a small hill, I raced into an area of bushes and trees with an old stone bridge that cut through it. The sun had disappeared from that side of the hill, and everything appeared as shadows in heavy shades of grey. In that breathless jumble of thoughts, my mind seized upon the only defence I had even vaguely contemplated as the words of Pensioner Ivchenkov sent me racing through the underbrush in search of a brick, a rock, a branch, anything to hit him with. I found a branch before Lavrenti came tearing across the top of the hill, and, hiding beside that stone bridge, I tried to make myself stop gasping for breath. I heard him stop. And then move ahead slowly, and then begin to run.

I swung with all my might as he passed, catching him across the shoulders, breaking the branch but stunning him long enough for me to leap out and tear at his glasses. They were held in place by a headband, but I managed to knock them off his head, and in the frantic scramble I kicked them onto the grass. For the first time, it was he who was overcome by panic, and it was awesome. As I knocked his glasses off, he yelled in a crazed kind of bellowing. He lashed out frantically with his hands, grasping my arm with a crushing power that just missed being fatal as my coat tore away, while he swung the small gun like a club. All of his careful plans

277

were instantly consumed in that inferno of panic as he began firing wildly. I flung myself over the edge of the small bridge onto the embankment as the bullets crashed into the stones. Suddenly there was a clicking sound. And then a kind of desperate grunting. I climbed up over the bridge and walked towards Lavrenti, who was now on his hands and knees, the empty gun in one hand, as he searched the ground for his glasses. He could make out at least my shape as I approached him. He rose to his feet. He was terrified.

"Come on, Dimitri. My glasses, damn you. This isn't part of the game." That strange smile was still there. But his voice constricted and his blind stare swept across me.

"The game is changing, Lavrenti. Academician Ivchen-kov sends his regards."

He managed a startled, fleeting laugh. "I'm sure he does, I'm sure he does. Now, Dimitri, my glasses!" He lunged at me, but I easily stepped aside. He fell onto the ground and began feeling quickly across the grass.

"This isn't part of the game, Dimitri!" he said again, his voice cracking. I had never seen him like this before.

Suddenly there was a collective wheezing noise that came from the top of the hill. A group of joggers appeared, and Lavrenti's eyes searched blindly in their direction. He jammed the gun inside his sweat suit. "Help!" he yelled. "I'm being attacked! Robbery!" He rolled over on the ground.

The joggers all bunched up in a tight little herd and kept running on the spot, wheezing and making protective huffing noises, like animals who had just spotted a dangerous predator. "Mugger!" they cried, and one of them blew a whistle that must have been heard all over the park. It took me a second or so to realize that it was me they were calling a mugger. Lavrenti, to his credit, thrashed across the ground as if I had just beaten him nearly senseless.

I dropped the glasses and fled. Running across the next hillside with those accusing cries ringing in my ears, I stopped just for an instant, gasping for breath, and looking back to see the joggers giving Lavrenti his glasses. That was all I needed to see. I ran, literally, for my life. Across the traffic-filled roads that wound through the park, I dodged cars as horns blared and tyres screeched. I reached Fifth Avenue and glanced back at the fearful sight of Lavrenti charging towards me. No longer was he loping casually, like some distant jogger. Now he was charging, tearing madly across the last hill, and even at that distance I could see his eyes through those thick glasses, magnified embers of fury in the near-darkness.

I reached a streetlamp and groped for a piece of paper in my pocket. The address was one I had written that morning, knowing it was not far from Central Park. I raced to the north, cutting across Fifth Avenue again and leaping through the blare of the horns as the relentless slapping sound of Lavrenti's feet hitting the pavement behind me seemed to grow louder.

I heard singing. Young, full voices rising up over the traffic noise, and I knew I was there. I raced up the steps and crashed through the doors of the huge church, lurching breathlessly down the aisle as the hundred voices of the choirboys trailed off into threads of a hymn, and the distinguished-looking man in the clerical collar hurried toward me. He squinted at me, and then a look of astonished recognition came over him.

"Dimitri!" the distinguished-looking man boomed in a resonant, pastoral voice that soared into the rafters of that enormous place.

"Man from the government!" was all I could croak as I sank to my knees in exhaustion and pointed towards the doors as Lavrenti burst into the church.

"Yours?" he asked almost hopefully.

"Yours," I gasped.

"Ours?" bellowed the Reverend Kent Filmore, signalling the hundred choirboys to take up defence positions. "In *my* church?"

31

From the moment the choirboys drove Lavrenti out of the church, I should have known there would be problems with this next scheme of mine.

But even back in Moscow, I had been certain I could get the church to save Enemy Number One. It all seemed so natural to me then. So easy. After all, wasn't the name of their God even emblazoned across their money? So if not the church, then who else?

I had planned to start with the Reverend Kent Filmore, simply because he was the only religious type I knew. And I was sure that in the years since we had buried Harry, he would have mellowed into a nicely pliable pastor.

I was wrong.

Outwardly the Reverend Kent Filmore had proceeded into a respectable middle age, with his now-curly hair framing his still boyish but lined face, with its saintly smile. But inwardly the flames of revolution were fanned nightly by the winds of his own prayers, crying out for social justice in whatever wrathful form the Lord chose to dispense it. He had read his Bible, and he had read his Karl Marx. And decided it was all pretty much the same thing.

Share and share alike.

So he decided it was his duty to lay Christian siege to his own government. His zeal was so pure that I grew embarrassed in his presence. Like a whore listening to a virgin talking about true love. (Nothing embarrasses a professional like the fervour he is supposed to feel but doesn't. Not since the early days of Stalin had there been that kind of revolutionary zeal, and most of those who possessed it had gradually become embarrassments, like guests who stay too long at a party, so they had to be taken out and shot. Now, for most of the pros, it was just a job with a lot of mandatory rhetoric, the occasional parade here and there, and the monotone speeches as you elbowed one another off the bureaucratic ladder on the way up to a *dacha* on the river and a chauffeur-driven Zil.)

But the Reverend Kent Filmore was pouring from the chalice of holy passion. For days, I had to listen to the furious denunciations of his own country's greed and imperialism that rang through his huge church.

I decided to (as Sam would say) cut my losses. I wanted to get away from him as soon as I could. At first I tried subtle discouragement, and told him how we Russians had shot all the priests we could get our hands on in our own revolution. But that didn't work too well. It just made the fire of martyrdom burn in his eyes.

So I stopped going over to his church. That didn't work either. He began phoning me at the embassy, wanting me to give talks to some of the groups at his church. I made excuses as long as I could. One day I came up with what I thought was the perfect solution. I would simply airlift in another Russian poet. That way I could stay in the background, as yet another Alexei enthralled the congregation with revolutionary poetry.

But much to my surprise, the suggestion didn't excite the Reverend Kent Filmore. It seemed that the current batch of Alexeis didn't quite fuel the passions the way the old ones had. I quickly discovered why. Our own revolutionary aura had worn a little thin during my absence from New York. Maybe it was from sending in the tanks to beat down our allies once too often. Or maybe it was because those old bureaucrats in the Kremlin just didn't look like romantic revolutionaries when they were shown propped up in the cold reviewing yet another parade of missiles.

So I dropped the idea of a Russian poet. But one day, almost absent-mindedly, I suggested a Cuban poet or two might do the job.

It was like opening the door of a blast furnace. I felt the searing heat of romance as the Reverend Kent Filmore thrilled to the very idea. It was perfect. The ashes from the Cubans' revolution were still smouldering, and they could dust off no end of raw revolutionaries and send them out to meet the masses with tales of the old days in the mountains. The very sight of these Latins oozed glories in the eyes of those who had merely dreamed of the deed. And because Cuba would have been bankrupt without Russia's money, we almost ran the country behind the scenes.

And a poet is a poet. Cuban or Russian. Who cared, as long as he served the purpose?

But the best part was that Anatoly returned to New York with the Cuban poet. Because of his job working with cultural groups in Havana, it was only natural that he should come too. It was a joyous, bear-hugging, very Russian reunion, and we laughed and told each other lies about how we hadn't changed a bit. Actually I immediately noted the extra weight he had gained, making him more distinctly chubby than ever. And I wondered what he was noticing about me.

But strangely, thankfully, I never thought for an instant of the fears and suspicions about him that had overcome me in Moscow. It was just good to see him again. Once more I felt like I had a brother.

Someone to talk to.

On the night he returned to New York, we found ourselves in the back pew of the Reverend Kent Filmore's church watching our triumphant production like a couple of Broadway producers counting the house on opening night. Right from the moment when the organ thundered and the choir belted out a Bolivian revolutionary song, I could tell that I was in for yet another promotion.

Once again, my backfiring attempts to get Enemy Number One to save itself were going to be the secret of my success with the old men in the Kremlin.

The church was filled and many of the congregation were elegant and genteel revolutionaries with substantial mortgages. My thoughts soared with the music and clicked on my mental projector as I saw wide-screen scenes of terror and confusion on their faces, as they were the first to be lined up against the bloody wall in the early days of this revolution they now wanted.

My father would have understood such images.

Scattered around the pews were the usual quota of diplomats who were really agents waiting to haul in their catch. There was almost a breathless excitement that filled that church. I recognized many familiar faces peering eagerly to catch sight of the Cuban poet. Miriam Nelson was near the front, wearing a mink coat, and Harold Leonard Dawes sat on the aisle, looking somehow frail yet impassioned in an elderly way. All through the church that same old whiff of romance was in the air. A meaning to life itself had been sensed. And decency. A sense of purpose.

Anatoly and I ducked out the back door and went to a bar on Madison Avenue.

We laughed like schoolboys. And we drank endless toasts to our founder, the late, lamented Alexei. Over the noise of the football game on the wide-screen television in the bar, I recited some of my best poems and got upset thinking about how Alexei, that fraud, had taken credit for them. People kept yelling for me to sit down. It was just like old times.

Especially when Anatoly's face began to sag like a melted candle and I knew he was going to announce the latest problems in his love life. "I'm in trouble," he said morosely.

"You're in love," I said.

"Of course. But this time it's serious."

"And she's an artist of some kind. Probably a dancer."

"So? Is it my fault if I admire physical perfection?" He stared down at his own large stomach. "Opposites attract. You've probably heard of her. Ilena Nikolev."

Anatoly was right. He was definitely in trouble.

He had fallen in love with the most recent of the Russian ballerinas to defect to the West. Which made her an Enemy in the eyes of the old men in the Kremlin, who would fling Anatoly into the most remote post in Siberia if they found out about his affair. I suddenly understood why Anatoly had been so anxious to get to New York. Ilena Nikolev was now dancing with one of the big New York companies. I remembered seeing pictures of her when she arrived. The publicity had been so intense that within a week she was almost as well known as Baryshnikov or Rudolf Nureyev. But I still couldn't remember what she looked like. Ballerinas all looked the same to me.

"We met while she was on tour last year," he said. "Even then she knew she was going to defect. The last time she came through Havana we stayed up all one night just talking about it."

"Pretty risky."

"I told you, we're in love. I've been manoeuvring to get back here since that night. I think I'll be here for at least six months now. Hopefully more."

"I thought you wanted to stay away from New York and all the spy business here."

Anatoly's eyes were becoming large and watery, like a hound's. "I do. You know I'm not cut out for all this heavy stuff that goes on here. But I'm in love. I've got no choice."

"Of course not," I said, thinking of all the trouble I

could see looming ahead. "How are you going to meet her? Do you know what they'd do at the embassy if they found out that you were going out with —"

"I don't want to know, I don't want to know!" he interrupted, waving his hand in front of me, the fear showing across his face and the beads of perspiration dribbling down his cheeks.

So we changed the subject and earnestly debated the merits of going back to the church. We really intended to return for the last of the poetry, but we managed to talk ourselves into believing it was too late. It would be almost over, we told ourselves. Much better to show up at Miriam Nelson's party afterwards. So we went to a few more bars on the way, and in one of them I began reciting my own poetry until someone turned on the jukebox to an old Fats Domino record, which was fine with Anatoly because he knew all the lyrics in Russian and sang with the exuberance of someone who wanted to take his mind off his troubles. I sat back and watched him, deciding that in terms of trouble, he was really in the big leagues, as they say in Enemy Number One.

I was touched by how he had trusted me enough to reveal all this. It was a dangerous thing to tell anyone. (Of course, a nagging little voice said, Wait a minute — this could be a trap. Because we were all supposed to report anything like this immediately to our secret police. And more than once someone had been doomed by an act of friendship, by not reporting just such a story, told by a friend who turned out to be working for the secret police. I hated thinking that way, and I cursed that voice. But all that business about the poison pill that was not poison kept haunting me. As did Lavrenti's jeers about friendship.)

After the third Fats Domino record I decided to hell with my fears. I would share my own dangers with Anatoly, my friend.

Maybe it was the vodka. Or maybe it was the old Warner Brothers western movie on the television over the bar, where the two Indian warriors slashed their hands and clasped them together in a ritual that made them blood brothers.

I decided that Anatoly and I should be blood brothers too. Sharing the perils together.

And what greater peril was there than showing him the Yagoda Building?

32

"Lenin is turning over in his tomb."

Anatoly stared up in awe at the Yagoda Building. "Marx will rise up and strike you dead," he yelled over the traffic noise. We were standing on one of the traffic islands in the middle of Park Avenue. Huge buildings loomed all around us, dark slabs in the night with broken beads of light shining from them. Anatoly and I began to laugh as we raised our vodka milkshakes in profane toasts to each other's idiocy. We danced around that island as horns blared and people yelled at us from the passing cars. In that life of keeping so much hidden, of watching every word, my old need just to forget all caution was momentarily enough to obliterate any fears. It was exhilarating to be so gloriously reckless.

We weaved precariously through the traffic, running over to the Yagoda Building, where we stood peering into that cathedral they called a lobby. At the far end, a security guard sat behind a marble desk. "You are a tycoon," said Anatoly, his mouth hanging open. "A capitalist, imperialist hooligan!" he said, laughing out loud. I hushed him up and in a fit of pride announced that I was going inside to get him one of the glossy company brochures that were in the office on the seventy-fourth floor that Sam had said was mine. (Actually, I think I was really just showing off. I wanted to prove to Anatoly that I really could go inside the building.)

Ever since getting back from Moscow, I had been very careful in my dealings with Yagoda. I didn't want to suddenly turn up after all those years and begin interfering with Sam and the normal operations of the company. (Although I did get involved in one thing — the company's annual party. When I heard about it, I began to think of it as my own personal party. I insisted we hire a ballroom at the Plaza Hotel. And a full orchestra! So it would be just as glamorous as those parties I had seen in the pages of *Life*.)

I had decided that before I could ever play any role in the company again, I had to familiarize myself with its operations. So I began to look for ways to go into our offices and get to know the business without attracting any attention. The solution was simple. I would pose as a member of the night-time cleaning staff. Just like I had done years ago in that first tiny office when Sam was hiring people. It was the perfect cover. I could wander through the empty areas of the company at my leisure.

When I told Sam of my plan, he thought I was crazy. He told me I would end up like Howard Hughes, the crazy hermit billionaire who owned half of Las Vegas. I was tempted to tell Sam that I would rather be thought of as a crazy hermit than be a prisoner somewhere in the Russian *gulag*. But I couldn't. So Sam just had to shrug and accept my scheme with his customary head-shaking grin.

As usual, Sam looked after everything, including getting me a locker in the subbasement where I could store my cleaner's outfit and security pass. The first time I descended to that locker room, I found a bottle of champagne and a note in Sam's handwriting that said *Congratulations on working your way to the bottom.*

I left Anatoly outside the building and went inside. A few minutes later I was going up the elevator with an empty garbage bin, wondering if someone from our secret police would be waiting, gun drawn, when the doors opened. I still couldn't get used to the idea of going in there. On the seventy-fourth floor, I entered the carpeted opulence of my office, found one of those glossy brochures, and then sank into that high-backed chair, allowing myself just a moment of swivelling opulence. That chair was like a leather throne.

I stared at all those lights. Below me! And I thought that in my home city, where my parents still lived, the tallest building was the headquarters of the District Soviet — and that was only a few storeys high. I put my feet up on the desk and said to myself, Comrade Businessman, this is the life.

"Get out of here!" said a voice suddenly, shattering my daydreaming. An indignant female voice.

Flustered, I looked over to see a girl — perhaps she was a young woman — out in the corridor. She was wearing a dark green cotton work coat with the emblem of the cleaning company on it. I could see she was very angry.

"Just who do you think you are? Coming in here to the President's office! And putting your feet on his desk!"

I didn't know what to say. Like a schoolboy caught cheating, I retreated with very little style. "Who are you?" was all I could think to ask.

"I clean here," she said, coming closer. She spoke with a slight accent that seemed somehow familiar. She was very young, perhaps in her early or mid-twenties, and pretty. Very pretty. Without any makeup, and her dark hair pulled back behind her head. For a moment I thought I knew her, but then I realized she reminded me a little of Audrey Hepburn in *Breakfast at Tiffany's*. (I must have shown that movie a dozen times to my trainee spies in Moscow. It was pure New York.) Her face had those same round yet delicate features, with wide eyes showing a kind of perpetual astonishment. Or maybe it was amusement. At that moment I wasn't sure.

"You don't look like a cleaning lady," I said, and then suddenly I froze with the realization that I had spoken to her in Russian.

She looked at me surprised and immediately answered,

"I didn't know there was a required look for this job."
She was answering me in Russian. For a moment I didn't
know what to say. Maybe it was her accent in English
that had made me do it. She disappeared into the
corridor.

"Where do you come from?" I called out, running after
her.

"Brooklyn," she said with her back turned to me.

"No. I mean before that."

She turned around with a kind of puzzled smile. No
words. Just that smile. And then she went back to her
work. (I was right. A definite Audrey Hepburn type.)

I kept following her. "What are you doing here?" It
was one of those questions people sometimes ask just to
ward off silence.

"Now, what does it look like I'm doing here?" she
said, becoming impatient. "I'm trying to finish my work
so I can go home. Not sitting with my feet up on
somebody else's desk pretending to be the President."

"Can I take you out for a drink afterwards?"

"No. Thank you anyway."

"Okay, then, a coffee."

She stopped for a moment and I thought, maybe. Just
maybe. But then she went back to her work. "I have
classes in the morning," she said.

"Classes?"

"Yes. Classes," she said very deliberately. And then she
pointed to a pile of cardboard boxes. "Now are you
going to take out that garbage or not?"

What could I do? I took out the garbage. And I decided
I was definitely not handling this tycoon business very
well.

I mean, would Rockefeller have fallen in love with his
cleaning lady?

33

I discovered later that her name was Nina. She had married very young but now lived by herself in a single room in the basement of her aunt and uncle's small house in Brooklyn. She had somehow got out of Russia, learned English, gone back to school at New York University during the days, and worked nights to pay for her tuition.

And in the elevator I could see her face in front of me all the way down to the subbasement. When I got outside I realized I had forgotten the brochure that I went in there for. But so had Anatoly. He looked pale and very nervous as he paced back and forth in front of the Yagoda Building.

"What's the matter with you?"

"Trunks," he said. "I can't stop thinking about those trunks in the basement of the embassy. The ones like they shipped Boris back in."

"Think about something else. Like your ballerina."

"I was. That's why I started thinking about those trunks."

He insisted that we go back to the embassy on our way to Miriam Nelson's. To see if those trunks were still there after all these years. There was no way I could talk him out of it. So we returned to the embassy, looking as sober and solemnly official as possible, and immediately headed down to the room just off the underground parking garage.

Those big trunks were still there. "But where's the other one?" Anatoly said, for some reason talking in a whisper. Overhead a swinging light bulb cast strong moving shadows that made me feel dizzy. "There were three trunks here when we left. And look there," he whispered. On the floor was only the outline, traced in the dust and grime of the decades, of where the third trunk had been. "It's been moved recently," said Anatoly in a small voice that quivered.

"It could have been moved two years ago," I said, trying to reassure him.

"So?" His voice was now a tiny rasping sound. "That's since Viktor took over."

Viktor was the new *rezident*, the man in charge of all spying and secret police work out of New York. In the two years he had been there, he had brought an impressive sense of order and priorities to the chaotic business of spying on Enemy Number One. With his slouching, paunchy appearance, his sagging face and pale, expressionless eyes, he looked like a peasant. Viktor would often laugh and make jokes to show that he was just one of us. But he was as cold as he was brilliant, and he demanded and often got the impossible from his subordinates, who lived in fear of his truly awesome anger.

Viktor loathed me. He saw me as a threat because he did not officially control me. Although Viktor could give me orders on certain sensitive operations, I was really reporting directly back to the old men in the International Department of the Kremlin. And because of my past prestige and success in the field of destroying Enemy Number One, I was considered roughly equal to Viktor, even though I did not have his day-to-day power. To Viktor this was intolerable. I was nothing more than a bureaucratic boil that had to be lanced.

"I wonder who he put in that trunk?" said Anatoly.

I stared at the outline on the floor and tried hard to reassure him. And myself. "Don't be ridiculous," I told him. "They don't put people in trunks anymore."

"Oh yeah? How do you know?"

I didn't. We went to Miriam Nelson's party. For a while just being in that crowded, elegant apartment overlooking my park and talking of interior decorating, city politics, revolution, and the newest restaurants provided enough of a distraction, and I forgot all about the trunks. Miriam Nelson gave me a welcoming kiss, showed me her latest book, and inquired about my father, searching my eyes for clues behind my noncommittal answer. Her face was now deeply lined, and her voice had taken on a brittleness of age that for the first time made her seem a little vulnerable.

Her large apartment was filled with people I remembered from my first time there, years ago, and many others whose names I recognized from reading the New York papers in Moscow. There were slightly dishevelled middle-aged radicals whose natural anger overwhelmed the defensive sensibilities of guests from the more elegant levels of society, and several men whom I had seen in photographs wearing blue jeans and long hair were now dressed like businessmen and were talking earnestly with the Cubans. Harold Leonard Dawes was locked in a conversation with an endlessly admiring woman who wore too much makeup. She was dressed in designer blue jeans, an expensive silk blouse, several large rings, and held a small poodle wearing a rhinestone collar. Occasionally she would talk to the poodle as if it was a child, referring to herself as Mama. Later the Reverend Kent Filmore spoke of her glowingly as a major contributor to many of his causes.

For some reason the Reverend Kent Filmore was beginning to irritate me. Maybe it was because he was a professional saint. I was always suspicious of too much goodness.

Anatoly mixed with almost no one. He spent most of his time beside a telephone in the living room, dialling a number that was obviously engaged. He looked nervous and out of place. When the woman with the poodle went over and sat near him, Anatoly just looked distastefully at the dog, which snapped at his ankles. At first he tried to push the poodle away with his foot when the woman was not looking, but that provoked a head-turning outcry from the dog and much soothing from its mistress. Anatoly became flushed with embarrassment at being singled out by the woman's angry looks, and quickly retreated to his vodka and his phoning. When he got through, his whole face changed and he talked furtively with sparkling eyes for several minutes.

"She still loves me," he said after he hung up. Then he sat staring out at the moving chain of headlights that cut through the black expanse of the park below us. "I've got to do something," he said bleakly.

"Like what?" I was worried someone might overhear him. Our corner of the room was packed with people, and next to Anatoly the woman was throwing pieces of smoked salmon hors d'oeuvres to her poodle.

"I'm not sure yet. I'm thinking about it," he said, staring off into those lights and emptying another glass of vodka. Then he said, "Make me a promise — a vow. Swear on the lives on your unborn children, that if you ever hear they're going to put me in one of those trunks, you'll find me wherever I am and tell me."

"Don't be ridiculous."

"Will you promise?" He was glassy-eyed as he stared at me. Feeling it was useless to talk anymore, I nodded. He reached into his pocket and pulled out a tiny clear-plastic bag with a small, tubular object inside it.

"Another pill?" I whispered in amazement.

"First I'd try to escape. But if I couldn't, then I'd take the pill. You're dead by the time you hit the ground."

"I thought you had only two of those."

"I did. But when I knew I would be coming back here, I started worrying about what would happen if they found out about me and Ilena. And I just go to pieces even thinking about that trunk. I get fits of horrible claustrophobia in my sleep, and I wake up in the night crying out, dreaming that I'm locked inside. The only way I could stop those dreams was to steal another pill from the Department V guy in Mexico City three weeks ago."

I stared at that pill. It was identical to the one I had made him give me back in Moscow.

"I'm not going to give you this one," he said, closing his pudgy hand slowly around the pill. By now he was fairly drunk, but his words were spoken with a heavy precision, just to make sure I understood.

I stared out of the window for a moment, surrounded by the commotion of the party, wondering what I should say. All my suspicions were suddenly rebounding back on themselves, mirror images of what I had felt that night in Moscow lying awake listening to the dog barking in the hallway. Was this business with the pills some kind of macabre trick being played on Anatoly? Or by him?

Finally, I decided that if it was my brother Yuri who had been alive and sitting there, I would tell him. "Something has been bothering me for a long time," I said.

So I told him about the other pill. And how his story about killing Ivchenkov for my sake had suddenly seemed very suspect. Anatoly sat listening to me glassy-eyed and open-mouthed. His reaction was not quite what I expected. He began to grin. "Terrific!" he exclaimed. "That means I'm not a murderer. If the pill I gave to you in Moscow didn't work, then the one I put into his coffee couldn't have worked either. That means he died from a normal, everyday heart attack! I probably just stole the wrong kind of pill."

Of course, there were other possibilities, but in the face of Anatoly's exultation they receded from my mind. "I'm so relieved," he said, gulping more vodka. "All these years my guilt has been tormenting me. I'm just not meant to kill anyone."

But then his smile faded quickly, and he stared at the pill in his hand. "But that makes this one useless. It's identical to the others. Look. Even the markings are the same," he said, holding it out to me, and then sinking back into the big cushions on the couch, suddenly feeling defenceless against the spectre of those trunks. The poodle snapped at his ankles again until he flicked vodka at it. Then it went back to gulping down bits of quiche dropped casually by its owner, who was now staring intensely at the Cuban poet she was talking to. Anatoly looked forlornly at the pill in his hand, shook his head, and then just tossed it toward a huge pot of ferns.

The poodle suddenly snapped at the pill in midair, gulping it down like a piece of quiche. For a moment it stared at Anatoly with a look of disdainful gratitude. Then suddenly its ears shot out as if they were electrified. Its eyes pinwheeled. It lurched one step toward Anatoly, who clutched at his vodka, his own eyes bulging in disbelief. It snorted once and then keeled into the carpet as if hit by a bargepole. The poodle lay utterly still and unnoticed by the throngs of people standing nearby.

Anatoly looked from the poodle to me and back again in a kind of glazed horror. I sat clutching the arms of the chair I was in. Anatoly stumbled to his feet, perspiring furiously and unsure what to do. He emptied his glass in one gulp and again looked plaintively toward me for assistance. I was immobilized, my thoughts fusing. Adjusting his tie, his eyes filling with guilt and his perspiring face turning red, Anatoly teetered across the prostrate poodle and tapped the woman on the shoulder.

"Excuse me, madam," he said, trying to be pleasant, "but hasn't your dog just died?"

34

I was no longer sure what to believe.

With that chic poodle pitching into the carpet while the Moscow guard dog lived ferociously on, who could tell what game was being played? And by whom?

But I had other, more immediate concerns to contend with. Like the Reverend Kent Filmore. He was driving me crazy with phone calls of effusive thanks and revolutionary exhortation. "Power to the masses," he always said now instead of goodbye. I couldn't even stand to be around him. There was just no defence against all that open-faced sweetness of his, the wholesome innocence that allowed him to rejoice in the absolute certainty that revolutionary justice and decency for the downtrodden masses was the Christian way to utopia. I wanted to shake him senseless, yelling at him that my father had shot utopians by the cattlecar-load when Stalin had ordered that saintly fools like him be taught their final lesson on revolution: it's really just politics with guns. But I knew it wouldn't have done any good. He would have just smiled patiently and told me I was going through a bad period, where my revolutionary consciousness needed raising.

The Reverend Kent Filmore's name had begun appearing in the newspapers. He addressed rallies. Gave speeches before large audiences. Was sought out by nervous politicians who feared his scorn. And condemned his own country, no matter what it did. I had created another monster.

Once again I thought of that saying the Christians have, about their Lord giving and their Lord taking away.

I decided to stop that pious zealot before he went any further.

My plan was brilliant in its simplicity. I would go right to the heart of the matter. No more politicians or church types or fuzzy intellectuals. This time I would use businessmen. The legendary capitalists.

I simply borrowed an office in the Reverend Kent Filmore's church and, without telling him what I was doing, called in half a dozen important businessmen. Over the phone I told each of them I was from the Russian embassy and would like to discuss business matters on a confidential basis in a place where no one would see us. It was blatant, but occasionally we did buy things from the capitalists. Things like wheat. One by one they came in to the church, marching uneasily past the clenched-fist posters, and listened intently to my proposal. I watched their faces turn red or tighten around their mouths in amazement as I offered to buy some of their most important military devices. Laser-optical mirrors. Submarine-tracking devices. Ball-bearing machines for missile guidance systems. The very tools of war that we could turn around and smash them with. The capitalists responded with a noncommittal grunt or a lot of throat-clearing, got up, and departed with a numb look in their eyes.

It only took one afternoon. I never intended to go back there again or have any further contact with those businessmen. But I gave each of them the Reverend Kent Filmore's name as the person to contact, knowing that they would stampede over to Enemy Number One's own secret police, the FBI, who would then descend on the church in droves of double agents.

On that warm early-summer afternoon, I walked back through slanting sunlight feeling joyously like their great folk hero Paul Revere. Hadn't he galloped through the countryside two hundred years ago warning the people of the enemy's approach? *Dimitri Revere.* I liked the sound of it. At Columbus and Broadway I bought a hot dog from a street vendor and gave him a dollar tip. I chuckled with hand-rubbing glee as I waited for the results.

It took only five hours. There was an urgent message to phone the Reverend Kent Filmore. The doves of peace fluttered from his excited voice when I reached him. "Bless you, comrade!" he said three times, before telling me that his church building fund had just gone over the top. The businessmen had checked with their boards of directors and were desperate to reach me, he said. And three of them had already made large donations to the building fund in the hope that the Reverend Kent Filmore would use his influence to steer some business their way. The construction of the new Liberation Wing of the church offices was now assured. "And, Dimitri, I almost feel as if I should name it after you."

"It's probably better if you didn't."

"You may be right. We don't want any undue attention. Bless you, comrade, and go in peace."

Of course, Moscow would give me yet another promotion for my work with the Reverend Kent Filmore and his church. I sat in my office with the door closed and stared out of the window for a long time.

What would Paul Revere have done?

35

Those days were probably the golden era of our espionage in New York. After Enemy Number One's disastrous Asian war, which they lost, we had a sudden upsurge in the number of spies we recruited from among those citizens who remained in a permanent state of suspicion and sometimes disgust with their own country. That war was a bonanza for us. We sort of counted on something like that happening every couple of generations — like the Depression of the thirties, when so many people were jobless. Those were always the times we loaded up on spies.

If any of our recruits felt uneasy about working with us, we just parcelled them out to the Cubans or the Bulgarians or one of the other outfits we worked with. It was a big, complicated job.

But we had some very hard-working, talented people on our staff. Which was occasionally a problem for me because I really had to keep up with my embassy competition in order to remain stationed in New York. Fortunately, the old men in the Kremlin were letting it be known they were impressed by my latest work on manipulating Public Opinion. It was my theory that public opinion in Enemy Number One was almost always a decade out of sync with reality. Whenever a wave of public opinion became fashionable and swept the country, it always seemed to be suited to solving their last great crisis. Not whatever new crisis loomed in front of them.

Like old Army officers sternly fighting a war with the outdated tactics they learned from their last conflict, the whole country marched from crisis to crisis demanding its leaders act as they should have done a decade earlier.

This time lag between reality and public opinion created a kind of perpetual confusion, which sometimes worked to our advantage whenever Enemy Number One was thinking about building more missiles or fighting another war. It was my job to lengthen this time lag and so increase the confusion.

Our best method was spreading outrageous lies. There was nothing unusual in this. They had their lies and we had ours. But I think we did it better through our front organizations around the world. Lying was simply a tool in that business, as a wrench is to a mechanic. Only an amateur would ever get upset about it or talk about the morality of it all.

At home in Russia we grew up learning to listen to lies properly. It was taken for granted that our leaders told lies to the people. But that was okay because the people had long ago stopped believing what they were told. And no one expected them to. It was all part of the ritual of ruling and being ruled there. And, as an antidote to having to listen to all those lies, the whole population had developed a sly, cynical sense of private humour, always looking for the real meanings behind every statement.

But in Enemy Number One we discovered an incredible bonus to our lying.

A lot of their people actually believed what we said.

I never quite figured it out. Maybe they just didn't have our experience in the matter. Maybe it was because we were so good at camouflaging the source of our lies. Or maybe they were all having such a good time they never thought about it much. I don't know. But what I did know was that it made my job very important.

So on the surface my life was very bullish, as Sam would have said. But I had a couple of terrible problems that were getting worse all the time. The first was Viktor, the new *rezident* in the embassy. The new Boris. He was constantly watching me, waiting for that one mistake that he could announce to Moscow with scathing frustration as he suggested one of his own people to take over my work.

Several times Viktor approached me, smiling, his pale eyes ceaselessly scanning for weaknesses, and suggested that we combine our efforts on certain projects. I always refused, with the same friendliness with which the suggestion was made, knowing that I was being offered a walk across quicksand. He would smile, shrug, and return to his office.

Where, I heard later, he would rage against me for hours.

Viktor lived for control. He ran his network with the supreme ego and precision of a symphony conductor. And I stood in the way of him achieving his full glory. Viktor actually believed that we would win, that our efforts were becoming so successful, and Enemy Number One was becoming so confused that someday soon we would smash them. He even began to convince me. I began to worry about what would happen if I ever defected and was found sitting behind my desk at Yagoda on the day Comrade Viktor and the People's Liberation Army came up the elevators without an appointment.

But Viktor wasn't even my worst danger.

Katya was.

One night about a month after we returned to New York, I sat alone in our apartment at the embassy, staring down at the streets. Behind me, draped casually across couches and chairs, were dresses. Beautiful, expensive dresses. The dam had broken. It had been unable to hold back the torrent of money that Katya had sensed from the moment we arrived. Our apartment was quickly filling up with those damn things, and it had got to the point where even I could tell a Dior from de la Renta; a Halston from a Givenchy.

It seemed like every few days another one of those pretty pieces of fluff would be smuggled into our apartment. Where I saw a rising tide of doom, Katya saw her dreams draped around her. And when the problem for me became one of sheer survival, for her it became simply a matter of closet space.

When I got angry, she would look genuinely puzzled and ask what was the point in getting upset when the answer was simply more closets. That was all. A place to put them.

If we had been caught, one or two of those dresses could have been explained away. Nowadays one could always claim success on the black market back home. The occasional foreign-currency transgression. The usual things. But no one could have explained that deluge of haute couture I was staring at.

Attempts to talk to her about the need for self-control were like trying to use logic with a junkie. It was the act of buying that now gave her a thrill, a rush of exhilaration that engulfed her and then subsided, leaving a terrible void that could only be filled by her next purchase. And with each new dress, her life took on the vibrance, the purpose that she had longed for since those bleak childhood days in that angry little room in the depths of Russia. Without them now, she felt she was nothing. They were her key to a glittering new world. Katya was a lock-picker at the most firmly barred doors of New York society, scheming outrageously for invitations to the best events. And some of those doors actually began to open, pried with the crowbar of money and the skilled knowledge of how to use it. If a painting had to be bought to get invited to a certain gallery opening, then it was bought. If a donation had to be made to a museum, it was made. Whatever it took, she did it.

Life had become a daily game to be won. And in

playing the game she changed physically, in ways perhaps only I noticed. In Moscow, her features had softened, but now a brittleness was descending on her. Whatever warmth there had been in her eyes was now sometimes driven out by an appraiser's stare, which made that beautiful face a mask. But she was still stunning, sometimes even sultry, except now I thought she worked at it. And her figure had so far defied gravity and normal ageing. Old men still peered into that splendid bosom and perceived their youth.

A few times I had found that appraiser's stare directed at me. Crafty peasant that she was, Katya knew that those golden eggs would continue to fall only as long as the goose was properly cared for. It was the only limit to her obsession, for she knew that one mistake could still hurl her back, without a dime or a kopek, into that world of unheated apartments in the depths of Russia. She knew that Viktor was the enemy, and that those pale eyes in that sagging face were what really counted, not the warm smile he always gave her.

Our marriage had evolved, or perhaps disintegrated, into a kind of mutual blackmail. I had taken those credit cards away, but for someone of her ingenuity that was only a minor problem. When she began charging purchases directly to Yagoda Enterprises, I had to give the credit cards back. When she heard that movie stars like Paul Newman had apartments in the Hotel Carlyle, she wanted to buy an apartment there. Or maybe the Pierre, she wasn't quite sure. I got to a point where I was made so crazy by all this talk that I actually asked Sam if I had the money to buy an apartment in those places. He just laughed and told me I could buy the whole hotel if I wanted to.

An uneasy truce prevailed. She didn't get the hotel apartments. But she did get the dresses. And the Broadway opening-night parties, the receptions at the best galleries, and even the big gala at the Metropolitan Museum. We went as Mr and Mrs Berezovska because I insisted on absolutely no link to our real life at the embassy. She had wanted us to be the Redfords, after the movie star. But I wouldn't allow it. (Whoever heard of the Sundance Kid with a Russian accent?)

And now I was sitting at the dining room table in our apartment, my strategies for destroying Enemy Number One and the instructions on how to tie a proper bow-tie laid out in front of me. In a couple of hours I would join Katya for this week's elegant party. Katya, of course, was already dressing. But not in our apartment.

Where else did one dress but in one's suite at the Plaza?

36

I stayed there for a long time just staring down at those New York streets, watching people walking in and out of the haloes of light cast by the streetlamps. People always walked so much more slowly in the spring. A couple approached from Lexington Avenue. When they came nearer I saw that they were old, perhaps in their seventies, and walked at a pace that said they had nowhere important to go. They were holding hands. I'm still not sure why, but I thought it was so strange to see old people holding hands. I envied them.

And I knew I had to see Nina.

It had been ten days since I was last with her. I had walked through those days with a weight hanging from my thoughts. Merely facing other people, especially Katya, had been a struggle. And I had to force myself not to phone her.

I had only seen Nina twice since that first encounter on the night I showed Anatoly the Yagoda Building. A few nights later I had returned nervously to the seventy-fourth floor, wondering if I should have brought flowers. All I wanted was a reason, an excuse, to talk to her. A strange form of luck had been on my side in the guise of the cleaning company's sleazy foreman. He was a neighbour of Nina's uncle and had got her the job on a part-time basis. The foreman told Nina several times what a favour he was doing her. He had slicked-back hair, too much cologne, and seven children. He ruled his night-time empire like a dictator, and he had decided it was time she should pay her respects to him on the couch in Sam's darkened office.

According to the foreman's cleaning company personnel list, Nina should have been working on the floor alone. So when I walked in, dressed in my cleaner's outfit, to find him trying to wrestle her onto the couch, he was completely taken by surprise.

"Get out!" he screamed at me, grappling for his pants. "And you're fired."

I grabbed him by the arm, wrenched him off Nina, and kicked him right square in the ass. He was a small man, barely coming up to my shoulders, and when I kicked him both his feet left the ground at the same time and a sharp little squeal burst from his mouth. He became hysterical, clutching his loosened trousers and screaming at me to leave the building. I just stood there, between him and Nina. (After all, is there any single experience that can make a man so outrageously noble as reducing another man to moral ashes for doing what has already flickered through his own mind?) When the foreman had been chased raving from the floor, I went back into Sam's office, where Nina was sitting on the couch staring out the window. I asked if she was all right. She just looked up at me with that same wide-eyed expression and shrugged.

"That was the second time he's tried," she said, buttoning the torn blouse she wore under her cleaning coat.

"That's ridiculous," I said. "You don't have to take that. Why don't you quit?"

"If I didn't have this job I couldn't afford my classes," she said with the same shrug. In that faint city light seeping through the venetian blinds, her face seemed as flawless and pale as porcelain. She fixed her hair, which had fallen around her face, pulling it up and behind her in the kind of ponytail she wore. "He'll try to fire you. You know that, don't you?"

"What choice did I have?" I said, thinking afterwards that it sounded like something the hero would say in the movies I had seen back in Moscow. I was glad I had said it.

"That's true," she said. Somehow I hadn't been expecting her to say that. And then she smiled at me.

That night we went out together after she finished work. We walked to a place on Third Avenue where the bar was surrounded by single men and women looking to be picked up and there were a few empty tables under the hanging ferns near the window. Seeing her walking in front of me through the crowded restaurant, I thought how much smaller than Katya she was.

"What happened the first time? With the foreman?" I asked when we had been seated at the table.

"He staggered away pigeon-toed," she said, looking too delicate for what I thought she was saying. "You see, I grew up with two older brothers who used to wash my face in snow every time I scored a goal on them when we were playing hockey. Having brothers is very useful for a girl. You learn a lot." She smiled. "But that was when we were little, and we used to play for hours in the snow when they'd pile it around the rink we made. I guess I miss my brothers the most now."

One brother was an engineer in Leningrad, the other was still living in their hometown, which was not far from where I had grown up. Both of them had been upset when she left Russia, and now they only wrote every year or so. She missed them in a way that only another exile could understand. She asked me about myself and I told her how I grew up, and about Yuri and my parents. But I was careful not to say anything too specific about my life in New York.

"Why did you come over here?" I asked, wanting to change the subject.

"My husband's family were allowed to leave Russia, so

I came too. I was twenty, he was twenty-three. A year after we got here he met someone else. A girl from New Jersey who really impressed him. I cried a lot, and waited for him to come back. I knew he would. But when he did, I realized I didn't love him anymore. Things change."

"I know," I said.

It was not too late, and we stayed in the restaurant for at least another hour. I did everything I could to let that moment go on and on, sitting across from her and watching her as she showed me the work she was doing in her classes, designing sets for theatre productions. In the bag she carried were her sketches and intricate designs of scenery pieces for the various plays her class had been assigned. Once she had wanted to be an actress, but in the midst of rehearsals for a local production back in Russia, she realized that it was the physical element of the theatre itself that excited her imagination, even more than the work of the actors. Since then, theatrical design had been the constant passion of her life, and only after her marriage ended did she begin her precious classes. She had seen every play on Broadway and had got copies of the blueprints for the sets from many of the designers. Two of them had offered her work on their next productions.

We walked towards Grand Central Station, where she always caught the subway home. On the way, we passed a building where the second-floor window was open and music could be heard. We walked over to the other side of the street, from where we could see people dancing in a brightly lit room. The sign across the window said FRED ASTAIRE'S SCHOOL OF DANCING. She stared at the dancers, her eyes taking on a kind of laughter all their own. "See!" she pointed. "Now there was another advantage to having brothers. I used to make them dance with me all the time when we were kids. I always had a

310

dance partner to practise with. Even though they hated it. But I used to love that old-fashioned kind of dancing."

"Do you think Fred Astaire ever taught there?" I asked, remembering all those old movies I had seen him in. Fred had been one of my idols when Yuri and I were boys. When we saw photographs of him dancing with Ginger Rogers in Father's *Life* magazines, we were both immobilized with awe. No wonder he got such a good-looking woman. Who else was as suave, as cool as Fred? After seeing those photographs, Yuri and I had slicked our hair back and swaggered past the girls in our town, suddenly jumping into the air and clicking our feet together. Which was what we thought Fred was doing in these photographs. When the girls laughed at us, we treated them with disdain. How could those peasants be expected to recognize sophisticated dancing when they saw it?

"Do you dance?" Nina asked.

"I'm terrible at it."

"No one's terrible at it. Not even my brothers. Look," she ordered, positioning herself as my partner right there on the street. She began dancing. I lumbered after her. "Don't be shy."

"Humiliated," I corrected her. "People are looking. I'm embarrassed."

"That's not the only reason you should be embarrassed." She laughed, looking down at my feet, which had just stepped on hers twice. I seized her hand and led her back across the street and up to Fred Astaire's school. "We just want to dance," I said to the receptionist. "No lessons. Just dancing." The receptionist called the manager, who finally let us in for the cost of one lesson.

So we danced. All that corny old stuff that Fred Astaire used to do. And I loved it. She taught me enough that I didn't step on her feet, and I stopped feeling foolish. And best of all, I was in love. Absolutely, ridiculously, in love. I would have given it all up that night just to be with her forever. It was like pulling dreams out of the air. I was Fred and she was Ginger. And I could see that Nina was happy too. I can still remember her eyes looking up at me with more than their usual sense of amusement as we danced across the floor.

Later, on the way to the subway, I thought about getting a taxi but decided not to when she began worrying over the money I had spent. "That was at least two hours' wages for you," she said. I just shrugged. "What will happen if the foreman fires you? He's a little tyrant, you know."

"I'll get by."

"How?"

"I'm resourceful."

She looked away for a moment. "You certainly are. Every time I asked you anything about yourself, you changed the topic."

I started to make up an explanation. "It's okay," she said. "I'm not prying." She was smiling.

"But I want to tell you."

"Not interested," she said.

"Look, I want to tell you about myself."

"Okay, so tell me. But the subway closes in ten minutes."

So I made up a story. A good one. About how I had jumped ship from one of the Russian freighters that had docked in New York five years ago. And how I lived in a downstairs room of a home in Queens, with only the owners' phone to use in emergencies. And so on.

And when I was finished she just looked up at me and said, "Oh, Dimitri, do you expect me to believe that?" And gave me a kiss on the cheek before hurrying off to catch the subway.

I was destroyed for the two days I didn't see her. I couldn't concentrate on anything except making sure that

312

the foreman was transferred to an ammonia factory on Long Island. Sam took care of it. Just shaking his head. When I saw her two nights later on the seventy-fourth floor I was nervous. But she seemed happy to see me and even invited me to the dance her class was holding at the university the following week. It was like being reprieved. I was ecstatic. And when I watched her as I was waiting for the elevator, I was so struck by the way her serenely delicate features looked out of place in that green cleaning coat that I decided to do something about it.

I decided to buy her a dress.

A beautiful, flowing dress to wear to the dance. A Dior. Or a Halston. Perhaps a Saint Laurent. I would go to Saks or Bloomingdale's or wherever until I found the best.

Which I did the next day. And I loved buying it for her.

Until I could find the right moment to give it to Nina, I had to find a safe place to store that dress. I came up with a brilliant idea. Katya's closet. I jammed it in between all the other dozens of dresses she had bought and forgotten about. On the night of the dance, I told Katya I was meeting a spy, put the dress and the Dior bag in my biggest briefcase, and went to Brooklyn in a taxi. But on the way there I was suddenly struck by the craziness of what I had done. What was I trying to do with Nina? Turn her into another Katya? Taking the very thing that had driven me crazy about one woman and encouraging it in another? The taxi arrived at her uncle's house before I had even begun to answer any of my own questions.

The house was one of those small, ugly brick structures that were built in rows stretching off into the infinities of outer New York City. Below a concrete porch with a wrought-iron railing was a narrow door that led to

Nina's apartment. Above the concrete porch was an aluminium screen door that separated me from her uncle, a fierce-looking old *kulak* who peered out at me as if I was trespassing. Her apartment was tiny, with a hallway separating the bathroom and kitchen from the only other room. Sketches and photographs of theatrical scenery hung everywhere in neat profusion.

When I gave her the package with the Dior label on the bag, she thought it was some kind of joke. She opened it with a perplexed look on her face and then when she saw what was inside, her mouth slowly fell open. She held the dress up in front of her, just staring at it and shaking her head. For a moment I thought she was going to cry. "Thank you. Thank you," she murmured. "But, oh, Dimitri —" Her voice trailed off. She never finished the sentence.

She changed in the kitchen and returned looking as if the dress had been made for her alone. She was stunning. The gold and green silk fell gracefully from her shoulders and swept around her in opulent waves as she walked.

"Has anyone ever told you that you look a little like Audrey Hepburn?" I said.

"Who's Audrey Hepburn?" she asked, sweeping around, the colours blurring into a kind of frame for those dark round eyes and the delicate features that looked strangely troubled. She reached out and took my hand. "Can I ask you a favour?"

"Of course."

"Please don't misunderstand what I'm going to say. But would you mind if I wore this another time?"

"Whenever you want —"

"Please." She interrupted me and reached over, kissing my cheek. "I really want you to understand. This is beautiful and I'm just overwhelmed by what you've done. No one has ever done anything like this for me before. But I'd feel better waiting till another time. I

314

know it doesn't make sense to you right now, but I'll try to explain it before we —"

"Don't try," I said, giving her a hug.

She went back into the kitchen to change into another dress, one that she made for herself a year ago. I was very upset, because I thought I'd done something wrong.

We went to the dance. Most of the people there were dressed in outrageous or even shabby clothing and seemed a lot younger than I was. Around the outside of the hall where the dance was held were pieces of stage scenery the class had designed. One of Nina's was there, a fantasy piece for a production of *Dracula*. From a distance it looked very large, but when you got close to it, you could see that she had played tricks with lines and perspective. It was really deceptively small. I was impressed and was pleased to see that she was hoping I would like it.

We danced, talked with her friends, and walked through small clouds of marijuana smoke. It was the sort of occasion where people naturally touched one another, holding hands or putting their arms around each other. I tried not to show my eagerness just to put my arm around her as we came off the dance floor. Some things never change, I thought to myself, feeling just as I had as a schoolboy years ago. And being strangely grateful for the feeling.

But something was bothering her. I could tell, not because she showed it, but because I could sense she was trying not to. When we returned to her home the old *kulak* was still staring fiercely through the aluminium screen door. She waved to him and introduced us. He looked at me like I was about to steal something from him. He was heavy and almost totally bald, with a mouth that turned down at the edges. He said hello in Russian and then told her to make sure I didn't stay too long.

"What's the problem?" I asked when we went inside.

She thought for a moment and then said, "Would you mind if I phoned you tomorrow?"

I made some excuse about being out all day, looking for another job. Until that moment she and the embassy had seemed like parts of a universe that would never meet. I could tell she didn't believe my answer.

"Dimitri, where do you live?"

"Uptown," I said. "In a place around Sixtieth Street." Which, of course, was true.

"Is that like uptown with a wife?" she said. "A wife who thinks you're out working tonight?"

I wanted more than anything to give a proper, rational, persuasive answer that would let her know I was not just your run-of-the-mill philandering husband. But my every emotion congealed into a verbal blob, which yelled back at me that I probably was. "Something like that," I said.

"Why didn't you just tell me?"

"It's not quite that simple."

"It probably never is. Does your wife understand you?"

"Pardon?"

"Forget it. I'm sorry," she said. "It's just that I've been through this once before with someone else. And I swore I'd never go through it again. But you know something? I was ready to. Because I knew you were married. I just *knew* it. But I wanted you to tell me yourself." She went into the kitchen and came back carrying the Dior bag. "I think you should take this back."

"I can't," I lied. "They don't take things back. And why don't you want the dress?"

"Because it reminds me of you sitting with your feet up on that desk, the first time I ever saw you. Pretending you owned the place. You're just a dreamer, Dimitri. But that was harmless compared to this," she said, holding up the Dior bag. "You don't make enough money in two months to pay for this. Someone's going to get hurt. I'm sorry, Dimitri."

That was the last time I saw her. Ten days ago.

But now, sitting there in my apartment, staring out the window and practising tying a bow-tie so I could join Katya at this week's elegant party, I made up my mind to go back and see Nina again. I was so desperate I felt I had nothing to lose. At least I could try to change what she thought about me.

I hurried out of the embassy, looking appropriately solemn, and spent the next hour jumping from one taxi to another. In case Lavrenti was following. I arrived at the Yagoda Building and went straight to my basement locker, where I changed, not into my cleaner's uniform but into the tuxedo I now kept there for such occasions as tonight's gala. Then I went up to the seventy-fourth floor, sat behind my desk, and waited, my heart hammering in my chest.

Nina arrived on the floor to find me there, looking like an ad for a men's fashion magazine. She just stared. "I would like to talk to you," I said, trying to sound cool and pleasant. She stared some more, then came into the office and sat on the couch.

"I have some important information I would like to tell you," I said, feeling pleased that I was so in control of myself.

I told her everything.

I told her how I had started Yagoda Enterprises with Sam years ago, almost as a joke. And about how I was really a Russian agent living at the embassy, which was why I'd been evasive when she asked me questions about my personal life. But really, I was trying to get Enemy Number One to save itself. When I finished she just sat there staring at me.

"Well?" I said.

"Oh, Dimitri," she said, shaking her head. "You jerk. Do you really expect me to believe that?"

37

My limousine was waiting.

I didn't want to be seen getting into such a car out on Park Avenue, so I had left instructions with the driver to park at the back door of the Yagoda Building. Beside the garbage.

"Never called for anybody by the garbage before," the chauffeur said. He was an older man with a craggy face and fine white hair under his peaked chauffeur's cap. I had the feeling I'd seen him somewhere before.

"Nothing wrong with garbage," I said.

"You've never driven for rock groups," he said in a cynical voice. When we stopped at a traffic light, I saw his eyes casually sweep across the rearview mirror, checking me out with practised indifference. I was sure that after his years of driving, he put his clients into categories within minutes of meeting them.

"What category?" I asked.

"Not a clue," he said.

I sank back into that blue velvet cocoon that seemed to float through the streets and watched New York glide by. That limousine was so big the whole Politburo could have fitted inside. It had a bar, a television, and a sink. It was somehow soundproofed, so the neon uproar of Broadway passed by as if I'd been staring into the silence of a goldfish bowl. The limousine was Katya's idea. The wealthy all had limousines, so she wanted one too, even if it was only for the night.

Katya had recently decided that the rich were truly different from the rest of us. Different in how they talked, walked, ate. And probably made love. But luckily for her, she decided it was a difference that could be learned if one worked very hard at it. And Katya had embarked on a crash course in which I was determined she would not get passing grades.

We were now arguing almost every day over all the outrageous things she wanted. The limousine had been such a battle. I had reluctantly yielded only after she threw a momentous tantrum when I refused to agree to her planned weekend in Palm Beach. The limousine was a sort of peace offering.

It was a peace that could not hold much longer. Behind the façade of our embassy routine, our life together was spinning ever faster. The sheer weight of those desires of hers created a centrifugal force all its own. And to make matters worse, I was becoming immobilized by my love for Nina. At that moment I would have given anything to be riding with her. It could have been on the subway for all I cared.

The limousine drifted up to the grand entrance of the Plaza Hotel. "Side door," I said.

The chauffeur's eyes looked at me in the mirror. "Side door?" He arched his eyebrows. "Right. Side door," he muttered. In the lobby I phoned Katya, who was waiting upstairs impatiently in the suite she had hired. Over the phone, I gave her a description of the limousine and told her I would be waiting for her inside it. When she emerged from the hotel, I was sitting as obscurely as I could in the back, hoping no one from the embassy would pass by. The chauffeur stood holding the door open. With great flair Katya got into the car. She had been practising for that moment all week in our living room, hoisting the front of her skirt an inch or so the way she had seen the wealthy women do it.

She gave me a kiss that would not spoil her lipstick. I told her how beautiful she looked. She did. Her blond hair was combed back from her face, making her lips and

319

eyes seem seductively wider. Or maybe it was all the makeup. The best money could buy. And the low-cut silver and blue gown flowed from her body, yet clung in all the intended places.

She looked rich.

The chauffeur was constantly looking into the rearview mirror as we drove to the other hotel where whatever it was we were going to was being held. As we approached, our limousine joined a line of other huge vehicles that were discharging their elegant passengers. I began to get nervous because there were crowds of people standing in front of the hotel. In an instant my nervousness catapulted into panic.

Right in front of that hotel was an entire delegation of visiting Russian officials! I even spotted two men I had worked with in Moscow. And with them was Viktor! I might as well step out into a firing squad as get out of that car.

"Is there a side door?" I said, my voice cracking.

Those eyes in the rearview mirror told me that I was marginally rational at best. "No side door to this place," he said. "Just the alleyway where the winos hang out. If it'll make you feel any better, though, I can let you off over there, next to that pile of garbage."

We were getting closer. "Give me your hat!" I said. He turned around and stared, the left side of his lip rising up almost to his nose. But when he saw I was serious, he just raised his eyebrows and gave me his hat. It fitted.

Two minutes later, when our limousine had finally edged up to the entrance, the chauffeur and Katya stepped out as the doorman held the rear door open for them. The chauffeur looked the doorman up and down, nodded, and then called out to me, "Be back at midnight." A smile that could have fallen off and shattered was plastered across Katya's face. I drove off, still rubbing my shins, which I had bruised climbing over the partition in the limousine. I parked it around the corner, went into the hotel through the kitchen, and up to the huge penthouse apartment where the reception was being held, in honour of someone's return from somewhere. "Job's looking better," said the chauffeur when I found him to give him the keys. "First I got the garbage. Then the lady." I told him to stay if he wanted to. With his black suit and tie he just looked like one of those who had decided against wearing a bow tie. He grinned, nodded, and headed off into the crowds. I was still wondering where I'd seen him before.

A pianist sat behind a grand piano playing sanitized melodies with a vacant look on his face as the hundreds of guests moved from room to room and out onto a terrace that overlooked the jagged silhouette of the New York skyline at night. Katya worked the room like a politician. When I joined her, she whispered, "Darling, isn't it exciting? I've met four people who are leaving for Palm Beach next week."

"Only four?" I said.

I began to work the room in my own way. The real reason I had decided to risk coming to these parties was because I thought I had finally found the way to begin saving Enemy Number One. Who else but the wealthy, the old blue-blooded families with castles of money surrounding them for generations? Who else but the wealthy had so much to lose if we succeeded in our plans for Enemy Number One? They would be shipped off to the dungeons and lined up against the walls of the country by the busloads.

This time it would work. My problem with the other groups was they didn't really have enough to lose. At least that was the only reason I could think of. But the wealthy had merely to ponder the fate of their counterparts in all the assorted revolutions around the world to know that they stood like a wheatfield before a scythe.

321

Why hadn't I thought of them before? I asked myself a couple of weeks ago, sitting in the corner at the first of these parties we went to. I was watching the tuxedoed parade of elegance, the sleek confidence, and the flashes of light from the diamonds that passed before me. And thinking of my father's stories.

Once in a while, usually when he had been drinking just a little, my father would tell his stories of what he had seen happen to the wealthy when he was a boy and the revolution came to his city. I could almost see the Cossacks galloping in as he talked, their swords sweeping down on the wealthy Russian landowners while their screaming families pleaded for a mercy that was never shown. My father was old enough to watch them throwing the wealthy into deep wells. And once, throwing a trunkload of elegant satin gowns in after them. Gowns soaked in kerosene, turning the well into a cannon of flame when the torch was tossed in. My father had seen the city's most prominent lawyer shot in the grand ballroom of his home while his wife, a woman of silks and perfumes, was spared a few more hours so she could be raped until the soldiers grew tired of her. And he had seen the sleek and the powerful trembling in rags, living in their own stables with the cattle, and hunted down at the whim of the city's Military Revolutionary Committee.

At all these elegant New York parties I had been careful not to say anything until I knew enough people on a first-name basis. I maintained my congenial role and always kept my conversation light, never attempting to steer any discussion into sombre areas. I would wait for the proper moment.

That moment came in the peach-coloured living room next to the grouping of Picassos and Chagalls, when someone casually mentioned that a European friend had just hired a bodyguard. "That's ridiculous," I blurted out.

322

"It's about as much good as trying to stop an avalanche with a haystack."

The conversation stopped for a moment until one of the men, a financier whose family I had read about in the files back in Moscow, smiled in the way of a true negotiator and said, "We're only talking about a small avalanche here."

"So were my family," I said. "But there's no such thing." And I created a story about how my family had been members of the landed gentry in Russia before the revolution. And for years all of them had just stared out at the firm, solid ground around them, never seeing the grim, silent revolutionaries who had laboured in darkness for years, hollowing the earth away beneath their feet until all it needed was a small jolt to send it all caving in. And then I told them my father's stories. By the time I had got to the raping of the woman of silks and perfumes, one of the men stopped me. "This is ridiculous," he said.

"I'm afraid I didn't come here to hear this," said a woman of clear, sharp features and blond hair turning gracefully silver. She walked away. Several others followed her, and Katya, who had overheard the last part, was hissing in my ear that the rich didn't talk about this kind of thing, while the host of the party, a heavy man with thinning hair, took my arm and said with a smile, "I know you people sometimes get upset about that sort of thing, but it's different here. Different people. Different customs. And please, I can't have you upsetting my guests. Now what can I get you?"

"Scotch," I said. Katya had told me to order Scotch. The wealthy always drank it, she said.

I drank a lot of it that night, as I wandered around seeing those guests and for some reason imagining how they would have looked inhabiting my father's stories. My mind started running away from me, and everywhere

I looked, my mental projector showed terrible scenes. I walked into the den and saw only flames, while the tall, elegant man with the farm in Connecticut was dragged through the cattle pens and impaled on the side of the barn and his dark-haired wife was dumped out the second storey, the stunning Givenchy dress she was wearing long since torn from her body. And their friends with the tans from their summer place on the coast were the lucky ones, lining up for their work cards, building the roads with their soft hands bleeding.

I wanted to get away from there, but Katya was furious with me, insisting we stay. To repair my damage as she put it. I turned away and saw the financier in front of me standing in rags in the snow, weeping for his children.

I hurried off to find the chauffeur, who was in the piano room standing around one of the food tables. I stared at him and suddenly I remembered.

"Hey," I said. "Didn't you play for the Brooklyn Dodgers?"

38

The chauffeur said it was the first time anyone had recognized him since before his hair turned grey. It made his whole evening. I switched to vodka, and for the rest of the party the two of us sat in the back of the limousine talking about the old days.

His last name was Baker, and I didn't want to embarrass him by admitting I couldn't remember his first name. But that face I could never forget. It receded easily in my memory, into the unlined features of the athlete whose photographs had for one day filled the newspapers after the game I had seen with the H-bomb spy. It was the last baseball game I saw, and I had all those years in Moscow to remember that one madly euphoric moment when Baker hit the ball so hard it almost went out of the stadium. I had cheered so much I had almost flung the H-bomb plans into the joyous mass of humanity, wildly celebrating yet another victory of our beloved Dodgers.

All these years later, I became just as excited merely talking about it in the back of that limousine. With Baker himself! (How many times do you get *that* chance?) For a few precious minutes we resurrected Ebbets Field out of the rubble before my eyes, as Pee Wee Reese made another diving catch while Campanella ripped off his mask to take the throw from Jackie Robinson. For these moments, it was magic, and Baker was carried away by it all even more than I was, emotionally reliving the one instant of glory in his life before he sank into the obscurity of the minor leagues. He had stayed in the major leagues only for twenty games before descending almost unnoticed through a series of lesser teams, ending

325

up in a crumbling stadium in Alabama with cold-water showers and a bus that he took turns driving to the next out-of-town game.

We talked and laughed until the first guests began leaving the party. "Would you like me to go up there and call for the lady?" he asked.

"How did you read my mind?" I had no desire to go back to that apartment.

"I took her in there, didn't I?" he said shaking his head. "Never had a job like this one before." He went to call for Katya and I sank back into the velvet plushness, deciding that maybe having a limousine for the evening was a good idea after all. I reached over to a cluster of chrome switches and dials and, turning one, found that a small light came on behind me. Another dial turned on the stereo. Another for the television, which slid out from a wooden console in the middle. I sat there contentedly pressing buttons and turning dials until I heard the phone ringing.

The phone? I was sure I hadn't done anything to make the phone ring. I wasn't even sure where it was. I groped around opening various compartments until I found it. It was still ringing when I picked up the receiver.

"Good evening," said a voice.

"And good evening to you," I said, matching the cheerfulness, until I lurched forward, my heart taking off like a rabbit. We had been talking in Russian!

"So how are you doing, pal?"

I couldn't answer. No words came out.

"Trying to recruit a few spies from the ranks of the filthy rich, are we?" he said in that same easy voice. The small mercy of him thinking that I was there for my embassy duties was lost as my fears flew in on themselves. "Shouldn't have any trouble there. They always make the best traitors," he said.

In my numbed state I was vaguely aware of a large shadow that had moved up on my left side not far from the limousine. I sat there utterly rigid, the phone jammed against my ear and only my eyes moving in the direction of the black Plymouth that eased slowly forward. It was the kind of car the government bought by the thousands.

Lavrenti sat behind the wheel smiling at me with one hand holding the telephone and the other giving me a little wave. "My, my, aren't we coming up in the world?" he said, looking at the limousine, "Things must be getting better in the Workers' Paradise."

For some reason I nodded.

"Now, Dimitri, you must admit that I've been patient. And it's more difficult to find you this time, pal. Not out on the streets as much? And I'm getting fed up. So how about you and me taking a little ride, huh? In this car." His free hand dipped ju t below the level of the seat and I knew he was holding a gun.

I sat there unable to move.

The smile faded from his face, and the look from those magnified eyes was like a knife. "Don't push your luck, Dimitri," he said. I saw what he had said instead of hearing it because the phone had dropped from my hands. I reached stiffly for the door handle.

But suddenly a blur of silk came between us. And then another one, as the departing guests began to leave. Groups of them were coming out all at once, heading for their cars and limousines. One of the limousines drove up and stopped between Lavrenti and me. All that could be seen through the side windows was a small crowd of elegant gowns and expensive suits. The guests got into the limousine, which drove away.

I stared out the window expecting to see a gun pointed directly at me. But there was nothing. Lavrenti had gone. I got out of the car and looked around, seeing only other

limousines and guests. It was impossible for Lavrenti to
have left without a trace. But he had.

Or was he just in my imagination too?

39

The catastrophes in my life have never been the isolated events that other people have. No car accidents or lightning bolts for me.

My catastrophes always have a clear, inexorable chain of events leading up to them. Looking back at them now, it all seems so obvious what was happening. I keep telling myself I should have known. But I'm not sure anyone ever does know. We all walk down the path backwards.

On the way back in the limousine, Katya pleasantly announced it was Palm Beach or else.

Or else? Baker discreetly rolled up the glass partition between him and us.

On Friday morning, Katya's suitcase stood packed in our living room. It was as subtle as a roadblock. The party she wanted us to attend in Palm Beach was that evening. "Have you any idea how far it is?" I said, trying to control myself. "It's all the way down to Florida."

"The Sandfords have a private jet. We'll be back by one A.M."

"The answer is no. Definitely not." I hurried over to turn up the radio, tripping over a Saint Laurent dress that I picked up and threw into a corner. "I'm going to burn that thing," I yelled angrily.

"Not until I've worn it," she said with a mixture of defiance and pouting she reserved for such occasions. "It's not my fault if there's not enough closet space."

"The Kremlin wouldn't have enough closet space for you. Have you ever, for one moment, considered not buying more dresses?"

"Oh, Dimitri, honestly. Sometimes you're just impossible," she said, putting on her coat. "Now it's all arranged. The plane leaves at four o'clock. I'll wait here until three in case you change your mind. If not, here's the phone number of the Sandfords' place in Palm Beach if you have to reach me."

"Where are you going?"

She looked surprised that I would even ask. "Shopping," she said.

I think secretly I was pleased she was going. That night the annual Yagoda party was being held, the one I had insisted be at the Plaza Hotel ballroom. Of course I had never intended to take Katya to it. The less she was involved with Yagoda, the fewer jewels and dresses I would have to contend with in our apartment. But with her out of the way in Palm Beach, at least I didn't have to come up with yet another lame excuse about meeting some spy late at night. I was free to go off to the party and play the mysterious host, standing in the shadows watching all those people having a good time the way they used to in those glamorous pages of *Life*.

I had planned the party down to the last detail, driving Sam crazy with questions about the orchestra and the decorations. Sam and I met every two weeks, usually on Friday morning, in a series of dingy restaurants scattered across Manhattan. Most of them were places I had used years ago for meeting my spies. For Sam and I these meetings were a way of staying in touch outside the office, and occasionally they were a little more than that. Sometimes I would tell Sam that he should take a closer look at a certain company. And perhaps even buy it.

Usually these suggestions of mine were brilliant. They should have been. They came from Russian intelligence, which usually got any important news before the stock market. Just by watching which companies our people at the embassy were trying to infiltrate, I could tell where

330

the biggest technological breakthroughs were going to come from. It was all very simple. And it re-established my credentials as some kind of wizard in Sam's eyes. My track record was incredible. Better than any investment banker.

Because of my argument with Katya, I was several minutes late getting to the coffee shop over on Eighth Avenue. It was surrounded by grocery stores with fruit displayed in baskets under ragged awnings, decrepit hardware stores, and bars with cracked marble façades and signs in dirty windows saying GIANT TV SCREEN. The early-morning sidewalks had yet to reach their normal crowded tempo. I could see Sam sitting in a booth with patches on the red vinyl seats. With his smooth features, his neatly trimmed hair, and his usual starched white shirt that was too big for him, he definitely looked more ageing Ivy League than Eighth Avenue. He was so absorbed in a newspaper he didn't see me arrive.

"Look," he exclaimed triumphantly when I sat down. Thrusting the newspaper in front of me, he pointed to a rocket lifting off a Cape Canaveral launch pad. "Ours!" he beamed.

"Ours?"

"Our satellite. We made it, Dimitri! Yagoda Aerospace. And last night they put it into orbit."

It was indeed. I stared at that photograph feeling somehow outrageously proud. "I didn't even know we had a company that made satellites." My little Yagoda! In outer space.

"We took it over years ago when it was really small and brought it along carefully. Company's booming now."

"Can I see it sometime?"

Sam smiled as he always did when I asked unnecessary questions. "I can probably arrange it. In the meantime

I've brought you a souvenir," he said, reaching into his big accountant's briefcase and removing something that looked like a distorted salt shaker made in white plastic. "It's a model of the satellite. The one we put up there last night."

I held it in my hands like a newborn baby. I was simply enthralled by it. "Thank you," I said several times. I asked so many questions that I was late leaving for the embassy. In the taxi on the way back, I just stared at that little model. My feelings were quite unexpected. I wished I had a son or a daughter to give it to and say, "Your father was the founder of the company that built it." Even though I really had nothing to do with that satellite, I understood for the first time why construction workers who had worked on huge bridges or buildings would take their children there years later, to show them where the bricks had been laid or the girders had been placed.

I even smuggled my little model into the embassy. I couldn't bear to part with it. Anatoly was waiting for me. "I'm in big trouble," he whispered, his face flushed and moist.

"What trouble?"

"The worst. I've been promoted."

The two of us sat in his apartment hunched over the stereo as it blared the overture to *The Nutcracker*. In the old days, when Anatoly had been worried about being overheard by electronic bugs, he had used the cool-jazz albums he collected. But now his meticulous apartment was filling up with ballet records.

"I'm having enough problems just handling the tension of sneaking out to see Ilena." His voice dropped to an even lower whisper. "I'm living in fear of photographers. They take her picture all the time now. She's a celebrity. Can you imagine what would happen if I ended up in the *New York Post*?"

There was no way to cheer him up. He was too

worried. With good reason. His promotion was a masterfully cynical ploy devised by Viktor to destroy Anatoly. He had just been put in charge of one of Moscow's more important spies. The problem was that the man was the most temperamental agent of them all, and as the value of his information increased, so did the tortures he wrought upon whoever was in charge of him. He was leaving a trail of burned-out Russians behind him, some on the verge of breakdowns.

Moscow didn't care what the problems were. The man was irreplaceable. His information was so strategically astounding that no matter what the problems were, he had to be kept happy and operating. Moscow let its will be known in the most severe terms. I had never even bothered to find out the man's code name, because thankfully I was now removed from that day-to-day espionage. But I knew that around the embassy he was the most dreaded assignment of them all. A variation of Russian roulette, because whoever was handling this man when the inevitable explosion came would be thrust in front of the full fires of Moscow's terrible wrath.

Just before lunch Viktor met me in the hallway, fixing those pale, expressionless eyes on me and smiling that dead smile of his. "How nice for our friend, Anatoly," he said. "He's been given an important assignment. The big time. But, of course, he'd better not fail."

I stared into that sagging face and dismissed the possibility with a casual wave of the hand. "No problem," I said, as if it was not even worth discussing, and then went immediately to Anatoly's tiny office, where I found him staring at the wall. "When are you meeting your spy for the first time?"

"In a couple of hours." His voice was high, like a record played too fast. His mouth hung open after he answered.

"Would you like me to go with you?"

333

"Oh, thank God," he said.

We drove through the tunnel towards Brooklyn. I tried to calm him down, playing the role of trainer, getting my boy in shape for the big event. "Don't worry about it. This guy is just like any other lousy spy. They're all neurotics, you know that. All you have to do is be firm with him. You'll do just fine."

"I reached my limit handling poets," he said. Blotches of perspiration had appeared on his shirt. "I should have stayed with them, getting drunk and arguing about the meaning of life. I never learn."

"Look, he's probably more nervous than you are."

"Impossible. He doesn't have Moscow breathing down his neck."

We cleared the tunnel and drove around for a while in a half-hearted attempt to see if anyone was following. Anatoly was like a robot. I had to remind him to keep making turns around different blocks of the area, which was part of New York's urban war zone. By the sides of the roads, cars lay scattered like picked-over bones of long-dead beasts. Tenements were burned out and adorned with graffiti ravings. After half an hour we headed toward a main street near the East River, where we parked the car and took the subway, getting off one stop later. We walked back toward the river and a warehouse overlooking the docks, where Anatoly's spy was waiting.

For some reason I had expected a bigger man. He was shorter than either of us, about fifty years old, with pale, smooth skin that looked as if it had never seen daylight. He reminded me of a mushroom grown indoors. He had gone almost totally bald, except for a fringe of hair at the side, which he grew long so he could comb it over the top of his head in an attempt to cover that glistening surface. Underneath his white shirt and tie, the outline of a blue T-shirt showed through. In his hand was a

334

cardboard tube, the kind they roll posters in.

"Sergei was never late," he snapped when he saw us. Sergei was his previous handler, the one he had driven to a nervous breakdown. "And why are there two of you?"

"It shows how important we think you are," said Anatoly. Mistake. The man was the kind who seized upon flattery and wrung the weakness out of it.

"Don't give me that crap," he sneered. "I want Sergei back here."

"He's been transferred to Moscow," said Anatoly, somehow managing to tell a lie and look stern at the same time. Attaboy, Anatoly, I said to myself. You're going to do it. And it looked like he was. Managing to hide his nervousness, he endured all the verbal fencing with the man, while I just watched, ready to step in if I was needed. The man wanted to know if he would be given a secret trip to Moscow. "And first class too." Anatoly assured him it was already being arranged. As were the medals he insisted on.

He was not the first spy to receive medals in a secret ceremony in the Kremlin. I liked very few spies I had met, but him I loathed. He was the worst kind, the small man who wanted to make himself big. Every intelligence outfit got its share of them, flattered them, praised them, and then dumped them when their usefulness was finished, happy to get away from the odour. I knew nothing about this man, not even his name, for which I was thankful because I wanted to forget him as soon as we left.

I stared out over the East River at the New York skyline and let my mind drift with the barges that were passing by. It was a form of self-defence.

When I tuned back into the conversation, it was dragging precariously. Anatoly had lost the momentum. And with it the control. The man was toying with him, taking him through the same questions over and over again. And he was still refusing to turn over whatever it was in that cardboard tube that Moscow cared so much about.

Finally, I could stand it no longer. "Look, we have to go soon if we're going to get your information to Moscow on time."

"Hold your horses, Ivan," he said, his flat Bronx accent grating in my ears. He was the kind whose lips come together in a little pucker when he thinks he's just scored a big point. "I ain't turning this over until I'm satisfied you characters know what you're doing."

"We've been over everything twice," I said.

"Don't go getting high and mighty with me, Mac." His face tightened around that thin, purple mouth. "You don't get good satellite stuff like this from anyone else, and you know it."

"What do you mean, satellite stuff?" I blurted out in a voice far too loud.

"Do I have to spell it out for you, Ivan?"

That terrible question careened through my thoughts. "Who do you work for?"

"Yagoda," he said disdainfully. "And why are you looking at me like that?"

40

I went berserk.

"Traitor!" I yelled, beating him over the head. "You lousy, disgusting little creep!"

"Help!" he shrieked, backing away, his arrogant blue eyes contracting into fear and servility. I wrenched the tube from his hands and chased after him. "Take it! Take it!" he screamed as I battered him with it.

"Thief," I yelled. "Stealing other people's secrets." The cardboard tube echoed off his head like the sound of a crazed woodpecker, as I flailed madly and chased him all over the dock. Anatoly stood there horrified, his mouth falling open and making unintelligible noises.

"Well, tell me what you want me to do!" the man pleaded, covering his head with his hands and running blindly, as I shredded the cardboard tube over his head until it was nothing but tattered strips.

"You're a disgrace to the country."

"Which country?" he screamed, trying to dodge out of my way by darting around the edge of the dock. I whirled around, lashing him with the remains of the cardboard and the secret plans to my little satellite, catching him off guard. For an instant he teetered on the edge.

With a quick kick I sent him flying off the dock in a blur of arms and legs.

There was an eternity of silence. A kind of metaphysical tranquillity that came from somewhere in the stillness of that awesome skyline. And then, from far away, as if from the depths of an infinite tunnel, came a splashing noise. In the middle of the dock, Anatoly stood almost perfectly still, like a rotund, pale statue. His eyes had glazed over as if he were inwardly reliving the moments of his own life as seen from its end. His mouth dropped open and tried to make words, but only sounds emerged.

Stiffly, Anatoly walked to the edge of the dock and peered over. The man was clinging to one of the concrete pillars that rose up out of the water. He was yelling something at us, but his words got lost in the choking and spluttering noises he made. Beside him floated the remnants of the cardboard tube and the secret plans inside it.

Silence.

A silence that seemed impenetrable as we sat in a bar on Third Avenue not far from the embassy. We had gone there because neither of us had known where else to go. We were locked in our wordless and terrified worlds, either too numb or too far beyond any normal responses, like tirades or apologies or accusations. The bar was dark, with the pale light from the busy street coming through a big neon-clustered window like a soft veil. Somehow it felt safe there.

All the way back in the car, we had been like robots. I had driven because Anatoly could hardly put one foot in front of the other. And now, with the jukebox turning on to some other country and western song, we both sat there thinking of Moscow, of places in Siberia, of our loved ones. I had drank two vodkas already, but strangely, Anatoly had the same untouched drink in front of him for as long as we had been in there. He just sat staring into it as if some answer would appear out of the vapours. I could almost see him change in front of my eyes. Every other time I had seen him in trouble, he had gulped down vodka in sweating haste and talked nervously until his words tumbled over themselves.

But now he was strangely different. A kind of calmness

338

had settled across his face, which was no longer perspiring. He seemed completely in control of himself. And it was he who finally broke the silence. "I'm sorry," he said. "I had no right to ask you to get involved in my problems. It was all my fault."

"No, it wasn't. I'll take the responsibility for it. I'll figure something out."

He stood up and shook his head slowly. I had never seen him so composed. "Wait here," he said. "I'll be back." He left, and I managed to remain calm until he disappeared from view, which was when my mind was overrun by the hordes of fear. Where was he going? To explain to Viktor? Anatoly, my truest friend. Whose career I had just destroyed. Not to mention his life. But he still might be able to get out of it by blaming it all on me. The Yagoda spy would probably back him up. If the spy could be found.

I changed tables so I could have a clear view of the street and checked to see where the back door was. The Friday afternoon traffic on Third Avenue was getting heavy, and I wondered if Viktor and the men from Department S could get close enough to trap me before I saw them in all those crowds.

Ten minutes later, I saw Anatoly emerge out of the confusion of traffic and people on the other side of the street. He was coming from the direction of the embassy and was walking slightly faster than before. He came into the bar, looking like someone who had an agenda forming in his thoughts. I stood up, not sure what to expect.

He embraced me in a bear hug, as only Russians can do well. "It's all right," he said. "You can go back to the embassy. I've taken care of everything. I've made sure they will think it was me who threw the spy off the dock." I wasn't sure, but I thought there were tears in his eyes. It was hard to see because he was standing against

339

the glare of the window. "I have to go," he said.

"Wait a minute —"

"Just trust me," he said. And left.

I stumbled out into the blast of warm air from the New York streets, but he had disappeared into the crowds. For a moment I stood perfectly still, as the noise and the colours of Third Avenue blurred around me. I forced myself to stay calm, sorting out what I had to do. It was not quite three o'clock. Katya would still be there, waiting until it was time to leave for Palm Beach. (I must confess the vision of her being hustled back alone to some dingy flat in Siberia with none of her dresses did flash through my mind. And for a moment I hesitated, savouring that image. But this present dilemma was not her responsibility.)

I had no choice. I had to go back to the embassy. And trust Anatoly.

I tried to phone her, but our line was busy. I ran to the car and drove the remaining few blocks to the embassy, urging myself not to panic as the parking garage came into view. I looked for any of our cars positioned at the end of the block to try to prevent my escape. There was nothing.

Everything appeared normal.

Slowly, ready to leap out of the car in an instant, I drove up to the embassy with one hand gripping the steering wheel, the other on the door handle. Nothing. I edged the car around and down into the parking garage, expecting men with guns to appear at any moment. But only the usual guard was there to wave me through into the gloom. I parked in the darkest part of the garage and for a moment just slumped back in the seat.

And then I noticed the light coming from that small room that opened onto the garage. The room with the trunks!

Noises were coming from that room.

Noises that knocked all the props out from under my wavering confidence and sent my worst fears crashing down around me. Memories of Boris being dragged screaming and kicking away, to be packed into one of those trunks, rushed over me, while voices yelled at me to run — anywhere, just run! A man backed out of the room. I couldn't help it, but I gasped as I saw he was carrying one end of a trunk. And out of that musty air came Viktor's face, those pale eyes cutting holes in me as he told me the good news about Anatoly's new job. Which he knew would draw me into his grasp like a leaf in a whirlpool. Why hadn't I thought it could be a trap?

And Anatoly — my true friend, on the soul of my dead brother Yuri embracing me and saying, "Trust me!"

Trust me, in the way Stalin had embraced his cronies at lunch and had them shot before dark. "Trust me!" I wanted to cry or rage or even laugh. But I was too seized with fear to do more than stare through that steering wheel at the terrible sight in front of me.

The second man appeared, holding the other end of that huge, terrible trunk. They were both embassy maintenance men, strong and tough-looking, who were occasionally assigned to handle other tasks requiring physical strength.

"Where to?" said the one holding the back end.

"Shhh," whispered the other man as they passed in front of me. "No one's supposed to see us. We're taking it up the back way. To apartment 31."

My apartment!

Why did I see Yuri in the darkness beckoning to me?

41

Wearing my green cleaner's uniform, I sat behind my desk in the carpeted silence of the executive floor and watched the sun sink through the concrete spires of the New York skyline.

It was early in the evening, but no one else was there, the staff having left to get ready for the annual party. I had made almost all my arrangements and phone calls, leaving the important one till last. Although I had prepared for this moment for a long time, I still was not ready for it.

I never would be.

In front of me was a file that I had kept locked in a drawer of the desk. It was the only thing I had ever kept in that office. In the file were photocopies of all the information the embassy had on Lavrenti and the people who worked with him. It was material that had been gathered to help us recognize our opposition and the way they worked. In some cases there were just surveillance photographs of various CIA or FBI men who worked in the New York area. But for others, there were complete histories, photographs, and even phone numbers. It was obviously material stolen right from secret official documents.

Lavrenti's photograph was in there, an old one when his face was much thinner, making his glasses seem even larger. He was smiling. Attached to his photo was a page that looked like it came right from his government personnel records. Most of his background was in there, and I read the account of his early days in Russia with a kind of fascination that only he would have understood.

It told of his parents being shot and the suffering he had endured before fleeing to the West and freedom.

It also told once again of his escape from the Village when the Germans had overrun it during the war. As I read that section, I could almost see Pensioner Ivchenkov's wizened indignation at the mere suggestion that the prison camp had been taken by the Germans.

Under Lavrenti's records was a photograph of his boss, the number-one man in New York. His name was Burgess, and from his photograph, he looked to be in his forties, with the fleshy appearance of a former college football player. There was very little information on Burgess, but there was a photocopy of the business card he used in his cover job as a marketing consultant to an import-export firm on Madison Avenue. On the business card was his home phone number.

I picked up the phone and dialled.

There was still a wedge of sunlight behind the skyscrapers when Nina arrived on the floor. She smiled when she saw me and came into the office where I was still sitting behind the desk trying to look engrossed in something. The last rays of the sun shone almost horizontally through the window, casting a flat orange light across her face, somehow making her look even younger.

"So, you still think you're the President of this place, huh?" she said in a teasing voice.

"Of course." I hoped I didn't look as nervous as I felt. I was thrilled just to see her again.

"Why be the same all the time?" she said with a teasing smile. "How about Napoleon for a change?"

"Very funny," I said, trying to look only slightly offended. "But I've already tried that. I'm too tall for him."

"Okay, so be Shakespeare, then."

"I was a poet once."

"That too?" She looked at me out of the corner of her eyes. "Oh, Dimitri," she said, going out to the corridor.

I followed her. "How's your designing coming along?"

"Terrific. No, more than terrific. I'm starting Monday as an assistant on a Broadway musical. Now excuse me, Mr. President, but would you hold this bag so I can put your executive garbage in here?"

I held the bag. "You know there's a company party tonight?"

"That's funny. I didn't see streamers and balloons in the boiler room."

"Not the cleaning company. This company. Yagoda."

"So what's that got to do with us?" She walked into Sam's office and started tidying up.

"I've got two tickets. Would you like to go?"

She stopped. And once again those delicate features clouded with an instant of indecision, and I thought, maybe, just maybe. "Oh, Dimitri, thank you, but that's impossible."

"It's not impossible."

"Somehow I don't think green denim work coats are in style right now." She whirled around like a model.

"What about the dress I bought you? Have you still got it?"

"It's at home. Still in the box." She became very guarded, and her eyes lost their playful look.

"I can arrange to have it brought here."

"No, Dimitri," she said firmly. "I don't want to go through all that again."

"Look, you're in the theatre business, aren't you? It's all fantasy there, isn't it?" For some reason I was almost angry. "So pretend this is just another play. Another piece of make-believe in your life. Pretend the script says I'm from the Russian embassy here. And pretend, just pretend this really *is* my office! Okay? It's all part of a play."

344

"It'll close on opening night."

"What do you care?" I said, aware that my voice was getting loud. "I'm just asking you to design the scenery."

She looked right into my eyes with a defiant stare, and for a moment she didn't say anything. "You know, Dimitri, I must tell you something. I can't for the life of me understand why — but I was worried that I wouldn't see you again."

I phoned Baker the chauffeur who was waiting downstairs in his limousine, and he went out to Nina's home, where he was given the dress by her aunt. On the way to Brooklyn, Baker phoned me from the car and said he remembered what he was going to tell me about the way Branca should have thrown a curve ball on that awful day, years ago, when our beloved Dodgers had lost the championship. Someone from the Giants had hit a home run in the last inning. When he returned with the Dior bag, I went down to get it from him. He looked at me in the cleaner's outfit I was wearing and said, "Look, tell you what. If you can't afford the whole shot tonight, I'll give you a special rate."

Nina insisted on completing all her normal work, although I noticed that she worked a little faster than usual. We changed in the subbasement, and as I stood outside at the back of the building waiting for her, I thought how much like a movie this moment would be, where the man in the tuxedo, suave and debonair as always, is waiting for the beautiful woman in the Dior gown.

But the only problem was the garbage. There was tons of it piled up all around. And it stank.

When Nina came out, she looked like she had stepped from the pages of *Vogue*. Her hair fell down naturally, almost to her shoulders, and the gold and green silk shimmered around her. "I feel a little self-conscious," she said.

"Unnecessary," I said, taking her hand. And it was.

When she saw the limousine with Baker holding the door open, looking as dignified as he could with his uniform and white hair, she stopped. "Oh, Dimitri, that's ridiculous. There was no need to go that far."

"Either we're doing the play or we're not," I said firmly. She looked at me in my tuxedo and then down at her dress.

She shrugged. "Props," she said, raising her eyebrows, and got into the car. I could tell Baker was surprised I was with another woman, but he had seen too much in his job to register even the slightest look. But inside, he discreetly raised the glass partition. As we floated up Park Avenue, Nina was like a cat in new surroundings, sitting forward and peering at everything in that blue velvet interior. Then she relaxed and sank back in the seat, looking at me and shaking her head. But at least she smiled. When we arrived at the Plaza, Baker put the glass partition down and asked, "Side door?"

"Front door."

"Thought so," he said, his eyes looking at Nina in the rearview mirror.

We drove round to the circular entrance, past the lines of horses and carriages that took people for rides through the park, and stopped in front of the canopy. As we walked up the carpeted steps, I took a deep breath and looked back. Just in case. Inside, we walked around the inner courtyard restaurant, looking through the palm trees and the huge columns that soared to the ceilings high above. Starched matrons and Latin military officials sat over pastries and cognacs while the wandering violinists wrung every gypsy tear out of their melodies.

We followed the silver-coloured Y signs down corridors, leaving the gypsy violins behind us, drawn toward a more powerful music, which grew less muffled as we approached the big doors that suddenly opened before us, overwhelming us with a swirl of colours and sounds. In that ballroom there were hundreds, maybe thousands, of people dancing or milling happily around the tables with white linen coverings and candles. All of the opulence of the old Hollywood movies had been especially recreated for that one evening. Just as I had asked.

"You don't need a designer," Nina said, taking my hand.

On the elegant Art Deco bandstand, the orchestra, dressed in tuxedos, played with a fierce joy that went out to the dancers and was returned in a circle of exuberance. Light danced off the horn section, which was taking turns with spirited solos that drew applause from all over the ballroom. There was a chemistry, a pure excitement to that moment. I saw Sam on the dance floor, and even he was caught up in it, his normal reserve, almost shyness, having been overpowered by high-spirited laughter.

Nina spotted him too. "That's the boss of the whole place," she said.

"How do you know him?"

"From the photographs of him and his family he keeps on his desk. He's very neat."

Sam saw me through the crowd and waved. I waved back. "How do you know him?" Nina asked, looking at me strangely.

"He's part of the make-believe," I said, as Sam threaded his way through the tables to reach us.

"Dimitri! You've gone public!" he exclaimed, giving me a hug. It was not like Sam at all. "Welcome to your own party. I never thought you'd show up," he laughed. Nina just stared. I introduced them, and Sam said, "I hope you two are dancers."

"We've been practising," Nina said.

"Anything you'd like the band to play?" he asked her.

Nina looked too surprised to answer and then said, "When I was a little girl back home, I used to dance to an old scratchy record of 'Begin the Beguine'."

"Wait a minute." Sam grinned and disappeared back into the crowds.

"Where's he going?" she asked.

"I don't know."

"Did he say this was *your* party?"

"Would you like to dance?"

42

So they played "Begin the Beguine."

They played it after Nina and I had found ourselves in the middle of the dance floor with the spotlight on us, while Sam stood at the microphone saying that he wished to let people know who had founded Yagoda Enterprises. As people around us dutifully applauded, I became embarrassed by the outrageous corniness of it all, yet secretly I must confess, I loved it.

And as the band began playing, we found ourselves alone on that huge dance floor for the first minute or so. We danced, oh, we danced so well, and I felt her tremble slightly with the same nervousness I felt. She looked up at me and said, "Do you expect me to believe this?"

"No," I said, and we both laughed while the dance floor filled up again. I held her as tightly as I could as we stepped into those forbidden pages of *Life* magazine that had once taken me to this world I had now created for myself, where Hollywood movie stars dance to "Begin the Beguine" and only Chicago gangsters ever get shot as jazz and the blues fill the night with dreams. And all around me I heard a thundering chorus of dead Bolsheviks scolding ferociously before retiring, grumbling in unison, to the backs of their limousines, while I danced in my reverie as I had done years ago when I knew I was really Humphrey Bogart and Clark Gable and Fred Astaire and not just a boy wondering why all the colours were grey.

In the middle of the dance floor, I kissed her.

And upstairs in the elegant suite with the big windows that looked out on the darkness of the park, the green and gold silk slid from her shoulders, floating to the floor like a veil as we undressed one another with the sound of the city drifting far away. I held her to me as we lay back across the bed with only the distant lights falling across us. I swept my lips across the warmth of her face and down to the gentle silhouette of her breasts. In my joy, my ecstasy, I was somehow aware that this was the very first time. Never before had I been vulnerable as I was at that moment. I don't know why but I was afraid I might start crying. For some reason I wanted to. Something inside me was letting go, a deluge dammed up for all those years. I buried my lips in the soft contours of her body as she trembled beneath me and softly called out my name. It was she who was weeping. Yet smiling at the same time and shaking her head. And then reaching down and guiding me inside her. It was the purest moment of my life. There was nothing else. No danger. No fear. No past or future. And a world with only two survivors. For that one tiny flicker of time we were locked together in the surging rhythm of our bodies until the moment when she cried out and I released myself within her.

I was free.

For what seemed like a very long time, we just lay there in each other's arms listening to the noises of the street and to our own thoughts.

"There are some things I have to do," I said finally.

"What things?"

"I have to make a phone call to Florida. To my wife."

In that faint light, I saw her smile. "To let her know you'll be late?"

"Very late," I said, kissing her. "It's a part of my life that's over."

"Please don't say anything just for my benefit."

I dialled the number that Katya had written on the piece of paper before she left this afternoon. A man with a very formal voice answered, and in the background I could hear conversation and soft music. Katya came on the line and told me what a marvellous party I was missing and how we had to spend at least a week in Palm Beach very soon.

"I think you should stay there for a while longer," I said.

"I'd love to, darling," she said excitedly. "The Sandfords are staying for the week and have already invited me. And there's a party at the Breakers tomorrow evening that I'd so wanted to go to. But how have you arranged it with the embassy? Just so I'll know what to say when I get back."

"I haven't arranged it. There are serious problems there."

"What problems?"

"There were men taking one of those big trunks up to our apartment."

"Oh, no. That was to be a surprise."

"What surprise?"

"When I found out about those trunks, I thought they'd be perfect to hang my dresses in. Until we get more closet space. What a shame, Dimitri. I wanted to surprise you with how neat the apartment is."

I sat there with the phone slowly descending in my hand until it hung by my side. Against the darkness of the bedroom window I could see Nina's reflection as she was dressing.

"Dimitri, that was what you wanted, wasn't it?" I could hear Katya's voice coming through the phone, sounding distant and metallic.

"Dimitri? Are you there?"

43

It was too late to change. What I had set in motion that afternoon now had a momentum that could not be stopped. And watching Nina's reflection in the window, I didn't want it to be.

The phone rang almost immediately. It was Baker, calling from the limousine parked downstairs. A Mr. Burgess had just phoned and left a number where he could be reached. I had decided it was safest to use the limousine as the contact point, and when I talked to Burgess earlier that night, I had told him only that he should wait near the southeast corner of Central Park at midnight, and phone the number I gave him.

It was exactly midnight. When I called the number Baker had given me, Burgess answered on the first ring. I could hear traffic noise in the background. I told him to meet me outside the hotel in half an hour.

"Five minutes," he said, his voice thinner and more tense than when I first talked to him. "And I'll meet you inside, not outside."

"I don't want that."

"I'm sorry, but that's the way it has to be. There are a few problems," he said, refusing to say any more. When I hung up, Nina was standing in the shadows of the bedroom, staring at me with her Mona Lisa smile.

"I have to go somewhere," I said, wanting her to ask me where and why and a hundred other questions, so I could explain all over again that it had nothing to do with being married. But she just slowly nodded her head, as if keeping an agreement she had made with herself.

"It's okay. I was beginning to feel a little insecure in

this place without my cleaning cart anyway," she said running a finger across the chest of drawers and checking for dust. And then she laughed.

"Look, I want you to know this has got nothing to do with my wife."

"Did I ask you any questions?" she said with a wide-eyed expression.

"But I want you to ask questions."

"Okay, I will. Would you like to dance?"

As the elevator glided closer to the ground floor, the music and the voices grew louder. The party was in its final moments, and when the doors opened we stepped into a blast furnace of coloured lights and laughing faces shouting over the big-band music that roared from the open doors of the ballroom. We stepped out into the throngs of people, and Burgess suddenly emerged in front of me, looking heavier than he did in the photograph. "I have a car waiting outside," he said without a word of introduction. He had a heavy, reddish face and short hair. He looked tense, yet there was an oddly delicate quality to his movements.

He stared at Nina with a moment of uncertainty. "You didn't mention anything about the lady being with you."

"She won't be involved in this," I said. "But we're going to have one last dance."

"Impossible," he snapped. "Your friends from the embassy have somehow found out about this. They're here in the hotel."

All my old fears surged back over me. Nina took my hand. "I think I'll ask those questions now," she said. That teasing look had vanished, and her eyes darted from me to Burgess.

"It's too dangerous to hang around here," Burgess said, looking at the partygoers.

And for an instant, I was telling myself that he was right, that I should kiss Nina goodbye and disappear into those crowds, running for my very life. But staring into that flushed face, I realized what I had known all along.

I had never really wanted to defect. It was like throwing my own body in front of the freight train of history, when all along I had fooled myself into thinking that I could painlessly turn the switches and simply send it down a different track. But now I had run out of those painless ways to get Enemy Number One to save itself, and there was just this last and only certain way of walking into the outstretched arms of its own government, loaded with information that would stun them.

And Burgess, this stranger in front of me talking over the noise of the crowds and the music, was really just the messenger bearing the news that from this moment, I was truly an exile, cut off from the unseen rhythms, the emotional seasons of all that vast and beautiful Russian bleakness, where sorrow and laughter rose from the memories before we were born. It was a Russia that had existed within me and sustained me because I knew it was mine to return to.

But it shattered. And the faces of my family vanished into that crowd, and my world filled with strangers at the moment I desperately wanted only those I loved. Suddenly there was no one left but Nina.

"I don't care," I said. "We're going to have one last dance." Burgess began to object, but I walked past him and into the ballroom, putting my arm around Nina and pressing her to my side. The dance floor was filled and the orchestra had built the evening to its final encore pitch when we stepped into the blur of motion, the soothing anonymity of all those people swirling across the floor. We put our arms around each other and danced to a music that only we heard. "What kind of trouble are you in?" she asked.

"I'm not in trouble," I said, smiling and trying to force myself to look calm. "I'm defecting."

She put her head down looking troubled. "Dimitri, wherever it is you're going, I'd like to go with you." For a moment the dancers parted around us and I caught a glimpse of Viktor hurrying among the tables, scanning the room with a quiet, desperate gaze. On the opposite side of the ballroom were two other Russians I had seen at the embassy only a few times. They too were peering into the mass of dancing people.

I grinned and hugged her. "Not right now," I said, as if I didn't have a care in the world. And feeling almost sick with panic. In my whole life it was the one time I wanted to be brave. Burgess suddenly appeared on the dance floor looking very nervous. He motioned to me, nodding his head toward Viktor.

"Our chaperone," I said to Nina. "He's here to protect your honour."

"He arrived too late. And stop changing the subject. Dimitri, where are you going?" The urgency in her voice cut through the music and the noise.

"I don't know. But there's a routine way they handle these things. You get taken to some safe house for a week or two until they've finished asking you a lot of questions. That's all. Don't worry about it."

"Don't tell me that," she said, her eyes sharper than I had ever seen them. "I'm going with you."

"Look, remember two things. I love you. And you're not going with me."

She stared fiercely for a moment until she pulled me closer to her. "Damn you," she said softly.

Burgess moved through the crowd, managing to look like he had lost his dance partner. "Look, this is ridiculous. We've got to go." It was Nina who followed him first, seizing my hand and squeezing it tightly in hers. We passed through the throngs as the music built towards its finale and Sam and his wife spun by me.

"Thanks for inviting us," he called out, laughing.

"Any time," I said with a big smile. "Listen, I'll be out of touch for a while."

"Ohmigod. Last time I heard that, you showed up a couple of decades later," he shouted and receded farther into the dance floor with a wave. Burgess was already at the edge of the crowd when he stopped abruptly, looking toward the entrance. One of the Russians stood in the doorway staring at everyone who passed by. We turned and, as casually as we could, headed back toward the far edge of the bandstand. Burgess was careful to walk just far enough away that the three of us did not look like we were together.

Twice I spotted Viktor, peering more frantically into the mass of dancers. Nina sensed the tension that shot like a current between Burgess and me, and we slid through the crowds more quickly, the music keeping time to my own fears. At the corner of the bandstand, we hurried around behind the decorations to an almost hidden exit door that opened onto a corridor and after that the main lobby. To Burgess's angry amazement, I insisted on taking Nina down to the limousine. We walked through the high-ceilinged courtyard restaurant, the gypsy violins mourning our passage all the way to the front doors and the carpeted steps under the canopy, where the limousines were lined up in rows.

"Take the lady straight home," I said to Baker, leaning into the limousine after I had opened the rear door.

"Do I come back for you, sir?" he asked from behind the wheel.

"No. Subway's fine for me." I grinned.

"Whatever you say." He shrugged with that wary look of his.

I put my arm around Nina as we stood outside the limousine. "Trust me," I said, wondering why it sounded like a strange thing to say.

She smiled at me, but not with her eyes. "Thanks for

the theatre," she said, running her hand across the lapel of my tuxedo. "Loved the costumes."

We kissed, and from somewhere behind horns blared, but we stood there in the noise of New York holding each other, until with a fleeting, uncertain look she brushed my cheek with her lips and then quickly stepped inside. I closed the door and Baker put the car in gear. It rolled a few feet forward, then stopped as the front side window rolled down.

"He should have thrown a fastball," he called out, his craggy face leaning into the light. "The Dodgers would never have lost if it had been a fastball."

"Of course," I said. The window slid up again and the big car glided toward the lights of Fifth Avenue. I stood staring at it, lost in a world of emptiness. And then it was gone.

Burgess seemed to come out of nowhere, his voice sharp as he smiled with his lips never parting. "Goddammit, let's go." We walked like a couple of tourists around to the side of the hotel, crossing the street. A few people were leaving the last showing of a French film, and the theatre's lights flickered off. Burgess hurried between the parked cars onto the sidewalk and looked back. "Shit," he muttered. Rounding the hotel were Viktor and one of the Russians. They saw us and called out to one another in Russian. Burgess seized my arm and pulled me up onto the sidewalk. We ran toward a plain black car, with Burgess grappling for his keys.

"Dimitri!" Viktor yelled.

I looked around for people on the street, for safety in numbers, but there was no one nearby. Viktor ran onto the sidewalk behind us, and the other Russian followed him. They were only a couple of car lengths behind.

An arm suddenly shot out from behind a parked Volkswagen van, catching Viktor off guard. A pistol pointed toward the other Russian. "Easy, comrades. This isn't the Workers' Paradise here, you know."

Lavrenti. *Saving* me!

"You are kidnapping our man," snapped Viktor.

"Doesn't look that way to me," said Lavrenti, stepping out from behind the van. I felt a chill just seeing him, and the idea that he now was defending me still did not register on all the reflex fears that came loose within me.

"Dimitri," Viktor called out. "It's all a misunderstanding. I know you're upset because of what happened to Anatoly. But we'll sit down and —"

"What happened to Anatoly?" I yelled, walking back toward them until Burgess grabbed my arm.

"You don't know?" said Viktor.

"C'mon, dammit," said Burgess, steering me back toward the car.

"Dimitri, this is a mistake," Viktor called out. "You have a brilliant future." Burgess almost pushed me into the car and slammed the door behind me. He got in and jerked the car out of its parking space, as Lavrenti backed towards it, never letting his eyes leave Viktor and the other Russian. He got in the back seat and the car lurched away.

"Are they following?" Burgess asked.

"I can't tell," Lavrenti said, his voice almost a whisper as he looked from side to side. Then he slumped back in the seat for a moment and stared at me, the streetlights washing over those heavy glasses, making moving circles of whiteness where his eyes should have been. "I didn't expect this, pal," he said. "Should play chess. Brilliant move. I *have* to protect you now."

"It's going to be trouble getting you out of New York," Burgess said nervously.

"Where are we going?"

"Can't tell you," he said. "I'm sorry, but this is necessary." And then Burgess sprayed something in my face as we stopped at a quiet intersection. I coughed, and suddenly everything before me seemed to stretch out like it was melting with all the colours running into one another and the sound of my own voice warping like a tape that was slowing down until my mouth could no longer form the words that waded out of my darkening thoughts.

And before it all went black I tried to get the words out and ask, "What happened to Anatoly?"

44

I woke up in what looked like a typical motel room. For what seemed to be hours, I lay there letting the edges form around the colours that slowly came into focus.

White walls and bright curtains with a lot of orange and green in them. Two big double beds and cheap furniture trying to look expensive. A big mirror and a television set with a label on the back warning against removing it from the room. And paintings of sailboats on the wall.

The only difference was the .windows. They were opaque so that the light came in, but only the smallest shimmer of movement could be seen indistinctly edging across the beads of glass. I could hear the noise of traffic from somewhere far away. And across the windows were heavy shutters, with big slats that I could look through but not put my hand into to get at the window.

I picked up the phone, dialled 0, and a woman's voice said, "Operator." I asked her where I was, and she said if I hung up someone would phone me right back. I waited for a few minutes and no one called. I turned on the television and changed the channels between three soap operas, an old Gary Cooper movie, a children's show, several reruns of old situation comedies, and a faint, very blurred Spanish programme that I realized was one of the Puerto Rican stations in New York. By the poor reception of that Spanish station, I knew I was probably being kept somewhere about fifty miles from New York in a place that used an old-fashioned television antenna to pick up the signals.

There was a knock on the door and immediately

afterwards the sound of a key in the lock. The door opened. It was Lavrenti. He looked at me coldly, slamming the door behind him. "Look, I think we should get something straight right now. I'm here because I've been ordered to be here. Because you pulled a fast one, pal. You changed the game again, didn't you? But before I turn the tape recorder on, I just want you to know that the first way I can figure to nail you, I'm going to do it, okay? But unfortunately, for the moment you happen to be a valuable piece of property, and the Constitution, the judicial system, and most importantly, my boss, would all be most upset if I were to do to you what I really want to do. So we're going to transact our business and get this part over with. Understand?"

"I like the idea of you, of all people, having to protect me."

"I'm sure you do, but let me give you a hint. Don't ever let your guard down." He threw a newspaper onto the bed. "Thought you might be interested in this."

It was the *New York Post*. On the front page was a big photo of Anatoly and his ballerina. RUSSIAN DEFECTS FOR BALLERINA! said the headline. I let out a whoop of joy.

"Easy, comrade," said Lavrenti.

"I want to see him," I said, staring at that photograph. Anatoly looked happy in a way that I had not seen in months, maybe years.

"Fat chance," said Lavrenti. "Not till we do some business and get you commies out on the street earning a buck. Then the two of you can talk till Lenin turns to dust, as far as I'm concerned." He put a tape cassette machine on the round table beside the window. "Sit down and start telling the story of your life."

For several hours, until I grew very tired, I talked into that tape machine. Lavrenti asked me questions and I answered, holding nothing back. And when I told him about Yagoda Enterprises, I watched his eyes widen, and he thumbed hastily through his files. I had known I would stun him with that.

"Wait a minute, what the hell are you talking about?" he said. "*You* own Yagoda?"

"That's right."

"I don't believe you."

"That's your problem."

"Prove it."

"Talk to Sam Smith. He's the chairman of the board."

"Keep talking."

"I'm tired. I want to sleep."

"Not till we're finished."

"I've got news for you. We are finished." I went over to the bed and collapsed onto it. "You go around spraying that shit in people's faces, so don't expect eighteen-hour days. That was unnecessary."

"You were starting to panic."

"Like hell I was. You were the ones who were panicking."

"Well, look on the bright side, then, Dimi," he said, using that old nickname with a cold stare. "If I had my choice it would have been something other than just a spray." He unlocked the door and left the room.

When I woke up it was dark outside, and on the television there was only an old movie with actors I didn't recognize. All the other channels were off the air. There was no clock in the room, and they had taken my watch away from me. I phoned the operator but there was no answer. I tried the door again, and the shutters over the window. Everything was securely fastened.

I looked through the pile of books and magazines beside the bed, and then went back to reading the *New York Post* article about Anatoly. It said that he too was being held in some secure place until he could be fully questioned about his activities. In the photograph, he and his ballerina were being hurried into an office building,

362

surrounded by intelligence officers and reporters. My own joy at seeing Anatoly so happy was all the more intense because the terrible suspicions that only yesterday had settled across our friendship like a shroud were now gone. And whatever else may have happened, at least he had been loyal, even courageous, in those difficult hours.

I sat there rejoicing, as if Yuri had come back from the dead. I was a little ashamed of myself for not trusting Anatoly as he had obviously trusted me.

Another day and more questions, all about Yagoda, but I kept steering the discussion around to information I knew would be essential to saving Enemy Number One. The names of agents I knew. Espionage rings. Illegals. Disinformation operations. I wanted to get it all out before I forgot about it.

"First things first, dammit," Lavrenti kept saying.

"There's nothing more first than this," I yelled back at him.

"Don't tell me my job," he hissed through clenched teeth. So we went on with questions about Yagoda until I got bored and switched on the television. The evening news was on, and I switched back and forth between CBS, NBC, and ABC, pretending to compare how each network covered the latest crisis in the Middle East. But really just wanting to get away from the questions.

That night I ate only half the food they sent in and paced the room restlessly. "I want to see Nina," I told Lavrenti when I saw him again.

"Not till we're finished."

"We're finished unless I see her."

"Don't try and play games with me. I'd love an excuse to let you rot in here for weeks on your own."

"I want to phone her, then."

"No way. You have no contact with anyone till this is over."

"Then get out of here."

"With pleasure." He smiled. His eyes were as cold and filled with fury as they were that first time in the park. He turned and walked out of the room.

The day turned into night and back again. I phoned the operator and demanded to talk to someone. I read magazines and newspapers and ate the motel food that was sent in. I watched television. And I dreamed of Nina as I paced around that room, lost in my obsessions of dancing with her again, of seeing her laugh from the corner of her eyes. And in the darkness I lay there remembering her warmth.

For some reason it was always at dawn, in that first pale light casting faint shadows through the shutters, that I would think of Russia and my parents and the same terrible homesickness swept over me. I would close my eyes and see the faces of my father and my mother. And imagine the streets of Moscow and the forest outside our city, which I would never see again.

It all ended one day when I could stand it no longer and found myself staring into the images on the television, knowing something was wrong. For several minutes, I just stood there transfixed in the flicker of those images, at first not allowing my thoughts to accept what I was seeing.

I was watching exactly the same news broadcast I had seen two days earlier!

Everything was identical. Every image of Washington, of London and Egypt and some place in Africa. Every line of narration. Every correspondent. I spun back and forth through the other channels. The other newscasts were the same too. And the Marx Brothers movie and the re-run of "I Love Lucy". I had been watching taped television shows, and someone had put on the wrong tape!

I ran to the phone and yelled into it, demanding that someone explain what was going on. I pounded on the door and then picked up a chair and hurled it against the shutters over the window. It splintered. I seized one of the legs and pried at the shutters until it snapped. I tore the drapes down and, using the curtain rod as a lever, forced the shutter until it began to come loose. When the curtain rod broke in half, I slammed at that shutter with what was left. I would have used bare hands if I'd had to. Just to see daylight, to breathe the air. I fought as if I was drowning, with a desperation that spun out of control when that first tiny chip of glass fell from the window.

I had pried one of the slats loose and then kicked at another one until it too yielded. Slamming that curtain rod into the glass until tiny shards exploded from the window. There were thin, strong strands of wire mesh running through the entire window, and the glass was too strong to shatter under the glancing blows. I tore off the remaining shutters and then destroyed the rest of the room, searching for something to batter against the glass. I found a metal strut on the frame of the bed and, scattering the mattresses and sheets, I kicked the frame to pieces.

And somehow in my fury I heard laughter. A distant laughter that somehow seemed very near.

I stood, breathless and drenched, the metal strut hanging in my hand like a club, and raced from one side of the room to the other, searching for the laughter that got louder.

"Lavrenti!" I yelled. And the laughter seemed even closer. I stood in front of the wall, groping across it, getting closer to the laughter until I could almost feel it.

It came from behind the mirror. I tried to wrench it from the wall, but it was built in, like the window that it really was. I hammered at it with the metal bar, but it was like hitting steel and with every blow, that laughter grew until it was a taunting uproar.

"Lavrenti, damn you," I yelled again, staring into that

mirror, my own face a mask of fury with his laughter coming from it, as if I was mocking myself.

I turned and raced through the shambles of that room, searching for something else to use as a weapon. I felt like I was suffocating, as if I had to breathe the air beyond that unyielding window or else I would perish in my own rage, dragged down by the laughter from which I could not escape. In desperation, I seized the television, which was still alive with the Marx Brothers movie, and swung it around until it flew from my hands.

It slammed against the window, catching the glass on a fault-line crack from my earlier assault on it. The glass shattered and fell away like ice on a wall.

I stood there gaping at that familiar skyline. The laughter became uncontrollable.

And so did my own terror.

How could I be in Moscow?

Lavrenti's Testimony

45

Let me tell you what it was like in those years after your father shot mine.

In the winters, when the gales blew and we were huddled in our rags around the pitiful stoves in those prison shacks, we would sometimes notice that one of us was missing. It was a mark of our love that we would go out into the blizzard, yelling into those lashing winds that froze our breath across our faces. Almost always we would find our missing friend, frozen into his clothes. They were so stiff you could break pieces off them.

I remember one of them, a boy about my own age who had been my closest friend there. I was the one who found him, standing frozen into the earth like a pillar beckoning blindly into that black storm. His arm stretched out, pointing to the forest beyond the barbed wire and the gun towers. His face was frozen — truly — into a smile so serene I was tempted to envy him. He had given up. He had chosen death.

But I could never make that choice. I never even considered it. You see, I was sustained by a fire so fierce the cold hardly mattered.

I was kept alive by you.

Nothing they did to me held any more terror than what I had already endured. And as long as I could tell myself that I would survive to come after you, I could not be crushed. That homicidal old fool Ivchenkov was driven to despair by my resistance.

But others took note of me too. The secret police at the camp found other uses for me. And I became one of them, working against my own people in those camps in ways that I am not proud of. But it was a means to an end. You. I would do it again. They arranged for my escape and gave me certain minor

369

tasks in distant cities. I never failed them. I knew it was all part of a plan. A testing. And when the colonel who had been my patron went to Moscow, I knew I would follow.

And I also knew they would never have gone to the trouble of arranging my escape from that prison camp unless they had something important in mind for me. The first thing I did when I got to Moscow was to look for you. You were never aware of me following you at the ministry school. Or when you first came back with your wife.

There was truly a bond between us, even in those days, don't you think? From the moment I saw you, my father, my mother, my sisters all rose from their graves and embraced me. You had become my life. My obsession. I knew you were aiming for New York. Where else was there after the dreams we shared as children? So I did everything I could to get there too. I know you can imagine my joy when I was chosen to be sent over there as an illegal. And all through my training in Moscow I imagined those streets of gold in New York, just the way you probably did.

Isn't Enemy Number One amazing? It is still truly the land of opportunity. I went there saying what they told me to say in Moscow. A poor refugee. Fleeing from the camps. Dodging Nazis on one side and Stalin on the other. There were millions like me at that time, and no one ever suspected. I worked harder than anyone else I knew, and succeeded in the way I had been told to succeed.

After all, who could ever question my reasons for loathing Russia? They looked into my background and verified the slaughter of my family and my own imprisonment. The people in Washington checked and rechecked everything they could and convinced themselves, as they should have, that there was a harvest of hatred which could be put to use.

But they could never look into my soul and see the only fury that mattered. They could never hear the silent voices of my family.

Working in New York for their intelligence agency was all

that I needed to draw us closer to this final moment. I worked hard for them, but I quietly took my orders from Moscow. As Burgess does. And I used both sides to edge you closer to the abyss. If I'd wanted, I could have left you dead on the Fifth Avenue sidewalks that first night. Clutching your ridiculous pink flamingo. But it would have been so meaningless.

And why end a play in the first act?

I relied on my little diversions to amuse me during those years. The cat-and-mouse chases. The costumes. The jargon. Pal. Even your chubby friend helped brighten an otherwise dreary period by poisoning Ivchenkov's son right in front of my eyes. I had excellent seats for that little performance, and I almost laughed out loud when Junior fell into his lunch. Just watching Tubby's eyes become like silver dollars after he dumped the pill into the coffee was amusement enough. I even saw the second poison pill clutched in his hand and decided that the joke was too good to end there. So I got Moscow to send someone into his room and replace that pill with a phony one. I often thought of him sitting in front of his victim in a panic, waiting for that pill to do its work.

As you can see, during those difficult times I had to seek amusement wherever I could find it.

And I must tell you, there were moments when I despaired and wondered if it would ever work out the way I wanted. The waiting was the worst part. Sometimes, as the years dragged on, the thought of ending it quickly did cross my mind. But I realized it was really no different than it was at the prison camp. There was simply no choice. I either had to follow our little game through to its proper conclusion or else I would have been better off walking into the blizzards and freezing into the ground with a smile on my face.

I had no other way but to end it here in Moscow. Otherwise I would lose that single instant of absolute triumph that I have craved for so long.

You see, I have been waiting all these years just to watch the face of your father when he comes in here.

371

I want to look into his eyes at that moment when he sees me. I have been told that I resemble my father, that people often see his face in mine. I hope so.

I want your father to look at me and see the victim and the victor. And know why his own son is truly doomed. The price will have been paid, Dimi. It will all be over.

But I must tell you something that will surprise you. I shall miss you.

Like any kind of lust, vengeance is a part of love, the way opposites are just two ends of a broken circle. You have been so much a part of my life ever since the days when we skated across the frozen river near our home. You remember, I'm sure you do. During all those years you have blessed my life with a sense of magnificent purpose. It will be so difficult to live without you.

But that's not much consolation for you, is it?

Dimitri's Testament

46

My father has just left.

In the months I have been here, I have been allowed no other visitors but him. When he arrived, he had no idea why he had been brought to Moscow and met at the airport by strangers who drove him to the Lubyanka in a secret police car. And waiting inside the prison, he still did not know why he had been ordered to appear there. Even when he was brought into the cold, white room where the door slammed behind him with an echo and he saw me sitting alone on the single bench, he still did not understand. He just stared at me across that big room, his fierce old eyes clouding with confusion. Another door opened and Lavrenti entered, smiling like the host of a party.

Then my father understood.

He stood there looking smaller and more frail than I remembered him. He stared at me and then over at Lavrenti, who burst out laughing. My father's face grew as red as his nose. "Why are you here?" he bellowed at me, his voice too powerful for his body.

"It's complicated." I wanted to spare him the details of my activities in New York.

"Don't tell me that!" he roared. "Why have they got you in here?"

I couldn't answer him. Lavrenti almost convulsed with laughter. He could hardly talk. "Do *you*, of all people, really have to ask?"

"I could have had you shot," my father said, the confusion in his eyes suddenly giving way to fear. "You know that, don't you?"

"You should have." Lavrenti laughed. "*My* father would have been more efficient. He would never have left his enemy's son alive to come back and have his own son shot." He slumped back against the wall, his laughter subsiding into an exhausted smile. His whole face seemed to change. To soften. He just stared at us.

"You have five minutes," he said. And then he left us alone.

A lifetime in five minutes. With everything to say and nothing to say. At first my father couldn't look at me. He just shook his head and stared at the floor. I started to explain. I wanted him to know it was all my own fault, that he was not responsible for the folly of my own demise. But he just waved his hand slowly in front of his face, motioning me into silence. He put his hand on mine, and for precious moments we just sat there saying nothing until he raised his eyes.

"In my generation we killed each other off, telling ourselves that our sons would be better for it," he said, looking at me. "Of course, we knew that was not really why were were doing it. But I thought you would escape all this." He was weeping. A single tear edged into the deep crevasses of his face. More than anything else I wanted to be brave for his sake, but seeing him like that made me afraid.

"I always suspected you were sentimental," I said, trying to act unconcerned.

"That was my problem. I should have shot the little bastard when I had the chance. And then thrashed the daylights out of you. Might have stopped this mess you're in." He turned his head and wiped the tear away with his sleeve.

Lavrenti returned with a guard. My father and I embraced, talked of Mother and what he would tell her, and said goodbye. Then he was gone, the door closing behind him as he turned for one final look, standing there like a shrivelled scarecrow, his electrified hair and unruly moustache circling those bulbous old eyes that now showed so much anguish.

And now I am alone with my memories.

Or almost alone. This morning, as I was being led down the corridor, the old man with the bulging eyes and the frog face stepped out of the shadows and stood in front of me. For an instant I thought he was there to exact the final mocking vengeance upon me for his ruined steamer trunk full of New York finery. It took me a second to realize that he, too, was dressed in a prison uniform. "Dimitri!" he called out, as if I was his oldest friend. One of the guards pushed him away from me. "I am innocent," he cried out. "I am only a scapegoat for the higher-ups. You know that." As the guards shoved him back to his cell, he kept turning around to look at me, hoping I would call out to him. Even when his cell door was slammed in front of him I could hear the muffled cries of my name being called out.

I am told he was caught smuggling diamonds into Moscow from Tbilisi. Many others were involved, more important in the Party than he, but they were never arrested.

I can hear a tapping noise coming from the next cell, where my neighbour is trying to pass on messages from that old man. He wants to be my friend, needs to be my friend, he says.

But I want just to be left staring at the walls, which have become a screen for the images of my past as I live my life over again. In my cell I am left alone, except for the times Lavrenti secretly returns to Moscow. He shows up outside my cell, peering through the bars like an angry owl, his magnified eyes blinking through the shadows. I know he is not content with his revenge. He feels there should be more to it than this, and the unrequited furies of all those years are tormenting him now. I have never broken down and wept or pleaded, or even said I was wrong in what I did.

I can tell he wants this from me. But I will not give it to him.

Sometimes he will laugh and ask me to tell him just once more about saving Enemy Number One. When I answer with just a grin, his laughter becomes metallic and forced, and he tells me of all the fantastic things *we* are doing inside Enemy Number One, as if to say that I wasted my life trying to save *them*. And why did I even care about it? But nothing he says can shake me loose from my tranquil grin, which unnerves him even more.

I have filled so many of my empty hours with thoughts of Enemy Number One. What I did there was not even a matter of choice. For me it was a need. It was almost spiritual, the way that the greyness lifted from those grim childhood days when we walked into the pages of *Life* and strolled the streets of Miami or Chicago or New Orleans, and suddenly everything seemed possible as our imaginations soared among forbidden delights.

And I would do it all again. Although who would I go to now? Who else is there left who could save Enemy Number One, when the fight between *them* and *us* is really just a matter of rot, like watching two magnificent old mansions slowly crumbling from within? Each was built by stronger, more daring men than their present owners, who now merely paint the exterior. And fervently scheme for the collapse of the others' structure before their own.

"Rot!" I yell at Lavrenti and watch the unspoken verdict of madness form in his eyes.

But this afternoon when we talked it was different, as if he was saying his own kind of farewell. I can sense he knows it will not be long before I am led down the corridor to the stark room with the white tiles. He was nervous, while I was as strangely calm as I am now. His

378

victory is not what he expected, and he knows that a part of him will die too. He brought me news from New York. Katya is now living in Palm Beach and is wealthy beyond even her own considerable dreams, thanks to the affections of an older man who made his fortune in Ohio real estate. Katya has her Rolls-Royce, her yacht, her dresses. She believes I simply abandoned her and wants to marry her new man. I am genuinely pleased for her. Anatoly is living with his ballerina and has tried to locate me in every way he can think of. He has become an impresario himself, staging performances by dance troupes and singers. Next year he has booked Carnegie Hall for three days. I am told that, except for his concern about me, he is happy with his new life. Sam, of course, does not expect to see me for a long time, and when he finally does suspect something is wrong — *if* he ever does — years will have passed. My little Yagoda, naturally, is flourishing.

It is only of Nina that I have no news. Out of fear for her safety, I have never told them who she was, and now I live from moment to treasured moment with her face in front of me, emerging from the dark walls in my long, echoing nights. I pretend I am holding her, dancing and laughing with her. She has taken away my fears and brought me my soothing cloak of madness, which will protect me right to the end.

The guards cannot understand why I dance around my cell and sing out the old songs from *their* movies and Broadway musicals. But the guards cannot see Nina, her hair flying behind her as we dance, her eyes teasing me with secrets. And the walls fall away like the flats of the movie sound stage I always knew they were, and we dance out across those golden streets where the big Buicks and DeSotos and Cadillacs pull up to the elegant saloons to let off the Chicago gangsters and their blondes, and the Hollywood movie stars who tip their hats as we pass.

And anything is possible as the backdrops change and the band comes out in different costumes and plays Dixieland and then rock 'n' roll and Broadway and whatever else we want. But I hear footsteps in the hallway and a clanking sound as the heavy door opens, and I keep singing songs in a loud voice as the men in uniform stand in front of me.

For a moment they just stare at me, and I realize that no one understands the lyrics.